THE JIHADISTS' RETURN

A DANNY QUIGLEY ACTION NOVEL

*To Keith & Darlene
Enjoy & Pass it on.
Russ McDevitt*

E.J. RUSS McDEVITT

The Jihadists' Return
A Danny Quigley Action Novel.

Copyright © 2016 by E.J. Russ McDevitt
Penticton, BC, Canada V2A 3J5
www.russmcdevitt.com

This is a work of fiction. All of the characters, names, incidents, organizations, and dialogue in this novel are either the products of the author's imagination or are used fictitiously.

ISBN-13: 978-1537553030
ISBN-10: 1537553038

DEDICATION

I am dedicating this book to my super wife Marie for her diligent scrutiny and editing of the material and her unwavering support over the years.

www.russmcdevitt.com

CHAPTER 1

MI5, Thames House, London, England

The Director General of MI5, Rebecca Fullerton Smythe came to meet Danny Quigley in the outer office with a huge smile and a hug, which made her secretary Janice, raise her eyebrows.

"Yes Janice, you would hug him too if he'd pulled an attack dog off you seconds before it tore your throat out, as he did with me."

The secretary's jaw dropped.

Danny was a tall muscular figure with long black Irish hair and a coiled sense of danger that he wore like a mantel. Janice was aware of his hawk-like face and pair of intense blue eyes regarding her momentarily. She shivered.

Rebecca turned to him. "Danny, you're a sight for sore eyes. You look hunkier than ever. Come on in. I already have some strong coffee ready for you, just the way you like it" she exclaimed, taking his arm and steering him inside before closing the door behind him.

The Director General (DG) was a tall attractive mid-forties woman with a fit-looking figure that reflected her passion for

1

hunting and shooting in her spare time, though the demands of her new role made these more difficult.

She was the third woman to be appointed to the exalted role of Director General in the MI5 organization, which normally had men at the top, usually some appointee from 'the old boys club'. Her field of responsibilities within the organization was counter terrorism, counter espionage, and counter subversion, which she ran with a staff of approximately two thousand people from the imposing eight story building on Milbank in London called Thames House.

From Danny's recent work with MI5, he had gathered that Rebecca, as he called her, had finally quieted all the initial criticism of her appointment as a result of her hands-on competence in running her organization.

He eased over to the window to marvel at the view of London and the river Thames below, as the DG filled the cups behind him.

"Like the view Danny? I rarely have time to even look out these days, but yes it is impressive I'll grant you. I'll never forget though that when you get to these dizzy heights, there's only one way to go."

"Yeah, downwards…that's got to give you a strong feeling of security Rebecca, right?" he teased.

He moved back and sat down, as she tasted her coffee.

"Doesn't matter a damn when you drop the ball once or twice and the sharks start circling. Anyway I didn't call you in to counsel me on my career. Tell me, how have you found the last number of months within MI5?"

He shifted uncomfortably. "You always wanted me to speak the truth Rebecca, so in that vein I can only say that I've been bored stiff. I mean in essence, you could have got any of your employees down on the floors below to do what I've been doing: background checks on potential Military recruits and Government employees, even MI5 itself, when you were recently recruiting linguists to fill sensitive positions. I did however get a buzz from the surveillance work that I carried out for that specific role. I could see the value in that, and in retrospect, the training I did a few years back at the MI5 training farm came in quite useful."

She nodded. "Yes, and I heard some excellent reports from the teams you worked with in carrying out those tasks. Basically Danny, I wanted to break you in gently to the culture of MI5, and to see if you could put your old Military instincts behind you and adopt a new set of skills, and if you like, gain some street smarts in the intelligence field too."

She nodded at his appearance. "I guess the long hair and beard made it easier to blend in, lounging outside some mosque in Bradford or London when you were assessing the background and habits for us on those new recruits."

He chuckled. "Yeah, you should hear my daughter pull my leg every time I take her out for a weekend."

"How old is she now? Allison's her name isn't it?"

"Like they say, thirteen going on thirty... and yes its Allison?"

"If she has your genes Danny, you sure have a handful on your hands there. What about your ex-wife, how's she doing?"

"Oh, she's got a new male friend. Seems a nice guy, and Allison seems to like him too, which is a good indication.

Fiona deserves a few breaks after my years away in the Regiment when she basically had to play the roles of both Mom and Dad."

Rebecca put her cup down with more noise than she meant to, and appraised him carefully.

"Danny, one reason I wanted you in MI5, and particularly on my team, was that occasionally I have the need for someone with your old Special Forces skills and mindset to operate under the radar, so to speak. Sure I have a SAS Saber team standing by in Hereford, should we need them. I know it's been a few years since you were in the Regiment, but you haven't lost your edge. You're still a kick-ass trooper, as you demonstrated over in Nigeria recently. I didn't have any interesting work for you to do some months back, but I had to grab you then or I suspect I would have lost you to some overseas contractors who'd give their eye teeth for someone like you to run their security details. So, am I forgiven for the boring stuff we dumped on you for the last while?"

He sat forward, his whole body language showing a growing anticipation.

"Do I gather that you have finally got an interesting challenge for me?"

She pursed her lips. "The answer's yes, but I should caution you that you might very well come to regret it. It could be dangerous depending on how it develops, and you might not be seeing Allison as much as you'd like to in the coming months. Still want to hear what the operation is?"

"You bet. After the last few months I'm ready for anything!"

"OK. To set the scene: the Paris, Brussels, Nice in France, the Istanbul airport and German massacres by ISIS Jihadists, made an indelible mark on the whole world."

"Yeah, those ISIS bastards are an evil breed. They almost seemed to come out of nowhere and spread like a plague."

"A plague is right, and no doubt you also heard the Prime Minister's concern when the chap who carried out a public beheading had a British accent. OK he's history now after the Americans got him with that drone strike, but some additional information has emerged. Three of the ISIS Terrorists guarding some business westerners who were captured and subsequently released, said that their captors spoke with British accents, and in fact were referred to as 'The Three Beatles.'

Also when Pro-democracy and Kurdish forces chased ISIS out of Manbij, in Syria, 25 miles from the Turkish border, we hear that the city was referred to as 'Little London', because of the number of Brits fighting there with ISIS."

He nodded. "Well it's no secret that large numbers of young radicalized British Muslims have gone out to Syria and Iraq to fight in Jihad. The Americans and their coalition partners are trying to sort this out with air strikes, and now the Russians are in there... good luck to them. This is getting serious Rebecca!"

4

"Exactly, and I can tell you it is a major concern for MI5 right now that U.K. citizens, highly trained in death and destruction and holding British passports, are coming home, and could become a cancer that could very well destroy our society from within. A recent report suggests that we have sixty thousand potential Muslim recruits here in the U.K., and three thousand of these have returned from terrorist training camps abroad... and they keep coming! Recent 'chatter' picked up suggests that the setbacks for ISIS in Iraq and Syria, are forcing them to start sending Westerners back home early, to continue the fight. This has gone beyond being serious Danny."

"Surely they can pick them off at the airport or entry points to the U.K. when they return? I mean there are laws in place now to charge them with carrying out terrorism activities overseas."

"Yes, the legislation's already in place that will enable us to seize their passports as they come back in and charge them if we can prove they were involved in terrorist acts abroad, but it's not that simple. Most of them leave the U.K. under the guise of going to study in the madrassas of Saudi Arabia or other Arab countries, and promptly slip off to become Jihadists in some terrorist group. We only hear about their involvement when they're killed over there, so proof of their terrorist activities is difficult to come by."

"What about the foreign airports that they fly back in from? Couldn't they provide some clues as to their departure points?"

She made a face. "It's not that simple Danny. These people are way ahead of the game and zigzag around from the countries where they're doing their Jihad in order to get to France or the Netherlands, where they catch a flight back or use the Euro Tunnel. Look how easily one of the Paris terrorists slipped back into Europe through Greece, hiding in one of those displaced migrant groups."

He leaned back thoughtfully. "So I guess this has something to do with why I'm here?"

5

"Essentially yes, but you'd be working as part of a team headed up by my Director of the counter terrorism section, Trevor Hawthorn. The team is a group of people who are a mixture of seasoned operatives and newly recruited young Asians who've been security cleared and have completed the initial training program at the MI5 farm. An operation like this has many segments, for example there'll be a research section that compiles all information coming in from various sources: GCHQ; Metropolitan Police Investigations; any undercover Agents that we have in place at the moment, as well as MI6, and overseas police sources such as Interpol.

The surveillance section has a major involvement in this operation as you might imagine. Fortunately, you've already made contact with them in your background screening checks and you'll be attached to them, but your role as I understand it, may be fluid.

Additionally, when and where required, we have a group that can break into buildings and premises to plant listening and video devices. We also have computer techies to provide support where required, and this could very well be a vital linchpin in fighting returning Jihadists."

"Sounds interesting. So specifically, what will my role be?" Danny enquired.

"I can't go into this any further, as Trevor Hawthorn will be holding a full briefing tomorrow morning downstairs in the training suite at 10 am. I want you to be there, and plan to keep the rest of the day free as you'll be meeting the team and discussing the overall objective of the operation in detail, including your own role at that time."

There was silence for a minute as Danny thought about her comments.

"Hmm… so tell me about Mr. Hawthorn. Who is he and what's his background? Oh, and who would I be responsible to during the operation?"

She poured another coffee for both of them, stirring the cups and looking across at him thoughtfully.

"I know where you're coming from with this one Danny. The hierarchy you were used to in the Military was simple.

6

You answered to a higher designated rank that, in the main, had got there through being tested in the prism of combat, and who'd earned the respect of the people under them. Trevor Hawthorn is an ex-Guards Major who worked in Intelligence and came over to MI5 three years ago on his discharge from the Military. He's done a good job in the counter terrorism division. I have no complaints there with him. He can be a bit pretentious - lets one know he's an ex-Guards Officer and expects to be called 'Sir' by the people under him."

Danny grimaced. "As you know, I'm not much good at 'yes Sir, no Sir, three bags full Sir'."

"No leeway there I'm afraid. You'll be answerable to Trevor Hawthorn and his appointed section head in surveillance Peter Sanderson who you've already met. However I'm always here if you have any real adjustment problems with the new arrangement, and I'll also be there tomorrow. Happy enough with that?"

His face reflected some conflicted emotions, but he knew this wasn't the time to bring any reservations to the fore. If he could survive the BS in the Army, he could handle the MI5 version of it as well.

He shrugged. "Sure, no problem there. Look, will the UK's decision to leave the European Union, have any impact on this whole thing?"

"Good question, and the answer is that I don't know. There is an anti-immigrant attitude that has come more to the fore since it happened, as the people who wanted to stay blame immigrants for influencing the 'leave' vote. We'll just have to wait and see, as the process to bail-out is being worked out."

They chatted around the topic for a few more minutes before he left.

Janice observed him as he went by. She thought he moved like her cat when it had just been let out of the house and was going prowling.

She shivered again.

CHAPTER 2

A Sunni village in northern Iraq, newly 'liberated' by ISIS

The British Jihadist Zain Abraham wasn't sure which sound was driving him and his British colleague Mohammed Youssef more demented as they squatted in the mud hut cleaning their weapons: the sound of fellow Jihadist Ali Rasheed sharpening his knife hour after hour, or the strange giggle that erupted from his lips occasionally, as if he was privy to some inner torment or ecstatic vision.

These were their Jihadist names, which they had chosen when they joined the group. No western Jihadist wanted their real names to appear in print back home, and that had been happening all too frequently.

Rasheed giggled again. "Did you see the face of that villager when he went for me as I started to drag his young daughter out for some fun? I tell you I got a bigger kick out of blowing his head off right then than I did with the kid. She was a right waste of time......hadn't a clue about pleasuring a man."

Mohamed stared at him. "You like them far too young as far as I'm concerned Ali. Not that Zain and I haven't had our fun over the past nine months with the women and girls we captured, but we're not bloody pedophiles either."

Ali jumped to his feet, rage suffusing his scraggy bearded face.

"Just who the hell d'you think you're calling a pedophile? I've seen your face when you were selecting your pick, and they weren't all grown women either, why..."

The door was slammed open noisily as a large fighter stepped in, removing the hood covering his Caucasian features that had prevented overhead satellites and drones from identifying him.

He carefully put down the weapon he was carrying and glared at the three Brits.

He had a large domed head, with a lanky thin body and a greasy black beard that he scratched as he dropped down onto the floor.

"I can't figure it out. You goddam Brits never stop pissing each other off over nothing! If Zain and Mohammed weren't the craziest fighters we've got out there, real warriors, always charging ahead and attacking, never showing any fear of dying, I'd have kicked your asses back to Limey-land long ago."

He shifted his gaze to Ali who had stopped sharpening his blade, "and your weird friend there who gets his kicks from cutting the throats of prisoners, even before they get a choice to convert......man he's pure crazy!"

He spoke with an American accent as he struggled to pull some papers from an inside pocket, then waved his hand dismissively as Mohammed started to say something.

"Anyway, new battle plans have just been prepared for you lot. It seems that with the Iraqi army and their coalition taking Fallujah, and setbacks in Syria, the ISIS leadership has decided to move to plan two: to filter as many Jihadists back to their home countries and continue the fight from there. It seems that the U.K.'s ripe for the picking already, with the efforts of young Muslims back there - Sharia Law and no-go areas, operating entirely outside British jurisprudence being unofficially introduced in many areas. You've no doubt heard of the Muslim group 'Muslims against the Crusades' which has launched a movement to turn twelve British cities to

9

operate as autonomous enclaves ruled by Sharia Law, including what they call Londonstan, into independent Muslim states. Muslim preachers now issue death threats against women who refuse to wear Islamic veils, and streets in Muslim areas have been plastered with posters declaring, "You are now entering a Sharia controlled zone". It seems that the time is now, and all they're missing over there are people like you who have learned the power of death and destruction, to change people's beliefs and attitudes. Now is the moment to go back there and rip that society to shreds using the fire and sword as instructed by the prophet. We're selecting a small number of trained fighters who have learned the art of war, to filter back into the U.K. and start recruiting and training young men and women for Jihad."

Rasheed giggled from the back of the hut. "I can't wait to get my hands on some of those high and mighty stuck up English bitches who wouldn't have anything to do with me when I was back there. "If Daddy doesn't like it......" he lifted his weapon.

The American grinned, showing yellowed teeth. "I ain't keeping YOU here any longer, that's for sure. We'd have no westerners left to ransom off, with you so eager to behead them all. However I'm in charge of the operation initially, and I'll be slipping over regularly to the U.K. to kick your butts and get Jihad active in destroying that nice English way of life. We already have a number of 'sleeper' Jihadists back there living nice quiet English lives, not wearing beards, not attracting attention in any way, just waiting for the call to action. That's where you guys come in. Get their Military training under way and start looking at targets and strategies. In the meantime, I'll be selecting more Brit. Jihadists from here with fire in their bellies, and shipping them back to you guys to establish them in different cities, getting ready for a big 9/11 launch over there. You'll be briefed later on the strategy, including getting the weapons and explosives necessary to cut a swathe through that country like we did here. I'll only be in this role for another twelve months, and then I'm heading back to the good old U.S.A. to start enjoying some of the rewards of Jihad."

Mohammed studied him bleakly.

"I didn't see you ducking and diving out front when we came over the border and chased all those gutless Iraqi troops all the way back to Bagdad. You're not a believer are you?"

The American roared with laughter.

"Oh, I'm a believer all right Buddy. I did four tours over here with the good old U.S. Marine Corps. We kicked ass in Fallujah and handed it back to the Iraqis after I carried the dead and broken bodies of my buddies off the field of battle. Look what the results were for our efforts in this God-forsaken country! The Iraqi army, as you pointed out, ran off with their tails between their legs at the first sign of a fight! I'm not dying for any more so-called 'patriotic causes', I can tell you."

He paused for a long moment as if reflecting back.

"You've read about how they're treating the Vets. back home: left to die; waiting for appointments at Veteran Hospitals; refusing to recognize injuries as proper permanent disabilities, and expecting our guys to go out and get an f---ing job when able bodied people can't even find one! Yeah, I've seen the light all right. You probably noticed me hauling a chunk of cash out of that bank we broke into in Mosul, and the booty I confiscated from some of the villagers when we shot up and blasted their homes on the way here. I even found one or two with small packets of diamonds squirrelled away in their clothing. Yeah, when I get home this time, it's first class all the way for me, Buddies. I'll be a Capitalist then and won't want any part of this Jihad shit. Mind you there's a whole bunch of Americans here who wouldn't agree with me, and who plan to bring the revolution back to the good old U.S.A. Well, good luck to them...I'll be set up for life."

He stood up, smirking, picked up his weapon, opened the door and stepped out into the bright sunlight. In seconds the door burst open again as he jumped back in, sprawling on the earthen floor. He sat up, ashen-faced.

"I forgot to put my hood on. An f---ing drone just went over...they probably got my picture! Oh shit!"

11

CHAPTER 3

London

Using the subway in London was the only way to make sure that one gets to a meeting or appointment on time. Danny was inside Thames House and ensconced in the training and briefing room with a cup of coffee ten minutes before the meeting.

A slim, late forties man with the cut of an ex-Officer was up front at the lectern, poring over some notes. Danny assumed this was Trevor Hawthorn, the Director of counter terrorism. And he was aware of a pair of hard alert eyes flicking in his direction as he came in.

Two other men who were chatting to each other came across and introduced themselves.

The first had the rugged look of someone who might have played rugby at some time in the past and still had that aggressive handshake and build, but he had a friendly open demeanor and manner.

"You must be Quigley. I'm Jeremy Sackville, counter terrorist investigations and research, and this is Phil Dawson who can break into your house in ten seconds if you get locked out some evening."

While Sackville was large, Dawson was lean and had the tough look of a jockey about him.

They both laughed at his perplexed expression.

Dawson touched his arm.

"What Jerry's trying to tell you is that I'm the chap heading up the team that breaks illegally into houses and establishments, and plants covert microphones and cameras."

Danny laughed with them. "That's a relief. For a moment there I thought I'd wandered into the wrong meeting room."

Seeing their expectant looks he went on. "Well you got the name right, it's Danny Quigley, and as for what I'm doing here, I haven't a clue at this stage. All I know from the DG is that it may be fluid, whatever that means."

Sackville looked at him speculatively.

"Hmm, I heard a few rumors that an ex-Saas type had joined the surveillance team for background checks a few months back, which is how I knew your name there a minute ago. A new addition to our normal operational package… interesting, especially if the DG has voted you in. Hey, you must know Peter Sanderson over there already."

He turned and called out to another man seated near the front of the room. "Hey Peter, we just met your recent recruit."

The man looked back and shook his hand dismissively, saying nothing.

Sackville looked slightly embarrassed. "Probably got things on his mind. As you know he runs the surveillance and counter surveillance teams."

Danny smiled wryly.

Sanderson had never been enthusiastic about him being imposed on his team without his prior agreement and selection. The specifics of his role had fortunately not necessitated any close contact with the head of the surveillance section prior to this, but he was aware of the man's frosty demeanor towards him.

Some more people drifted in including Rebecca-Fullerton Smythe the DG, and a young attractive Asian woman. Within minutes the meeting was called to order.

Trevor Hawthorn looked completely at home up front addressing the group, and he wasted no time in getting started.

"Good morning and welcome. I believe you all know each other, and our newest member is Danny Quigley back there

13

who, I noted, has already introduced himself to most of you. We are pleased to have our Director General join us, and she came in with Alina Tariq who works with Peter Sanderson as a field supervisor in his section. The other few people in the room, you can introduce yourselves to later.

"Why are we here? Well, it's not an unfamiliar topic as the media have been hammering it recently: returning Jihadists with British passports that, we suspect have been involved as terrorists in Iraq and Syria. Now our concern is that they will not be going down to the job centers looking for work, but planning to undermine the very core of British society: through violence and destruction, helped by young naïve Muslims that they will radicalize and train. Our job is to nip their plans in the bud in every way possible, either by stopping them at their entry points with the new legislation that allows us to do so, or putting surveillance on them and finding out where they're going and who they're contacting. I'm not one for big graphic names like the Americans have for their projects, but I've nevertheless selected the code word for this project - 'Trojan Horse'. I think you'll agree that this probably describes pretty well what it's about. Any comments so far?"

Phil Dawson, the break-in expert, had one. "Why let them back into the country in the first place if, as you say, they'll just go ahead and radicalize a whole bunch of potential terrorists?"

"Excellent point, and one that I intended to cover later in my briefing, but let me fill you in on our thoughts in this area. Firstly, if we have proof of terrorist activity abroad by young returning Muslims, we can arrest them, confiscate their passports and charge them in court. That's one option. Unfortunately we generally only hear about their terrorist activities when they get killed in Iraq or Syria, and the media have their grieving families on TV saying that they never knew anything about their radicalization to the ISIS cause. Be that as it may, and indeed it may be true to some extent, as with teenagers of my own I can testify as to how close-mouthed they can be."

There were some chuckles and knowing looks around the room.

Hawthorn continued:

"Lacking any proof, we can still pick them up on suspicion and question them about their itinerary: countries they'd visited; the route they took getting back to the U.K. for example. We could ask for proof of their attendance at specific madrassas in the Middle East, as some of them do issue documentation for attendance. Indeed we have established relationships with a number of legitimate Imams over there, which the investigation section under Jerry Sackville will be chasing up.

In the same vein, we'll be cultivating the co-operation of Interpol and other Police Forces overseas to work with us on 'Trojan Horse' as it ramps up. So, if we have proof of terrorist activities with these returnees, we'll arrest them and charge them, but we all know what happens then in this enlightened and democratic country, don't we?"

"Yeah, we all know what happens…they get bail, and are basically walking around free until their trial comes up. We could do with a Guantanamo here to throw those bastards into!" Phil Dawson said tersely.

Hawthorn nodded. "Exactly Phil, but be that as it may, we're stuck with the system. Now that brings me directly to your role in this. The problem, of course, is that once they're out on bail, they have time to approach, radicalize and train young Muslims here in the U.K. Before you know it, we have an underground fifth column, with a growing hatred for Britain and all it stands for. We need your team, or teams as the case may be, to put these people under 24/7 surveillance on their arrival by plane, ship or Euro Tunnel. We need to find out where they're living, who they're meeting with and attempting to influence. Any questions so far?" he asked, looking around.

Jerry Sackville raised his hand. "No questions as such Sir, but I have a couple of ideas for Phil's group that would make their surveillance work somewhat easier."

Hawthorn pursed his lips, glancing down at his notes for a moment.

15

"OK, but could you take that up with Phil himself later so that I can carry on. I have another meeting scheduled with our Home Office contact, which we have to keep in the loop. We're also asking them for a large increase in funding for this operation, and I feel positive that we'll get it. Good news for all of you, especially Phil's team working all the hours that God sends them. Any other questions?" he asked impatiently.

Peter Sanderson raised his hand and quickly glanced back at Danny sitting off to one side.

'Oh, oh' Danny thought 'here it comes'.

"Yes, I do have a query that concerns my section. Why do we need to bring in someone like Quigley back there, lacking the culture and disciplines of our organization here at MI5, when we in surveillance already have a tried and tested team who've worked together, and trust each other? I understand he's ex-Sass, but he got out of the Regiment over 4 years ago. His skills would be pretty stale by now and probably out of date. Anyway, the DG has an SAS Saber team on standby when we need it" he said pointedly.

With that Rebecca stood up and walked across to the lectern.

Hawthorn stood back. She looked around the group.

"I'm delighted that Peter brought this up at this point in time, because it helps me to address the topic without it becoming a problem within the operation that we're putting together. With regards to Danny Quigley's qualifications within MI5, you probably wouldn't all be aware that while he served in the SAS Regiment, he worked closely with us in MI5 on a number of operations where he was seconded to us for his specialist skills. He was also trained at the farm in all the type of stuff that any active recruit has to undergo before we let them loose. The last few months I've deliberately placed him in an area where he was involved in screening those people who require clearance prior to taking up top-level government jobs and our own more recent MI5 recruiting requirements. Not a great challenge for Danny, but he never grumbled, and in the process did inculcate some of the essence of what we're trying to do here in our security organization, so I'm happy with where he's at right now. Prior to coming here five months ago, I sent him out to Nigeria to screen some applicants for highly sensitive jobs within our Government. While there, he uncovered a plot by a Nigerian terrorist group to place a job applicant in the foreign office, that would have allowed him access into the House of Commons, at which time he would have been wearing a suicide vest. Danny managed to stop the plot by uncovering some fake references over there in Nigeria."

There were murmurs around the room.

Jerry leaned over and patted Danny on the shoulder.

Rebecca held up her hand, stilling the conversations.

"On top of that, while he was there he uncovered a plot by Boko Haram to bomb a church, where the parish priest was the brother of one of his SAS mates in Hereford. Danny, along with six men and two women, led a pre-emptive strike across the border into Cameroon, where they wiped out a Boko Haram group of up to fifty highly trained fighters. "

On hearing this, there were shocked looks around the room, and Peter looked like he would sooner be somewhere else right then.

Rebecca motioned to Danny.

"So much for his skills being stale. Now, this new operation has some new elements to it, and I'm going to ask Danny to volunteer some thoughts on it. Danny, can you come up here please?"

He wasn't one to seek up-front opportunities to address people, but his previous experience in carrying out briefings and presentation while in the Regiment was obvious as he took over the front position, as was his confident stance.

He looked around the room carefully, reading their body language and formulating his thoughts as he did so.

"OK, here's the bottom line. Your typical radicalized young Muslims coming back here, will be different than the nice biddable young ones you know, who have been brought up and educated in Britain with good law abiding parents who tried to steer them in the right direction: get an education and that will be your passport to a good job, and so on. Those

17

exposed to radicalization, brainwashing, and mental conditioning, will come back with a hatred for everything that the west stands for, especially democracy. You can see it in their eyes. Far above everything else they pick up over there, is the deliberate brutalization to de-sensitize their western upbringing and morals. Shooting and beheading prisoners is part of their forced indoctrination, as is kidnapping, raping women and children. In fact they're taught that these are their rights – won in battle. They learn to fight, use weapons, and are easily molded into suicide bombers with promises of immediate rewards when they die. I doubt if any of you were faced with someone coming at you, firing a weapon and screaming 'Allahu Akbar'. Well, I have."

"Jesus" Peter Sanderson whispered, "What did you do?"

"Nothing else I could do. I sent him up to his seventy virgins that had been promised him, with the help of my MP5."

He allowed the silence to build up in the room before his final remarks.

"So, what I'm telling you is that this new operation will have considerable dangers for those of you out in the front line here in the U.K. It's a new ball game, and I'm urging you to develop a new respect for your enemy, a new alertness, and a new awareness that this could be a new front line in a battle where you could be a casualty. I'm looking forward to working with Peter where I would welcome learning of his experience in surveillance, and I'll be available wherever anyone needs some extra guidance in survival and staying alive. This may seem alarmist to some of you, but these Jihadists are really vicious people, and they're coming your way, and if we don't contain them, life as you know it here in England may never be the same again."

He stopped.

Rebecca could see that half the people in the room were still mentally assimilating the information they had just heard, while the rest were wondering what could soon be happening to their quiet safe way of life.

One person had certainly got the message.

18

Peter Sanderson walked over and shook his hand vigorously.

The Director General look pleased.

Shortly afterwards the meeting wound up.

CHAPTER 4

"THWACK!"

Alina Tariq's body jumped as one of the twisting, straining figures she was watching was slammed down onto the judo mat. Suddenly the crowd stood up and exploded into shouts and clapping, and her face cleared with relief.

The one standing with a huge grin on his face was Danny Quigley.

She stood up too and, leaning forwards caught the arm of the woman in the seat in front of her.

"What does that mean?" she asked loudly.

The woman glanced back, her face reflecting her excitement.

"Danny's got his 5th Dan. He's just thrown his competitor, who could be a number of grades above him!"

"How can you tell from here?"

"Danny is a 4th Dan black belt. His opponent is wearing a red and white belt. That means he could be a 6th, 7th, or even an 8th Dan black belt. All three grades wear the same color. With his technical demonstrations over the past few days coupled with his competition skills, especially the one you just saw, Danny will undoubtedly achieve his 5th Dan black belt."

The woman looked closer at Alina's face. "Your boyfriend?"

"Ah no, just a work colleague dropping in with a message. I know nothing about judo" she replied.

The woman laughed. "It probably looks dead boring to you. All that pulling each other around and no apparent action like you see with wrestlers on TV. When you know something about it though, it's easier to understand: the grips, attempted throws and attacks, the feints, hand movements designed to create reaction in an opponent and move them to a weaker state... the escapes as you encounter resistance, the use of multiple aggressive attacks, all the time maintaining contact as your Uke, sorry that's opponent, resists."

Alina looked confused. "You obviously know judo. Are you a follower or a competitor yourself?" she asked tentatively.

"I'm a brown belt, hoping to make black belt next year. You get marked on how you do Katas, that's a laid out series of technical movements out on the floor, supervised by independent judges from the National Judo Association, and you're scored zero to ten points on each technical movement. For Ist Dan black belt for example, you need 190 marks in order to pass."

Alina was impressed with her obvious involvement in the sport. "So what would Danny have had to score... his...ah... 5th Dan you said?"

"Yeah, that says it all. It requires 800 points to pass! That's some achievement! I should tell you for markers, that Ist Dan as I mentioned, has a pass mark requirement of 190, 2nd Dan 320, 3rd Dan 520, 4th Dan 700 and 5th Dan as I just mentioned, 800 marks. We all know of course that Danny, when he was in the Military, used to spend his leave practicing in Dojos in Japan and South Korea, which shows when you're in competition at this level. Oh, and you have to be at least 29 years of age to go for your 5th Dan in competition, or age 34 if you're only demonstrating the technical movements."

The woman laughed and clapped her arm.

"I'm in overdrive right now, but Danny getting his 5th Dan is such a mega achievement for our club here. If you want his

21

attention you'd better grab him before we drag him off to the pub after he hits the showers."

Danny did a double take when he spotted her.

He had just waded through the many club members and visitors from other clubs, who were clapping his shoulders and shouting congratulations.

When he reached her his eyebrows raised in query.

"Hey, what's up? I wasn't expecting you here."

"Don't worry, no panic as such. Mr. Sackville wants us back in this afternoon for an important briefing. As you know we were all asked to leave contact details as to where we would be at all times, and you weren't answering your mobile phone, so I was dispatched to get you."

He grimaced. "Oh shoot! I was out on the mat in competition and you can't carry a phone out there. Have I time for a quick shower? I'll have to defer the belt presentation ceremony for a later date" he said with some chagrin.

"Well you do have time for a shower and indeed a coffee afterwards if you'd like, before we head in. Sorry about the belt presentation. I spoke to a female club colleague of yours, a brown belt she said, and who was looking forward to dragging you off to a pub somewhere to celebrate. I'm told your win is a big boost for the club here."

"Oh, that would be Erin, she's as keen as mustard and lives and breathes judo. It's her whole life."

He picked up the unspoken question in her expression. "She's just a keen club member Alina. No relationship beyond that."

She lifted her hands dismissively. "Hey, none of my business Danny. I'm just the messenger here. Look, I'll go and move the car, as it's parked illegally, and you know these London Traffic Inspectors. How about I meet you across the road in that coffee shop as soon as you've showered. I doubt you'd be left alone after your win if we went upstairs to the deli here."

They parted as she turned and headed towards the door, aware of the many male looks she was generating from her slim attractive build and dark hair.

22

She smiled to herself. Hmm… perhaps joining a judo club might be better than that computer-dating agency that some of her single friends were suggesting to her.

Outside she was just in time to stop a Traffic Warden from ticketing her car. He stormed off when she appeared.

She had to travel two blocks to find an underground car park where she ended up on the 4th floor. When she finally reached the restaurant, breathless, Danny was already sitting in a seat near the back, his hair still damp from the shower.

"For a moment I thought I'd got the wrong place" he smiled as he slid a seat out for her.

She shook her head. "This city Danny, my God, it can be a nightmare at times, but you know what? I wouldn't live anywhere else in the world."

"Yeah, me too, and I've seen a lot of other countries as you can imagine."

The waitress came over. Danny ordered a coffee and she chose a herbal tea. They both relaxed while the waitress quickly returned with their order.

In their previous two rather hectic meetings he hadn't really realized how attractive she was. Now he suddenly became aware of the dusky color of her skin, her brown eyes, long dark hair and quiet self-assurance. He caught her studied look as she finished stirring honey into her cup, leaning forward as she did so.

"Danny, you know what? There was something about the club I just visited over there…the intensity and the interest of the spectators…the people themselves, so involved. Tell me a little about judo, it's history and background for example. I'm still confused about the ranking system that your colleague Erin briefly fired at me."

"Okay, where to start, that's my dilemma? We could spend a couple of hours on this topic."

"I really meant a broad-stroke background on the sport itself and how you personally got involved" she prompted.

"I can do that for sure. Let's see, a Japanese chap called Kano Jigoro in 1883 was the founder of what we call the Kodokan Kyu-Dan ranking system. This has built-in challenging tests as you can imagine - in the technical knowledge of judo, as well as the understanding and application of the various techniques, as one progresses up through the grades."

"Tell me about the black belt system Danny, please. I mean, how high can you actually go?" she asked.

He laughed, obviously enjoying her interest.

"A trifle complex here. You see, no one has ever been promoted to a rank higher than 10th Dan black belt, but theoretically the judo ranking system is not limited to 10 degrees of black belt, if one reaches a stage above that. Kodokan has never awarded more than fifteen 10th Dans. Now in Jan 2006 a remarkable thing happened, three individuals were promoted to this rank simultaneously, and that was the first ever at the same time, and the first in 22 years. I even remember their names. They're ingrained in the memories of all who follow judo: Tosmiro Daigo, Ichiro Abe and Yoshimi Osawa."

"Erin told me a bit about how the 6th, 7th and 8th Dans all wear red and white colors, and today you apparently beat one of them. She pointed out that you had trained overseas when you were in the Military."

"Well yes, my extra training, competing in various overseas clubs, gave me the edge today for sure, especially the time I spent in Japanese dojos. You asked how I got involved in the sport. Well initially, I was in the Parachute Regiment where we were all single, gung- ho individuals who wanted to learn how to look after ourselves. Afterwards in the Saas, as troopers, I was taught a more deadly form of unarmed combat. I mean, if you're in action, you can't dance around like we do on the mat in judo. You have to finish off the enemy before they scream and alert the group you're coming against."

"From the rumors floating around Thames House, you were in that position quite often, in and out of the Saas" she said, gazing intently at him.

He shrugged. "It's not something any of us who've been there would talk openly about. Let's just say I'm lucky to be sitting here in front of you right now, and the reason is that I keep training, staying aware and alert at all times, and dare I say, even now, sitting here in this coffee house."

He leaned forward. "Enough about me Alina. I met you and a number of the counter intelligence group the other day but never had a chance to speak one-to-one with any of them, especially yourself as Second in Command to Peter Sanderson. How about filling me in on your background and situation? For example, are you married and perhaps have some children?"

"No to both those questions Danny. I did marry someone I met in college several years ago, but it didn't work out. He was a Caucasian and my parents were dead set against the whole thing - marrying outside my own race, for example, was shameful to them. Well I proved them right didn't I? It didn't work out."

He could see that she found the topic difficult and moved on.

"So, what did you major at in college and how did you end up at MI5?"

"Oh, I stupidly took an Arts degree which was totally useless when I started job hunting. I worked as a shop assistant for a few years and ended up in the ultimate store, Harrods, where my language skills helped with their Arab visitors. Did you know that at times they actually close the store to the public, when some Arabian Prince is visiting London with his retinue of wives, children and staff?

Believe me, it was always worth their while! Someone from the Security Services spotted me one day and suggested that I try for an interview. There was a growing recognition within MI5 that they should become more diversified with the large Pakistani and Asian population in the U.K., so here I am."

"How did you get into counter surveillance then?" he asked.

"Basically boredom with translating documents and sitting in on job interviews and doing some background screening which I believe you've been doing recently."

He nodded. "You got it in one. It is boring! I'm not sure how much longer I would have stuck it out if the DG hadn't thrown me a lifeline. So how did you move on from there?"

"Basically I threatened to leave if I didn't get something more exciting or interesting to do. It happened to fit in with some new initiatives they were planning, so I ended up at the MI5 farm and completed the training with top marks. According to my boss's yearly job reviews, I took to the practical aspects of the position like a duck to water. You know, following people around, blending in and maintaining my focus on getting results on whatever operation or project I'm on."

"Hey, I'm impressed, and hopefully we may be doing some work together in the future. I'll tell you sometime about a lady I worked with in Nigeria. Was she a kick-ass female if ever there was one? Wow! So I have the highest regard for the ability of women in difficult situations, I can tell you. By the way, she's a nun now."

She looked shocked. "A nun!" She glanced at her watch.

"God, the time just slipped away. I'll have to leave my car where it is. We can just make it back in time if we get moving and catch a subway without delay."

She grabbed his arm as they both stood up. "A nun, you say! I've got to hear about this later."

They eventually got off the subway and headed for the escalators, and Danny was pleasantly surprised when she linked arms with him. He wondered if it was simply a Pakistani tradition. However, he liked it!

CHAPTER 5

It was Jerry Sackville who had called the meeting.

A large contingent of the counter surveillance section was present. Danny counted upwards of thirty people, and he made a mental note to introduce himself to them later if and when the opportunity presented itself. Some of the people he had met before in his background screening project, and others with Alina more recently, including an additional five women.

He couldn't pinpoint the precise genealogy of all the people present, but half were white people and the rest a mixture of Asian, and some Africans, possibly Nigerian. One of the criteria of being a good surveillance operative was the ability to blend in, and he could see that a number of the agents could be described as individuals who would not dramatically stand out in a crowd. However part of the agenda later in the afternoon was bringing in a make-up artist from the theatre who would demonstrate how to change appearances instantly, when and where required.

Sackville called the meeting to order.

"Thanks for coming in at short notice, and for some I know, very short notice. The Director, Mr. Hawthorn is at a meeting with the Home Office and couldn't be here. The reason for the urgency of this meeting is as follows:

As my section is responsible for counter terrorist investigations and research, we have been flat out establishing clearer lines of communication with our overseas contacts in Embassies, our MI6 contacts, Interpol, Travel Agencies and companies overseas. There was a black hole in Turkey for some time with the complexity of relationships there, where at some level they were funding ISIS in addition to filtering would-be Jihadists from various countries across the border into Syria. With the worldwide coalition established by the U.S.A., it seems that Turkey is now starting to realize that you can't embrace an evil like ISIS and remain untouched by what's going on around you. After all they are a NATO country as well. The bottom line here, and the reason for this meeting is that we have received information of three Jihadists who just crossed the border from Syria, and who appear to be heading back here to the U.K. The Turkish police tell us that when they went into a travel agency there, they specifically asked for a route that would be circuitous enough to camouflage where they had started out. They didn't specifically state that, but it was blatantly obvious what their objective was. Fortunately for us and our efforts in reaching out to the Turks, the Travel Agent had their pictures taken, ostensibly to facilitate their journey."

He paused for effect. "Here are their pictures."

With that the pictures of three men shot up on the screen. The whole room leaned forward. Danny was particularly struck by the hard edge to the men's faces. It used to be called 'the thousand yard stare' for soldiers returning from battle. Men who had been unceasingly under fire, beyond what a normal man could withstand for very long.

Jerry turned off the screen.

"You'll all have copies of these three after the meeting and their names which they're travelling under and which match their U.K. passports. Now the travel plans of these three bring them from Istanbul to Vienna, and then into Amsterdam Airport this evening, and they're booked into a downtown hotel, and fly into Heathrow in the morning. The plan I'm working on has two of your team flying out tonight to Amsterdam and following the three suspects back on the same plane, obviously without giving their identity away. We know we can arrest all three as they land, on suspicion of carrying out terrorist activities abroad, however we feel that these three

28

have a more dangerous role to play here than just returning to normal life back in the U.K., so we intend to have a team follow them when they disembark and see where they lead us."

One of the people in the room, a man, raised his arm. "Could we collect their bags when they land here, and plant some bugs in them?"

Jerry looked around at the group.

Danny raised his arm. "The problem with that would be that they would be alerted to their bags being pulled in, and suspect that bugs had been planted. It's an excellent idea, but could I suggest that we get the Dutch police to plant some devices after their bags are checked in for Heathrow? Something pretty undetectable, and not touch their bags at all when they land in the U.K.?"

Jerry smiled broadly "I'm glad you mentioned that Danny, because you're one of the two people we chose to fly over to Amsterdam this evening, and Danielle will accompany you. Your cover is being a young honeymoon couple returning from some tropical paradise. Your task, now that you brought it up, will be to interact with the Dutch police in planting those devices. I'll give you the contact details and set up the arrangement when this meeting ends. Your task is to follow them on the plane, not too closely, and observe their movements, particularly if they communicate in any way with others on the flight. There could be more than three of them travelling, so keep and eye out for any covert attempt at communication, equally when disembarking at Heathrow and coming through immigration and customs. Your task will be taken over by one of Peter Sanderson's surveillance teams at the Airport, at which time we will bring yourself and Danielle back here for debriefing and further tasking. Now apart from the Amsterdam trip, which I will fully brief the team on, are there any questions? I hope there aren't because time is getting on."

There were none.

There was however a great buzz of excitement in the room as people turned to speak to each other. They all remembered the 2005 subway and bus bombings in the city, and realized

29

that this could happen again, but with much more deadly consequences if they didn't manage to contain the highly trained and now brutalized Jihadists, bringing a new style of violence and savagery back to their homeland.

CHAPTER 6

On the flight to Schiphol Airport in the Netherlands, Danny found out further background information on Danielle Ackerson, his companion on the flight. The feisty, tall, thirty-one year old was married with two children aged three and five, and she was an ex-Metropolitan Police detective. Her husband Paul was a School Principal and soccer referee in his spare time. They were renting an apartment in central London, close to the school where her husband worked.

Danny was impressed with her studied professional air, and despite her obvious good looks, he could see her quite easily displaying a tougher side, carrying out her previous role as a Detective. She was dressed for the short flight in slacks and a yellow blouse with a colored scarf around her neck, and a short fawn jacket. They were both travelling with carry-on bags, and on the flight out they weren't concerned about being 'in-role' as honeymooners.

"So, from Police Detective to MI5 Intelligence Officer" he mused, "that begs the question Danielle, why this particular career change?"

She glanced across at him, her hazel eyes appraising him carefully.

"Basically harassment from male colleagues. I've found that bringing this up with the macho male species, I don't usually get much sympathy. With respect Danny, you would certainly qualify in the macho league, wouldn't you agree?"

"Oh shoot Danielle, ten minutes into the flight and I've put my foot in it. I'm sorry. If it helps, I've worked with some really competent and capable women, who could kick ass with the best of them, so I sure don't have any hang-ups about working with them, and if I may say so, working with you personally."

She relaxed visibly.

"I think I gathered that when you were speaking to the group the other day. You didn't appear to be concerned about impressing anyone and you looked and sounded comfortable in your own skin. When the Director teamed me up with you for this trip, I felt that we could work well together. Perhaps at another time and place Danny, I might share some of my police background experiences. They weren't all bad, I can tell you that right now."

They chatted for a while as the airline stewardess came along dispensing soft drinks, and avoided discussing details of the operation with other passengers around.

Once landed in Schiphol, they went along to the security section as arranged, and met with two Dutch Police Officers. They produced the latest 'bugs' obtained by Trevor Hawthorn from MI6 and demonstrated just how they were to be installed in the Jihadist's baggage. They also supplied copies of the pictures of the three men taken by the travel agent in Turkey. MI5 had already briefed the Dutch by Skype earlier in the afternoon so Danny and Danielle were out of there within 15 minutes and on the way to the Bastion De Luxe Hotel in one of their shuttle buses, where separate rooms had been pre-booked for them. The hotel was twenty minutes from the city center of Amsterdam, and they agreed to have supper there after they had freshened up. They both laughed when she shared that, in fact, she and her husband had been there before, on their honeymoon.

Danny had been there a number of times too, so neither needed to go on the Grand Canal tour again, despite its delightful experience. Once they were booked in they checked their watches and agreed to meet in the lobby in 30 minutes. Danny had the receptionist arrange for a taxi to be standing by.

Amsterdam was always a delight no matter how many times one visited it. They spent some time strolling around the numerous bridges overlooking the canals and marveled at the number of cyclists still out on the roads despite the shades of evening closing in. Finally they wandered down a small roadway, which seemed off the beaten track, and into an establishment that had a 'food and drink' poster on the outside window. Inside they saw that it had a long bar with seats spaced out along the front, and realized that it probably served what they would call pub grub rather than an a la carte menu.

They hesitated inside the door and were immediately accosted by the barman who came up to them.

"Here for food or drinks or both?" he asked, speaking in English.

They looked at each other.

"Food really." Danny answered, "what's on the menu this evening?"

"Ah you're English, great we love the English in Amsterdam, and they love our food. You're lucky this evening, we have some really delicious specials still available back in the kitchen."

He gestured across to the area where there were half a dozen tables, just two of them occupied.

"Why don't you both sit down and I'll run through the specials with you, and get you a drink while you're waiting for the food?"

So that was how they spent a pleasant hour, both relaxing and chatting with the business of the day taken care of. Danny hesitated for a moment before ordering a beer which he would usually pass on were he on an operation that required his full alertness, but with Danielle ordering a glass of wine, he was happy to go for his old Regiment drink, a Stella beer.

The barman was telling the truth, the specials were delicious, and they worked away, enjoying the food with little conversation.

They had just finished when the peaceful atmosphere in the bar was disrupted by four young men who lunged into the room laughing loudly at some joke being shared between them. The men were the large, blond haired type that could be seen anywhere in the city, and who were normally well mannered and courteous. However these were different in that they were loud and truculent in addressing the barman, who was already beginning to look uneasy. They argued with him when he brought their drinks, claiming that he'd got it wrong, one of them tossing a full beer bottle into the back area of the bar.

Finally they appeared to settle down, somewhat.

Danny and his companion looked at each other, and by mutual agreement decided to leave. He touched her elbow.

"I'll go and pay the barman and have a quick trip to the washroom. Will you be OK for a moment Danielle?"

She nodded.

"No problem Danny. Go for it."

He went to the end of the bar, and as the barman came through from the kitchen, he gestured to him with the universal 'give me the bill' hand sign. Almost immediately the group of men at the bar started to heckle him.

"Hey, what's the matter man, don't like our company?" one of them shouted.

"We'd like to get to know your friend, I think she'd like us, especially after a long haired wimp like you" another roared, thumping the counter.

Danny didn't reply, not even acknowledging their presence, and mentally made a decision to forget his trip to the washroom. As he was putting his money back in his wallet he leaned forward and whispered to the barman.

"I'd call the police if I was you Mate. These chaps are bad luck."

"They're from the university. We get a lot of business from them during the day. My boss would fire me if I called the police."

He spoke a bit louder as Danny was moving off.

As Danny walked back to the table this gesture seemed to inflame them.

"Hey, what did you say to him?   Did I hear him say police?"

34

When he got back Danielle was already on her feet and moving towards the door. The catcalls increased in volume with some very personal comments directed at Danielle that made him hesitate, but she tugged at his arm as they went outside and moved across to the sidewalk. They both breathed a sigh of relief.

"Jeepers Danny, for a moment there…"

She spoke too soon. The bar door slammed open behind them and the four men spilled out into the street. There was obviously only one thing on their minds – trouble! All four marched aggressively towards them shouting.

"Don't rush off, we'd like to have a little fun with you. Well not you, but your sexy friend there."

Danny knew a bad situation when he saw one. Still, he wanted to avoid a confrontation that might involve any sort of police presence. He could imagine the headline in the British papers;

'MI5 Agents involved in a brawl in the Netherlands'.

He had to defuse this as quickly as possible, if he could.

As he turned and walked a few paces back toward the group he could hear Danielle's concerned voice behind him. "Danny…"

The men were bunched up with one of the larger guys a couple of steps out in front. He halted when Danny came up to him, and raised both his hands.

"Hey look guys, we're just out for a couple of drinks and a quick bite. We don't want any trouble, OK Mate?" he asked.

The big guy laughed and, turning, he shared the remark with the others in Dutch, then turned back still grinning, and nodded his head.

"Mate is it? Couple of Brits we have here then? Treated me like shit when they kicked me out of Oxford. Well, I'm not your Mate, but we'd like to do some mating with your friend back there with the cute ass. Get it?"

Danny knew he'd lost it. Talking his way out of this situation was out of the question. He knew what he had to do and decided to get under their skin and make them react more emotionally rather than the studied way they were starting to edge up on him. He leaned back, peering up at the first man. "You know what, I thought you chaps were German back there in the pub...all that blonde hair...the arrogance, the master race attitude..."

The man reared back, his eyes widening in shock and swung a massive roundhouse blow at his head. Danny blocked the blow and delivered an incredibly fast chop to the man's carotid artery, followed by an elbow smash to his jaw.

He was already falling when he shoved the inert form in front of the two men on his left and gave a savage side chop to the exposed neck of the man on his right, kicking down on the right side of his knee and hearing it crunch.

The second attacker was already falling, when he jumped sideways across the sprawled figure on the ground, blocking two punches from the third man who, from his stance, looked like he knew some martial arts. The two traded several brutal blows as the fourth man jumped back and reached into his pocket.

"Look out Danny, he's got a knife!" he heard Danielle warn.

At that moment the figure he was trading blows with, missed a blow and slammed into Danny. Hours of training and conditioning kicked in and, using his hip and the back of his ankle for leverage, he lifted him into a high hip throw and slammed him down onto the pavement.

He would normally have followed him down and finished him off but he only had a second to hurl himself sideways as a knife slashed past his ribs.

He did a fast forward roll and was on his feet in seconds, turning to meet his opponent, lunging at him with the knife.

Danny didn't like people who pulled knives on him. He'd seen a martial arts expert in a TV interview advise the presenter to "run like hell" if someone pulled a knife on him. He knew it was good advice, but right then it wasn't an option.

He backed up as the man came for him, slashing and stabbing.

He was watching for his chance.

It came.

He turned slightly as the knife came at him again, clasped the arm tightly and levered upwards on the elbow joint...breaking it.

The man screamed and dropped to his knees.

On his right hand side he glimpsed the attacker that he had used a hip throw on, struggle to his feet, and without thinking snapped an incredibly fast side knuckle strike to the bridge of his nose, sending him flying back onto the ground, clutching his face and moaning.

On hearing a noise he turned and saw Danielle kicking the first attacker in the crotch, dropping him in a heap on the pavement. The man had apparently started to get back up onto his feet. He heard a shout from the pub doorway and saw the barman staring at them.

Danielle shouted.

"Let's get out of here Danny. We can't afford any police involvement."

He grabbed her hand and they ran round the corner. They crossed a main thoroughfare and Danny started looking for a taxi.

She pulled his arm.

"Not here Danny, too close to that pub. The police will check with all taxies in this vicinity. Let's keep moving."

They kept going and even jumped on a bus, not caring where it was going. It seemed hours later that they made it back to the hotel. They were both too exhausted to even sit down and discuss the evening.

It was Danielle who said it.

"Let's just get to bed and we can discuss this in the morning. I hope we've covered our tracks on this evening's incident. If it's any consolation to you Danny, I don't think you had any way out of that situation back there. They meant business and I heard what they had in mind for me, so thanks for what you did."

On that note they went their separate ways.

CHAPTER 7

It was obvious that neither had enjoyed much sleep during the night. Danny had tossed and turned, re-living the incident outside the eatery the previous evening. He wished that somehow they could have avoided the situation completely, but short of turning tail and running which was not in his nature, he couldn't see any way of avoiding the affray.

Danielle looked worn out, and had obviously managed very little sleep either.

They looked at each other across the small hotel breakfast table where other early travelers were bustling around them with paper plates and cups of coffee.

In a quiet moment Danielle leaned forward and spoke in a low voice across the table.

"You look like I feel Danny. I can tell you that if we wander in to Thames House looking like this, the rumors will start flying...you know?"

He grimaced, shaking his head. "The funny thing is that on my previous trips to Amsterdam I found the Dutch to be very friendly and made us Brits welcome, which goes back to the Second World War I'm told. So much for a pleasant stroll around the canals and a quiet meal. Sorry about that Danielle, but thinking about it most of the night as it happens, I can't see how we could have avoided it. If this gets back to Thames House we're in deep shit, well I am anyway."

She reached across and briefly touched his arm.

"You know something Danny, I enjoyed my honeymoon here and always found the Dutch with their excellent English, both courteous and helpful. However I can't see any way we could have walked away from that bunch. They were looking for trouble and we looked like easy meat. I heard what they said about having their way with me, and they weren't kidding. All I can say is thanks Danny, for sticking up for me back there."

He relaxed momentarily.

"Well, I liked the way you left an impression on that big-mouth with a perfectly aimed kick. Thanks for watching my back."

She leaned back shaking her head.

"You must be kidding. I probably saved that poor bastard from having some of his limbs broken."

She studied him closely. "If you'll pardon my French, and especially at breakfast for a supposed honeymoon couple, and especially from the female of the species, you were like a fucking buzz-saw out there last night. Like something switched on, and once you started moving, nothing could stop you. I used to watch my uncle working in a sawmill when I was a child, and he had that same mechanical approach... grinding away at the timber coming at him up the line. I don't know how to describe it any differently. I never saw anything like it Danny. You were like a goddam grinding machine out there! Alina said you were into judo, but that wasn't judo you were using last night."

He put his hand up to his face thoughtfully.

"Well, there was a competition in South America a few years ago between different martial arts styles, judo, karate, kung fu and some others, and guess what? The judo chaps came out in front, mainly because opponents, sooner or later, had some body contact, and then the judo people had a distinct advantage and were able to slam them to the floor in a hip throw. I decided to get highly trained in that but also in other combat skills, mainly because I have an intense passion for all styles of self-defense. You've triggered a train of thought here. I just realized that I've improved. If I'd had that run-in

39

four years ago, those four thugs could have been dead right now."

She paled. "Jesus Danny, what d'you mean?"

"Well basically the Military initially break you down until all your moral conditioning, upbringing, and normal thought processes are swept aside. Bear in mind that this happens in a group as well, so it accelerates the process. Then they re-build you into a deadly form of their own making. Basically from there on in, they're teaching you to kill as quickly and efficiently as possible, not only with a variety of weapons, but especially using your whole body as a tactical weapon."

She looked confused. "But surely this is just the normal practice in Military training, isn't it?

"Yes and no. Think about it. Out there in Afghanistan, myself and a group of eight or sixteen troopers, depending on the mission, climb into choppers and head out into bandit country to find an enemy. A Military General once described his men in battle as 'like an iron peg hammered into the frozen ground in the winter'. Well Danielle, that was us when we hit the ground.   Operating as a team we were basically indestructible, and the enemy couldn't touch us in battle. When we encounter an enemy we finish them off quickly, and perhaps grab a prisoner, if that's part of the mission. Then we head back to Base, get some food and sleep after the de-brief. The following night we might be off again. We're like aliens in an alien landscape, and the only thing that helps us survive is our training, our single minded focus, and our fierce loyalty to our mates fighting alongside us."

"So where's this leading Danny?"

"Leading to the day they say goodbye to you when your time's up and you decide not to re-enlist. They shake your hand and say basically 'Look, you're a civilian now, forget all that stuff we taught you and be a good boy out there you hear, or they'll lock you up and throw away the key.' Not only that, but I could recount stories about myself and the ex-Regiment lads heading down to the job centers and having some pimply twenty year old telling us that we don't have the skills employers are looking for."

"So, reading between the lines here Danny, if you had run into those louts from last night four years ago, your training would have kicked in and you would have finished them off?"

"In a nut shell, yes. I've managed to place what I would call a behavioral wedge between the old Danny Quigley, the assassin, the sniper, the destroyer of the enemy, to now using as much force as is deemed necessary to sort out the situation."

She shook her head helplessly, "and you call what you did last night as using as much force as was necessary? Oh man, we should have had you as our trainer in the Metropolitan Police Academy, when I joined up. They would have loved you!"

Any further conversation was interrupted by an announcement that the shuttle bus was outside and would leave in ten minutes for the Airport.

They had an agreed routine worked out with the Dutch security people and it was the same two individuals from the evening before who, when they arrived, helped them by-pass the various passport and security checks. They were brought through to a small room, which looked like it might have been used for interviews or interrogations. It was there that Danielle got to work, watched with interest by the security people.

She produced a comprehensive theatre make-up kit and proceeded to work on Danny first, the task being to change his outward appearance.

That was not difficult as she simply created more fullness to his jaws and face with some implants slipped inside his mouth. Then she highlighted his eyebrows, and finally had him put on a plain pair of reading glasses.

One of the watching security detail whistled in appreciation.

"That's amazing, in just five minutes" he exclaimed.

Even Danny had to agree.

She took another couple of minutes to get him to change his military stance and take on more of a slouch to suit his 'geeky' glasses.

The transformation on Danielle took some extra time but the effect was equally impressive. Her main change was putting on a red wig and highlighting her cheekbones with make up which made her look younger and more chic. Danny felt they looked more like a honeymoon couple and unlikely to be recognized by the Jihadists, if they were part of a surveillance team later in the week.

It had been arranged for them to view the three suspects without being seen, as they went through passport control and security checkpoints. Dutch Security had already arranged to divert the baggage of the three men and plant the bugs carefully, without disturbing anything that might be noticed when they opened their bags later.

With some time to spare, they checked the pictures and reviewed their names one more time: Zain Waheed, Ali Hossain and Mohammed Shareef.

"Hard looking bastards" Danny commented.

"Hmm...the research people told us that most of them take on a Jihadist name when they go over and join a terrorist group, but they can hang on to their first name to avoid confusion when they're being trained and spoken to. Obviously the names we're looking at are their legal identities here in the U.K. It can be a trifle difficult when they get killed over there as it can take some time for the relatives to get word of their demise."

Danny's brow furrowed. "I have a bad feeling looking at the faces of these three individuals Danielle. We should lift all three of them at Heathrow and wring them out for information. Letting them loose on the ground in London's asking for trouble and will just result in more young Muslims being turned into twisted killers and suicide bombers" he grumbled.

"I guess Military life was simple, Danny. Just hose them down with an MP5, and that's it. Here in Britain we have to consider the legal issues and things like human rights, civil rights and a media that will hang you out to dry with a minimum of supportive material. Plus we have to obtain evidence that'll stand up in court and put them away for a good number of years, where they can no longer harm or radicalize any more impressionable young Muslims. It's just a game my friend and you have to learn to play it. We usually get there in the end, if that's any consolation."

At that point one of the Security personnel came in and gestured for them to follow him to the viewing window where they could watch the three Jihadists filing through.

Things started happening quite quickly after that.

Security had personnel controlling the lineup of people coming forward, one by one to passport control. They made sure that the three men were kept in the line for the checkpoint closest to the viewing window. They had no trouble recognizing them. The freshly shaven cheeks were a dead give away for starters, but Danny was struck by what he would have described as an insolence in the first one as he strutted up to the passport window.

"That's Mohammed Shareef" Danielle murmured as the first man's passport was being checked. They were looking at a tall, gaunt faced individual, with a hard alert stare, whose lips were set in a tight thin line. His head was moving around, and when his gaze flicked to the smoked window they were watching from, Danny felt a stir inside. He knew he was watching a stone-cold killer. The man suspected he was being watched. No doubt he had been well briefed for the trip. As he was released by passport control the second man came forward.

Danielle said nothing, but pointed to his picture and name underneath.

Ali Hossain was smaller than the first and looked a far cry from what they considered a Muslim fighter would look like, with a roly-poly walk and tentative steps. Danny thought he looked like some sort of bird, with his beak like face and jerky head movements.

Danielle shuddered.

"Can you feel it Danny? This one is pure evil! I can feel it from here. I felt like someone just walked over my grave. God, I bet he's got some history wherever he's come from right now."

He nodded.

"Yeah, I'd say he's a right piece of work for sure. Not someone I'd recommend you get stuck in a lift with, even if you are an ex-cop."

The third man Zain Waheed was different from the first two in that he looked more like a slim athletic schoolteacher or coach. He sauntered up to passport control as if he didn't have a care in the world. It was only when he also looked sideways momentarily at the viewing window that Danny saw the hard black gimlet eyes, and the cruel measuring look to his face.

"Another hard man" Danny muttered. "This guy's bad news for sure. I'd say he could out fight just about anything one could throw at him."

"Come on Danny! You can tell that merely by looking at him for a couple of minutes?" she queried skeptically.

"I've spent years in the company of hard dangerous men, and right now from the moment I saw his face I can tell you this, he qualifies as one of them."

Both were silent as they watched the last of the men walk through.

Danny was more convinced than ever that they shouldn't be letting them walk free when they reached Heathrow.

What was that saying about 'letting the genie out of the bottle'?

The MI5 pair didn't want to draw attention to themselves by organizing priority boarding, so they mingled with the other passengers and boarded when the seat numbers were called. However it had been arranged for them to sit several seats behind the Jihadists, in the opposite isle with Danny occupying the outside seat. Danielle sat in the middle and the window seat had deliberately been left vacant.

They weren't expecting anything untoward to occur on the flight, their objective being to keep the trio in sight, and in particular to watch for anyone else showing an interest in them.

The flight settled in to its normal routine... safety instructions and takeoff, followed by the usual trolleys in the aisle offering free coffee and nuts. A few people stood up when the stewards had removed the trolleys, and went forward to use the washroom. Danny had discussed with Danielle that he would go forward as well at some point, passing the three men, and familiarize himself more closely with their faces, without making it obvious.

He nudged her, then stood up and started moving forward slowly. As he did so another man also rose from a couple of seats ahead of him.

Danny wouldn't have noticed what followed if he hadn't been so close to him and trained to spot even small movements.

It was as smooth as a well-practiced spy passing a message in London's Hyde Park to a colleague. As the man in front of him passed the trio, his right hand brushed the elbow of the outside Jihadist, and Danny briefly spotted a small flash of white being dropped in his lap.

A note, he wondered?

When he passed the trio's seats seconds later, there was no sign of any piece of paper, but the man seated on the outside had his hand clenched tightly.

Danny casually followed the man in front as he proceeded up the aisle, then he slipped into a vacant seat just short of the washrooms. He wanted to get a frontal view of this fourth man as he exited the toilets, as he was obviously associated with the three Jihadists.

MI5 had no information on this fourth person and they would have to hustle when they landed at Heathrow, to try to establish his identity.

The washroom door opened and his target came out, slid the door closed behind him and passed Danny without a glance.

In that moment Danny was able to get a full view of the man -- a big burly, completely bald white man with a sort of western plains looks to him. In fact he saw that he was wearing cowboy boots, jeans and a black shirt. The ISIS color!

He had a broad forehead, with sunglasses anchored on the top of his head. Danny noted the studied confidence bordering on arrogance, as he strode past.

Knowing how alert and possibly paranoid the three Jihadists might be, Danny also went forward and used the washroom. After a suitable time he emerged and went back to his seat. None of the three men even glanced up at him as he passed, but his stride faltered momentarily when he heard a peculiar high pitched laugh coming from the smaller of the three men. He felt his muscles tighten at the sound and noticed that even the passengers in the immediate area seemed disconcerted.

Once seated again, he produced a notepad, made some brief notes of the incident and passed it to Danielle.

She stared sideways at him.

They would have to hustle at Heathrow if they were to find out the identity of this fourth mystery person. Somehow, they would have to contact the waiting surveillance team in time and get Danny forward into a viewing spot where he could point out this person of interest.

Sometimes plans made in a hurry work out magically and fall into place.

This one didn't.

Danny had made an assumption that the fourth man was a U.S. citizen and would be in the line up for foreign nationals as apposed to EU citizens where the three returning Jihadists would pass through. He managed with Danielle, to get set up on this window. One of the MI5 Heathrow surveillance team rushed in breathlessly as the line started moving forward.

The fourth man never showed up

It had been arranged that Security at Passport Control would merely give a cursory check on the other trio coming in, to allay any suspicion they might have.

Legislation in the U.K. now allowed a deeper screening and interrogation, leading to confiscation of passports where deemed necessary. In preparation for this morning's flight, Security prompted by MI5, placed a younger looking male Security Officer in the kiosk. They instructed him to look rattled and under pressure, not giving them a fuller check than was necessary.

Two of the surveillance team watched them pass through without incident and reported later that they had exchanged triumphant looks, once through Security.

Danny had got it wrong.

The fourth man must have had a EU passport, passed unnoticed through the Airport and was now in the U.K. Danielle checked and found that the three men had taken a train into central London and the surveillance team reported that there was no sign of the fourth person of interest.

The bugs in the baggage were apparently working, but the only sounds being heard were of a train rushing through the English countryside.

They were into the next phase.

Danny and Danielle took a train in and grabbed a taxi after the short journey to take them to Thames House and a de-brief.

47

CHAPTER 8

The meeting room had Jerry Sackville of counter terrorism, Peter Sanderson and Alina Tariq of counter surveillance, and Phil Dawson of the bugging section all waiting. Also some 'techies' involved in the ongoing monitoring of the planted bugs in the suitcases.

There were some nods of approval as the two entered the room and after some re-arranging of chairs and people grabbing tea and coffee drinks, the group settled down to hear the report of their trip to Amsterdam. There were a number of small tables set up in such a way that it provided an empty square in the middle where the presenter could stand and run the meeting.

Danielle succinctly reported the operation from the start of the day at Schiphol Airport where they observed the terrorists boarding the plane, and the trip across to the U.K. It was Danny's picking up on the passing of the presumed message to one of the trio that caused the most interest. However the mix-up at Heathrow brought groans from the group.

Jerry looked interested in his opinion that the fourth man was an American.

"It's not unusual for people in the U.S. who have Irish parents or even grandparents, to be able to apply for an Irish passport. It takes some time, but it means that when they land at a EU Airport, they line up with locals. Could be useful to a terrorist.   Your friend could have done that, so don't blame yourself for that call, Danny. Anyway, give me a description as best you can. That could be a starting place."

When he had done that, Danielle brought up Danny's reading of the Jihadists as being very dangerous people.

No one questioned that, but Peter Sanderson was interested in how he should factor the information into his counter surveillance teams' strategy.

Danny didn't mince his words.

"Your people should have some sort of back-up protection if they run into trouble. In my opinion these trained Jihadists, wouldn't mess about if one of your team were lumbered. I'm assuming the opposition may have undergone some counter surveillance training. I don't know what spread of people you intend to use… front, back or parallel teams for example, but the Point Agent should have someone like myself covering their back and working close in to them. I mean Peter is the expert here and I'll be guided by his experience and ideas on this. All I'm saying is that these men have the look of soldiers who've been in action, and could do some nasty things to our people."

The meeting would have progressed on from there but for the fact that the meeting room door crashed open and Trevor Hawthorn, the director of counter terrorism, stormed into the room.

He marched directly up in front of Danny's chair and slammed some paperwork down on the table in front of him. His face was red and angry to such a level that he was spitting when he spoke.

"You really fucked up this time Quigley! I knew it was a mistake when you were sent across to Amsterdam with Danielle. D'you know what you've done, you idiot?"

"Actually no, as it happens" he replied, almost with a measure of disinterest in his voice.

Jerry tried to intervene. "Look sir we were in the middle of a de-brief and working out some strategies here. Surely this, whatever it is, could wait and be discussed in a more private environment?"

Trevor turned on him. "Stay out of this Jerry and don't interfere. Let me lay out what this ex-squaddie has been up to first."

He glared around the room as if daring anyone else to interrupt him.

"Now" he continued, "Quigley here, last night in Amsterdam, assaulted four young Dutchmen so seriously that all four are in hospital as we speak. Most of them are suffering from broken limbs and other injuries."

There was a collective gasp around the room.

"That's right, MI5 will be all over the papers in a few hours with mud on our faces, and furthermore the families of these four have stated their intention of suing us for their injuries by this madman here who thinks he's still in the mountains of Afghanistan. What a fucking mess!"

Silence fell on the room.

It was Danielle who broke it. "Can I explain how all this happened Sir, because Danny didn't start it…he was protecting me from an imminent assault."

Hawthorn turned on her and snarled angrily "save that for the courts…right now we have a major public relations disaster descending on us."

Danielle raised her hand tentatively. "Just how did Danny's involvement, come to light Sir?"

Hawthorn sneered. "Thought he'd got away with it eh? Well by coincidence the two Security people you met at the Schiphol Airport saw the description of the two people involved, which was provided by the barman who witnessed the incident, and they phoned it in to the Dutch police."

Danny straightened up. "I gather you're not interested in our explanation of events. Is my assumption correct?"

Hawthorn slammed his hand down on the table. "That's SIR to you Quigley, and by the way you're fired" he shouted. This time spittle flew out of his mouth and landed on the table.

Danny chuckled almost in amusement, stood up and leaned across the table until his face was almost touching Hawthorn's. "I don't know if the squaddies in your Guards Regiment ever told you that when they really despised some clueless Officer they called him SIR all right but they spelled it C-U-R........on that basis I'm more than happy to address you as Sir." There were muted sniggers around the table.

"Get out Quigley now! Right now " he screamed, "and leave your pass at the front door. Get yourself ready for some really nasty criminal police charges coming at you from the Dutch police."

Danny turned and left, conscious of Danielle's concerned expression following him in the now silent group.

On exiting the building he was handed an envelope by desk security with his name on it. He tore it open and found a slip of paper with four words on it: 'Danny, call me, Rebecca.'

Outside he stopped and took a deep breath.

He decided to pick up his gear at home and spend some time at the gym. He might have lots of gym time after today.

He never made it to the gym.

There were two voice mail messages on his telephone.

He recognized the source of the first one...Scotty McGregor at the SAS Regiment in Hereford. The second one was from Rebecca, wanting him to call her.

He called the Regiment first and was kept waiting while someone ran off to get Sergeant McGregor who was apparently at lunch.

Scotty wasn't even breathless when he came on.

"Figured it was you Mate. I only called you an hour ago when we got back from some gentle field exercise for a new lot just in."

Danny laughed, despite the difficult position he found himself in with MI5.

"You say 'gentle' Scotty, but I know these poor lags were throwing up their breakfast when you were finished with them."

"You know something Danny, I'm in the best shape of my life chasing these wankers around every mountain in Wales. Anyway, I've only a minute as we're off out again. Here's why I called. They got a message from some lady in the States looking for you, and because of our history, they hauled me in to talk to her."

Danny scratched his head. "Geez Scotty, I've no idea who might be looking for me at the Regiment after being out for so long."

Scotty laughed. "I wish I had your problems where the female of the species is concerned. Personally I don't get it. What do they see in you when I'm available Mate?"

"Oh for Pete's sake Scotty, take me out of my misery. Who the hell was it, and what do they want?" he pleaded.

"OK Danny, here it is. An American woman by the name of Naomi Richards. Does that name ring a bell?"

"Actually no...look fill me in some more on her Scotty."

"Well, she was a First Lieutenant with the U.S. Military Police and she said that you did a Rambo with her one evening, clearing out some troublesome American soldiers in some pubs up near London."

Danny clapped his forehead. "Of course, the redhead...a real cute lady I can tell you, and missing her husband who was posted to Afghanistan... a Seal as I recall."

"I'm sure you helped her get over missing her hubby Danny. You were always good at that," said Scotty, needling him.

"Scotty, for God's sake, give me the rest of it, and NO there was nothing between us back then, you bastard."

Scotty laughed again. "All she gave me was her telephone number in California...here it is."

He proceeded to read out a long number, which Danny wrote down.

There wasn't much time for further chat but Scotty confirmed that he was taking his discharge in two weeks time from the Forces and moving to Nigeria, for a top-notch security position with an oil company, after first taking his accumulated holidays.

Danny was already aware of this, as he was partly responsible for the offer when they were both in Nigeria recently. They agreed that Scotty would spend a weekend with him up in London, before heading to his home in Scotland. He also provided a mobile phone number where he could be contacted in the meantime if necessary.

His next call was to California after mentally figuring out the time difference.

He got straight through, and despite the lapse in time since they had met previously, he immediately recognized Naomi's voice.

"Hey, it's Danny Quigley here…I believe you were looking for me Naomi?"

He heard her intake of breath. "Oh my God, it is you! I'd recognize that British voice anywhere! Your friend Scotty didn't waste any time!"

"He's busy training a new bunch who just came in but still managed to leave me a voice mail at my London address and I just finished chatting with him. He was on his lunch break."

"Chatting! God it brings it all back Danny…those cute British accents, and the pubs! Those pubs! I sure missed jolly old England after I left…the best posting I'd ever had, despite missing my husband."

She fell silent.

It was Danny who picked up the conversation. "So, you were trying to contact me?"

There was an obvious question in his voice.

He heard a sigh at the other end. "It… it sounds so ridiculous when I try to say it now Danny, especially when I'm looking for help on the other side of the world, and the problem's right here."

"Problem?" he prompted.

"My husband disappeared 6 weeks ago, and there's been absolutely no trace of him since. We've involved the police and they did their usual missing person routines, checking hospitals etc. Nothing's turned up at all. I'm obviously very worried about him Danny."

"I can see why you would be Naomi, and by now you must be going out of your mind. Tell me, what has his Unit done about it? He must be AWOL by now for starters."

"Surprisingly no. He's not being declared AWOL. My paycheck's still coming in. Oh, I'm now out of the Military and have been doing some part time work as a temp at a police station, running files around to lawyers and courthouses. I'm really marking time until they have their next recruiting drive and I'll apply for a job with them. I'm told that my chances are pretty good."

"I'm still missing something here Naomi. For example, what's your husband's C.O. telling you about the situation? What about his colleagues at the Seals training unit? Those guys are usually so close that you couldn't pry them apart. They must be turning every nook and cranny over trying to find him, surely?"

"A good question Danny, and here are the answers for what they're worth. I did manage to get a meeting with the C.O. on the Base and basically, I felt he was very dismissive and fobbed me off. The police would find Colin eventually, he suggested.   He wasn't on the Base, and his buddies had checked his usual haunts. You know the Seals, they have their favorite watering holes, and apparently he hasn't been in any of them since he disappeared. I get the feeling that his old buddies are avoiding me right now for whatever reason. I can't imagine why. I call the local Detective that was originally on the case every day, but I get the impression that his focus has moved on to more current cases. He told me stories of other married men who disappeared and did so because they'd run off with some other woman, and eventually returned with their tail between their legs. So there you have it."

There was silence again on the other end.

Danny finally asked the question that was starting to puzzle him.

"I'm not quite sure why you called me Naomi. I certainly sympathize with your situation and can't even imagine what you must be going through, but beyond that I must confess I'm puzzled as to why you called me."

She sighed again. "Well Danny, to hear myself say it right now, yeah it does sound weird, but I'm at my wits end. I'm getting the run-around from all sides, especially the Military, to which he has unreservedly given the last several years, putting himself in harms way time after time. I can't figure it out. My last desperate thought was that the Seals, Special Forces that is, are a breed unto themselves, and maybe, just maybe, they might be willing to open up to someone like you, who had been in that same special category, and they might open some doors for you. Right now I'm desperate Danny and need some answers. I can't go on like this. Can you understand?"

'Oh man, Oh man' he thought 'how do I react to this one?'

He wondered if he could fall back on the important and politically charged operation he'd been involved in, but again he'd just been fired!

He was suddenly aware of a bright light welling up inside his stomach and flowing into his head. Oh shoot, not that spiritual dimension that a few people had sensed in him recently, and which he denied emphatically.

Was this why he had just been fired an hour ago?

He couldn't believe it when he heard himself say that he would get on a plane as soon as he could and head over and visit her.

He would call her when he had made airline arrangements and get the other details of where to go when he landed.

He hoped he wouldn't regret it!

He sat for a while, shaking his head.

'Quigley, you've done it again you idiot' he berated himself.

Then he called Rebecca.

Would he have news for her!

CHAPTER 9

Danny was taken aback when he was joined in the dim recess at the back of the pub in Soho where they had arranged to meet. She had made some changes to her appearance that almost created a totally new identity.

"I like that reaction from you my friend. If I can fool you I can fool anyone" she greeted him.

"Hey Rebecca, what's this all about?" he asked.

"I just worked out a way to slip out of Thames House without my two blood hounds following me around. It was driving me crazy. A woman likes to be able to mooch around the shops like everyone else, even if it's to buy a few presents or cards for a special occasion. When that make-up chap was in recently showing the counter surveillance people how to disguise themselves, I sat in and picked up some pointers."

He smiled knowingly. "You're probably not fooling anyone back there Rebecca. Letting the Director General of MI5 drift in and out at will? Come on! The front desk Security for starters, would have spotted you from day one, unless you bribed them. I bet they merely let you out on a longer leash, and are watching you right now."

She glanced around, alarm creeping over her features.

" You really think so Danny?"

He nodded. "I'd be willing to bet on it. After my five months in surveillance, I can tell you that we can follow even the best-trained people from the Russian Embassy and they wouldn't have a clue. Of course we might have to invest in a pretty sizeable crew: teams, spread out three hundred and sixty degrees around them, with cars running in parallel streets and agents with subway tickets at the ready if they headed down to catch a train. Anyway don't feel bad. I like the new look."

"Oh shit Danny, they must be laughing at me back there."

"I wouldn't worry about it, unless of course if you're pulling that stunt to visit your lover during your lunch break. Then you'd end up in the Sunday papers sooner or later" he needled, leaning back as she took a halfhearted slap at his head.

"Not my style really, unless of course you're volunteering for the liaison."

He flushed, and decided not to lock swords with Rebecca's intellect. Equally, he suddenly felt unsure of his ground.

Had he just heard an oblique invitation, he wondered.

He was aware that she had tilted her head back as she said it, an appraising half smile on her face.

She laughed openly, then reaching across and slapping his shoulder. "Gotcha going there for a instant Danny."

"You're one piece of work, Rebecca, for sure" he said feelingly. "Now, what did you want to see me about, though I probably do know already…the Dutch fiasco, right?"

"Here's the thing Danny, I brought you in to MI5 over the objections of Hawthorn and a few others. This could start undermining my position and start a call, probably from the Home Office, to replace me, so I need to have all the facts at my disposal to fight back. I've interviewed Danielle and got her version of the story, and my reaction was that, unfortunate though the incident was in terms of the timing, you had no way out of the situation, so now let me hear your version of events, which obviously should be similar to Danielle's."

They had ordered some drinks and pub grub and the waitress appeared at that point and placed the plates down in front of them.

Danny decided to start the ball rolling before eating, and briefly recounted the series of events leading up to the assault in Amsterdam. She had started eating, but stopped him at times to query some point he brought up.

When he mentioned what the main troublemaker had come out with prior to the assault, about 'being kicked out of Oxford' she put her utensils down and made some notes in a pad that she had placed on the table earlier.

"Hmm…that's an interesting piece of information. I'll follow up on that. The initial blast from the press tomorrow will be damaging to your case and MI5 in general, but lets see what we can save from the situation."

He carried on, to the event in the airplane coming back, and his 'take' on the fourth man. She shrugged her shoulders. "You can't win them all my friend. This one slipped through, but only for the moment. We have a pretty competent police presence here in London, and he can't escape us forever. Oops, I almost forgot. Jerry our intelligence guru just had a picture through from the CIA here in London, of a Jihadist that a drone managed to take going over one of their encampments in Northern Iraq, and as he looks like a westerner, he wanted you to take a look at it." She passed it across.

"Hey I've been fired Rebecca. I'm not involved anymore in this whole thing" he protested mildly.

"Just look at it Danny" she said tiredly.

He picked it up and she sat forward when his eyes widened. "Holy cow, this is the chap on the plane, the fourth man! I'll bet he's an American after all."

"You were right on that one. In fact the Americans have positively identified him as Frank Skinner, originally from South Carolina and a twenty-year veteran in the U.S. Marine Corps. Did a bunch of tours in Iraq and took his discharge two years ago. He was documented leaving the country shortly after his discharge, and there's no record of his return, unless he slipped across the Mexican or Canadian border."

He examined the picture more closely.

"A U.S. Marine Vet. with Iraqi experience. He would be a great asset to ISIS wouldn't he?"

"Yes, but what's he doing here in London, and with three more Jihadists in tow? What are they up to?"

They chatted for a while longer and she advised him to go to ground to avoid the hordes of reporters who would be seeking him out for a statement. He told her he would be heading off to California and would stay in touch.

They walked outside together and she looked around almost furtively, to see if she could spot any of her stalkers.

Danny tapped the back of her coat grinning. "Hey, I was only kidding in there. They probably haven't a clue that you're out, gadding about."

She glared at him. "I don't know what to believe now Danny! I'm almost glad you're leaving the country."

He knew she didn't mean it.

CHAPTER 10

Mud dwelling in the City of Kunduz in Northern Afghanistan

They didn't bother tying Jamilla Mehsud to the chair.

The beating and slapping that had been handed out over the previous hour had reduced her to a quivering wreck.

The watcher's cruel face never altered expression as the two women, observing the code of 'purdah', wearing burqas, which completely covered their eyes, delivered the beating with curses and shouts, tearing strips off her clothing and ripping out chunks of her hair.

Finally the watcher stirred. "Enough. Bring in the girl" he instructed.

The women hurriedly left the room and returned almost immediately dragging a small child, no more than eight years of age, who was wailing with fear. They shoved her roughly into a chair, and even though she was obviously no threat to anyone, they tied her hands to it with cords.

The watcher nodded approvingly and stood up, moving across to Jamilla, still sobbing and now casting terrified glances at the small girl sitting across from her. He spoke in pedantic English but with reluctance.

"I was a school teacher so I had to learn the language of the infidel, but I apologized to Allah every day I had to use that disgusting language. I use it now because you've been living among the infidel in Kabul and London, and I have it on good report that you even loved one of them, so you're to be treated like one. The Pashtunwali code of hospitality will not apply to you my dear. Now, you come back here after years away, bearing gifts for your nephews and niece here. She doesn't look very happy, does she Jamilla? Your presents haven't done her much good have they? All you've done is bring grief on your family. You don't know me. Do you know why I'm here?" he asked, lifting her face from its slumped position on her chest.

Her glazed eyes tried to focus on him but failed.

"Ah, not up to conversation are we? The women were a trifle rough with you then. Nothing to what we have in store for you, you infidel slut, unless you provide me with all the information I need right now."

He slapped her suddenly, snapping her head back. "Answer me…do you understand me?" he shouted, leaning forward, the spittle from his mouth landing on her forehead.

She managed to lift her eyes. "Yes" she whispered.

He gestured to the back of the room and a young boy hurried forward with a small table that he set to one side of the 'watcher'. He then placed a notepad and a pencil on it. Another boy scurried forward with an ancient wicker chair, which the man slowly lowered himself into.

He leaned back, speaking quietly again, but never taking his eyes from her.

"You never met me, because I'm from a Pashtun tribe in Pakistan. Related to you, it shames me to say- a cousin I'm told."

Her eyes opened wider and some intelligence crept into them.

He nodded. "Yes indeed. I can see that got your attention. Some years ago when some of your family came through here from Pakistan with some other men, one of those men was your uncle, and the other a young cousin. As a favor, you were taken with them from your village here, to bring to your aunt

61

in Kandahar. I want to know what happened to them. Before you answer I should say two things"

One is that we have debriefed your aunt some time ago, Unfortunately she never survived our little chat, but we did get some answers from her. The second point is that if you lie to me or refuse to answer, take a look at your niece now please" he instructed.

She lifted her head with a great effort and peered across the room, dimly lit by a shaft of morning light. One of the women was holding the girls head back by her hair, and a sharp knife across her throat, which the villagers used for butchering animals.

She gasped. "Oh no!" she shouted. "Please don't hurt her! I'll tell you anything you want to know!"

She broke down, sobbing, tears running down her cheeks.

If the watcher was pleased, it wasn't reflected in his expression.

"Good, we understand each other Jamilla. Now to proceed: what happened to the group that left here?"

"They were killed," she whispered.

He slapped the chair impatiently. "Louder, I can't hear you."

"They were killed, shot," she answered more loudly.

"Where?" he demanded.

"In Afghanistan on the road to Kandahar."

"Who shot them?"

"A British soldier."

"One British soldier! Was he alone?" he asked harshly.

"Yes, alone" she answered, glancing across at her niece.

"So one British soldier killed all three of them, is that what you're saying?"

She hesitated, biting her lip.

The watcher nodded to the woman with the knife who made an aggressive movement, pressing it tight against the girl's throat.

"Lie to me once or refuse to tell me the truth and her death will be on your conscience. Now speak the truth," he shouted, leaning across to her.

"The British soldier shot the other man and my uncle." She paused.

The watcher slapped her face again. "Go on," he demanded.

"I…I shot my cousin."

The watcher looked astounded. "YOU… SHOT… YOUR… COUSIN!" he bellowed.

She dropped her head to her chest. "Yes," she whispered.

"You shot him, but why?" Now his voice dropped to a whisper.

"He and my uncle had been trying to have their way with me as a woman, all the way from my village here to where we ran into the British soldier."

"You betrayed your family culture and heritage for that? So they wanted their way with you. So what? A woman in our tribe belongs totally and wholly to the men. So they were probably not right to attempt that with you, but the stress and danger of the journey, who can blame them to seek comfort along the way? But to shoot your cousin for that, and help a British soldier into the bargain? I know the story after that Jamilla. You're aunt was very clear on it. You helped him escape, even to helping him kill more of our friends the Taliban. You spent a week alone with this British soldier out in the mountains. Did he, as you put it, have his way with you during that time?"

She raised her head defiantly. "No, he was too much of a gentleman to try that."

"Ah, I see…a gentleman. Not an enemy of our Pashtun tribe or the people of Afghanistan…so did you want him to Jamilla, that's what I want to know?"

Her head dropped again, and then shot a glance across at the trapped girl.

"At one time, yes, but that was all," she replied quietly.

The watcher nodded in satisfaction. "I called you a slut and that's what you are for all to see. Now to other matters. The men travelling to Kandahar were entrusted with a mission for our fight against the Americans. They carried precious diamonds from the mines of India with them, to purchase

63

weapons to allow us to continue the fight. What happened to those diamonds Jamilla?"

"The British soldier found the diamonds, but told me to keep them," she answered quietly.

The watcher looked astonished again. "Told you to keep them, but why?"

"He said that I should use them to help me become a doctor, which would help my people."

"I don't understand! An infidel soldier refused to take a fortune in diamonds, and told you to use them for yourself and your people? Can you explain that to me?"

A slight smile, almost of satisfaction crept across her face.

"As I said, he was a gentleman. Not the enemy we've been taught to despise and hate in growing up."

He slapped her again, his eyes raging at her. "So, it didn't take much to win your heart and forget the teachings of your family. What happened to the diamonds? Your aunt told me she split them three ways and converted them to cash by sending them to the Netherlands with one of the Dutch NATO employees. So, tell me how the monies were disposed of after that. Remember, I know most of this, so don't even be tempted to lie or cover up anything."

She tried to sit up straighter, as she struggled also to recall the details from some time back.

She carried on in a monotone voice. "My aunt kept one third of the money, and used it to set up and run six health clinics in Kabul and the surrounding areas. I understand it was all spent supporting them. My share, I spent going to England to train as a doctor, but I returned before qualifying and have been working in different areas of Kandahar, Kabul and the surrounding villages since then, as a health worker. Most of the funds given to me have just about run out supporting the clinics and my work."

She paused.

He stirred. "You mentioned that the funds were split three ways. Where did the third share go?"

"To the British soldier" she replied, averting her gaze.

"Ah, I see, this gentleman, as you refer to him…. and how and when did he receive this money?"

"I gave it to him in England when I was studying to be a doctor."

"And he took it then? I remember he was too much of a gentleman to take the diamonds back in the mountains," he needled.

She nodded. "Yes, he took it…. Reluctantly," she added.

He didn't rise to her slight protest.

"So you must know the amount of the money you passed to him. Approximately how much was it and how was it set up for him to get his hands on it?'

"He mentioned that it was 1.3 million Euros, about two million U.S. dollars, and it had been set up in his name in the Cayman Islands. I gave him a pass book, and all he had to do was turn up there with a passport to claim it."

She slumped back down in the chair, completely exhausted.

The watcher sat back thinking. "Hmm… two million dollars. As the Americans would say, a nice piece of change. D'you know what he did with it? Has it all been thrown away on useless efforts, like the other shares?" he demanded.

She sighed tiredly. "I've no idea," she answered.

Looking at her, he believed her.

"The British soldier's name, Jamilla…what was it?"

"He's no longer a soldier and I've no idea where he is, if that's what you're after."

The watcher shook his head. "I'm tired of this game you play. I asked you for his name."

He turned to look across at the women holding the girl.

"NO! Jamilla screamed. "I'll tell you…it's Danny Quigley."

She started sobbing again. "I'm sorry Danny," she muttered, "so sorry."

The watcher wrote the name down and turned to her again. "Nearly there, that wasn't so bad was it? Just a few minutes more and we're finished. Now, there was an air strike in the mountains connected to your time there, and we believe your friend the British soldier was responsible for it. The family of a very important and influential man was killed in that air strike. His name was Mohammed Qureshi, and under the code of 'badal', a tradition of revenge, one death must be answered by another. The memory and honor of his Pashtun family means that they'll never forget their sacred duty to exact revenge on whoever has wronged them, however long it takes. This has taken them some time to put together, but now that Karzai is gone and the new administration's installed and is negotiating with the Taliban, we have access to information that we didn't have before. We have contacts in Kabul that stretch to the British establishment in London, and we'll soon have information on this man Danny Quigley. The British, of course, refuse to heed the lessons of history where Afghanistan's concerned, which is why the Afghan people will win back their country in due time. Time is on our side."

He stood up and made a gesture to the women who released the girl and hustled her outside, still wailing uncontrollably.

The watcher removed a pistol and placed it against Jamilla's forehead.

"Your worst crime I leave to the last. You killed your brother in London."

Her head shot up. "I did not," she shouted back at him. "He shot himself."

The watcher smiled, but no smile reached his glacial eyes.

"Ah, she fights back. Your brother called home the night before he was killed with the information that a man, presumably this Quigley, went into your apartment and stayed the night with you."

"But we didn't...I mean..." she started to protest.

He cut her off. "Don't deny it. He saw you both come out together the following morning. That's what killed him - the knowledge that you were sleeping with an infidel. On the phone home he said he no longer wanted to live, so whatever happened later that day doesn't matter. You're the one who really pulled that trigger."

He paused. "Killing one's brother...the ultimate crime, even mentioned in the bible I believe...Cain killing his brother Abel...and what happened to him? Banishment from his tribe for all time...hardly a fitting punishment for your terrible crime, Jamilla" he murmured, lifting her head higher and cocking the weapon.

He paused reflecting. "Hmm...I wonder... could you be of any further use to us... in finding this Quigley? "

CHAPTER 11

California bound

He didn't particularly like long haul commercial flights.

They always brought back haunted memories of him and heavily equipped troopers heading for one more drop into a battle zone, and the trip home, usually with wounded colleagues and sometimes body bags... and with the adrenalin still coursing through one's veins.

He could usually sleep for a few hours on a commercial flight, but the continuous movements inside the aircraft, with periodic announcements, were unsettling.

The new awareness of the potential for catching the frightening Ebola disease on a flight made everyone uneasy and suspicious of who they were sitting beside. The pre and post flight checks on passengers only heightened this feeling. At least the food was good.

There wasn't a direct flight available to San Diego, his ultimate destination, so he had to settle for a stop in San Francisco for two hours before catching a short haul south, arriving late in the evening. He knew he would be a total wreck and jet lagged on arrival after the long flight, and had dissuaded Naomi Richards from meeting him. Instead she pre-booked him into a hotel close to the Airport and agreed to meet him there for an early breakfast.

On arrival, at the San Diego Airport he moved slowly through the Ebola screening checkpoint, and eventually emerged with his baggage. He managed to catch a shuttle bus to the hotel as it was pulling out. He'd forgotten just how large American hotel rooms were, but the best part was an incredible power shower with multiple jets that he could have stayed in for hours. When he hit the bed he was out like a light, and his last thought was the knowledge that he would get an early call and didn't need to be worried about sleeping in.

He had forgotten just how attractive Naomi was and felt a thump in his stomach when she strolled lithely across the lounge to where he was waiting. Somehow she looked taller than the five foot eight Military Policewoman that he had briefly worked with back in the U.K. but there was no hesitation in the warm hug she gave him, which he returned in kind.

"Danny Quigley, as I live and breathe!" she exclaimed. "I never thought I'd see you again after our short time working together back there in England. My God, you do look trendy with that long hair and fashionable beard!"

He hadn't forgotten her gorgeous hazel eyes or her clearly defined facial features, like those of a top model. The red hair of course topped it all. It defined her and he could see several of the men in the lounge throwing glances her way... probably thinking what a lucky devil he was, which he agreed with.

He surprised himself when he felt a catch in his throat, and wondered if he was dwelling on times past when he was still in the Military, on top of his game and loving it.

"Hey Naomi, you haven't changed a bit, and that red hair looks fantastic now that you don't have to stuff it down your military hat anymore."

"You remembered? Yes my hair was the bane of my life back then...trying to discipline servicemen, and my hair slipping out from under my hat. So much for cutting a stern figure! "

As he stepped back to look at her he could see that, while her red hair was now worn longer than he remembered and she looked extremely healthy, there was sadness around her eyes.

'Probably why he was there' he thought.

Still feeling slightly uncomfortable with the new circumstances, he steered her into the restaurant and they both busied them- selves stacking their plates from the self- service counter and the coffee machines. Finally they managed to find a table over in a corner, and by mutual agreement tackled their breakfast in silence.

He liked that in a woman. The ability to be silent without feeling the need to keep a conversation going, and enjoying the meal at the same time.

When he was down to the toast, and having slipped across for a second coffee, he sat back and looked across at her.

Naomi hadn't finished all her breakfast but looked like she'd had enough.

He glanced around at the busy breakfast room.

"Probably not the place for unburdening yourself at this time, but could you give me a broad stroke on this amazing place, the Seals Base at Coronado, that I've been hearing about over the years. I mean, in the world of Special Forces, this is the crème de la crème... well after our SAS Regiment of course" he said smiling.

She had been struggling in her mind, wondering how to broach the subject of why she had appealed to him to come over and help her, and was relieved at the opportunity to postpone it until later.

"Coronado, ah well, let's see: known as the Naval Amphibious Base Coronado, NAB. It was commissioned in 1944 and it's across the bay from here at Point Loma in Ventura County, situated on what's called Silver Strand. The Seal Base itself is on Tulagi Road and you'll find that all the streets are named after world war 2 battles such as 'Guadalcanal, Tarawa, Tulagi, Bougainville' to name a few. The Base itself is one thousand acres, nine square miles, which contains enlisted family housing and a state park. Colin and I stayed in the enlisted housing when he was posted back here.

He had no option with the 24/7 nature of the training. There is, of course, the main Base, training beaches and even a recreation marina.

It's not just for the Seals, Danny. NAB Coronado is also home to 30 other tenant commands with approximately 5,000 personnel, and its primary purpose is providing administration and logistical support to the amphibious units.

You asked about the Seals, well there's 257 acres south of the Base allocated for training, and you probably already have some ideas of what it's all about, right?"

He shook his head. "Yeah, brutal from what I hear…and that 'Hell Week' - continuous training with only a total of 4 hours sleep for the full week… what is that Seal saying?   It's like a mantra in their training: 'The Only Good Day Was Yesterday'… 'Oh man!'"

"You don't know the half of it Danny. I'll try to fill you in as we go along. Just be aware that my husband Colin, all the time he was here, was dishing that out to those poor bastards who were here to fulfill their ambition to be Seals. God help them!"

"Yeah, I know quite a lot about Special Forces' training, but while I did the Special Boat Service course at Poole in the U.K. to top up our SAS training, from what I've heard, we came nowhere near the sheer slog and pain that the Seals are put through out on those brutal beaches that eliminate so many good men."

"Whatever you've heard Danny, increase it by five hundred percent! The stuff they throw at these guys is a man killer. Therein lies part of the problem. Those who make it are the elite…and they know it, and I have to say it, they are indeed super human beings."

"I've met some of them in Afghanistan and they impressed me all to hell. They were warriors for sure," he agreed.

She glanced around. "Sorry, started slipping into some personal insights there. I'll come back to this later.

Now, outside the Base there is an actual city of Coronado, which is 9 square miles, 23 km in size, and has a population of 30,000. As you can imagine, a lot if not all of their business comes from the Coronado Base. It's got an awful lot going for it in other ways apart from the families of Servicemen coming to visit them. I should say that I'm not living on the Base any longer. I moved out 6 weeks ago. I'll fill you in later…OK?"

They chatted for a few more moments, then Danny excused himself and spent the next fifteen minutes collecting his bags and checking out.

He joined Naomi who had pulled up to the front door in a late model Toyota. He threw his bags in the back and jumped in.

He was stiff from his trip over and asked her if it was possible to go for a walk somewhere, preferably on one of those California beaches that everyone dreamed about.

The weather was beautiful…up in the 70's.

It was almost like being on holiday…almost, but not quite.

CHAPTER 12

They flopped down on the deck of a small snack bar overlooking the beach they had been walking on for the past hour. Danny was feeling much better, having got the kinks out of his limbs with the fast-walking Naomi.

The waitress left after leaving some refreshments on the table. Danny couldn't wait to try out a California milk shake he'd experienced before and had never stopped talking about back home. Naomi settled for a root beer and a donut.

They had got rid of all the small talk up along the beach and now they both accepted that it was time for Danny to be brought into the full picture.

He slurped the first three inches out of his mug and took his mouth off the straw long enough to prompt her to get started.

She sighed. "OK, sitting out here overlooking the beach, it's hard to believe that I have problems, mega problems. I suppose the best way is to go back to Colin and I coming back here, he from Stan (Afghanistan) and myself, as you know, from England. Despite the fact that we had both missed each other a lot with being posted to different areas, myself in the Army Military Police and Colin in the Navy Seals, he seemed a bit miffed at being hauled out of Stan without much notice, leaving his Unit buddies behind. He'd expected to leave with the rest of his Seal team in four months time. At first he asked me if I'd been responsible in some way. You know, the whining wife going over his head and claiming marriage problems. It happens all the time apparently."

"Don't I know it? It's not the exclusive scenario of your U.S. Forces, I can tell you. We have it in the U.K. as well, particularly with Special Forces where you can virtually disappear overnight and can't even tell your spouse where you're going."

"Well anyway, I denied any responsibility which is true, but I didn't tell him that you'd put in some leverage for me back there in the U.K. He would have killed me had he known.

As we were finally together, I suggested to him that it was a good time to have children and I didn't hear any objection from him. Combining that with living on a Navy Base with Colin's crazy hours, and being an Army MP with transport and other difficulties, I decided to get out of the Military. So, happy wifey at home, hoping to get pregnant and being there with a nice hot meal when he dragged his ass in after ten, fifteen or more hours out on the beaches and obstacle courses. You know something Danny, for a while it worked out. I was really happy and fulfilled. Then something started to slip in our relationship.   Colin would become more pensive, and seemed to pull away from me somehow. Oh he was courteous and attentive, opening the car door and so on, but emotionally I felt a barrier creeping in. I put it down to the pressure of work, which was enormous. You've no idea! He also hated being party to the number of basically decent and focused young men he had to send back to their Units. He still believed in the screening out process in the entry requirements for the coveted Seal designation, but he still found it hard to see those young men, giving their all as it were, and still being rejected. I could be wrong in assuming this was responsible for the invisible barrier that had come between us. Our lovemaking had decreased considerably, and one night when I'd gone off to bed and Colin was at a graduation for another class, I found him in the morning in a bed in the spare room. I didn't think much of it as I assumed he hadn't meant to disturb me. However, that's where he slept each night afterwards.

74

When I tackled him after a couple of weeks he said something like "I just can't handle it anymore." I couldn't tell if he meant that the Seal training energy requirement left him unable, or incapable of sustaining a physical relationship with me. I should say that the Seals pride themselves on having all sorts of family outings for the kids and the wives, and he still brought me to them. His behavior and attitude was such that no one would suspect things were an absolute disaster at home. You're knowledgeable in the way of the world Danny, to know that a woman has basic physical needs as well as a man. I don't mind admitting that I enjoy sex and miss it, and when I brought this up to Colin he just shrugged, and either left the room, turned up the TV or went out somewhere with his buddies for a few drinks. I didn't begrudge him the few beers with his friends, as they certainly needed to let off steam and chill out. I suggested that we get some counseling, and there were excellent facilities for this on or off the Base. He dismissed the idea, and said it would affect his career in the Navy and possible future postings. I'm afraid I kept harping on it and one day when I got up; I discovered he'd packed some basic things and moved out somewhere. No note, phone calls or anything. Total silence!"

Danny had been sitting there, frozen in stillness. He realized he had been holding his breath in for too long, and let out a loud exhale.

"God Naomi that must have been absolutely horrible for you! I can't imagine…."

"Yes, and to make matters worse, I called his Unit and he hadn't turned up there either, so I, not the Unit, called the Police and a couple of detectives came out and completed a missing person's report and told me that they normally wait a few days after checking hospitals, as most missing persons turn up. Well he didn't, and after checking with the Base again - same story there. I called the Police again, and the same two Policemen came out and asked more questions.

'Had we been having marriage problems etc.?' Those kinds of questions. Two Navy Shore Police Investigators came out and interrogated me as well, and I was surprised to hear that Colin hadn't yet been posted as AWOL. Three of his Seal buddies came out one evening, and they surprised me when they suggested I play it cool and leave it to the investigators to track him down. Play it cool! For Pete's sake Danny, I was going out of my mind by that time! My next step was to call his Commander and he reluctantly agreed to meet with me. He also suggested that I leave the tracing of Colin to the proper trained people, but of course I let him know that I was in fact a trained investigator and intended to keep looking, and if that upset some people, so be it."

"Good for you Naomi" Danny interjected.

For the first time he reached across and placed his hand on top of hers...then withdrew it.

She looked startled, as if the gesture of comfort was alien to her, and for a brief moment he saw the mantle of sadness slip from her face.

She carried on with her story.

"Anyway, I kept calling him every few days until he stopped taking my calls. After a month some of the housing people came round and suggested I move off Base to make room for some new posting coming in. I could see a common thread - I was not wanted on the Base anymore. Oh, I could have dug my heels in and stayed on, as I doubt if they would have actually had me physically removed, but I moved out to an apartment in Coronado a few days later. Another thing that surprised me is that I'm still getting Colin's pay check in my bank every month."

"What's surprising about that?" he asked.

"Well I know from my Army experience that when someone goes missing, they cut off their pay check. Most of the time in the Army, it's the wives who call up and tell the MPs where their husband is hiding. One house we went to where the missing soldier was supposed to be, we couldn't find him inside, until his wife, saying nothing, pointed to a large unused chimney, and that's where we found him...pretty black and very reluctant as you can guess, to go back to his Unit."

There was silence between them for some time.

Danny nodded as if coming to some decision. "Well, it's pretty obvious that there's some sort of cover up going on and that you're not included in it. The Military are pretty darn good at covering up when they want to, so you're up against a brick wall for starters. I want to immediately get us started on finding your husband. I also need to make some phone calls."

Danny had her drive him to a small hotel not far from her apartment and she came in while he unpacked and got settled away. It was then that he made his phone calls, which she could still follow, as she brewed some coffee in the small kitchen.

When he'd finished she came round with two cups and sat down on one of the two lounge chairs.

"You don't mess around, Buddy, do you?" she exclaimed.

He grimaced. "You know what, we could hang around for days getting the run around and achieving absolutely nothing. I know the Military and there's only one thing that scares them…a higher rank tearing strips off them and perhaps threatening their next promotion, particularly the Officer ranks who build their little steps up the pyramid ever so carefully with selected postings, and the right contacts who are in a position to maneuver them into being noticed by people of influence."

"Jesus Danny, you sound like it's some sort of a game! Quite an indictment of our Officer class. Remember I was one of them."

"Yeah, sorry about that Naomi. It is a flipping game to them. Almost a paranoia when you get to a certain level, especially in the Navy, trying to get to be a Commander on an ever diminishing fleet of ships, which opens the door to the higher echelons of power. You were just a young 2nd Lieutenant, and the bug hadn't bitten you yet."

She shook her head. "I don't entirely agree with you, but one thing I will say, and that is to keep your views to yourself around the NAB Base and outside in the city. The navy way is like Mom and apple pie around here, and you'd get your block knocked off anywhere if you were heard making such comments."

77

He grinned. "Message received and understood."

The phone rang then, saving him from burying himself any deeper. It was Bret Zeitner from the CIA in Washington, one of his previous calls.

"Danny, you keep popping up all over the place and by now I know it means trouble for someone...hopefully not for me or any of my friends."

Zeitner had been involved in some other challenging situations, one in which Danny had been responsible for foiling an attack on the American mainland.

He laughed. "Don't worry Bret, your ass is covered on this one for sure. No fall out I promise you."

"I'll only relax when you've left the country. I've arranged a meeting on the NAB Base at ten hundred hours tomorrow morning with the Seal Commander. He wasn't a happy bunny, but I did mention a certain top-ranking individual who could sabotage any future promotions merely with a phone call, so that's number one."

"Bret, you really play hardball don't you?"

"You have to with these Rambo types, and yes I did go for the crotch."

"You sure did! I'm not going to win a popularity contest with him when I meet him."

"Just go in and tell him that you expect him to cooperate fully on this. Don't mess about. He was curious how you had the leverage to call Washington, and I told him that the Vice President himself had presented you with a citation at the London Embassy in Grosvenor Square a couple of years ago. I didn't tell him any more than that."

"Got it...OK, I can live with that...and the second thing?"

"I have an FBI contact in San Diego who contacted the police in Coronado and set things up for you... here's their names."

He read out some names, which Danny scribbled down...a Superintendent Cole Ranger and an Inspector called Mike Collins.

Zeitner carried on. "You can actually slope around there in the next hour and catch them, or if that doesn't suit, just call and make an appointment. They can fix you up with those requirements you asked for as well. Now, I'm running late for a meeting so good hunting, or should I even say that? Look, how about dropping in to see me in Washington before you leave the good old U.S.A. I want to make sure you're actually leaving!" This with a loud raucous laugh.

The phone call had been on speaker and Naomi sat there with her jaw dropping.

"Shoot Danny, you really are a mover and a groover!" she said, shaking her head.

He grabbed his jacket.

"Lets get going then and get this show on the road...onwards!"

They raced out of the hotel.

On the way he spotted a rental car company and had her pull over.

"But I'm happy to run you around while you're here Danny" she protested.

He was getting out of the door and turned sideways to her.

"I have another angle I'm concerned about and will fill you in later on. I'll follow you to the police station when I come out. Just watch for me. I'll flash the lights."

The reception was empty apart from two smartly dressed women behind the counter. One of them looked up and smiled at him. "Yes, can I help you Sir?" she asked.

"You sure can. It's no mystery that I'm here to rent a car. What I'm looking for is something that doesn't stand out...perhaps a Toyota or something like that."

She looked surprised. "Oh, you're English...we have loads of English tourists coming in and renting autos, but I have to say they're usually looking for something like a soft top Ford Mustang to fulfill their dream of driving up the beautiful California coast. I've never been asked for something that doesn't stand out."

He smiled. "No doubt you're right. However please check and see what you've got in at the moment."

She frowned and dropped her head to a computer screen on the desk in front of her, then looked up.

"There's nothing there in that category right now Sir I'm afraid."

Her friend, who was listening, called across to her.

"A Toyota just came in, but it's not washed or cleaned out yet."

Danny snapped his fingers. "I'll take it. That sounds like what I want."

"But Sir, our policy is never to rent a car that isn't spotless. Let me get the crew to service it for you and we'll have it bright and sparkling in about ten minutes."

He shook his head. "No, I want it exactly as it is, dirty or not. If I can't get it I'm out of here," he said firmly.

The two assistants looked across at each other.

Danny slapped his British driving license and his credit card on the counter.

"Come on, let's get the paper work going. Someone's waiting for me outside and we're on our way to a meeting at the local Police Station with Superintendent Cole Ranger and his Inspector Mike Collins. I'd appreciate you expediting this transaction a.s.a.p."

Whether it was him mentioning the police officials' names or not, he was outside in five minutes, flashing his lights.

Naomi stared at the car and shook her head as if baffled.

He pulled in behind her as she moved out into the traffic.

CHAPTER 13

London

Fiona frowned when she heard the doorbell ring. There were few callers in their particular area apart from the odd visit from a neighbor across the street. Still she had no hesitation in swinging the door open.

Standing there was a well-dressed and presentable man, probably around late thirties, with a smile on his face. He looked like he might have been Asian, though like many English people, she wasn't great at guessing people's backgrounds.

"Mrs. Quigley?" he asked, in quite passable English.

"Not really, I'm divorced. Who are you looking for anyway?" she asked.

"A Mr. Danny Quigley actually. Is he in right now, I have something for him."

A slight look of impatience crossed Fiona's face. She was already running late for a hair appointment.

"Look, as I just mentioned, I'm divorced and there's no reason why Mr. Quigley would be here. He moved out some years ago."

"Oh, sorry to trouble you then. Can you give me his present address please as I have an important message to give to him?"

She shook her head.

"Sorry but I certainly wouldn't hand his private address out to some stranger who turns up on my doorstep. Anyway, he's not even in the country right now, so giving you his address wouldn't be of any help to him. What's so important anyway, about this 'something' that you have for him?"

His smile dropped and she started to observe hard lines creasing his face. Fiona suddenly felt uneasy and looked up and down the street, hoping to see some neighbors out walking along, or cars pulling over.

He looked skeptical.

"Out of the country you say? So where has he gone to?" the man asked, reaching into his coat pocket.

She tensed, not knowing what his intentions were, but all he withdrew from his pocket was a small fat letter. She breathed again and stepped back slightly.

"I've no idea where he's gone to, and quite frankly, as I've said, I would have no intention of releasing that information to someone who just appears on my doorstep."

"Yes you do Mum, he's gone to California, like he told us the other evening."

It was the voice of Allison who had suddenly materialized alongside her. Fiona's head snapped sideways.

"Allison, stay out of this!" she said tersely.

Allison looked from her to the man on the doorstep, and her hand came up to her mouth.

"Oh sorry Mum...I thought..."

Fiona pushed Allison behind her and started to close the door.

The smile had come back on the man's face.

"Ah, your daughter Allison I believe... California, very nice, very nice." He handed her the small envelope. "I'm sure you'll be in touch with him, so please pass on this message to him."

He gave a half mock salute, turned and left. As he walked back down the steps he waved and a long sleek black car appeared, almost it seemed, out of nowhere. He jumped in and the vehicle took off with a squeal of rubber.

Fiona was left standing there looking down at the letter in her hand. She turned and looked into the remorseful face of her daughter. She suddenly had a bad feeling about the whole visit and was too shaken to give out to her right then.

'Danny' she thought 'What is this all about?' She sat down abruptly on the settee, staring at the letter in her hands, then finally stirred, having been completely unaware of Allison creeping off with a guilty look on her face.

Should she open it, wondered Fiona. Should she call Danny at the contact number he'd left? Should she open it and then call him? Was it just a previous associate or contact dropping off some harmless information that could wait until Danny returned? Somehow she doubted that. Could it be some disturbing information that would interrupt whatever he was involved in right then?

It suddenly occurred to her what she should do, and she picked up the phone. She'd had Rebecca's direct number at MI5 since Danny started working there five months previously, and in a moment was through to her.

Rebecca listened to her account of the recent visitor to her door, and agreed that there was something untoward about the visit. Fiona got the impression from her short sentences that she was actually in a meeting at the time.

Finally Rebecca asked her if she was free immediately to come in to Thames House. She would send a driver for her.

Fiona was, but first she had to send Allison across the road to a friend's house, because today was a teachers training day or something, which meant no school. She made a brief call and cancelled her hair appointment.

She had barely time to change and put her makeup on before the MI5 driver was at her door.

On arrival at Thames House she found that her pass had already been organized and she was escorted up the elevator to the fourth floor, where Rebecca and a dark skinned lady were waiting for her.

After greeting her, Rebecca turned and introduced her to the lady who was present.

"Fiona, this is Alina Tariq, who works in the counter surveillance team and is an acquaintance of Danny's...an admirer as well I believe, right Alina?"

She flushed. "Only in so far as I watched him in a recent judo tournament competition where he won his 5th Dan belt. I was there to summon him to a meeting, as he'd switched off his mobile phone. I didn't understand the moves of judo, in a way it looks quite boring, but Danny's impressive to watch for sure."

Fiona smiled, picking up on her slight embarrassment.

"Danny has his admirers I know, and let's face it, he's one impressive chap when you see him in action."

Rebecca coughed. "Speaking of action lets take a look at what we have here. Tell me again in more detail, what happened at your home this morning. Take your time. Anything and everything could be important, OK?"

They had all sat down at this stage. Fiona took the envelope out of her purse and placed it on the Director General's desk.

Then she recounted the visit that morning, speaking slowly, and trying to include as much detail as possible, including her impressions.

Alina was taking notes.

When Fiona had finished her account, Rebecca sat back.

"OK. Good so far. Now some questions. First could you make a guess as to what his country of origin might have been? By that I mean was he a Pakistani, Iraqi, for example, or are you not at all sure?"

"I'm sorry Rebecca, I'm not terribly good at this."

"No problem. Alina here has dummied up a file of different racial faces and downloaded it on to my computer."

She swung the computer round so that she was looking at the screen.

"Now, I'm going to work through some of these, and all you have to do is shout out when you think you see a picture that has some defining features not unlike the chap who called on you. Here we go"

Fiona was quite intelligent and had a fast take-up on what they were attempting to do. It only took a few moments before she raised her hand.

"That face reminds me of the man who called this morning. I mean it's not him obviously, but has the same sort of profile and color."

"An Afghan" Alina volunteered.

Rebecca nodded. "No doubt at all. Now Fiona, describe the car that picked him up."

"Hmm…let's see…a long dark car, more like those chauffeur cars that run VIPs around. Very clean, like it had just been washed. I had the impression, though I'm not one hundred percent sure, that the driver wore a uniform. I can't think of anything else. Remember, I was somewhat disorientated."

Rebecca nodded, leaning forward. "No, you're doing fine. One last question regarding the car. Was it carrying a diplomatic plate on the rear? You know, the CD insignia?" she asked.

Fiona shook her head. "I'm sorry, I…I just can't recall. As I mentioned, I was a bit shook up" she said apologetically.

"That's all right. Now d'you mind if Alina plays a little mind game with you to help your recall ability? Just takes a couple of minutes."

"Look, whatever works. I called you after all. Yes, go right ahead."

Alina moved her chair closer and touched Fiona's arm.

"This is something we sometimes use to help witnesses recall more detail of things like traffic accidents or a crime that they saw."

Fiona nodded. "As I said, I'm quite open to anything."

Alina touched her arm again encouragingly.

"Good, now Fiona, just get yourself sitting comfortably and close your eyes. If at any time you feel uncomfortable during this process, you merely have to open your eyes and you're back in total control. Now run your mind over the various muscle groups in your body and mentally tell them to relax, release and let go. Visualize a balloon letting all the air out...feeling secure and peaceful."

She paused for a moment, her eyes watching alertly as Fiona started showing signs of allowing her body to relax, then her quiet voice started up again. "Now Fiona, I want you to go back to the incident on your door-step this morning when that man called. Be open to any or all of the impressions you were recalling right then...what you felt, what you saw, what you heard. When you've processed the whole incident again in this way through your memory, I want you to concentrate on the back of that black car in particular as it was driving away, to see if you can spot any writing on it that was something you don't see on the average British car. Do that now" she instructed.

A small smile came across Alina's face as she watched Fiona's head turn, as if she was following the vehicle in her mind. She waited another minute.

"OK Fiona, that was good. I could see that you really got into that recall process. Now you can open your eyes and tell us what you saw, if anything, on the back of that vehicle."

Fiona opened her eyes and, straightening up, she looked, a trifle dazedly around the room.

"Wow, that was amazing! I saw everything in real live living color...even the color of the man's tie. It was solid red, but you're not really interested in that. The back of the vehicle? Yes, it did have a CD sign on the back of it. So there, does that help?"

Both Rebecca and Alina nodded excitedly.

Rebecca blew out noisily. "You'd better believe it Fiona...we're pumping on gas here! Let me make a quick call downstairs."

The other two women chatted as the D.G. was mumbling into the phone behind her desk.

Finally she slammed it down. "I'm asking Jerry Sackville, who runs the counter terrorist investigations section, to come up here and bring pictures with him of those people who we believe are in Intelligence at the Afghan Embassy. It's something we do with all Embassies, and they do the same to us worldwide. It's a game we play. The Afghans haven't a large Embassy as yet, but with Karzai gone, the new lot has put more resources into London. Let's see if we can spot your friend from this morning, shall we?"

Minutes later, Sackville knocked on the door and was introduced to Fiona.

"Ah, the ex-wife of the legend Danny Quigley. I'll bet you could tell us a few stories about the man himself?" he prodded.

Rebecca raised her hands. "Just calm your curiosity for a moment Jerry, and show us what you've got on the Afghans" she instructed.

"Yes, right, sorry about that D.G. We haven't had that long to winkle out the few members of the Embassy that we think run the Intelligence Section. However I've brought along about twenty of the prominent people we see out and about, doing the things and attending the events that people in the Intelligence business are known for, so, here we go."

He passed a bunch of pictures across to Fiona who placed them on the D.G.'s desk, and started working through them. She had reached the last five pictures, with the rest of the room starting to look disappointed, then lifted one picture up.

"This is the one. The chap who came to my door with the letter.   I'm a hundred percent sure about this," she said emphatically.

Jerry took the picture from her and checked a file that he opened in front of him.

He pursed his lips nodding. "That's Akmal Massoud, a well known, well connected Afghan name, and one that we'd figured was in Intelligence. He arrived here two months ago and has been pretty active in the political circles around town. Mind you, that may not be his real name, as they prefer to work under the radar as much as possible.   SO…what does this tell us D.G?" he enquired.

"That someone well connected with the Afghan Government has just sent a message in a plain envelope to Danny Quigley, for whatever reason, and who is now out of the country. Question, do we open it, or open it and inform

Danny of the contents? Fiona, you should be the one to answer that. The letter was handed to you personally this morning."

She looked around at the group, all watching her, some with curiosity, others with a sense of eagerness.

"I believe this is somehow important to Danny and I believe we should open it."

She started to hand it over to the D.G. who stopped her and looked across at Jerry.

"Fingerprints Jerry. Shouldn't we...?"

"We should indeed," replied Jerry who pulled on a pair of rubber gloves from his briefcase and, reaching forward, took the envelope from Fiona.

They watched as he carefully opened the letter with a letter opener from the D.G.'s desk and removed the contents.

They all stood up and leaned forward to get a look.

There was a collective gasp from the group.

Inside was a small square of cardboard backing with two items attached to it: the first, and most visible was what appeared to be a two-inch tuft of hair, and the second? Jerry moved his head down closer to peer at it. He finally looked up.

"It looks like a small diamond, stuck to the cardboard" he said in astonishment.

"A diamond?" Rebecca echoed.

"A piece of what looks like human hair and a diamond" Fiona added.

The group sat back and looked at each other.

Finally the D.G. turned to Fiona. "Does this make any sense to you?" she asked.

She shrugged helplessly. "I've absolutely no idea whatsoever what this is about." There was a brief babble of conversation amongst the group, all equally baffled.

Something seemed to occur to the D.G and she picked up the phone again. When she put it down all eyes were on her.

"Well, we can sort out one thing in a couple of minutes. We have someone downstairs who happens to be an expert on diamonds and their value. I told him to come up and bring his doodad with him. You know, his valuation eyeglass they all wear when doing their job. I for one am very interested in what he has to say."

They didn't have long to wait. In a few minutes a thin middle-aged man came in carrying a small kit, which he opened out on the desk. Jerry had him put some gloves on before he picked up the card then, placing his eyeglass in position, he scrutinized the item for what seemed a long time.

"Hmm" he muttered. Moving across to the window, he spent a further long couple of minutes, peering at it.

"Well, I'll be damned!" he muttered again.

Rebecca slapped her desk.

"For God's sake, take us out of our agony Ken! Tell us about the diamond!"

He looked up. "No doubt from the Himalayan diamond mines."

"It's value Ken, it's value?" she entreated.

"Oh, yes of course. A guestimate only, mind you. I'd have to get it valued outside by a top notch expert but...I'd say probably about twenty to thirty thousand U.S. dollars, give or take."

Jaws dropped around the room.

There was another collective gasp.

It was Rebecca who finally managed to articulate what everyone was thinking:

Why had the Afghan Government contact sent Danny a valuable diamond and a tuft of hair in a plain envelope?

It was then that she leaned closer to the envelope and spotted something in smaller writing scrawled on the bottom of the cardboard. It read 'call me' and listed a number.

She read out the number and the message.

It was Jerry who jumped in.

"That's a number for Afghanistan," he pointed out.

They were no further ahead in solving the mystery. In fact the mystery had deepened.

Rebecca stroked her face thoughtfully.

'Diamonds? What was it about diamonds and Danny Quigley that had come up in a conversation with him in the past'? she wondered.

89

Only one person could solve this puzzle and he was six thousand miles away and with no set plans for his return.

Why should he?

After all they had just fired him.

CHAPTER 14

Police station, Coronado, California

They weren't kept waiting very long. Within five minutes of approaching the front desk and being escorted up to the second floor, a squat, tough looking man, probably in his early forties with an Irish face and wearing a military brush cut, strode into the waiting room.

He came across smiling, with his hand already outstretched.

"Inspector Mike Collins. You must be the two we've been expecting: Mrs. Naomi Richards and Danny Quigley, is that right?"

They both smiled back, especially Naomi who felt she had been getting the run around in her previous contact with the Police.

As Danny shook hands, and not one to miss an opportunity to create some initial rapport, he peered closely at the Policeman.

"With a name like Mike Collins, probably short for Michael Collins, you've got to be Irish?" There was a question in the statement.

Collins stared at him. "You got that right. My parents came from west Cork and my father never let us kids forget where we came from...jolly old Ireland, and that movie 'The Big

Fellow', where Michael Collins was played by Liam Neeson. That made me really appreciate my Irish name."

He took a step back and looked at him. "Quigley, Danny Quigley...now that's got to be Irish as well?"

Danny grinned. "Yeah, born in Ireland and came across to Wales when I was eight years old."

"Ahah, so that's where the English accent comes in...still a bit of a lilt in there that I'm catching. Probably picked up a touch of the Welsh Celt accent while you were there."

Naomi pushed good humoredly between them, laughing.

"You bloody Irish! If I'm not careful you two will be off to the nearest pub to drown the shamrock and I'm still stuck with my problem. OK guys?" she teased.

Danny winked at Collins. "Sounds like a good idea to me Mike, what d'you think? I always find that problems get solved much more readily when I have a couple of pints inside me, or is it that we just forget about them after a while?"

He ducked back as Naomi took a mock swing at his shoulder.

The chuckling was still going on when they moved across and went inside to meet Superintendent Cole Ranger. He was the opposite of Collins, being tall and lanky with silver hair, probably in his early fifties and with a set of piercing green eyes that scanned them quickly.

When he shook Naomi's hand she nodded to the other two men.

"When Irish eyes are smiling!" she grumbled. "Is this always what happens when men with a connection to the old sod meet up?"

Ranger threw his head back laughing. "You should see him on St Patrick's Day! Drinking green beer and disappearing into those Irish pubs across the bay. Anyway, you didn't come here for that, did you?"

They chatted for some minutes, then Danny summarized Naomi's dilemma in trying to locate her husband. When he got to her opinion as to the Police Department's involvement and apparent lack of cooperation, the two Policemen glanced at each other and, if by some unspoken agreement, Collins slipped out of the room. They chatted together until he came back several minutes later, carrying a file, which he placed in front of the Superintendent, who gestured at it enquiringly.

"So what's in the file Mike? What did you find out?" he asked. Then turning to his two visitors, "Mike's dug up the file that was written up by the missing persons team who were probably in touch with you, right?"

Naomi's face tightened.

"If you don't mind my saying so Superintendent, those two were a waste of space. I was a trained investigator in the Military and I wouldn't rate their abilities very highly at all. They basically suggested that my missing husband had probably driven down to Tijuana for the weekend and would turn up sooner or later."

The Superintendent glanced across at his Inspector. "What does the file say Mike?"

He shrugged. "Not much really. Probably in line with what this lady says. This is a Navy town after all, and the roads on Friday night are filled with young Navy personnel heading off for some fun. On Sunday nights our guys are out there on the roads catching them coming back all juiced up. It used to be Tijuana in Mexico until the Marines put it out of bounds as being too dangerous any more. In fairness, the missing persons team were not far off the mark in the sense that ninety five percent of AWOLs turn up after a couple of days, broke, and with sore heads, and are thrown straight in the Brig."

"Well my husband Colin didn't turn up after a couple of days and I phoned repeatedly to your missing persons team and just kept running into a brick wall. I got the same result from the Base Commander as well: 'leave it to the professionals', he kept repeating…"

Collins lifted the file again. "Sorry, neither Detective is in the building right now, but the file does say that they visited the Base Commander as well and were told that the Navy investigators were looking into it, and in the meantime they were posting her husband as AWOL."

Naomi threw her hands in the air wearily.

"That's not technically correct because normally the Navy stops putting their pay cheque in the bank when someone goes AWOL. I should know…I've chased enough AWOLs to know how it works. I'm still collecting mine on a regular basis."

Danny raised his hand. "We also believe that the Base Commander had something to do with having her ousted from her enlisted quarters there, because she was stirring up too much trouble for him. There's something weird about this whole thing Superintendent. I intend to stick around until I get to the bottom of it," he said firmly.

Mike Collins grimaced. "OK, sooner or later it has to be brought out into the open. This is, after all, a Navy town, and the top and bottom of it is that we pretty well live off the Navy here. You should see the huge amounts that are contributed to charitable causes in the town, and the large numbers of volunteers who are involved in all sorts of things as well, so to a large degree it's a case of 'I'll scratch your back and you'll scratch mine'. In a way you're talking politics, but not to the extent that we're soft on Navy personnel when they wreck a bar, or punch out a taxi driver, or hijack a car to get back to Base some Saturday night. The system has been going on for some time, and I hate to admit that it works." He paused.

"Well, most of the time anyway," he finished lamely.

The Superintendent nodded. "It sounds, Ma'am, like your husband just fell between the cracks, and for that I do apologize. So, what can we do for the pair of you now? I'm quite prepared to facilitate in any legal approach you intend to make. I understand from your CIA contacts that you, Danny, have a reputation that, if we are to believe half of it, you're a cross between Rambo, James Bond and Clint Eastwood on one of his bad days."

Naomi jumped in. "I saw him in action in a pub in the U.K., sorting out a bunch of our hard-assed paratroopers all on his own, and you could barely scrape them off the floor when he'd finished with them, so you better believe what you've heard about Danny. That's why I brought him here from the U.K. He's a great admirer of the Seals, but he doesn't play second fiddle to anyone…do you Danny?"

94

He didn't reply as the two policemen both gave him a long measured look.

Finally Collins leaned forward. "Well, I guess we can expect some fun and games around here for a little while. Just a warning…if you do break the law in any way, and get caught doing it, we'll have to get involved, and that'll probably mean charges being made, even if you are a nice guy AND Irish with it. Now having marked your cards, I believe there was a couple of things you wanted us to provide for you."

Danny nodded. "Right, and the first thing's pretty easy. Naomi and I would like to have a direct number to program into our cell phones or mobile phones as we call them in the U.K., in case we need you real fast. The second is, I would like to be able to plant some bugs in any vehicle that I might want to follow, and the tracking equipment. The final and last thing that would be useful would be to obtain a weapon and ammunition with the appropriate license to carry it."

Mike Collins barely blinked. "No problem with the direct number for your phone. This will get me 24/7, even at home…the second is equally no problem. You're in luck actually, because we've recently had our surveillance equipment updated, which means that even if a 'perp' had a sweep done on his vehicle, it would be difficult to locate this bugging device. Have you heard of this stuff Danny?"

"Fortunately I was in counter surveillance with MI5 in London and we do have some really cool stuff that we use. That sounds like what I'm looking for Mike."

"Talking to the converted then…excellent! Now as to the weapon - reassure me that you're not going to start a shooting war around here Danny. That's the last thing we need right now. You couldn't take it on the Base anyway, unless you were guarding the President."

"You know what, if you'd said no to this, I wouldn't have quibbled too much. It's just that with this ISIS thing going crazy right now, and these 'lone wolves' coming out of the woodwork, I've no idea if my name might come up as a target on some list. There's a new Government in Afghanistan, and I don't know if they'll dig into some of President Karzai's previous connections."

"Sorry, I don't follow." The Superintendent looked puzzled.

It was Naomi who answered. "Look, Danny was presented with an award from President Karzai as well as the Prime Minister of England AND our own vice president Biden at our London Embassy. It's classed as top secret information."

Both men sat back looking shocked. "Jesus, what on earth was the award for?" Collins' voice was almost a whisper.

"He was responsible for taking out a hundred and sixty Taliban and Al Qaeda when he was inadvertently left behind in a joint Delta/UK SAS mission, back in the mountains of Afghanistan. The one hundred were as a result of an air strike he called in, and the sixty he took down personally in various ways, that I don't want to go into right now."

"Whew…" Ranger shook his head as if to clear it.

"You know something Danny. I'm going to personally put you on that plane when you're leaving. I won't even sleep at night from now on as long as you're cruising around this town. I might even contact my SWAT team if they need an extra body for some raid they're planning."

Danny laughed, "Funny you should say that. My contact at the CIA said exactly the same thing. Now is that weapon available or not?"

The Policeman nodded across to Collins.

"In your court Mike."

"OK, right…. have you been qualified on any range in the use of firearms in North America during the last twelve months, otherwise we'll have to do that locally and it won't be today."

Danny pulled out his diary and turned some pages at the back.

"Eight months ago I was qualified by a Leroy Hesseltine of CSIS, that is the Canadian Security Intelligence Service, at an RCMP firing range outside Vancouver. I'm sure you would have no problem contacting him, and he could fax back my qualification license to you here. Would that work for you?" he asked.

Collins looked across at his superior, who nodded.

"OK, I can let you have a weapon and some ammo right now, on the back of getting that information down from Vancouver, so lets go get you some of the new bugging gear and the lady can program my contact number into her cell phone and yours. I'm sure the Superintendent would love to hear some more stories about Rambo here."

A concerned look crept across Cole Younger's features.

"I nearly wished you good hunting" he grumbled, "but now I'm even reluctant to do that!"

Mike Collins clamped his arm around Danny's shoulders and they both left the room grinning.

The Superintendent sat back. "Irishmen…fucking Irishmen! Get them together and you can be sure that a war is about to happen. You know what? I think I'll go on vacation next week!"

Naomi was relaxing and enjoying herself.

"Superintendent, with a name like Cole Ranger, you must get bugged all the time with people calling you The Lone Ranger, would I be right?"

"Naomi, I can tell you, I never get a moment's peace when I'm introduced to some new group. I wished many a time that my parents had called me anything else rather than that…. well as long as it wasn't 'Sue'!" he exclaimed.

Naomi enjoyed his short rant as she proceeded to program in the phone numbers of the two policemen. She also felt vastly relieved at the reception they'd had from them. Things were starting to happen, and she knew that Danny would continue to ramp up the momentum in his own unique way.

CHAPTER 15

MI5 London

The Director General had summoned the small group together for the following morning, and even though Fiona had to cancel some appointments, wild horses wouldn't have kept her away.

Jerry Sackville and Alina were present too.

Rebecca didn't waste any time getting going.

"Right, thanks for coming in Fiona and the rest of you as well. I know that you people downstairs are up to your eyeballs at present. I'd like to start by asking Jerry what he's come up with since yesterday...Jerry?"

"Right Ma'am. Firstly we traced the telephone number on the package, to a small village or town called Kunduz in the northern part of Afghanistan. Secondly, I've asked our listening post in Cheltenham to start monitoring all calls out of their Embassy here in London. So far no results, but regrettably we may have missed the boat as the person who delivered the envelope to Fiona here may very well have gone back directly to the Embassy and phoned to their contact in Afghanistan."

"So they would then know that Danny is over in California" said Fiona.

"I wouldn't doubt it at all" Rebecca replied. "

Fiona looked anxiously across at her.

"So is he in some danger over there? I mean, can they trace him to California?"

It was Jerry who answered. "In this day and age Fiona, anything's possible. I'm not sure about the caliber of the Afghans Intelligence Service over there, but they might use some other Embassy's Intelligence Agency contacts. If he were travelling under his own name, using his credit card to pay for hotels or car rentals, it wouldn't be difficult to locate him. I could locate him in ten minutes using the resources we've got downstairs, so there you have it."

Alina nodded. "So, we really have to alert Danny then. If he didn't know he was being stalked, for whatever reason, he could be in danger from some sort of attack against him."

Rebecca looked around the group. "Alina's right, I need to get in touch with him a.s.a.p. I was hoping we could sit on this for a few days until Danny sorted the problem out over there, but I'm not prepared to see him taken unawares, if this unknown group actually have something sinister in mind for him. If, in fact, all they want him to do is call them, then it sounds like all they want is information or a dialogue."

Fiona shook her head. "Knowing Danny, I doubt it. Bad things just follow him wherever he goes. Be prepared for the worst where he's concerned, and you won't be far off."

The D.G. took control. "OK, that's it then. I'll get in touch with him as soon I can wake him up. He's still sleeping over there. I'll keep everyone in touch, and Fiona, I'll have Alina as your contact until we sort this out. I'm undecided if we should be providing yourself and Allison with some protection at this time too."

Fiona stared at her, her eyes widening.

It was a sober group who quickly exited the room.

California

The phone woke him at six and his old Military habits had him alert and on his feet immediately.

"Hello" he said "Quigley here."

"Danny, Rebecca here. I waited until a decent hour instead of waking you up and bringing you some disturbing news. Are you wide awake?"

"Yes Rebecca, old Military training. Awake and ready to rock and roll. What's up?" he asked tersely.

She gave him a brief overview of the situation back in London, leaving nothing out, including Fiona's visit to Thames House.

As she spoke, he made notes on some hotel notepaper on the desk, including the telephone number he was supposed to call.

He didn't realize that he'd been holding his breath until he suddenly exhaled.

When she had finished her report the first thing that came to mind was Fiona and Allison.

"How is Fiona taking this Rebecca?"

"She's not a happy bunny I can tell you right now, especially when I raised the possibility of giving her and Allison some protection. I mean we don't really know if she needs it, but the chap who called to her door was creepy according to her, and mentioned Allison by name, so someone has done their research on you."

Danny rubbed his forehead in frustration. "For crying out loud. Here I am right in the middle of this situation and I should really be back there, trying to sort that out."

"Speaking of sorting it out, let me ask you a question Danny. What is the diamond thing all about, and at a value of around twenty five thousand U.S. Dollars? Before you answer though, remember the topic came up before, when you met up with that young Afghan woman here in London. I forget what she was called. She went back home as I recall it, shortly after her brother was shot in that underground garage in the city. I should have followed up on my instincts at the time and got you to explain further regarding the diamonds."

He groaned. "I can't believe this is coming up after all this time Rebecca."

"Come on Danny, give... there could be lives on the line here, and some of them could be your own family, for Pete's sake!"

He nodded to himself, trying to get his head around the situation.

"I should know that nothing stays hidden forever. A question for you first. What color is the hair and is it human?"

"It's black as a crow and has been tested downstairs...it's human all right."

"OK Rebecca, here's the story of the diamond or diamonds as is the case, and I hope you're not going to drop me in it with the Inland Revenue back there."

He filled her in on the story from his last operation in Afghanistan and the girl Jamilla, who eventually made her way to London as a young woman to become a doctor. Also how he only found out at that time that a fortune had been lodged in an off shore account in the Cayman Islands in his name, for quite a large sum. He mentioned the amount.

She whistled. "One point three million Euros! My God man, that's over two million dollars!" she gasped.

"Yeah, I guess it was around that at the time. I've no idea what the exchange rate might be now."

"Danny, we're talking about a lot of money here and you know what, this is probably what this is all about. They're holding Jamilla, and she's told them the whole story, probably under some sort of duress. Odds are that tuft of hair is hers, just to get your attention...and the diamond is peanuts to them because they want the whole lot back. Would that be your take on it? Oh, just how much is left in the account at this stage? I can't see you as a big spender in any way shape or form."

He was silent for a moment as he tried to digest what he was hearing, and which he was gradually coming to accept.

"Well Rebecca, I only heard about this some fifteen minutes ago, and as you can imagine, I'm still trying to get my head around it. My family being in some potential danger worries me most right now, so I'd suggest you get them off to a safe house immediately. Fiona will absolutely hate this for sure, but I'm coming round to your take on this. They've probably tortured Jamilla and got the whole story from her, and quite probably a lot more details from that trip in the Afghan mountains back then. The money? Well, I used about a hundred thousand dollars of it helping out a Delta chap called Hanlon, that I served with back then, and some expenses that I had…flights and hotels in the U.S. at that time, and later that trip to British Columbia in Canada, so most of the funds are still there. As you say I do have a rather low key lifestyle."

"Danny, you take the cake, you really do! A millionaire for the past few years, and I never had even a hint about it! Now, what did you mean about Jamilla providing more details about that trip in the mountains with her? I can't see the significance."

He shrugged, forgetting she couldn't see him.

"Probably none, but nevertheless it was considered top secret by U.S. Intelligence at the time, and I as you know, like everyone else in the Military, had signed the Official Secrets Act in the U.K. so it never came out."

"I don't follow you Danny," she said.

"Okay, well some years back, I called in an airstrike in the Afghan mountains, killing over a hundred Taliban and Al Qaeda as you've already heard, I believe, but it wasn't mentioned that one of those killed was one of their top Al Qaeda leaders called Mohamed Qureshi. We heard later that his Pashtun tribe, as was their custom, swore to get revenge on those responsible for his killing, which basically is me. I never heard anything more about it, and I never returned to Afghanistan."

"I don't buy this side of it. I think you're seeing enemies all over the place now Danny. Look it's been some years, and yes, these people do have long memories, but let's keep our minds focused on what we do know. What d'you plan to do? Are you going to call this number and find out for sure what they want?"

"Right, thanks for that…you're logical as always. Now, what to do? Well, for one I need a couple more days here to sort this situation out. If I call this number, the clock starts ticking right away and I'm stuck here. They obviously know where I am and that I may not be immediately contactable, so it may give me some time. One way or the other I'll be back there within two days, and I can call the number from Thames House with the entire technical backup that I'll need. In the meantime please inform Fiona what's going on and get her somewhere safe for the moment. How does that sound Rebecca?"

"Danny, I think you're right on the button. Just know this… I don't know where this is going but MI5 and myself are behind you one hundred percent, and I'll have your family moved as soon as I hang up. Get things sorted out over there and get back here just as soon as you can."

He glanced at his watch, took it off, and dived into the shower. Naomi had agreed to meet him at a nearby diner for breakfast, and they would then head for their meeting with Commander Nathan Byrne at the Base.

She was already there sitting in a booth in the back with two large cups of coffee on the table.

He slid into the seat opposite her and grabbed the drink.

"Am I ready for this Naomi!" he said, taking a long swallow.

She made a face. "I thought you Brits were always so precise with keeping appointments. I think the waitress was starting to feel I'd been stood up."

"Hey, sorry about that. I had a rather disturbing telephone call from MI5 in London."

"Disturbing, in what way Danny?" she asked, beckoning the waitress over.

He waited while she took their orders and left, then looked across at Naomi. He didn't want to go into the history of the whole situation that revolved around his time in Afghanistan. For starters, she would feel quite guilty at expecting him to continue helping her here in the States. He also wanted to park the whole situation back in the U.K. until he could properly focus on it. He did mention that some old enemies had surfaced and might cause some trouble for him and quite possibly his family.

That got her attention. "Shouldn't you be back there with them, if there's a question as to their safety?"

He nodded. "Yes, I would certainly like to be there for them, but I really do want to clear up Colin's disappearance first, and I feel we're getting close. In any event Rebecca at MI5 is arranging to bring Fiona and Allison to a safe house as we speak, so they're in no danger."

"A safe house! That sounds like something serious. I'm really starting to feel quite uneasy about your family being in some danger. I mean Colin's situation will evolve in time, and as far as I know, he's not in any danger as of right now. Why don't you get a flight back today and be there for them?"

"Well Rebecca and I agreed to give this situation here two more days, then I'll head back. Hopefully we can put some pressure on the people at the Base to open up to us. They have to know something. I'm convinced of that for starters, so let's get this meeting over with and see where we are then. OK?"

He could see he hadn't fully convinced her, but further conversation stopped when the waitress came back with their orders.

Danny always enjoyed breakfast and especially the American style of serving it up. Naomi seemed to agree with him as they both fell silent and settled down to reducing the pile of food on their plates. After his second coffee he sat back.

"I meant to ask you how you knew about my Military operations back in Afghanistan that you told the Police about yesterday. How on earth did you dig that up Naomi?"

She laughed.

"Remember how my Military Police detachment Commander Colonel Bob Kokaski approached your SAS senior Officer Major Wainwright about having some really hard-ass trooper work on the problem we were having with some of our boys in the local pubs? Well your name came up.

Quite simply, the Colonel accessed your background with a little collusion from your Commander. I recall that your CO referred to you as 'a walking killing machine', which prompted my boss to dig a bit deeper. He wanted to reassure me to some extent, when you chose me to accompany you on what looked like a suicide mission at the time. So there you have it...that's all there was to it."

"So much for the Official Secrets Act. My CO just spilled his guts." He shrugged. "Oh well, what the hell. Let's talk about our meeting."

She straightened. "I was about to bring this up, so what's your plan?"

"Quite simply, they're covering something up and I intend to go in there and shake them up. I have some heavy leverage back in Washington, and I intend to wave that around."

She reached across and tapped his elbow.

"These are Seals we're talking about here. The Crème de La Crème, as you said yourself, and they don't scare easily. I know, having lived with Colin and met his buddies on a number of social occasions. They don't buckle to man or beast. All I'm saying is, be very careful in how you phrase any threats you make, or even imply."

He nodded somberly. "Don't worry, I get it. In a way I was there once - not a Seal of course, but I understand the mindset of men who have been trained to mete out death and destruction without a second thought. There isn't much fear left in you, and especially when you realize how weak and vulnerable the average human being is, and how easily they are to take down."

"Good, I wanted to emphasize that...and you seem to have taken it on board. Now what car do we take?"

"Good question. I want both cars to head for the Base, and I'll park as close as I can outside, preferably not in view of the Guard on the front gate. This will become clearer after we leave the Base, if things work out as I've planned. I would envisage both of us switching over to my hire car at that time. I won't say any more for the moment, as I'm not really sure how things will turn out with this meeting. "So," looking at his watch "let's hit the road, and here's hoping for a good result."

They exchanged a big High 5, left some bills on the table and hurried out.

CHAPTER 16

The Guard at the gate took their details and checked a list he was holding, then he seemed to take forever wandering around the vehicle, checking the sides and back.

Finally Naomi called across to him. "What's the problem? I've been in here dozens of times and the Base Seal Commander's waiting for us."

He looked up from his file. "Oh yes, sorry Miss. It's all about being more alert with this ISIS threat. The concern is that they might follow a civilian car from the Base and plant something in it, if it was parked outside. Just more security, that's all."

He waved them on.

They managed to park around the back of the building they were going to, as all the visitor slots were occupied. Danny paused for a moment as he went in the front door, glancing at the designated parking with the names of those it was reserved for.

"I see your Commander has his spot nice and handy to the front door," he muttered.

She glanced at him, puzzled, as he pushed through into the reception area. He hung back again, looking out through the curtained window to the parking lot, as Naomi went forward and announced them. In a moment a young women in naval attire came through a side door and greeted them.

"Ms. Richards and Mr. Quigley, will you follow me please?"

Without another word she turned and went back through the door, holding it for them, then started up the stairs to the second floor, where she went through another door into a small reception area, and pointed to some seats.

"The Commander will be out in a couple of minutes. Please take a seat while you're waiting."

Danny preferred to stand, and occupied himself strolling around the area, examining the numerous pictures on the wall…mostly Military.

When he felt someone's eyes on him, he turned.

A tall lean man was standing in his office doorway regarding him. He looked tanned and fit, dressed in a short-sleeved shirt with the epaulets showing his rank, and as Danny swung round he detected coldness in a pair of narrow grey eyes focused on him. This quickly turned to a half smile as he stepped forward with an outstretched hand.

"Mr. Quigley, and of course Ms. Richards, I'm Commander Byrne…come in, come in…we've been expecting you."

'We?' Danny wondered but he realized the connection when he saw a second Officer waiting back in the room beside what he assumed was the Commander's desk.

If the Commander wore a half smile, this Officer didn't have any. In fact he looked downright unfriendly. He was as thin as a rake, with even thinner grey hair and a pair of penetrating, almost black eyes. He didn't offer to shake hands either when he was introduced as a Lieutenant Commander Greg Fitzpatrick. The Commander casually mentioned that he was the Base Legal Officer.

Danny's first thought was that the room was probably rigged with listening devices. 'Careful Quigley' he thought.

No refreshments were offered.

It was the Commander who started.

"First off, I don't even know why you're here. I understand you're an old acquaintance from the U.K. who Mrs. Richards, then Lieutenant Richards, carried out some police work with."

Danny straightened and looked directly at him.

"That's correct, it was a short Police action over the course of one evening, and I haven't seen her since then until she called me in the U.K. a few days ago to help her out. She's obviously concerned that her husband has disappeared and wanted me to help locate him."

"How extraordinary! With all the Investigative Agencies available to her she calls across the pond for some ex-Military Policeman!"

Having delivered his put down, he glanced at the thin man and got his first smile…one of approval.

"Well I actually work for MI5 in the counter terrorism section. We carry out quite a lot of investigate work."

The thin man's face clouded. "MI5! No one informed us of this." He looked at Commander Byrne, and then a smirk crossed his face.

"Commander, MI5 have no legal brief in this country, and in fact they can act in the U.K. only and have no police powers whatsoever" he said triumphantly.

Danny pretended to look surprised. "Police powers? Who said anything about Police powers? Why, have you people been doing something you shouldn't?" he asked with a half laugh.

"This is no laughing matter Quigley. I'm a busy man running a Base with thousands of people that I'm responsible for. I don't even know why I agreed to see you."

Danny snorted in derision. "Commander, let's cut to the chase. I've been connected with the Military family for years, right across the board, working with NATO and getting to know people from all across the globe, and there's one common denominator among all of them: family matters… family matters Commander - those people who are left to look after the home and the children and keep the light burning brightly until their people get off that plane and embrace them again."

Here he turned, raised his voice, and pointed dramatically to Naomi, "and you, for whatever reason, let this poor wife down when her husband disappeared. Fobbing her off with

109

lame excuses and telling the local Police that you would sort it out. I even believe that you had her quietly removed from her enlisted quarters as she was becoming a nuisance to you…calling up every day, as any wife would when her husband vanishes without trace."

The Commander's face reddened. "That's a lie. I deny it. The Shore Police Investigators still have an open file on it, and continue their investigations."

The thin man burst in. "This is a ridiculous accusation and I demand you take it back. We had Mrs. Richards removed because her husband went AWOL" he sputtered.

Naomi jumped in. "So you were involved in having me removed: a point of legal order then. Why did my pay continue if he was really AWOL? That's not supposed to happen in the Military, and that means the Navy too."

"An oversight no doubt. We'll put a stop to that immediately, I can assure you."

Danny stood up, took out a notebook and pen and started writing. He pointed at both of them slowly as they stared up at him, almost mesmerized.

"I now have one more name for my Admiral contact in Washington, as well as your good self Commander… Lieutenant Commander Greg Fitzpatrick. There's something rotten going on here, and I intend to get to the bottom of it if I have to tear this whole Base apart. The Police we just visited in downtown Coronado, Cole Ranger and Inspector Mike Collins, can confirm I'm quite capable of doing that."

He turned to the door. "Let's go Naomi, these two make me sick. They're a disgrace to the Seals and their uniform. Let's see how long they're wearing it!"

They strode out, leaving two astonished people staring at each other in shock.

Once in the car he turned to her.

"Drive up, and stop for a second by the Commander's car. I want to leave him a present. I checked the reception area and his car is out of the view of the receptionist."

"Sure you know what you're doing Danny?"

"You betcha! Just get moving at the slow Base speed limit."

It went quite smoothly.

The car stopped, he got out and reached for a piece of paper he had put there moments before, stuck underneath the windshield wiper of their vehicle. On getting back inside again, the paper slipped from his hand and he bent down to pick it up off the ground. As he did so, he attached the bug under the rear of the Commander's car. Then they headed out the main gate, both swopped cars and waited. Naomi got behind the wheel.

Only then did she ask him.

"Danny, I know I'm pretty naïve in some things, but what the hell are you playing at? I thought you were going in there to inveigle some further cooperation from them, and quite honestly, I've never seen two senior ranks so insulted in my life!"

He grinned. "Yeah, I stirred 'em up didn't I?"

"Stirred them up? I should say so. I bet the lines to Washington are burning right now. You're in deep shit Quigley! What's that in your hand that you're fiddling with?"

"It's a trace for that bug I planted in the Commander's car. If I read him, correctly he'll be flying out of here very shortly. Why d'you think I went for his juggler back then? That's what you do with an enemy, and get him to do something stupid."

"Like what?" she asked hoarsely.

"Like leading us to Colin, wherever they got him stored, or held, depending on how this plans out."

"Look ..." she started. "Shit, here he comes...son of a bitch! That's why you settled for this scruffy car isn't it?"

He didn't answer her. He was busy operating the scanner as the Commander's car tore past them.

She pulled out behind it, first allowing another car to pull in front of them.

"You can leave even more space if need be. We won't lose him in any event with this scanner, but we'll need to get closer if he looks like he's slowing down for some sort of building or destination. I have a distance camera here and some clever stuff to change my appearance if I have to follow him on foot."

About twenty minutes later that was exactly what happened. The vehicle in front signaled to leave the main street and pulled into the parking lot in front of an apartment block. There were a number of cars parked, and Naomi managed to cruise into a vacant spot directly opposite the vehicle they were following, and conveniently blocked by two other SUVs.

The Commander went up to the outer door of the apartment and let himself in.

"Obviously had a key" she commented. "What do we do now?"

"We just wait. We'd be too exposed to try to follow them. If I'm right, he's going to be coming out again soon, and what I'm going to need is my camera."

She shook her head. "You called it dead right so far Danny...you're something else. You put a ferret in the burrow and the rabbits are scurrying."

"Speaking of which, here they come!"

The Commander came out first, followed by two large burly men dragging a struggling man between them.

"That's Colin" Naomi screamed.

Danny dropped his camera on the street and was racing to the sidewalk where the group had just stopped as the Commander was reaching for the car door.

Danny jumped in front of him and grabbed his arm.

"The game's up Commander...stop right there."

The Commander looked desperately behind him at the two burly men.

"Get him," he screamed, "or we're all done for!"

One of them dropped his hold on Colin and reached under his coat.

Danny was already moving and grabbed his wrist as he was pulling out a large automatic pistol, then he hit him three times, incredibly fast, finishing with a chopping elbow smash that felled him like a tree. Not even changing his stance, he delivered a savage back knuckle strike to the nose of the second man, hearing it crunch, followed by an unearthly scream. As he clutched his smashed face, Danny kicked him in the crotch, dropping him like a stone.

He turned in time to see Naomi holding the Commander in a full nelson before proceeding to bang his head repeatedly into the vehicle. Danny pulled her back and the Commander slumped to the ground.

"Speed dial that Police Inspector and get him here fast, before we gather a crowd."

He then rushed over to Colin who was blinking rapidly, and looking around dazedly.

"Hey, it's OK now old Buddy...we got you...you're free. Hey, your wife Naomi is here."

Just then she came up alongside him.

"The Inspector's on his way and he said five minutes with full lights on. He's got medics on the way as well" she said.

"Great stuff, and nice job on the Commander. Here, hang onto Colin - I think he could do with a hug. I've got these two to take care of."

He dashed over to the car and came back with two thick cords that he swiftly used to tie the two up. He discovered a second weapon on the other thug and sheath knives tucked into a scabbard attached to the back of their belts.

The Commander was still moaning on the ground when Michael Collins' vehicle screamed into the parking lot. He jumped out.

"What you got Danny?" he shouted.

"Probably kidnapping of this poor chap here, the Seal who disappeared, and who I believe was drugged and held somewhere in this apartment block against his will. The whole thing was engineered by this chap lying groaning on the sidewalk - a Navy Commander called Nathan Byrne, if you can believe it, and probably another Officer back on the Seal Base called Greg Fitzpatrick. I suspect there are more people involved as well. Your best chance to rope all of them in is, I suggest, getting that other Officer off on his own and questioning him. He's a legal beagle so watch your P's and Q's. I'll bet he'll cut a deal pretty fast."

113

Collins looked around as Danny handed him the weapons he'd confiscated.

"These two you tied up - are they Seals?"

"I doubt it Mike. Their reactions were far too slow for them to be Seals. Probably some thugs hired by the Commander here."

Just then the medics rolled up with klaxons blaring, and four more police cars came tearing in.

Danny raised his hands in the air. "It's all yours Mike. I'm going to go and sit in the car. It's blocked in anyway."

Collins looked at him. "Jesus Danny, our guys were working on this for weeks, and you come and wrap it up in one day. What was behind all this anyway? Why the kidnapping in the first place?"

"I've no idea Mike, but I'd like to know when you can debrief that poor guy over there. In the meantime I'm going to have a nap. Wake me up when you find out."

Collins stood staring after him as he climbed into the scruffy Toyota back in the lot.

CHAPTER 17

After an hour. with the group milling around and Police cars coming and going, people headed off in various directions.   Mike Collins woke Danny up and told him that Naomi had accompanied her husband in an ambulance to the hospital and would come back to the Police Station as soon as she could to give her statement. Some of the Police had travelled with them and were going to wait until Colin was able to make his report.   The Commander and his two thugs were taken off to be booked and interrogated. Another team had proceeded to the Base to arrest the Lieutenant Commander Greg Fitzpatrick.

On Collin's instructions, he was to be kept isolated until he personally interviewed him, after he had collected all the statements.

He proceeded to take down Danny's account of events, sitting alongside him in the Toyota. Danny also passed over the kit he had been given by Mike Collins...the weapon, ammo and surveillance kit, which had been in the car with him.

On finishing writing down Danny's statement, Collins looked closely at him.

"Look Buddy, why don't you head back to your hotel and get a couple of hours shut eye. You look all in. Probably jet lag mixed up with all the excitement around here. Come back to the Police Department afterwards and we'll probably have all the facts in hand by then and fill you in."

It sounded like a plan, but he had no sooner got inside the hotel than his phone rang.

It was Rebecca. She sounded grim and didn't waste any words.

"You'd better get back here, right away Danny" she barked.

"What's going on Rebecca, you sound terrible!"

"Danielle has been murdered," she said tersely.

He could hear the agony in her voice.

"Jesus, no!" he gasped. "What on earth's happened?"

"She was on this new operation tracking the chaps who came back recently, and they must have copped on to her. A witness coming along the street said that someone dashed out of a doorway, grabbed her, dragged her to a waiting car and threw her inside. The door must have been opened by someone inside the vehicle."

"Oh shit!" Danny exclaimed. "Where was the minder back-up that we agreed on at my last meeting? He should have been up close to her, surely. What happened?"

"You're not going to like this Danny, but after Trevor Hawthorn fired you, he cancelled the back-up plan you'd proposed."

"Cancelled the back-up? Oh God no! I told him they were really bad bastards and we couldn't leave our surveillance people unguarded. Just wait till I get my hands on that son of a bitch" he snarled.

"You won't need to. He's resigned his position already."

"I don't like the thought of him walking away scot free. You said murdered, how d'you know this?"

"She was found dumped in Hyde Park in the early hours of this morning. Initial finding is that she was raped and beaten to death, probably tortured beforehand."

"How d'you know for certain that it was caused by the people we had under surveillance? I mean it could have been a spontaneous act by some group to kidnap some female, any female, couldn't it?"

116

"Two things really. One is from a piece of information you supplied from that flight back from Amsterdam when you walked past the returning Jihadi group and you heard this chilling laugh from one of them. Well our witness heard a similar laugh as the door was slamming in the car that Danielle had been thrown into."

"And the second reason?" he asked, his voice cold as ice.

"The witness spotted faces through the windshield and he said they were Asian, Pakistani."

He was silent, his mind reeling, still trying to come to terms with the terrible news: Danielle, a lovely lady, married and on top of her career!

"OK Rebecca, it's hard to take in like this…a call on the phone, as you'll appreciate."

"I do Danny, I most certainly do, and we're all in shock here, which is one reason I need you back right away."

"There's something you're forgetting Rebecca aren't you? I was fired, remember, over that incident in Amsterdam

…..brought disgrace on the MI5 and all that."

"Oh that? Well I do have some good news for you there. Remember the barman in the restaurant where the trouble started? Well his boss for some reason fired him. He then went back into the Police and changed his statement to the effect that the four Dutch people started the brawl. At MI5 we then went up to Oxford to find out why one of them was kicked out of there. Did we unearth a can of worms! The Dutch chap had sexually assaulted a woman at the University and she was advised by the Directors not to go public, as they would expel him instead. Apparently she's since dropped out of the University, emotionally she's a mess, and very much regrets allowing the whole incident to be swept under the carpet. With our encouragement and support, she's now suing the Dutch chap who assaulted her. It's all gone public and the Dutch man's family has dropped their intention to sue you over the incident. So, a lot's happened here and you're a hundred percent back on the team. I'm re-hiring you right now to your old position, so get back here a.s.a.p." she urged.

After she rang off Danny sat there, letting the whole shocking news sink in. Normally fast in his reactions, he sat trying to get his head around the deluge of good and bad news he had just heard. Then he sprang into action.

His first call was to the San Diego Airport. He booked a flight to San Francisco with a non-stop connection to the U.K. for the following morning at 5am. He didn't have a lot of time.

He contacted the car hire company and arranged to drop the car at the Airport. His next call was to Mike Collins, and he apprised him of his early departure. Mike told Danny that he might have to come back at some future date for the trial of the kidnappers. Danny had been right about the legal beagle back at the Base. He had spilled his guts about it all, looking for immunity. Apparently the whole thing was about the fact that Naomi's husband Colin had realized he was gay, and had decided to 'come out' publicly. Commander Byrne and his Second in Command decided this would be a terrible blow for the reputation of the Seals, especially after the previous very public 'outing' by another member, only recently, so they grabbed Colin with the intention of convincing him to keep 'mum' about his new sexuality. When that failed, they started torturing him and injecting him with drugs to pacify him. According to Lieutenant Commander Fitzpatrick, when Danny had stormed into their office and threatened to move heaven and earth to find Colin, Commander Byrne made a decision that there was only one course left - to kill Colin, and that was what they were planning to do when Danny intercepted them outside the apartment block.

"So, Danny old Buddy, if you hadn't scared the shit out of those two nitwits on the Base, we would have had a murder on our hands sooner or later. I get the feeling they were getting nowhere with Colin Richards, and couldn't see any way back. They couldn't let him loose after what they'd done to him. You simply accelerated the whole process. I take my hat off to you. Now, you're heading for the Airport in the morning, so I won't have a chance to buy you that pint we talked about. Hey, you'll be back for the trial though, if nothing else. Take care, you hear?"

118

He had one more call to make...to Naomi.

He kept it short. Things were going crazy back in London and he was taking the first flight out, but so much had happened to her in the past few hours that he was sure she wasn't registering fully what he was telling her.

She had heard from Mike Collins that her husband was being taken out of the apartment as they arrived, to kill him.

"Danny I really don't know what to say about all you've done for me - for us over here. I can handle the news of Colin realizing that he was gay. At least I'm not in the dark any more...I've got answers and I can go on from here...not with Colin obviously, but now there's a hope for some sort of future. I can live with that, but tell me one thing please: what exactly was your strategy today when you went in to the Base and approached the Commander? Even as a former Police Investigator, I didn't understand what you were trying to achieve?"

He chuckled. "Well, for starters I'm ex-Military, so I understand the Military mind and especially it's hierarchy and its strong sense of entitlement in the Officer class. Take the Commander as an example: all his life as a privileged Officer, it's been, 'yes sir, no sir, three bags full sir'...everyone below him in rank deferring to his every mood and decision. Lower ranks being paraded into his office, charged with some Military misdemeanor, and he was both judge and jury. His office was hallowed ground in other words, and he was almost like some deity dispensing his wisdom on the peasants, untouchable, and surrounded by his minions who insulated him from the real world out there. So, I deliberately attacked that protective screen and threatened to undermine his whole illusory fiefdom. The totally unexpected shock of it burst his comfortable bubble and he made a completely irrational decision to go and get rid of the problem, once and for all. Remember, I'd threatened his career by mentioning that Admiral, even though I really had no idea who my contact in the CIA had approached. Commander Byrne panicked and reacted rather stupidly."

"But if we hadn't followed him to that apartment, Colin could be dead right now...."

"Yeah, I hadn't really thought that a top ranking Naval Commander would take such extreme steps Naomi. We were lucky there, for sure."

"You know something Danny, I don't think you were relying on luck entirely. You read that situation pretty well, and you had the back-up car and equipment ready to follow through, so I take my hat off to you for that. What a result! Wow!"

"Thanks for that, and yes, I'm really happy that we got the whole thing sorted out."

"Me too, and one more thing before you go. I'd really like to personally thank you in a more appropriate way for all you've done for me. How about you check out of your hotel and come round here for a super meal that I'll cook up. You can kip out on the lounge pullout bed, and I can get you to the Airport in lots of time for your flight in the morning. How does that sound?"

He smiled for the first time since he'd got the terrible news from Rebecca.

"Hey, you know something Naomi, I can't think of anything I'd rather do, especially with you. I'll be over there shortly after I drop the hire car off. I was originally going to drop it off at the Airport in the morning."

And that was it... he never got as far as trying out the pullout bed.

He made the flight... only just!

CHAPTER 18

Danny had always found the trip going back to the U.K. much tougher to take from a jetlag point of view, but was lucky in that he hadn't really adjusted to time in the U.S., and there hadn't been any delays on his flight connections. Notwithstanding that, long haul flights from the west coast were hard on the system, and he would have loved to sleep for several hours but he couldn't.

The funeral service for Danielle had already started, but he managed to squeeze in the door of the church and joined the crowd standing at the back. A few people frowned at his late arrival but he shrugged and made what he hoped was an apologetic expression. The church was crowded to capacity and he spotted some MI5 personnel and one manager from MI6. He couldn't see the front of the church, and in a way was glad that he didn't have to get too close to the grieving family - especially Danielle's husband and her children.

He usually found funeral services long and difficult, and he'd attended a few in his Regiment days, however, he couldn't stop replaying the time he'd spent with Danielle in Amsterdam, and how utterly impossible it was to accept that she was no longer on this earth, walking around, laughing, talking and so full of life.

The service was nearly finished when his eye caught a movement by a side door, several feet in front of him. He froze!

He couldn't believe his eyes!

Trevor Hawthorn was pushing his way out of the church.

Here, he thought, was the man who was responsible for Danielle's horrific death, and he had turned up at her funeral!

Danny caused more frowns when he elbowed through the crowd and caught the church door as it was swinging closed.

Outside, he caught a glimpse of Hawthorn moving swiftly away towards a small roadway off to the side of the church grounds.

"Hold up there you bastard!" he shouted.

A startled face turned back towards him, then Howard turned and started a half run away. Danny sprinted after him and caught him by the shoulder, spinning him around. The man's face was white with fear and his voice was almost a scream.

"Get away from me. I'll report you for assault and threatening me."

Danny took his hand off and laughed in his face.

"What about the people who threatened Danielle and assaulted her? Too bad you weren't as diligent with her as you are at protecting your own worthless hide, and you call yourself an ex-Officer? You're nothing but a useless piece of shit, Howard!"

"And you're nothing but a killer, Quigley" he spat. "I'll file charges that you threatened to kill me. "

Danny looked at him for a moment, shaking his head, then he leaned forward and whispered in the terrified man's ear.

"I never threatened you...the tiger never growls when it's going hunting at night ...remember that."

Then he turned and bumped into Alina coming up to him.

"Everything OK Danny?" she asked.

"Oh yeah, Alina. I just had a few words with Howard there. Seems to think I threatened to kill him. Hmm...nice thought, but he's not worth spending 10 years in prison for."

She looked from one to the other, measuring the mood of the situation, then she caught Danny's arms and pulled him away gently.

"Come on Danny, this isn't the time or place" she said quietly.

Sensing his opportunity, Howard turned and scuttled off, glancing back fearfully before disappearing out of sight.

"What a f…ing nerve, turning up at her funeral service" Danny muttered.

She nodded. "You got it in one. He probably thought he could slip in and leave early without being noticed."

She canted her head sideways, looking closely at him.

"Did you really threaten to kill him? I wouldn't blame you if you did, mind you."

"Well, not in so many words" he offered lamely.

"What exactly did you say then?" she asked.

He shrugged, starting to feel embarrassed by the whole incident. "I told him that the tiger didn't growl when it was going hunting at night."

She slapped her forehead. "Oh man, and you don't call that threatening him? No wonder the guy shot away from here like a terrified rabbit."

Danny grinned. "Yeah, he did didn't he? I hope the bastard has some sleepless nights. I doubt his conscience brought him here though."

"Hey, don't be too hard on him. He was probably feeling guilty by this stage, especially on a morning like this. Come on, I'm taking you out of here right now."

She grabbed his arm.

"You're coming with me my good man" she said, using the tone of a Policeman making an arrest.

"You got me Officer, you got me" he mimicked, then changing his tone "hey where are you taking me anyway, Alina?"

"Home with me for starters, where you're going to have a nice long shower to help you get over your flight. While you're doing that, I'm going to prepare one of those big breakfasts you get in an upmarket B&B. After that we'll see how it goes. Rebecca wanted me to get you back into Thames House late this afternoon, so you've loads of time to brief me on your trip to California."

And that was how it played out…almost.

The shower was fantastic, and he felt the tension of the last few days fall away. She was spot on about the breakfast too. It would have been a credit to any four star hotel in London, and he didn't stop until he had finished the lot and moved across to the couch with his third cup of coffee. She sat beside him with her own cup, and he smiled inwardly when she quizzed him about Naomi who he had flown out to help a few days before.

"I bet she was very grateful when you were able to sort out that whole mess for her" she prompted.

"Hey, I know where you're going with this…" He slapped her shoulder lightly as if in reprimand, "but no, she wasn't that kind of grateful you Jezebel" he lied. "Anyway, I'd just got the word about Danielle's murder."

Her faced dropped. "Sorry Danny, I didn't mean to make light of it. Hearing about her murder must have been a terrible shock to you, and especially hearing it cold like that from several thousand miles away."

Danny didn't quite know what happened to him next. He was suddenly convulsed with sobs, and he felt tears flowing down his face.

He shook his head. "Jesus, what's happening to me? This must be some sort of post-traumatic stress catching up with me from my military days… I don't believe it…this isn't like me. Oh shit!" he groaned.

Then her arms were around him and she was rubbing the back of his head…"Hey, its okay Danny, it's okay…tears are good, just let it all out. There's nothing happening to you that isn't part and parcel of being a normal feeling human being…"

He clung harder to her, and gradually his sobs reduced.

"So what was that all about Danny? You're the kick ass Saas chappie who walks through walls without a thought, as far as we at MI5 think, and now suddenly you seemed to fall apart!"

He shook his head dazedly. "Jesus, I thought I'd got over this …left it all behind."

"Got over what Danny?" she asked.

He was silent for a long moment, then he stirred, looking off into the distance.

"I spoke of this to a man called CC Courtney in Ireland, some years back. He was helping me adjust to being a civilian again. He could see that I was carrying a lot of stuff with me and started probing around some of my past."

"From the Military you mean?"

"Yes, exactly. I was, as you say, pretty hard-nosed about the operations we were on where we had to go in and, well, essentially kill people. Like most of the others in the troop we would simply switch our minds off and do the job like we'd been trained to do, then just walk away afterwards. We'd learned to park the violence and the experience. For some of them that didn't work out too well. It came back later, and sometimes when least expected. They ended up with what everyone now knows to be Post Traumatic Stress. In one incident I shared with this man Courtney, I did dissolve into tears, but I felt that somehow I'd been cleansed of the memory at that time."

"Is that the incident that's come back to you now?"

He nodded. "We'd staked out a terrorist camp in Africa in an attempt to rescue some oil workers who'd been kidnapped. I don't need to tell you all the details. Suffice to say that when we hit them at dawn with a deadly fusillade from 16 troopers' automatic rifles, we cut them down like wheat before a thrasher."

"But you were only doing your duty Danny," she emphasized, hugging him closer.

"Yeah I know, but when we went and looked at the dead bodies lying twisted and broken in the mud, they were all children...children soldiers from ages eight to thirteen years of age, holding rifles and machetes in their small hands."

"Oh shit!" Alina whispered.

He nodded again. "Yeah, some of the troop who were married and had kids went home couldn't function again as front line soldiers. Our Pastor actually resigned from the Unit afterwards. Two of our mates ended up topping themselves."

"And it suddenly hit you, sitting right here after all these years... what, four years or so?"

"Yeah, just like that, I saw those little forms lying there. I don't know, maybe it was seeing my daughter Allison recently, with her slim delicate arms and form. I've no idea Alina. I'm sorry... it came out of nowhere. I thought I was the original Rambo and that nothing could reach me."

"Danny," she whispered, "it just means, as I said before, that you're becoming more human, and that can't be a bad thing."

Neither of them knew what happened next.

Her face had been inches from his tear stained face when he turned to her. Suddenly they were kissing, tearing the clothes off each other, and in minutes were naked on the couch, making love with a desperation that totally consumed them both.

The time seemed to float by.

From the lounge they moved into the bedroom. This time it was slower and better.

They dozed for a while. It was Alina who finally jumped and glanced frantically at the time.

They both needed a shower, which delayed them further, and they barely made it to Thames House in time.

Rebecca looked at them for a long moment. They both tried to look casual and unconnected. Danny spotted her lower lip twitch.

They weren't fooling anyone.

CHAPTER 19

Already present were Phil Dawson, who was responsible for bugging and burglaring, Peter Sanderson head of counter surveillance, and his 2IC Alina Tariq, Jerry Sackville, counter terrorist investigations and research. Missing was Trevor Hawthorn, former Director of counter terrorism, who had resigned.

The welcome back for Danny was muted and brief, reflecting the somber mood of the group who had attended Danielle's funeral only hours before.

Rebecca Fullerton Smythe dived straight into her briefing and presentation.

"Danny has filled me in on his trip to California where he managed to sort out a problem involving a former American Military Police colleague. Some nice work there. Now we can get this ship back on the road.

Just to update Danny, under torture Danielle must have disclosed our bugging operation of the luggage of the returning group by the Dutch Police as all information from that source has dried up. We still have the Unit downstairs keeping an ear to this original contact, just in case. It has to be said that, sooner or later under extreme interrogation methods, we all talk, and this is no reflection on Danielle. The terrorists have also left the address they were at...no surprise there, so we have our work cut out to re-establish that contact. We're working in the dark otherwise. We also had to assume that our names and contact details are known as well, so what would that mean? These people play for keeps, and your families, women and children are fair game, as you know. So the first decision I made was to inform the team here of the situation: have Scotland Yard provide a 24/7 protection screen around each of you at your place of residence, and have you move out a.s.a.p., not necessarily to safe houses as such, but different addresses if feasible. This, for example, could be a relative who lives in the greater London area. If not feasible, MI5 are covering the cost of hotels, guesthouses or B&Bs of your choice, bearing in mind that Home Office funds are not unlimited. Alina just changed her address three weeks ago, so few of us knew of her new address and that included Danielle. Any questions so far?"

Danny raised his hand. "Just a thought…could we set up surveillance on our people's vacated residences on the off chance that the terrorists themselves will start watching them? We might just strike it lucky."

Rebecca nodded. "Good thought Danny. We've been a bit shaken up since Danielle was murdered, and haven't really re-grouped as yet."

She looked across at Sanderson, the head of counter surveillance. "What d'you think Peter?"

"I like it…could be a good place to start, and Danny having actually seen these people would be a great help. I'll set it up straight away."

Rebecca was about to comment when her phone rang. She shook her head in irritation. "I told them not to interrupt this meeting." She picked it up and listened.

They all noticed her change of expression…surprise and delight. She hung up and turned to the group.

"That bugging we set up on the terrorists…a signal started coming in again. I don't know how or why, but it seems we're back in business. Jerry, what's your read on this? How could it happen?"

Sackville's forehead creased up in thought.

"Unusual, but it happens occasionally. Let's say the Dutch Police who were told to bug the suitcase, did so, and had a device left in their hand. They might have just shoved two bugs in one piece of luggage, and the terrorists stopped looking when they discovered the first one. Danielle wouldn't have known this, and so the team we were targeting wouldn't be aware of it either. Why would it start up now? I've no idea. If it's back working, then we lucked in," he concluded.

The piercing eyes of Phil Dawson looked skeptical.

"Ma'am, I've seen everything in counter surveillance. They could be setting us up to lure out some of our people and kill them. They could have hung on to one of the bugs, deactivated it, re-activated it and planted it as a come hither to our group."

The group fell silent as they assimilated Dawson's input.

It was Danny who broke the silence.

"In any event we need to provide our surveillance people with an armed response team right on their backs to prevent any further debacles such as happened to Danielle. By the way Ma'am, I'd suggest Jerry contacts those two Dutch Police and query them on where they planted all the bugs. It might just shed some light on this."

Rebecca stood up.

"Danny and Phil are spot on. "Peter, can you chase this up right now please?"

He nodded and slipped out of the room.

She carried on. "This could be a break, but it could equally be a 'come on' to get us out there in the street where we're vulnerable, so apart from Phil and Danny, I want all of you to head back downstairs and start working on some strategies and contingency plans. We can't afford to lose this cell, but equally we can't put any of our teams in a position where they can be picked off at will. Oh, a piece of information. I'm not replacing Trevor Hawthorn at this time. We're in too critical a stage at the moment, so I'm taking over his brief as Director of Counter Terrorism. Let's get to it, people."

As the small group left the room, she gestured to the scattered chairs and indicated that Danny and Phil should pull in closer to her desk and sit down.

She brought out the package that had come in for Danny while he was away, and passed it across to him. He looked at it without comment, and placed it on the desk in front of him.

"Right, the next item on the agenda is this package that was handed to Danny's wife on her doorstep by a man who subsequently turns out to be with the Afghan Intelligence section of their Embassy here in London. Out of concern for Danny's family, we've moved them to a place of safety for the moment. A move, I can tell you that his wife is not at all pleased about, so Danny, I'm sorry to say, you have some fence mending to do. Now Phil Dawson is fully in the picture here as he has to be, and in a few moments we're going down to his department where he's arranged for you to call this number in Afghanistan and record it. We've established that it came from a small village called Kunduz, back in the foothills, and we're surprised that there was no effort at this stage to protect the source of this, considering that the Afghan Intelligence Service is involved. We won't know exactly what they want until you contact them, but there's no doubt in my mind they want the money back that Danny has in the Cayman Islands. To mark your cards Danny, it's the law that you cannot be seen to fund or support terrorism in any way, so you would face some serious charges if seen to be attempting this. Any questions so far?"

"Just a thought Rebecca. If I could find some source to produce a bunch of very genuine looking fake diamonds for an exchange with these people, would I still be in trouble here? I mean they probably wouldn't have some diamond expert sitting back there in that village, so that might give me some time while they authenticate them in Kabul or back in Pakistan."

She smiled grimly. "Assuming that we're going to let you go on such a foolish mission in the first place, no, fake diamonds would not put you on the wrong side of the law on this. Seriously though, you don't have an eight-man team of hard-assed troopers watching your back on this. It would be a one way suicide mission Danny, and I for one, want no part of it."

After kicking the topic around further, they followed Phil downstairs into his well-equipped laboratory where an operator was standing by.

Phil put a set of headphones on Danny's head, dialed the number, and handed the receiver to him. It rang several times and was then answered. It was an English speaking voice.

"This must be Mr. Quigley, back from California I believe, very nice… better late than never. I was just about to terminate a mutual acquaintance here."

Danny's voice tensed on the phone and he leaned forward "Look you…." but Rebecca's hand tightened on his shoulder warningly.

He carried on more calmly.

"I was just wondering how you knew it was me calling, and who am I talking to right now?" he asked.

"Ah, someone with you there, warning you about that temper of yours. Yes, she's a pretty woman… or was, should I say. How did I know it was you calling? This is a dedicated line strictly set up for you Mr. Quigley, so it shows the importance of these negotiations. My name doesn't matter, nor does your agency's recording or tracing of this call, the location of which I'm sure is already known to them. On completion of our chat today, we're leaving this location with our mutual acquaintance Jamilla. You won't be having any more contact with me until you put an advertisement in the Financial Times under the heading 'Afghan Investment Opportunity' with some twaddle you can dream up, and a contact number. We'll call you back."

"You sound very sure of yourself "said Danny." I have two questions for you Mr. Nameless, three actually. How d'you know that I have any funds left at all, after all these years, and how do I know that Jamilla is still alive, and that you would even consider letting her go under any circumstances? Under your code, I understand she's committed a very serious crime."

The man laughed. "Good questions Mr. Quigley. Yes, this negotiation is going as I expected… good! First of all, I'll let you talk to her in a moment…very briefly I caution you, but long enough for you to know that she's alive…not well, I'm

131

afraid. The money? We've researched you very well globally and you don't appear to have expended any large sums of money. Guarantee? Well yes, why would you hand over such a large sum of money without it? We could agree to release her to someone from the British Embassy in Kabul, immediately we're in possession of the funds. Our code would be satisfied then by this exchange and Jamilla would no longer be in any danger."

"Yeah sure. I wasn't born yesterday. Doesn't your religion allow you to lie to the infidel if it helps you achieve your aims? And what about me, if I'm the one delivering the package?"

The next minute all three at the table jumped back, startled, at the keening cry that came down the line. It was the voice of Jamilla.

"Danny, Danny, don't come. They'll kill both of us…"

Danny lost it. "You slimy bastard. If it's the last thing I do, I'm going to come over there and tear you apart…you…" he screamed into the phone.

There was merely a laugh at the other end.

"The Financial Times Mr. Quigley, and time is running out…."

The line went dead.

They sat looking across at each other, awestruck.

"Son of a bitch!" Dawson whispered. "He never replied to what might happen to you, did he?"

Rebecca said nothing. She sat there gazing at Danny with a tremendous look of compassion on her face. She had never seen him look like that before.

Finally he stirred.

"Here's what I want you to do for me Rebecca. That money's been nothing but trouble since it was given to me. I never asked for it, nor expected it in the first place. Tell me how to get the funds out of the Cayman Islands and dole it out to the following: the Sally Ann and similar type organizations here in London, and a share to organizations that help treat PTSD in soldiers and their families. OK, I know two million dollars isn't much in real terms, to create an effect, but it might make a difference. How's that?"

She looked shocked. "Are you sure about this Danny? What about Jamilla? This could be a death sentence for her!"

He didn't answer right away…just sat there looking off into the distance. Finally he looked at her.

"The money doesn't make any difference now. Jamilla's outer form is already dead… I just felt that… her heart gave out under what that bastard just did to her, but you know what, her spirit lives on as bright as ever Rebecca. I'm still going to put that ad. in The Times, and subsequently meet up with our friend on the phone." He stared at her. "He hasn't got much longer to live either," he said quietly.

Danny got up and left, without a further word.

Rebecca and Phil Dawson sat staring at each other.

"Jesus Christ, what was that all about? How could he tell that she was dead?" he breathed.

She went on thoughtfully. "It just occurred to me Phil. Danny hasn't been the same since he went over to Canada and was involved in that debacle on the west coast. Something traumatic must have happened to him over there. There's a stillness about him that wasn't there before… a detachment at times that can be disconcerting. Some might call it a bit weird. I'm going to try to talk to him about this soon."

Dawson made a face.

"It hasn't affected his performance in any way as far as I can see" he commented.

She looked at the door Danny had just walked through. "Precisely, and if anything I'd say he's better than ever at what he does…long may it continue" she said fiercely.

Back in the village in Afghanistan, the watcher stepped back from the form tied to the chair, whose battered body had suddenly quivered and snapped forward with a rending scream. His face was red from the effort of the beating he had just handed out, and sweat beaded his forehead. He roughly grabbed one of the women.

"Quickly, see what's wrong with her. Bring here round" he shouted. The woman came close and examined her, listening for any breath.

There was none.

"She's gone," she whispered. "You've killed her."

He turned away, his eyes desperate.

'Can we still get the diamonds?' he asked himself 'or is that opportunity as dead as Jamilla is right now?'

A cold dread gripped his heart.

Would this man Quigley have his own code of revenge when he found out, and come for him... ?

The watcher took some time to collect his thoughts, as the two women carried Jamilla's limp body from the room. He couldn't believe how stupid his reactions had been when the woman had screamed out a warning.

Shaking his head again, he picked up the phone and dialed a number in Kabul. A man answered and listened to his version of what had just happened.

They spoke in the Pashtu dialect, and the English version was as follows:

"So it seems your purpose in taking this woman prisoner is probably a waste of time now, would you say?"

"Not necessarily. There's still a chance I can pull it off."

The man laughed mockingly. "As the English saying goes 'you just killed the goose that lays the golden egg'. Why would this man Quigley part with all that money without confirming that she's still alive? This is part and parcel of any kidnapping negotiation."

"I may still be able to get him to part with the money first. He badly wants to free her, I know this."

"Hmm, I somehow doubt it and your chances of success are pretty nil at this stage. The family of Mohammed Qureshi, killed by this Quigley, waited before seeking revenge for his death, to allow you time to get back the value of those diamonds that were stolen. This doesn't seem possible now, so they'll be proceeding with their own plans. Now that he's back from the U.S. we have good intelligence as to his whereabouts and movements in London, so you'd better move fast if you expect to achieve any results from your present strategy. I wouldn't count on Quigley being around very much longer."

The line went dead.

The watcher sat there staring at the dead phone in his hand.

CHAPTER 20

They weren't the best circumstances for following a suspect on a dark night, with the streets slick from a recent burst of rain. The small team had been thrown together at a moment's notice at Thames House when the bug was activated again, and a surveillance vehicle driven by Peter Sanderson, had tracked it to a Soho restaurant. Alina was waiting well back in the darkened doorway of a closed shop when the Jihadist emerged and stood for a moment, looking up and down the street, before heading off. Fortunately he wasn't wearing headgear and Alina briefly spoke into her collar mike to Danny who was keeping her in view, 30 yards back, and Sanderson who was behind Danny in the van with the bugging equipment and an operator. They had two vehicles on parallel roads, and another some distance further up the road ahead of Peter Sanderson's van.

"Target just emerged and is heading north...appears to be Zain Waheed from the brief view I had of him when he stopped under the outside light...am following - over."

Danny clicked once and Peter squelched twice to acknowledge.

Alina scooted out from the doorway, and started following Waheed who didn't appear concerned about any possible surveillance on him. He was simply strolling along casually. She heard again the echo of Sanderson's warning that the Jihadists might be setting them up, and stayed on high alert, listening for any vehicles coming up behind her, or the sudden appearance of other figures joining the terrorist she was following.

From his vehicle, Sanderson, with a running commentary, kept her and Danny informed of any suspicious cars passing him. They had covered about half a mile in this manner when Alina's voice cut through urgently.

"Danny, can you get up here right now!"

Forgetting caution, he raced up the street catching up with her as she peered round a corner.

He caught the back of her jacket. "Hey, what's up?"

She pulled back and faced him. "We got a problem Danny. A bunch of tattooed skinheads just came out of a pub, saw Waheed passing, grabbed him, and slammed him up against a wall. They're starting to give him a right pounding. I've no idea how to handle this."

Danny took a quick peek around the corner, confirming what she had reported. He thought quickly and caught her shoulder.

"OK, I'm going in there to help him and see how it turns out. It could be a break."

"But Danny, it could still be a set up...shouldn't we consult Peter back there?"

"There isn't time Alina, and the moment will pass if I don't act right now. You fill Peter in."

He extracted his ear bud and collar mike and shoved them into her hand, then slipped around the corner.

Back at Thames House Danny had quickly utilized the expertise of one of the makeup department to change his apparel and appearance to one of a scruffy street person. He had been using this method for the past six months' surveillance work, and had built up some genuine contacts both on the street and the places where street people could get a meal and a bed for the night.

He was aware that Danielle had, more than likely, under torture, provided the terrorists with a description of the personnel in the immediate MI5 team involved, so he'd had to completely change his appearance and character-especially his

137

erect Military stance. Now he ambled up the street and stopped opposite the group who were beating the terrorist.

"Hey, what's going on here?" he shouted, coming closer to them.

He could see there were five skinheads involved in the assault and one of them pulled back and snarled at him.

"Get the f...k out of here, or you'll be next, you lay-about." He pushed Danny back roughly with his right arm.

Danny broke it.

Before he had even time to scream, he moved forward on the group and savagely kicked two knees that were sideways onto him, hearing them crunch. Two more collapsed to the pavement. The remaining two suddenly became aware that something was happening and turned, transferring their aggression to Danny with swinging fists and kicks. One presented him with an ideal opportunity for a foot sweep, as one of the thugs missed with a kick, and his boot stamped back down to the ground. As the thug hit the ground, Danny dropped straight down with his knees on his rib cage, breaking it, and hearing an anguished scream. As he came back up on his feet to meet the last thug, he saw that he didn't need to worry. Waheed the terrorist had flung himself at the man and was delivering a flurry of blows to his head and body, sending him flying back against the wall. There were now five thugs lying screaming and moaning on the pavement.

Waheed looked across at Danny.

"Hey thanks Man…where the hell did you come from?"

Danny pretended to be shook-up and raised his hands, backing up.

"Shit, I don't want any trouble Mate. I'm outta here before the cops come." He turned as if to leave.

The terrorist jumped forward. "Wait, don't leave. You can't leave like this after helping me with those yobos. It's a good idea to get out of here, but don't run off just yet."

Danny pulled away. "Look I just want to get away from here. I can't afford any Police getting involved. I'm glad I happened to be passing and helped you out. These bastards beat up a mate of mine last week...he may lose an eye...so I was glad for some payback." He turned away again.

"Wait, wait," the man pleaded, and pulled him off up the street and around a corner, where he stopped and turned to him. "Where'd you learn to fight like that anyway?"

Danny paused, looking more directly at the man as if hearing him for the first time.

"I was in the Parachute Regiment for 8 years...did it all...Iraq, Afghanistan, you name it. Then when I got back to the U.K. they discharged a whole bunch of us. I couldn't get a job so I ended up on the street" he said bitterly. "I was just on my way to a men's hostel, trying to get a meal and a bed for the night."

The terrorist was now studying him carefully.

"You mentioned that you didn't want any Police involvement. Surely that assault on me back there wouldn't cause you any problem?"

Danny shrugged. "I got into some trouble a couple of weeks ago when I was asking for some money outside a tube station and some American tourist pushed me out of the way. I decked him, but I ended up being charged and I'm up in court shortly for it. I can't afford any more attention from the Police at this stage Mate."

The terrorist held his arm firmly. "Well, you don't need to worry about a meal or a bed for tonight, because you're coming with me to meet some friends of mine who might be in a position to help you. I agree with you, let's get out of here. Those dammed CCTV cameras could be our undoing if we don't go...and keep your head down" he shouted, as they hurried off.

CHAPTER 21

Back down the road, Alina jumped into Peter's car. "Jesus Peter, Danny's gone off with Waheed. What the hell can we do?" she asked.

"Follow them for starters. It'll turn out to be either a great opportunity or a complete disaster for ourselves and Danny Quigley."

She grasped his arm tightly. "Get going Peter, and don't lose them, for God's sake!

Just then the telephone rang in the van and he grabbed it.

Alina couldn't make out who it was from, but it was brief.

Peter turned to her.

"Good news from Jerry. He managed to contact those Dutch Police who planted the bugs. They did have one left after doing the baggage, and they slit a sole in a runner and shoved it in, then stuck some adhesive in to seal it. In their opinion it could have been possible that the adhesive might have stopped the bug from activating, but with the runner in use, and some wet pavements, it could have kicked in shortly afterwards."

"Thank God for small mercies" she said fervently. "At least it's not a set up as you feared."

Up ahead, Danny hurried along with Waheed for a good mile before the terrorist made a right turn down some narrow streets, coming to a small broken metal gate, which led them into a neglected garden. It fronted a sprawled brick two-story house with an attached garage. The house showed lights inside. The door opened almost immediately, and they moved through it fast, with Waheed pulling Danny in behind him. From the flight over from Amsterdam, he recognized the roly-poly, bird-like figure that had let them in…Ali Hossain.

The terrorist looked disconcerted for a moment, trying to factor in the sudden appearance of a stranger in their midst.

Waheed clapped him on the arm. "Hey, it's okay…this guy just saved me from a beating back down the road. He's on his uppers Man, and we're going to give him a meal and a bed for the night."

Hossain reared back. "I don't know about that, you know our instructions…no one comes back here. Mohammed isn't going to like this."

"What won't I like?" A tall, gaunt-faced individual with tight thin lips pushed past Waheed and stared at Danny.

He had previously described the man he'd watched through the immigration mirror at the Airport as ' a stone cold killer'.

"Just who the f…k is this you've brought here Zain?" he rasped.

"Oh it's OK Mohammed, he stepped in and saved me from a beating from some yobos out on the street about twenty minutes ago. He's ex-army, down on his luck, and shit, can he fight! He was heading to a hostel. The least I could do was bring him back here for a bite to eat and a bed for the night."

The next thing Danny knew was that the man pulled a pistol out from his waistband and stuck it into his face. Then he turned and snarled at Waheed.

"You stupid bastard, you've probably been set up, and brought back one of those people from the Intelligence Service!"

He grabbed Danny roughly and hauled him back through an open door into what was a long L-shaped lounge, where a solid looking man was waiting, having overheard some of the conversation from the front door.

Danny recognized him as the American, Frank Skinner, whose picture had been snapped by the drone in Iraq and who had subsequently been identified by the CIA as a former Marine.

The American stepped forward. "What the hell's going on here?" he demanded.

Mohammed looked angrily at him. "Waheed brought this one back with him...says he saved him from a beating by some punks. I think he's been set up by MI5 for Christ's sake."

Danny struggled to face the group. "Hey, for crying out loud, you don't need to shove a gun in my face. I was on my way to the goddam shelter and stopped to give your mate a dig out. Look, just send me back out on the street for Pete's sake. I've no idea what's going on here, and I couldn't give a shit...all I was trying to do was help your friend there. As I mentioned to him, a mate of mine was beaten up by a bunch like them thugs last week, and will lose an f...ing eye."

In the van, Alina gasped. "They've pulled a weapon on him. What are we going to do?"

Peter touched her elbow. "Relax, it's Danny Quigley in there. He could easily disarm that chap with the gun and sort out the rest of them as well. Lets see how this plays out Alina."

Inside the house Mohammed rasped impatiently: "I still think it's a set up."

Waheed laughed. "Yeah sure...get this. He broke the arm of one of the attackers and smashed the knees of two of them, and to cap it, he dropped down on one of their chests and I heard his ribs crack. Some set up! How could MI5 get this kind of commitment from its staff, tell me? Hell, they'd have to keep recruiting full time to keep people on the street."

Mohammed paused, lowering the pistol slightly.

Frank pushed his way forward. "Well, there's one quick way to find out if he's the genuine article."

He turned to Danny. "Get your clothes off right now, all of them," he instructed.

Danny allowed his jaw to drop, and looked confused.

"My clothes off? Jesus, what's with you guys? "

Mohammed shoved the weapon back in his face. "You heard Frank...clothes off now!"

Danny looked dazedly from one to the other and started to undo his shirt. Frank reached forward and tore the front of the shirt down, the buttons popping.

"Shit, that's the only shirt I got" he started to protest. Then as Frank made to reach for more of his clothes he said, "OK, OK, hold your horses for God's sake" as he started to peel the shirt off, and the sweater and vest underneath too. He handed them to Mohammed who dropped them on the floor in evident disgust. "These are filthy," he said.

Danny shrugged. "Try sleeping in a cardboard box under a bridge for a few nights Mate, and see how you smell" as he bent over, removing the rest of his clothes.

He finally stood there in his underwear.

Frank looked at him. "In pretty good nick for someone living on the street" he observed.

Danny made a face. "I was in the Military up to 8 months ago…three square meals a day. Then I got kicked out as this lousy Government started cutting right across the board. I went down to the job center and an eighteen-year-old kid told me I hadn't the skills that any company needed today. They fu…. ng needed me in Iraq and other places to do their dirty work, and I wasn't good enough to get even the most basic job back home? Oh and then what happened? My wife sued for divorce, had me kicked out of the house, and there I was, simple as that, out on the street…the only friends a bunch of street people, and you know what? This is the twist… I ended up in a different army…the fu…ng Salvation Army," he fumed bitterly.

Frank looked at him thoughtfully. Then stepped close to him. "Lift your arms up high over your head" he barked.

Danny did so. There were streaks of dirt all up the inside of his arms.

Frank leaned forward, sniffed his armpits and recoiled. "You fu…ng stink…" He looked around at the group.

"Lesson for you people… if I picked up even the faintest smell of a deodorant in this situation, you'd probably have a spy on your hands."

143

He spoke directly to Danny again. "One last thing, turn around."

Danny shook his head and slowly turned around.

Frank caught the frayed elastic top of his underwear, pulled back on it and glanced inside.

He looked like he was about to throw up. "Oh man, you must have been wearing these for a month. They're streaked with …oh never mind. I can't understand how an ex-soldier would end up like this."

He turned and glanced at Mohammed, and at the same time reached up and slowly brought down the weapon he was holding.

"And this is the MI5 Agent they've sent to infiltrate us? Get real…. I'll tell you what this is…it's a real life lesson in why we're going to bring this brutal unfeeling country to its knees, and you must now realize that we're no longer alone. There must be a multitude of pissed off people in this country, like our new friend here, who would love to get back at the corrupt politicians in the U.K., who've been living off the fat of the land, and now it's payback time, and we'll show this unfortunate bastard just how to go about it."

He turned to Danny. "Sorry for the misunderstanding my friend. You do have a bed for the night, but first you have to shower and we'll get you some fresh clothes. What's your name anyway?"

"John Fisher, I'm known as Jack. Jesus am I glad to see that pistol's no longer sticking in my face."

CHAPTER 22

In the van the two occupants looked at each other. "Looks like he pulled it off" Peter said, breathing a sigh of relief, "but what do we do now?"

Alina still looked concerned. "I'm just worried that when he takes them up on that shower and change of clothes, he won't look much like a street person anymore. How did Danielle describe him I wonder, if indeed she did? That Mohammed chap could get nasty all over again if he senses something isn't quite kosher with Danny."

Peter was thinking hard. "You know it could unravel if they start to check up on something Danny said, that he'd been charged a couple of weeks ago with decking some tourist. We need to get some of the newspaper websites altered to support his story, not the major ones 'cos it wouldn't rate even a mention, but the smaller street versions that you find lying in the tube and places like MacDonald's."

"Great idea Peter and don't forget, he's now Jack Fisher" she added.

They arranged for one of the other cars to take over the surveillance of the terrorist's building, and headed back to Thames House.

When the door to Rebecca's office swung open at 7am she looked up, expecting to see Danny entering her office. Instead it was Peter Sanderson, with Alina right behind him.

The DG tensed. "Oh God, please tell me nothing's happened to Danny? Your team were out there last night weren't they?"

Peter nodded as they both sat down opposite her.

"Happened to him? Well, yes and no" he answered.

"Just give me the details for crying out loud!" she demanded.

So he took the next ten minutes to fill her in and left her sitting aghast.

"Oh shoot, Danny's in the lion's den! Where does this go from here Peter?"

"It's a major turn-around for sure, and from what we heard over that bug, Danny appears to have pulled it off. Here, let Alina play back the recording for you and see what you think. This is from the bug in the terrorist gym shoe, so at times it's a bit weak, but it paints a pretty clear picture."

They spent the next half hour listening to the recording that started with Waheed being assaulted, and Danny's intervention. When she heard the brief sound of blows and screaming the DG shook her head. "Quigley's something else when he goes into combat...Jesus!"

When the tape finished, they all sat back in silence.

Finally she stirred. "I don't know whether to be excited at this development or in fear and trepidation for Danny if they cop onto to him. That chap Mohammed's probably still a danger, and they may follow Danny when they let him leave, if they even do. I'd suggest you have a team doing counter surveillance when he does leave. Danny could easily give them the slip, but that would be a dead giveaway. What was his contact routine when he was on the street for the past few months and keeping up his cover?"

"He would pop in to the Sally Ann for breakfast and collect his back pack, which they keep in a cabinet there for the street people. We had access to his back pack and used it to collect any information he had, and to leave him messages."

The DG nodded thoughtfully. "Do we still have that contact there, you know the supervisor Kevin something...the chap who knows what Danny was doing and who was co-operating with us and covering for Danny?"

"Yeah, no problem…it's Kevin Whitehouse. He's a retired Copper so he knows the score. What did you have in mind?"

"Here's the thing Peter. Once you've established whether the terrorists are following him or not, get in and see this Kevin with one of your Agents who's known to Danny. Arrange for him to join the line-up of volunteers dishing out the food, and let Danny know the score…whether he's been followed or not. With his street smarts he would pick up on this pretty fast."

Alina interrupted. "Why would he be in the line-up at all this morning, if the terrorists have already given him breakfast? In fact why would he go to the Sally Ann at all now, with his new friends?"

Peter was also struggling with this. "Look Ma'am, it's quite possible that these terrorists might want to hang on to him for a few days and sound him out some more. Feed him information on who they really are—Jihadists, and watch how he takes it."

The DG nodded. "Both your points are quite relevant and it could just spin out that way. I probably know Danny better than either of you, how he thinks and how he might play this one. They'll either let him walk out, or they won't. If they don't, we'll keep a watching brief, a really tight one, and if they move him, be ready to swing a large team into action and follow them. Danny's going to know that we're on tenterhooks about his situation and will want to establish some means of communication with us. He'll finesse something about a regular arrangement that he has to meet up with his old Mates at the Sally Ann, as they might start looking for him if he doesn't turn up, and report him missing. The terrorists wouldn't want any Police getting involved. He could tell them that he'll just have a quick coffee with his Mates and leave. Get someone in there to slip a note into his backpack and confirm a future drop, if and when he has some further information. How does that sound?"

147

They both looked at each other.   It was Peter who answered.

"It's your call Ma'am, and it's probably the best we can do. I need to get someone to seed some of the newspaper websites for two weeks back to cover Danny for that assault he mentioned where the Police were supposed to be involved."

They spent another half hour going through the arrangements that had to be set up to monitor the new development.

A new sense of urgency had entered the room.

CHAPTER 23

The plans of mice and men!

It didn't quite happen as the Thames House team expected.

Despite the tension of the situation, Danny slept well, especially after a brief shower and getting some clean clothes that unfortunately didn't quite fit him.

He got some hostile and guarded looks when he joined the terrorists for breakfast, which was cereal and fruit. Ali stared thoughtfully at him, a puzzled look on his face. They waited until he had finished eating, to quiz him on his daily routines. He could sense their urgency in trying to assess how he could be of use to them, or if he would even be willing to translate his anger with the establishment into some sort of cohesive action.

The American started the ball rolling.

"None of us know much about living on the street as it were Jack. Fill us in on what you would normally be doing today, for example?" he asked.

"Hmm, let's see. Well this morning I would have gone to the Sally Ann for breakfast and to meet up with my Mates. I've had breakfast here now, of course, but I need to collect my small backpack that they allow us to stow there overnight. I should say, we don't always stay at the Sally Ann as they get a full house pretty fast. Churches, for example, might take one night a week each, to provide a bed and a meal for the homeless in their basement, so we move around quite a bit. We have our favorites too, as you can imagine. It may be difficult for you to understand, but most street people have lost their families, and in effect your friends on the street, just a small group of them mind you, essentially become your new extended family.

If I didn't show my face in there this morning they might start to get worried, and could even go as far as to report me missing to the Police. We are after all, unemployed, and have no schedules to keep or meetings to attend, apart from the odd drop-in to a hospital ER if one has a medical problem. Our street family, as it were, would normally consist of four to five people max, but we don't drift around London as a group. The Police don't like that and are continually hassling us. We might agree to meet up for a free lunch meal at some other charity kitchen and carry on from there. I did try for social security at the start, but you need to provide evidence that you're trying to get a job by showing them signed interview forms from a company you applied to. Well, you can imagine…with no fixed abode, address in other words, and dressed like I was last night, I wasn't even allowed into company reception areas." Danny paused, trying to keep his body language looking deflated and his head down.

The American kept the ball rolling.

"You say you have to go down to the Sally Ann this morning. I mean, we offered you some help last night and we're quite prepared to go farther. In effect you wouldn't need those guys or the Sally Ann if you can help us out in a few places. How d'you feel about that?"

Danny lifted his head and spread his hands. "Heck, I'd love to be able to tell the lads that I've been offered some work. I couldn't just not turn up though… that would break the code of the street man. They would start scouring the old haunts around the city, and as mentioned, would probably report me missing. Anyway" he looked across at Skinner "what's this help you might want from me?"

Mohammed leaned forward impatiently. "Look Fisher our friend Waheed here says you're shit hot at unarmed combat.

150

We've all done some of that but we'd like to be much more effective at it. We might have some other friends who would be interested too."

Danny shrugged. "Sure line em up...I'm your man. D'you own a gym or something?" he asked.

It was Ali Hossain who cut to the chase.

"Look Fisher, last night we picked up that you're really pissed off at the Government who used and abused you in the Military, and you ended up on the street. Our question is, if given the chance, are you willing to fight back and start really hurting this fu...ing bunch of corrupt leeches that are running this country?"

Danny sat back, a startled look flashed across his face.

"Christ, how dumb can I get? It must be associating with these street people that's fried my brain! I should know...the papers and the TV are full of it. You people are Jihadists for God's sake!"

Silence fell on the room. Mohammed reached back, extracted his weapon from his belt and placed it on the table.

Danny sat there nodding. A smile crept across his features.

"I like that...using the skills they taught me before they kicked me out, to kick them in the gullies and bring them to their knees. Oh yes, but just one condition."

"What's that?" Skinner asked, almost in a whisper.

"I want to make some money out of this. Oh I'm aware of your motivation, but I'm not a Muslim and have no desire or intention to convert to Islam, so my reasons are strictly mercenary. If that's acceptable to you, then count me in. I really have nothing to lose at this stage."

The American slapped the table. "A man after my own heart. I have to tell you I fully understand your motivation Jack. It's mine too, but these true believers will be disgusted with your reason for joining them."

Danny looked puzzled.

"While you're on the subject, I'd love to know what actually motivates these chaps. I mean, is it all about the Muslim religion?"

Skinner chuckled. "That's the sixty four dollar question my friend. I have to tell right off, that I don't have the complete answer. Yeah sure, some like Zain and Mohammed are radicalized from the Internet or some bloody mosque that they attended. Ali just wants to screw as many women as he can without having to ask them. Others that I met were addicts of game-playing on the internet and got bored with it...now they want to kill real people in real time. In fairness, some, like young men back down through the ages, just want adventure or to test their mettle out there somewhere. Some get sickened very fast when they witness the brutality of ISIS, beheadings and worse."

He fell silent then, thinking he'd said too much.

Then continued:

"Anyway, two things: Mohammed has a few more checks to do on your background before we go any further, and number two, we'll give you a lift down to this Sally Ann and wait for you while you set your friends' minds at rest that you're not lying dead under a bridge somewhere.

OK with that?"

He was.

Back in the surveillance vehicle, Peter and Alina gave each other a High Five.

"He's in, by God! Danny's pulled it off!"

She nodded somberly. "Let's hope their further checks don't turn something up."

CHAPTER 24

After breakfast Zain Waheed and the American Frank Skinner drove him down to the Sally Ann and parked outside.

"I'll go inside with you" Frank announced, "and eyeball this bunch you seem to think so much of. You've got me curious now. I never really thought of street people as anything more than a bunch of lay-abouts who don't want to work, and want us tax payers to sub them."

As he said this, the American handed him a wad of cash.

He was taken aback. "Shit, you don't have to do this Mate. I haven't done anything for you guys yet" he protested.

He took a quick look at the cash and could see that it was over two hundred pounds sterling. He stuck it in his pocket.

Skinner's eyes gleamed. "You said money was your motivation and that's something I understand Buddy."

Danny realized that this visit was part of the 'checks' that the group was still running on him. Essentially, they had no intention of letting him out of their sight until they were 100% sure about his intentions. Fortunately, he had already laid the foundations over the past six months, to back up his identity as a street person...or his 'legend' as it is referred to in undercover roles.

The first person they met inside was Kevin, the retired ex-Co who was part of his cover story.

"Hi Kevin" Danny fired off at him as he stood to one side behind a greeting table. "Hey, this is an American friend,

Frank Skinner who's going to give me some work for a few weeks. Is it OK if he hangs here until I let the lads know what's going on?"

"Absolutely Jack, no sweat. Hey, you're all cleaned up and sweet smelling. Your Mates won't want to sit with you back there" he retorted with a smile.

Danny headed off down the back and grabbed a cup of tea as he passed the big silver urn, then sat down at the end of the table, hearing the clamor of questions and cat calls coming at him.

Some of them pretended to find his new appearance hard to take, skittering their chairs off to one side and holding their noses.

He sat there chatting with them for some time, then went for his backpack.

There was a note stuck on top, filling him in on the information regarding the bug that had reactivated and caused some concern. Obviously the team had decided to use this method of sending him a message rather than planting an Agent in the line-up of volunteers spooning out breakfast.

Also lying on his backpack was a new belt, an exact match for the one he was wearing, with one exception. According to the cryptic note attached to it, the buckle was the latest technology in bugging that could not be detected by any scanning devices and had much more clarity in the sound. He was also told that the system of drops was now reactivated, if he had information and was in a position to plant it.

He couldn't see that happening as long as he and the terrorists were joined at the hip, and monitoring his every move. He quickly searched through the backpack to make sure nothing was in there to trip him up, and slung it on his shoulder.

At the front the American was chatting casually with the Sally Ann volunteer, Kevin. "So, Jack has been coming in here for some time then?" he asked.

"Well, only since his wife kicked him out of the house some months back and he ended up on the street, poor bastard. He got the odd painting job for a few days, but all the bloody

154

foreigners here in London undercut these lads in here. You'd be surprised who ends up in here. Ex bloody CEO's who pissed their life away with drink or gambling. Others found that their wives were playing around and their lives just fell apart. Government cuts made a lot of the mental health clinics and hospitals close down, and the patients were turfed out onto the streets with no support, no families to look after them and no skills to help them get even the most basic of jobs. You wouldn't believe what's happening in this country. I tell you what, I could fu...ing weep many a day when I hear their stories."

Skinner nodded, as if sympathetic to his views. "Jack seemed much attached to his friends here. We wanted him to start work today, but he insisted that he come in and tell them what was going on. He said that his 'family' as he called them, would have started looking for him otherwise...might even report him missing to the Police."

"Naw, Jack wouldn't walk away like that from the lads... very close they are. Hey, look at that back there."

Skinner turned and spotted Danny placing some cash down on the table.

"He's a good lad is Jack...will share whatever he has with them. That'll probably buy them a lunch or supper later on today. No, whatever work you give him, he'll pop in now and then to say hello to us, that's for sure."

"Speaking of Police, Jack said he was in a spot of bother with some bloody tourist some weeks back."

Kevin heard the question in it.

Fortunately he had already been briefed earlier that morning.

"Yeah, one of your lot, an American, made the mistake of pushing Jack. Jesus, that's like picking a fight with Rambo...ex- Para! Sure he's up in court sometime in the future but I'd guess that tourist will drop the charges. I mean, he might have to fly back to the U.K. and give evidence if Jack pleads not guilty, and the courts are soft on veterans here. No, I'd guess it won't amount to a hill of beans in the end."

Just then Danny wandered back to the table.

155

"Hey Kev, not giving away all my secrets are you?" he teased.

"No, I was just telling your friend here about that tourist you thumped recently, and that it'll probably blow away before it gets to court. Shouldn't affect any work your friends have lined up for you."

Danny's heart froze when he heard the remark, then realized that the team had got here already, having heard the tape recording from the terrorist cell.

'A close call' he thought... 'too close, that's all it takes to blow an operation'.

The two men left together with the American talking in a jocular manner as they got into the car.

He looked across at Zain. "We've got a real live one here my man.... he checks out. I have a good feeling about him. He's going to be a real linchpin in my plans to fu...ing blow up this goddamn country. Let's get back to the house and start the ball rolling."

In the surveillance van Peter chortled. "Nice piece of evidence for the courts, and the new recording is crystal clear. You hear that 'blow up this goddamn country'...couldn't be more specific than that now could you?"

CHAPTER 25

Back in the terrorist's house, Mohammed gestured to the American and they went into the next room. In a few minutes they came back in together.

Skinner walked up behind Danny and clapped him on the back.

"It looks like you're OK Buddy. We checked out the websites of some of the newspapers a couple of weeks back and spotted a mention of your run-in with the Police. Not much on it really, and only in two of the small editions - freebies and so on."

Danny shrugged. "Yeah, stories about a street person in a tussle with some tourist are not exactly a major news event, " he pointed out.

"Exactly what I said to Mohammed. Now it looks like you're clean, and not some plant from the Intelligence Services. Notwithstanding that, we operate on a need to know basis, and that means we're not going to involve you in the plans and strategies we intend to put in place here in the U.K. Possibly at a later date Jack, when we see your value to us and you've proved yourself as a new member of this group. Does that make sense Buddy?"

"Sure, sounds OK to me Frank. Remember, I'm ex-Military and we always keep things tight in planning operations. Quite frankly I'd be disappointed if you didn't, as your plans wouldn't even get off the ground for starters, and I wouldn't be making any cash out of it, speaking of which...."

Frank grinned. "OK, OK, I knew this would come up. A couple of hundred Pounds probably just whetted your appetite, I'll bet. Tell you what, Ali has booked an old gym not far from here for the afternoon. Zain saw you in action last night, but we'd like to see if you have the ability and skill to actually teach people as well. The two don't necessarily go together. Then we can talk money my mercenary friend, and you won't be disappointed, I can tell you. Money isn't really a problem with this operation."

Mohamed pursed his lips, obviously still unhappy with his motivation. His eyes swiveled to the American.

"Ask him that other question Frank," he prompted.

"Ah yes, of course. If you can't help us with this, it doesn't affect our agreement to do some work with you. The question is, being ex-Military and all that, do you have any contacts with people who could supply arms and explosives... the whole ball of wax...weapons, ammo, RPG's, C4, possibly IED's?"

Danny looked shocked. "Man, this is moving far too fast for me! Teaching unarmed combat's one thing, but weapons and explosives? I mean it's not unusual for the troops coming back into the U.K. on Military transports to be able to slip a rifle or a pistol through as a keepsake, but a cache of weapons? Not on your nelly! On the other hand, your question as to whether I have any contacts..."

A silence fell on the room. Danny stood up and started pacing up and down, rubbing his face thoughtfully.

"Do I have any contacts?" he murmured, almost to himself.

He stopped and clicked his fingers. "Wait a minute...wait just one fu...ing minute...!"

"What is it Jack? What's just hit you Buddy?" Frank asked.

"The Para's that I was attached to did four tours in Northern Ireland. We worked with an informer in the IRA, a chap who was into everything as well as working with us for money. You name it, crime, stolen cars, and protection

158

rackets…. which we turned a blind eye to. Rumor has it that he acquired a whole bunch of small IRA weapon caches when the peace process came in. I wouldn't be surprised if he hasn't still got most of them hidden away somewhere."

Frank looked skeptical. "Wait a minute Jack. As I understand it all those weapons were scooped up under that American deal. It was part of the signed and carefully monitored agreement on both sides."

Danny chuckled. "Hiding weapons is an art the Irish have invented, going back over six hundred years. I've heard rumors now and then that there's still a sizable chunk of weapons around. Mind you one would have to be careful with stuff like C4 explosive that's been around for some time, but weapons and ammo would still be quite serviceable, assuming they were properly stored and maintained."

Frank still looked puzzled. "Why would this guy deal with you anyway, assuming he's still in business over there?"

"For starters, I was his main contact when he was acting as an informer, and I built up a pretty good relationship with him. It helped that I was born in Ireland, though I went across to Wales when I was eight years of age, but yeah, if he's still alive, shady deals are part of his DNA.   Just a possibility. Obviously I don't know for certain, things change, but could be worth checking out. I haven't a clue at this stage Mate. The chap could be dead and buried by now, and buried in a bog somewhere, knowing Northern Ireland." The group looked around at each other.

It was the American who summed up their thoughts.

"Jack, you've just made our day, and you're suddenly looking a lot more valuable to us and that means a lot more money for you my friend. Let's take another look at this when we get back from the gym."

Ali still wore a quizzical and somewhat puzzled look on his face.

CHAPTER 26

As Danny changed into a sweat-suit they had loaned him, he realized that he was in somewhat of a quandary.

Instructing terrorists to be more deadly at unarmed combat could have serious consequences for him or members of the Security Forces down the line. He wasn't certain if he would fall under the provisions of the law regarding aiding and abetting terrorists, yet he had to offer them skills, which they at present didn't have, or needed a deeper knowledge of.

With the terrorists, first of all he had to establish where they were in their knowledge, skills and competency, and what they realistically wanted to achieve.

Like many TV viewers, he had seen Jihadists running around, high-kicking targets and disarming each other. He hadn't been very impressed, so once at the gym, he led them through some of their previous training drills, which involved punching, kicking and restraining prisoners.

It was a bit ragged, but he could see that it probably suited the type of tasks they would more likely be involved in - hauling people out of vehicles, striking an opponent with hands and/or feet, disarming an enemy and so on.

There was no doubt that Mohammed was quite competent and superior in skills compared to the others. He had probably trained Jihadists in Iraq or Syria previously. Still, Danny felt it wouldn't be wise to show him up in any way on the mat, considering his latent suspicion and hostility towards him, so

160

he initially led them through some movements to enhance some of the strikes and punches they were already trained in.

They liked the routine, and as they warmed up, started getting more committed and involved. Even Mohammed relaxed and appeared to be enjoying the exercise.

Then he led them through some really effective arm, wristlocks, and take-downs, which he emphasized would be much more effective in restraining a prisoner rather than a straight arm lock or full nelson. It gave them more control, and left them still free to use their feet if attacked from another direction.

They had a brief break, then he asked Zain the tall slim terrorist who had the look of a teacher, to try the much-vaunted high kick that the Jihadists appeared to spend a lot of time practicing on the numerous videos released to the Internet. He deliberately avoided asking Mohammed.

They faced each other on the mat.

Zain looked aggressive. "I warn you, I'm going for you man…I could really hurt you!"

Danny wanted him to go for him. "In your dreams Mate" he taunted.

He launched himself at Danny with a ferocious high kick which Danny avoided by moving his head slightly, blocking the kick easily with his right hand and rolling that same arm around the leg where he held it up there for a second, for all to see. Then he snapped an incredibly fast kick at the man's crotch, stopping just an inch from his target, before putting the man's foot down.

There was a collective gasp from the group.

Zain wasn't happy. "Hey, I wasn't ready, and you already knew what I was going to do. Let me try that again."

Danny smiled, holding his hands wide. "Fine with me. Why don't you take a number of kicks at me from different angles?"

Danny was even faster this time, and Zain was firing kicks with increasing frustration as his every effort failed to penetrate Danny's defense who added a further dimension by finally doing a leg sweep on the man's remaining leg, sending him crashing to the ground.

On the last fall, Zain got up off the mat in a fit of temper and attacked Danny with a series of punches and body kicks, which he blocked easily. Moving backward under the man's attack, he stopped his momentum by slipping him into one of the arm locks he had previously demonstrated to them, and brought him down to his knees grunting in pain. The American moved over and tapped Zain on the shoulder.

"Hey man, it's only practice here. Cool down, for Christ's sake!" he shouted at him.

Zain relaxed and looked up at Danny.

"Sorry Man. I got carried away there. I should have known from seeing you in action the other night, not to mess with you. Shit, that arm lock really hurt my shoulder."

He had them.

The remainder of the afternoon was spent unlearning the vulnerable high kick, and re-learning the new approach, which they took to with a vengeance. When they incorporated the leg sweep with gusto, there were a number of bruised legs and hips suffered from the session, but they were a happy lot.

They had a brief shower in the gym and Skinner took him to a nearby pub for a drink.

The Muslims frowned on this and headed home for prayer.

The American lifted his bottle of beer.

That was fu...ing fantastic Buddy! Its exactly what we needed back in our training camps in Iraq and Syria, not that useless shit they were teaching!"

He gave Danny a measured look. "I wonder. I just wonder if in any way shape of form, that might be possible."

"I haven't a clue what you're talking about Mate. Let me get you another beer. That mat work always gives me a huge thirst."

Fifty yards down the block, Peter was shaking his head.

"Well Alina, you're not going to be seeing lover boy any time soon. From the sounds of it, he may sooner or later be on his way to Iraq. We'd better fill the D.G. in on this new tilt to

162

things, apart from the fact that the terrorists seem to be taking the bait hook line and sinker."

She nodded. "How the hell is he going to get any sort of normal life back now that he's practically a prisoner with this group? What do we tell his ex-wife, who's still sitting in a safe house and expecting him to call? Danny has to hang in there until he finds out what the Jihadist's plans are, and other contacts that will be involved here in the U.K."

Peter snorted. "Don't knock it girl. Think where we were just a few days ago. This is progress, Baby!"

CHAPTER 27

Fiona, Danny's ex-wife was not a happy bunny.

Living in a so-called 'safe house' was not her idea of living at all. Allison was not allowed to go to school as the Afghan man who had seen her at the door of her house, might kidnap her there. Fiona was advised not to go to work for the same reason, and was delighted to hear from Rebecca, who updated her on the state of play where Jamilla was concerned.

"So, Rebecca, you're telling me that because of this potential agreement with the kidnappers for the moment, I'm probably not under any threat now and can go back home. Is that right?"

"Yes, in so far as the kidnappers think Danny's going to make the swap happen. He, however, believes that Jamilla died receiving a beating that actually took place as he was trying to talk to her, so there's no way he's going to part with any funds. He's playing them along for the moment, but he intends to find this Afghan torturer and take him out."

"God! I can't get my head around this Rebecca! Danny somehow believes that she died right then?"

"Sounds weird, I know Fiona. You know something? I believed, watching him then that he did go through some sort of psychic experience. It was strange. Phil Dawson thought the same."

"OK, OK, I don't quite get it, but essentially you're telling me that I have a window of time when I or Allison, shouldn't be in danger. Am I reading this right?"

"Look Fiona, I can't give you a one hundred percent guarantee because some of these people are head cases to begin with, but logic suggests they wouldn't upset the apple cart if the kidnappers believe the exchange is still on. That's all I can say. If anything changes, I'll let you know. While I'm on, I have to say that Danny is at a very dicey stage of a covert operation, where he probably won't be able to visit you for some time. I can't tell you any more, for obvious reasons Fiona. I'm sorry."

"Well, can you tell me if he's in any danger? Should I be saying something to his daughter Allison?" she asked.

"I can't add anything to what I just said, but I'll keep you posted."

"So he bloody well is in some danger...shit... the Special Forces Regiment, and now fucking MI5! Right, I get it and I'm getting out of here right now as well!"

Rebecca heard the phone slammed down.

Fiona didn't waste any time grabbing her and Allison's things.

She had no problems getting the Intelligence Agents who had been guarding them, to drop her daughter at school where she raced in, eager to catch up on the gossip.

At her home she wearily collected the mail scattered on the floor and threw it on the kitchen table. She ignored the flashing red light on the telephone, but made a quick call to her office telling them she would be in shortly.

Because she was late, her usual parking space was taken, and she went round the block twice before practically abandoning her recently purchased mid-range Subaru behind a construction site that had not been completed for some reason. Rumor had it that the builders had gone bust.

It was a relief to get back in to the normal but demanding routines of being an interior decorator in a highly successful business.

The day passed quickly.

Joey Charnock's teachers, and especially the school counselor, heaved a great sigh of relief when the teenager finally dropped out of school. Not surprising when he had missed most of the school year curriculum for a variety of reasons, one being his regular appearances in juvenile court for breaking into houses and nicking things that he tried to sell in pawn shops. Not a smart thief, he more than often got caught and ended up back in court again. The school tried to suspend him indefinitely but the boy's parents sued them, and a liberal court agreed with them. The parents believed that the school was responsible for the boy's wayward ways, even though the father was in jail himself at the time.

Joey did have one gift however, at which he excelled.... stealing cars. He could break into all but the most advanced of vehicles in moments, and speed off.

An enterprising car-jacking firm who regularly shipped hundreds of stolen cars off to the Continent and the Far East, became aware of Joey's talents, and brought him on board.

Joey had finally found his niche.

In the first three months after he dropped out of school he made more money than he had ever made in his years of pilfering. He had a future now, and to hell with all those people who had put him down, both in school and his home neighborhood.

Today he was nosing around an area where he had high hopes of finding an upmarket vehicle that he could nick and flog on. It wasn't working out too well until he came across a Subaru sedan parked, as he liked it, out of sight of office windows and residential apartment blocks. He took a quick look round and started manipulating with a wire coat hanger to get inside. Faster than any AA call-out, he was sitting inside in a half a minute. He pulled down the ignition wiring and spotted the two wires he had to join together.

Back in her office Fiona jumped at the sound of an explosion, and a number of the windows rattled loudly. Her partner Julie came hurrying across and looked out the window.

"God, look at that! The flames are shooting up from behind that old abandoned construction site. The place will be full of fire engines, police and ambulances in a few moments. I'd suggest we close up and try to slip out of this area immediately or we'll be stuck here for hours. "

Fiona stood up, shot across to stand beside her, and looked out.

She put her hand up to her mouth. "Oh no! I parked my car behind that building. You don't think...?" she blurted.

Julie stared at her. "Surely not. Hell, it could be anything, a gas stove or a propane tank. Let's dash over and see for ourselves. If you're actually blocked in I can run you home."

When they turned the corner, the first sirens could be heard in the distance. Fiona felt her knees weaken and she sagged to the ground, Julie catching her at the last moment.

"What is it Fee?" she asked.

There was no answer, just the sound of Fiona's gasping breath.

"Fee, was that your car?" Julie asked her anxiously.

She saw Fiona's head nod up and down, then she burst into tears.

CHAPTER 28

Some time later Fiona was back again at the safe house with Allison. Rebecca raced up the steps and stopped to have a few words with Alina at the front door.

"What a debacle! Can you believe it? I told her it was all right to go home this morning. How's she taking it anyway?"

Alina made a face. "How d'you think? She's pissed off big time. Giving out stink one moment, and the next sobbing her heart out. Who can blame her? She can't go to work, her daughter can't attend school, her ex has virtually disappeared, and now someone's trying to blow her up, and she doesn't have her car anymore either, but she hasn't mentioned that yet. Oh, it's been confirmed from the scene that there was a bomb in the car, and there's an unidentified person dead in the vehicle Ma'am" she finished.

"Any further information from the bomb squad?"

"I talked to one of the investigators, and when they established that Fiona was the legal owner of the car and hadn't loaned it to anyone, like a mechanic for example, they speculated that someone might have been attempting to steal it."

"Unlucky beggar whoever it turns out to be...lucky for Fiona though. How did we get this wrong Alina?"

"Who's that out there? Is it Rebecca?"

It was Fiona's voice from inside.

She hurried into the lounge where, on seeing her, Fiona got up and threw herself into her arms, sobbing."

She held her for a long time and managed to gesture to Alina who had followed her in, to bring a drink of some kind. Fiona sank back into the seat with Rebecca alongside her, still holding onto her hands as her sobs subsided. Alina came back in with a glass of water and two white tablets, which she handed to Rebecca.

"Here Fiona, take these...they'll calm you down a bit" she urged.

Fiona nodded, swallowing them without further comment.

She took some deep breaths and finally turned to Rebecca.

"Can you please tell me what's going on? What exactly is happening to me? I seem to have lost complete control of my life, and this afternoon I was nearly killed in a bomb attack. Presumably I was the target this time, not Danny. Is that how you see it?"

Rebecca shook her head. "I won't lie to you Fiona. We're as shocked as you are. We thought we had a handle on the situation with the kidnapper as we discussed this morning. Why would he risk the exchange at this critical moment? It doesn't make sense. In trying to re-evaluate it, driving over here, I recalled Danny telling me when we were discussing this, how he'd called in an airstrike that killed over a hundred Al Qaeda and Taliban, when he was left behind on a joint SAS/Delta operation. One of the people killed was a man called Mohammed Qureshi, a Pashtun and one of their top leaders. He got a decoration from President Karzai for that as you recall, and the incident would have been filed away in a highly confidential file somewhere. Now with Karzai gone and a new bunch in power in Kabul, including former Taliban enemies, I wouldn't be surprised at what information is being unearthed and passed out, probably for a price, to interested parties."

"Like the family of this chap Danny had killed," Fiona said tiredly.

"Exactly, and I have it from a good source that the Pashtuns have a code that demands revenge for family members being killed, no matter how long it takes."

"So, you're saying there might be a second group involved who couldn't care less about any exchange for this Jamilla?" Fiona concluded.

"It could be. Its just speculation at this stage. I mean why did they wait so long to start what we saw happen today? I've no idea, unless there was some contact between them. Perhaps they didn't have anyone on the ground here in the U.K. with the expertise needed, until now" she finished.

Fiona sank back into her seat, despair contorting her features.

"So killing Danny's family members is part of this revenge game? Doesn't matter that I've been divorced from him for years now... great, just great! So where the hell does this leave me?"

"At this stage, I've no idea. I'm so sorry Fiona."

She reflected on this, her face stony. "Danny Quigley, you have a lot to answer for. When I see you again I'm going to fucking kill you!"

Both the DG and Alina glanced at each other. Right now, Danny didn't need any more people in the equation who wanted to terminate him. Fiona was standing in a long queue.

CHAPTER 29

Danny was now part of the team, but it appeared they still had some reservations about him. The American was going out with Mohammed and Zain, leaving Ali behind, presumably to keep an eye on him.

Danny was becoming increasingly aware of Ali's close scrutiny and wondered about it. The other three Jihadists, as was their custom, went directly from the kitchen to their vehicle in the garage. This avoided any curious neighbor becoming suspicious of Asian-looking people coming and going, with the heightened reports in the media of potential terrorists.

That left both of them watching the latest version of the BBC news, which they had already seen a number of times.

Ali switched it off and sat across the table, watching Danny with a curious look on his face.

Danny decided to sound him out.

"So tell me Ali, this Jihadist thing you're involved in, - what's the big turn-on for you that you get out of it? I mean, I'm going to get me some money for sure, but here you are, a young man stuck in a house with your three Mates and myself, who I suspect you don't particularly like anyway, with no chance to go out and have some fun for yourself. I don't get it!"

"By fun you mean women, I take it?"

"Well, that's one part of it of course."

Ali sniggered with that chilling sound that made Danny's hair stand on end. It reminded him of the first time he'd heard it in the plane coming from Heathrow. The same sound that the witness heard when Danielle was pulled into the car and abducted.

"What do I get out of it? I'll tell you. When we were over in Iraq with ISIS, we had our pick of the young women and girls in the villages that we captured. Killed their men and screaming mothers, and just took them, where and when and how we wanted them."

He sniggered again.

Danny felt himself tense, his anger rising.

Ali carried on. "When we create total chaos here in the U.K. and tear every structure down, we'll take our revenge on all those stuck up English bitches in exactly the same way. They'll never say no to Ali again, I can tell you."

He glanced speculatively across at Danny.

"I've already had one of them, Jack, since we got back - very tasty bit too. We all had a go... she loved it... kept begging for more."

Danny lost it right then.

The thought of this excuse for a human being, boasting about ravaging the attractive young woman Danielle who accompanied him to Amsterdam, a wife and a mother, with her whole life ahead of her, made him forget everything but smashing this smirking animal in front of him into the ground.

He kicked his chair back and stood up, leaning across the table.

"You slimy, useless son of a bitch. You sit there boasting about yourself and your pals kidnapping, raping an innocent young woman, and then killing her. I'm going to kill you right now..."

Ali never moved.

He just smiled, reached behind him, opened a drawer and pulled a pistol from it, which he pointed across at Danny.

He laughed again...that sniggering laugh.

"I thought that might get to you Jack, or whatever your real name is. Ever since you came in the door the other night, there was something about you that made me think I'd seen you before. I couldn't say anything to the others. You were a gift to them… teaching us unarmed combat… finding us weapons. I would have sounded paranoid, but this morning when I was waking up, it came to me. I'd seen your walk on that flight from Amsterdam, going up the isle to the washroom and coming back. I notice things…sometimes the weirdest things. Now pick up your chair and sit down, and we'll wait right here for my Mates to come back. They'll be here in thirty to forty minutes, and will I have something to tell them…Mate."

Danny knew he was in dead trouble.

"Hey, look Ali, you don't need to point that gun at me! You're mistaken by a long shot. Me on a plane? Hell I was living under a bridge up to…."

He picked up the table and fired it across on top of Ali, sending him and his chair crashing back into the wall. Danny followed, jumping round the edge of the table and reached for Ali who struggled to sit up, his hand emerging with the pistol swinging towards him.

Danny blocked it, and at the same time leaned forward, sending his ridged knuckles directly into Ali's throat, crushing his larynx. Then he grabbed his head in both hands and twisted it violently to one side. He heard a crack.

Ali was dead.

Danny didn't have a minute to spare.

Knowing that the surveillance vehicle would be parked nearby and picking up full details of what had happened, he shouted urgently.

"Get the car up here right away. One dead terrorist to get rid of. Go directly into the garage. I'll have the door open for you."

He picked up the gun and opened the drawer with the idea of putting it back in there, but saw there was a second weapon lying there…an automatic. An idea jumped into his mind and he stuck Ali's pistol into his belt instead, then he rushed through into the garage and raised the door, using the monitor.

Within minutes, the surveillance car was driving slowly up the driveway and into the garage. He immediately closed the door.

It was Alina, white faced, who jumped out first, followed by Peter.

"Jesus, what went wrong Danny? The whole thing's blown apart" she exclaimed.

Peter was at his side. He didn't waste any time talking.

"Tell us what you want Danny?"

"Ali's dead. Take him out of here and do what you want with him. As you heard, we only have about thirty minutes before the others come back, so let's grab him and put him in the trunk."

Danny and Peter carried Ali outside without a word and dropped him in the trunk, which Alina held open, then slammed shut.

"What about you Danny? You're blown here. You'd better come with us" she shouted.

"I may not be blown. I think I can talk my way out of any responsibility for him being missing. I'm going to wait for them to come back."

Peter was shaking his head. "It's a total long shot Danny. They leave him here as your guard dog, and he's missing when they get back! Come on, there's no way they'll buy that. Get in the car right now and let's go. This situation's hopeless."

"Maybe not. Now here's something I want you to get Rebecca to put in motion. Have her get a story in the evening papers, today especially. The rest of the media as they bite…that Police arrested Ali Hossain at the Euro train trying to buy a ticket to go back to Iraq or Syria to fight with Isis… after having come to the attention of the Police earlier by robbing two betting shops using a pistol…this one. He handed it to him. She can distribute the picture of Ali that we have on file. Then have him off out of sight somewhere as far as the media and public are concerned…new legislation allowing much longer detention or whatever."

Peter's eyes widened. "That's a super idea Danny, and might just buy you some time."

He didn't answer, but ran to get the monitor to lift the garage door.

"You'd better get moving. We haven't time to debate this. I'm hanging in here for the moment."

"OK Danny, if that's what you want. One thing I have to tell you. Fiona's car was blown up yesterday when parked outside her office. She was inside the office at the time and is OK. We suspect that another group besides Jamilla's kidnapper is here in London, so we have her and your daughter back in the safe house."

Danny looked shocked. "Oh my God, and I'm stuck here in the middle of this and can't even get to see her. Look, can you lay on a direct line in the back of the Sally Ann and I'll try to manage another drop in there. I have more to tell Rebecca and yourselves."

Alina looked at him worriedly, and gave him a quick hug.

They leapt into the car, which then eased slowly out of the garage, and disappeared up the street.

Danny quickly closed the garage door and went inside. He proceeded to tidy up the scene so that everything appeared to be exactly as the terrorists had left it…except that Ali was no longer there.

He ran various scenarios through his mind, then sat back and waited.

CHAPTER 30

They came back early and barged into the kitchen, seemingly in a hurry, then they stopped and looked around.

"Where's Ali?" the American demanded.

Danny shook his head. "I've no idea. He just got up and left about twenty minutes ago. I'm surprised you didn't spot him along the road somewhere."

Mohammed frowned. "He left, just like that? He was supposed to stay and keep an eye on you."

Danny looked puzzled. "Keep an eye on me...why would he have to do that? I thought I was on the team, for God's sake! You bloody people! What the hell do I have to do? I couldn't care less what you chaps are up to. I just want to get my hands on some cash, and you know what? I haven't seen very much of it as yet."

Zain pulled a chair out from under the table and slammed it down, sitting directly in front of Danny.

"Stop trying to change the subject. Let's get back to Frank's question. Just where the fuck is Ali? Where did he go in such a hurry? He knew we were coming back in a few moments, and now we find he's missing." He leaned forward till his face was inches from Danny.

"Something smells here, and we're going to find out exactly why Ali is suddenly missing, so start talking" he demanded.

The American intervened.

"Hang on a minute. I want to know what led up to this. Something must have happened. Ali wasn't the greatest brain on the planet after all. If something was on his mind, you'd think he would have brought it up before now. Danny, talk me through exactly what went on here before Ali, as you say, just walked out."

Danny looked thoughtful. "Hmm...let me see...yeah, he started on about all the women and girls he'd screwed over in Iraq after they took over villages, particularly young girls, and how he missed it. He said he enjoyed killing the fathers and mothers who tried to stop it, and that it would be a long time before he'd be able to get away with it here in the U.K." He paused.

"Go on" Mohammed insisted.

"Right. He said you guys had grabbed some woman off the street and had a good time with her. He didn't say it in so many words, but I gathered she was probably killed. Then he started going on about his DNA being on the woman and how smart the Police were here in London, and that they would be coming for him any time soon. He got very agitated... muttered something about getting back to Iraq and having some more fun before it was too late. Next thing I know he grabs some weapon out of that drawer over there, the front door bangs shut and he's gone. When I heard you people I thought at first that it was him coming back."

"Jesus, he told you about the woman! What was he thinking?" Zain said wide-eyed.

Danny shrugged, saying nothing.

Down the street and having already disposed of their load in the trunk, the two MI5 Agents looked at each other.

"Has he pulled it off d'you think?" Peter asked.

He got his answer.

It was Zain who exploded onto his feet. He opened the drawer, took the automatic out, strode across to Danny, grabbed him by his hair, and shoved the weapon against his forehead.

"It was me who brought you into our group the other night. Well I'm going to sort this out once and for all." He jacked a round into the weapon and released the safety catch.

"Now start talking Jack you bastard, if that's your name, or in ten seconds I'm going to splatter your brains all across this kitchen."

Danny had no options left, so he took a gamble.

A lot has been written about the action/re-action scenario when one fires off a weapon. If one is close enough to an enemy holding a weapon on you, they can rarely re-act fast enough when you take some sort of offensive action.

Back in his Regiment days, the troopers went through endless rehearsals of disarming an opponent in various situations and with numerous weapons. There was nothing dramatic about the move he now made: a left hand chopping sideways against Zain's wrist holding the weapon, and a right hand scissor chop against the weapon.

This resulted in it dropping to the floor, which Danny picked up and leapt back against the wall… covering them.

There was silence in the room.

Danny shook his head from side to side.

"Jesus, you guys! What the hell do I have to do to convince you that I don't really give a shit what you're up to as long as I make a few quid and this goddam Government gets kicked in the crotch? You hear me?"

He turned on the safety, and tossed the weapon across the table to the American, who picked it up.

Danny carried on. "Now, I have some phone calls to make to chase down my contact in Northern Ireland to see if he still has access to the weapons you're looking for."

He turned for the door.

Frank held the gun up.

"Sorry, I can't let you go Jack," he said quietly.

Danny laughed. "Pick me up tomorrow morning at around ten, outside the Sally Ann. I may have some news for you, but let's have some quid pro quo. How about some specifics as to when I get my hands on some real money, for starters."

He turned and walked out.

Nobody moved, except the American. He put the gun back on the table…very slowly.

Out in the street Danny started walking. As he turned the first corner he glanced back momentarily, but didn't see anyone following him. He speeded up and spotted the MI5 car as it scooted out of a side street and pulled up beside him.

Peter stuck his head out. "Jump in Danny…the other team confirmed that no one has left the house after you, so you're clear. Let's go."

As he got in, Alina reached back and caught his hand.

"Danny, you sure know how to make people live on the edge. That was hair trigger stuff back there. I assumed you put the weapon down on the table. We heard a thump. That was pretty ballsy stuff my friend. We couldn't have rescued you in time. As you know we have no powers of arrest."

Peter nodded. "For a while back there we thought for sure that you'd be the second body to come out of that house this morning. I've no idea how you figured you could pull it off. We'd better get you in to see Rebecca first, and then your ex-wife. From what I hear from the safe house about Fiona, the house you just left might be a whole lot safer for you right now."

CHAPTER 31

When he arrived in the office with Alina and Peter, Rebecca enfolded Danny in a long hug. Jerry Sackville, the counter terrorist specialist and Phil Dawson the bugging and burglar agent, were already there.

She stepped back. "Jesus Danny, you had us really out of our minds for a while! How did you know they'd let you walk out of there? You sure cut it down to the wire!"

"I didn't really, but I had a weapon stuck up against my forehead and it would only have gotten worse from then on in. My positioning in the room was paramount in that I could move and have them all under my control. Then there was the shock factor, where their minds were trying to get a grip on the sudden reverse of events, and of course an automatic makes a pretty loud noise when fired, so it could have aroused some nosy neighbor to come and check it out."

Jerry was nodding. "Also the fact that you dangled the possibility that you still wanted to stay in for the money, and that you were planning to make some calls regarding weapons for them."

Alina looked exhausted. "I tell you, Peter and I were sweating bricks sitting in the car, especially when Zain Waheed made his move and threatened to blow your head off!"

Rebecca caught Danny's arm as he sat down.

"We were the same here. Phil had a direct link from the recording vehicle, so we were able to listen in as well, and we hadn't even got a SWAT team standing by! We were also busy getting rid of a body and getting your instructions set in motion regarding Ali being picked up. Nice one there, by the way."

"That's set up then?" Danny enquired.

"Yep, as we sit here. We'll have to make Ali really disappear in case some family members want access to him, though in this case, who would want to claim him? They know that if they did, they would immediately become suspects, being connected to a Jihadist."

"So, if the group reads or sees the news then, I should expect further contact with them at the Sally Ann in the morning? What d'you think?"

Danny looked around the group as they sounded this out.

"You dangled nice bait there. OK, they might just turn up, having decided to eliminate you as a threat, so you'll need to be on your guard Danny," Dawson pointed out.

Rebecca slapped the desk. "OK, that's settled then. Just an added dimension from your conversation with Ali, when he owned up to basically killing Danielle. That implicates the rest of the group in it as well, and would give the Police grounds for laying charges against them. We have a recording of his statement of course. What does the group think?"

Jerry shook his head. "Essentially we're like the proverbial tethered goat at the moment. Sure we could have the Police pull them in and hope to get them off the street, but with the justice system the way it is, some lawyer would have them back out again shortly, and they'd be up to their terrorist activities once more. I'd say let them run and see where it leads us. The American interests me. What's he doing here, unless he's involved in some larger scheme for the U.K.?"

Rebecca looked across.

"What d'you think Danny? Peter said you had more stuff you wanted to run by me as well."

"I agree with Jerry. The group is the only game in town right now. Assuming you agree with that, I was going to propose two moves that would facilitate me getting really deep inside.

One is to try to second an old Regiment colleague called Jimmy Patton, originally from Belfast, to play the part of a greedy professional criminal with possible knowledge of an arms cache. We could place him back in Belfast and initially have him play a rather skeptical role, as if suspicious of a sting operation. Then perhaps he thinks about it and starts sounding out some old IRA members regarding possible weapon caches, still buried in an old barn or a bog somewhere. The fact that this Jihadist group was actively seeking weapons and explosives would look good for any future prosecution."

Peter looked doubtful. "How long could you string them along Danny? Surely they'd want to see the goods sooner or later?"

"No, I agree with the idea," Jerry cut in. "If we get them running along a track that'll keep them busy, surely it'll keep them from other more devious plans here in London."

"The problem is that when they eventually find out," Peter added, "as they will, Danny's head's on the block again, and he might not be so lucky next time."

He shrugged. "Let me worry about that for now. My other request is for a secondment from the Regiment. That's for another colleague, Sergeant Scotty McGregor, to come up to London and provide me with some back up. I'm naked out there right now, and this situation could suddenly go tits up in a moment, as seen earlier tonight. I know, as MI5 personnel, we're not allowed to be armed out on the street, but I suspect in the new circumstances, with Jihadists coming out of the woodwork as it were, that a permit for Scotty to carry could be arranged."

"Wait a moment Danny," the DG objected. "I have a whole Saber team from the SAS standing by at my beck and call right now. What's wrong with activating some of them?"

"Look, I want people I've worked with in the past and who know how I think in any tricky combat situations. Despite their real time training and readiness, the Saber team could take too long to get operational in working with me. Bear in mind that I worked with both these men recently over in Nigeria. Their performance was seamless."

There was silence in the room.

Finally she started making some notes on the pad in front of her.

"OK Danny, I'll give you that one. When you made calls like this in the past you were usually right. I'll get on to the Regiment right away."

She made some more notes, and finally looked up at him.

"We need to discuss your wife's car being blown up. What's your reading on this, and what are your thoughts regarding the ransom for Jamilla, who you believe is dead anyway?"

He suddenly looked weary. "You know something Rebecca, I haven't a clue right now. I had an automatic stuck in my face an hour ago, and I only learned about Fiona a short time before that."

She took a closer look at him.

"I'm terribly sorry Danny. We never gave it a thought. We were so caught up in this. Okay, the ransom, you can park that for the moment until you decide to place your ad in The Times. They would assume that getting the money together would take time. I've put out an assignment to a jeweler, known to us, to organize a consignment of authentic-looking fake diamonds, if you ever plan to go face to face with this kidnapper in Afghanistan. That will be your call when the time comes, and bear in mind, an MI5 brief doesn't work outside the U.K., so we won't be able to help you if you decide to take that route. Now, the bomb in your car. There's obviously, or probably, a second group here in London who are quite prepared to take violent action against you and your family. You know quite well that it's impossible to provide 24/7 protection to anyone, and I have to say that your ex-wife Fiona has reached the end of her tether on this one. She's fed up with being in the sights of numerous people who appear determined to terminate you and her, and your daughter as well. You'd better get round to the safe house and have a long chat with her, and I don't envy your task."

Jerry raised his hand. "Danny, the DG and I, with Peter's help, have decided to put a tail on that Intelligence Officer from the Afghan Embassy, who originally called on Fiona regarding the ransom. Remember the package he gave her?"

He nodded. "With what in mind?" he asked.

"Basically, to see who he contacts, get some pictures of any meetings, check out the people he's seeing, for starters. It could be a dead end, but you never know. It's better than nothing. Oh, and we have the Police and the Bomb Squad trying to find out where the explosive used in blowing up Fiona's car came from. Unlikely that it came through by the diplomatic pouch."

The meeting came to an end shortly after with the DG instructing Peter to take Danny round to the safe house.

CHAPTER 32

Alina went off duty after the meeting and headed for the nearest subway. She threw him a look of sympathy before she left, probably thinking of his forthcoming meeting with Fiona. He followed Peter down into the Thames House garage and, in a few moments they were outside and heading off for the safe house forty minutes away.

When they turned the first corner Peter glanced back in the rear view mirror.

He didn't even notice the black cab that had pulled away from the curb when they passed... there were dozens of them coming and going on the busy streets of London.

Ten days previously, Al Sinclair got a surprise when he went to answer the doorbell in his council house in the town of Luton, an hour's drive north of London. His surprise turned to shock when he saw who was standing there. It was Omar Bashir, who he'd had previous contact with in Afghanistan prior to his discharge from the Military in his last two tours in that country.

Sinclair had been part of a Military Police team that had been put together to guard the massive pool of U.K. and U.S. Military equipment being sold off by the joint Quartermaster's section: anything and everything, new or used, that was not being repatriated was being sold off to enterprising Afghans - Omar Bashir being one of them.

Sinclair, like a lot of the NATO troops, didn't particularly like Afghans and was surprised when Omar, a regular visitor to auctions at the compound, stopped to chat with him a number of times. The man finally dropped a hint that there were opportunities to make some easy cash in the planned withdrawal of the troops from the country. Sinclair and his Mates had speculated numerous times, about the well-known reputation of the Afghans for corruption that went on, right to the top of the Government. Most soldiers were pretty cynical about this and shrugged their shoulders. They just wanted to get the hell out of the country.

Equally, they grew bitter at the stories coming back from their previous Mates in the Forces, who had been let go, due to cutbacks, shortly after they got back to the U.K.

At one time ex-Military Police were snapped up by civilian Police Forces. With the shocking disclosures of the Abu Ghraib prison in Afghanistan of Military Police degrading and humiliating prisoners, all that ended, even though the perpetrators who had carried out these atrocities were American and not British, they were all tainted with the same brush.

All these demoralizing details resulted in Sinclair, heavily disguised, slipping out of the Base one evening and visiting Omar's residence, by invitation. He accepted that it could have been a trap, but on weighing the risks, he took the chance and informed one of his colleagues, Tim Bresnin.

He was glad he did.

The meeting resulted in Sinclair being involved in a nice little money-spinner for his last two tours. It meant that he had to first of all pull in four of his MP colleagues who guarded the compound, and turn a blind eye at certain pieces of choice equipment being quietly removed during the night. One lot had been some guided explosive GPS shells that could be fired from 25 miles away and land within 20m of a target. They were 3 feet in length and weighing 106 lbs., and one of the MPs had ended up in the Military Hospital with a hernia as a result of lugging them out. The skim-off over the eighteen months meant a sizable amount of funds, set up in an Isle of

Man bank account, that Sinclair filtered out in equal shares to his Mates.

Everybody was happy. No one was getting hurt, and most of all those that were let go from the Military had a nice cushion to fall back on.

He was unlucky in that he had told his wife about the offshore account. Shortly after he got his discharge, she sued for divorce and took everything from him: his house, savings, and car, even his dog. He was left renting a shabby flat with shiny well-worn lino on the floors.

Now a well-dressed Omar Bashir stood on his doorstep.

Bashir stuck out his hand. "Al, I see you're surprised. You forget old friends?"

Sinclair blinked. "Shit, what the hell are you doing here? The last time I saw you, you were in Stan. I wasn't expecting a social visit ah…Omar," he stammered.

"You nearly couldn't remember my name Al. I'm disappointed, after all the business we did together."

He peered past Sinclair. "You invite your old friend in?"

He moved past him through the doorway, without waiting for an answer and looked around, raising his eyebrows.

"Where's your wife and children Al? You told me you were married - couldn't wait to get back, you said a number of times when we met for some business. I thought you lived in a nice little house with a picket fence and all that."

Sinclair closed the door and turned, looking embarrassed.

"She divorced me when I got out…took the lot" he said miserably.

The Afghan looked at him shrewdly. "Ah, I see. Well, I think you'll like my little proposition then. You'll have to pull in some of your friends for this deal, but the money is something that will get you out of this flat my friend… as long as you have no scruples…"

He didn't, when a sum of ten thousand pounds for each of his Mates was mentioned, but he did when the Afghan told him what would be required of them. He finally agreed when he was shown a secretly taken video of him agreeing to the scam in Omar's house back in Afghanistan, that would have put him in prison in the U.K. for at least ten years.

It helped stiffen his resolve when the Afghan increased his fee to fifteen thousand.

Even scruples have a price.

CHAPTER 33

When they pulled up to the solid looking metal gate at the entrance to the safe house, a Guard came out from a telephone-sized booth with a clipboard, and glanced through the driver's side window.

"It's OK... Quigley's team," Peter said, showing his ID papers.

The Guard nodded, and went back inside.

The gate slowly slid open and Peter started to ease through it.

Out of habit Danny glanced back through the rear view mirror but saw nothing that alarmed him.

"OK Danny?" Peter asked.

"Yep, clear. Just another of those black cabs dashing past."

They proceeded up the short driveway and pulled up by the main house, which looked more like a stockbroker's mansion than any safe house Danny had seen before.

"Yeah, I know" Peter said, answering his unspoken question. "It used to belong to a drug lord, and was confiscated by the Inland Revenue. We grabbed it."

An armed MI5 Officer immediately met their vehicle and relaxed when he saw who the driver was.

"Evening Mr. Sanderson."

"Evening Bert. This is Mr. Quigley. He's going in to visit his wife for a short chat."

Danny saw the man's eyes crinkle.

'Word sure gets around' Danny thought.

Peter got out and glanced behind the Guard.

"Where's your Mate?" he asked.

Bert nodded towards the house. "Just getting a brew inside to bring out for us. Bloody cold out here. Oh the front door's open" he added.

When they got there and walked through, they were met by two alert looking Officers with hard looking faces, who checked Peter's ID again and waved them through. They could hear the clinking of cups from what must have been a kitchen annex.

They proceeded along a long winding corridor, which made a left angled turn, then they made a right turn into some sort of drawing room. Peter went straight across and opened a solid door, which led into a large lounge.

The two people inside looked up, and one of them rushed straight across into his arms.

His 13-year-old daughter Allison.

"Oh Daddy, Daddy, where on earth have you been and are you coming to take us home?" she asked pleadingly, standing back and looking at him eagerly.

Before he could reply, Fiona was standing alongside him.

"I'd be interested in the answer to that as well Danny, considering I'm stuck here, thanks to you in the first place" she demanded.

Peter eased off to the side, rolling his eyes.

Danny turned to her, knowing that he didn't have an answer that would satisfy her.

When the black cab sped past the safe house gate, a second almost identical type of mundane vehicle trailed behind it.

It had three men inside.

The black cab had pulled over, and the car stopped behind it.

Two men and Omar jumped out of the cab and climbed into the front passenger seat of the car. The other started walking back towards the safe house, with a brisk gait, as if having his nightly stroll.

Omar looked around. "You all know your instructions?" He didn't wait for an answer.

"OK, let's go!"

The car turned around and headed back towards the safe house. As it pulled up to the front of the gate, the man 'strolling' was coming to the edge of the driveway, about six feet from the back of the car.

The Guard came out of the small booth, holding a clipboard and looking anxious.

The driver leaned out and beat him to whatever he was going to say. "Quigley's second team to get briefed for the relief shift" he snapped brusquely.

The Guard hesitated. By then it was too late.

The stroller had moved in on him and fired two swift shots with a silenced weapon, into the side of his head.

Two men leapt out of the car and dragged him off into some bushes where they tore off his uniform.

In minutes the stroller was wearing it and standing inside the booth. His first task was opening the gate, and the car moved through. The two men jumped back in and the car sped up the driveway.

Coming to the house Omar stared through the front window. "Only one Agent at the front, that's a break," he commented.

"Probably doing a recce round the back" suggested Al.

They had rehearsed it thoroughly. The car drove fast to the driveway in front of the doorway, where the Agent was holding up his hand to halt them.

When it stopped, one of the men in the back jumped out and shouted, "There's an attack coming on Quigley. They sent us as back up!"

He hesitated, and at that particular moment the second man in the back seat jumped out and shot the Agent directly in the face, also with a silencer. Then they were out, and racing towards the front door, all carrying weapons.

Omar came behind carrying a camera.

CHAPTER 34

Inside, Danny froze in midsentence, as a picture spiraled into his mind. A black cab!

"Cripes, the black cab" he whispered.

He pointed to another door leading off from the lounge.

"Where does that go Peter?" he asked.

"It's the library I believe," he whispered back.

Fiona stared at him. "What is it Danny?" she gasped, seeing his shocked face.

He turned and whispered urgently to Peter. "Get them all inside that library right now and push anything heavy you can find, up against the doors."

"What is it Danny?" he rasped, seeing his alarmed expression.

"Is this one of your frigging games Danny?" Fiona demanded, trying to shake off his hands that were pushing her towards the door.

Only Allison seemed to understand. "Daddy wants us to go inside. Something's wrong outside I think."

Despite the protests from Fiona and some doubt showing in Peter's expression, he managed to hustle them inside the library and closed the door in Fiona's protesting face.

He wasn't armed, and looked around the room for some sort of weapon. All he could see was a heavy brass poker by the old fireside that had probably had a fire in it at some time in the past. He picked it up and hefted it, then went back to the door and listened. He saw there was no key on his side.

Still no sound.

He switched off the lights and quietly eased the door open then felt to see if there was a key on the outside of it... none there either. He stepped out into the dimly lit corridor.

It was far too quiet.

He started creeping back along the corridor, stopping for cover behind some pieces of bulky furniture and what at one time must have been a gun cupboard, now empty. Coming up to a turn in the corridor he knelt down, crawled up to it, and slowly peered round.

'Was he imagining all this?' he wondered.

Then he saw it.

Off to the side of the front door was a small walk-in cupboard that was probably used for hanging coats and storing various items.

Sticking out from the cupboard, flat on the ground, was the shape of a man's hand, not moving, with the fingers outstretched, and a weapon lying a foot away from it.

Shit...one of the Agents was down! Was the weapon lying there as a trap, or had whoever was here just killed him and didn't have time to properly conceal the body?

He couldn't wait them out.

He'd always acted in dangerous situations in the belief that offence was better than defense, apart from which, he needed to get his hands on that weapon. He got up and, gripping the metal tongs, made a move across the carpet towards the Agent on the ground.

He'd only got four steps out when a bright flash exploded in his face, blinding him. His initial thought was that a flash-bang had been thrown in the room, but his eardrums hadn't been affected. He took the only option available to him, lashed out left and right with the metal tongs and kept moving forward. He caught someone a solid blow and heard a scream of pain, as something crashed to the ground. A man's voice cursed, then he started shouting "Quigley's here! Quigley's here!"

Danny's eyes started to clear somewhat.

He noticed that his desperate swings and movements had brought him to within six feet of the fallen Agent.

He dived in a forward roll, grabbed the weapon and heard the spat of a silencer as bullets scythed within inches of his head and crunched into the wall behind him.

Coming to his knees, he fired directly at the flashes and heard a scream, followed by a thud as something hit the ground. The Agent's gun didn't have a silencer, and the noise was tremendous inside the confines of the corridor.

'Dead or playing dead?' he asked himself.

He hadn't time to wait it out.

There had to be others in the building.

He heard a slithering sound and saw, with his recovering vision, someone crawling around the doorjamb of the front door.

He fired two quick shots in that direction, but heard only the tinkling of broken glass.

'Where the hell were the other Agents?' he wondered.

Had the intruders gone right down the corridor, or gone left and by-passed the lounge in their efforts to find them?

He went right, and after several steps came across the body of the man he had shot.

He was dead.

At the next corner he came upon the body of a second Agent.

He didn't have time to check his pulse for signs of life, but he had seen enough dead people to accept that it was too late.

The person who had killed him must be somewhere ahead,

waiting for him, and obviously not worried about any further opposition in the MI5 safe house.

Danny couldn't wait. His family was still vulnerable back in the library.

He had an idea.

This time he did feel the Agent's pulse and confirmed that he was in fact dead. His weapon was still in its holster under his armpit. He took that one as well and stuck it in his belt.

Then he took a deep breath, lifted the dead Agent bodily and slung him across his shoulder, legs dangling down his back, and chest against his. He ran straight round the corner, holding the body with one hand and his weapon in the other.

Within seconds, three or four bullets thudded into the Agents body as he charged straight across the corridor to where he could see the flashes.

He kept firing.

In the end it was the body he was carrying, that flattened his attacker, as he was half way to the floor with at least two of Danny's shots having gone through his chest.

He was about to drop to the floor himself when he heard the scream.

It was Allison's.

He turned and ran back down the corridor, pulling the second Agent's automatic loose, and making sure it was ready to fire.

Oh no, the first door was standing open!

He rushed through.

That scream again!

The library door was open as well. He rushed through it and would always remember that specific moment: a hooded man was standing with his back to him, pointing a weapon at Fiona who was standing in front of Allison, arms outstretched, and shouting

"No, no, not a child! You can't shoot a child!"

The man pulled the trigger a split second before Danny did, but it was too late.

Fiona slumped to the floor. The bullet had taken her directly in the head.

Danny kept pulling the trigger.

He heard that scream again.

This time Allison had thrown herself straight down on top of her mother.

He heard a strained voice from the behind a fallen set of fragile chairs.

It was Peter.

He was holding his shoulder, which was oozing blood.

"Sorry Danny, I couldn't do anything. I'm so sorry."

He had a quick thought and ran back to the front door and outside in time to see a non-descript vehicle spin around in the driveway. He was also in time to see a startled brown face looking sideways at him as the car sped away.

His weapon was empty.

He couldn't even fire what would have been futile shots after it.

Turning, he saw the inert form of the outside Agent who had greeted them earlier.

He didn't need to check his pulse.

Back inside, he turned the full entrance lights on and looked around for a phone. He called the DG first and did a quick report.

"How's Peter? Is it serious or can he hold on for half an hour?" was her first question.

"I can slap a pressure bandage on it, and he can hold for the moment" he replied.

"OK, here's what I want you to do Danny. Fix Peter up first, then run down to the gate and open it for a team and myself. It may already be open with that car taking off. You'll probably find that the Gate Guard is dead as well. I want you and your daughter out in one of our cars. We'll get her to one of our clinics for observation. I'm slapping a national security blanket on the whole situation to curtail the media. Our story is that Peter is the hero in all this. Yes I know, taking out three bad guys and suffering a wound himself, but we can't involve you there what with your relationship to the other group. I'll call the emergency services when I get there. Now brief Peter, if you have a moment while I'm heading over. Bye."

Danny looked around.

The first thing he saw lying on the floor was something he didn't expect. A camera! Probably what had flashed in his face?

But why would one of the attackers come with a camera?

He pulled a tissue from his pocket and, picking it up, placed it by the doorway to take with him.

He made a quick check of the Agent lying sprawled outside the coat cupboard, whose weapon he had managed to pick up earlier. Spotting another form on the cupboard floor he stepped inside. It was the fourth Agent, also dead.

He turned and raced back to the library in time to lift a sobbing Allison off the inert form of her mother, and sit her in a chair.

Then he located a first aid pack nearby and did a fast repair job on Peter, filling him in on Rebecca's imminent arrival and her strategy as he did so.

He didn't look happy.

"That story won't hold up for very long when they start to put the pieces together…. a bunch of dead people, and perhaps the Gate Guard as well. You can't button this up for very long even if it is a national security issue."

Danny didn't have time to answer.

He turned and knelt beside Allison who had thrown herself back beside her mother, and held Fiona's hand for a brief moment.

He knew he would find who had done this and avenge her, no matter how long it would take. Allison clung to him as she staggered back along the corridor and outside, where he sat her down on the steps after a quick word of encouragement.

It took him another couple of minutes to get down to the entrance to the safe house.

The first thing he spotted was the prone form of the Gate Guard lying partially concealed by the hut. The gate was closed, probably a deliberate ploy to slow down any pursuit by the vehicle owner who had fled previously.

He managed to get the gate swinging open without any difficulty, and went out to the road, looking up and down.

He saw the black cab parked thirty yards up on the side of the road. Probably abandoned by now, but he didn't have time to check it out. He dashed back up the driveway in time to stop Allison from stumbling up the steps, calling out for her mother.

Just in time, the MI5 team, led by the DG rolled up and stopped. He gave a quick update including the presence of the

197

abandoned black cab outside the main gate. Also details of the camera, which she placed carefully in one of the MI5 vehicles.

Within minutes Danny and his daughter were in one of the other team vehicles and heading off, while Rebecca and her team raced up the steps.

CHAPTER 35

Danny didn't know how he managed to stroll casually out of the Sally Ann the following morning and climb into the passenger seat of the waiting car. The American, Frank Skinner was the driver with Mohammed Shareef sitting in the back.

Both men tried to look relaxed but Danny could see etchings of relief on their faces.

Frank thumped him on the shoulder as he settled in and locked his seat belt.

"So, what's up Jack? How's your street family doing inside...they still on the take, separating you from your money?"

He laughed, making an effort at humor.

"Oh yeah, for sure. They're curious about my new job offer, but I fobbed them off, as you'd expect. I think my days are numbered inside for what it's worth. You know something, some of the lads are on the street because of some lousy break like my own for example, but you'd be surprised just how many don't really want to give up their life on the street."

Mohammed snorted from the back. "A bunch of fucking losers if you ask me. You're better off without them."

Danny knew they were angling to get him to cut loose from the Sally Ann contacts, and went along with it, but not too readily.

"You could be right, but I'll give them credit, they look out for each other, and as I said they're like family. They gave me a leg up when I needed it."

Skinner nodded. "I agree with Mohammed. It's time for you to move on Jack. You mentioned some real money. Can you imagine if that lot got a sniff of what you'll be getting your hands on shortly? They'd be a goddam security risk. The first time the cops pulled them in they'd be spilling their guts about their old friend Jack, a former street person, coming into some real money!"

Danny rubbed his chin thoughtfully. "Hmm... you've got a point there Frank, which I hadn't thought about. Now that you've brought it up, when do I start to see some of this cash you keep referring to?"

The American chuckled. "You're starting to sound like a stuck record my friend. I like that. It shows where your heart is. Do you have a bank account?"

"I did have, prior to my ex-wife taking everything, including the bank account. With no job and no abode or address, there was no point in even trying. I hadn't really given it any thought up to now."

The American cursed and banged the horn at some white van that cut in, close in front of him.

"These stupid Brit. drivers, they're a frigging menace on the road! Now here's the thing, I mentioned that money was no object on this operation. OK, we're not talking a bottomless pit here either, however, it wouldn't make any sense for us to hand over a chunk of money and you carry it around on your person, now would it?"

"No, I guess not Frank. I hadn't thought of that. Look, how much money are we talking about here anyway?"

"I'll come to that in a minute. Here's the thing. There isn't any room for any more people where we live. We have another group of our people coming in next week from Syria. We were discussing this and figured that we could set you up in a separate place where we could stash them away for a few days and then move them on up the country.

200

By setting you up, I mean pay the down payment and first month's rent. Then with that address, you could organize a bank account for yourself, and we could start paying you some real money. How does that sound Jack?"

Danny swiveled sideways eagerly. "Real money! Just what's your idea of real money Frank?"

Frank threw him a sideways measured look. "Oh, say five thousand pounds to start off with, and we look at the extent of your input to the group as we go along."

Danny shook his head dubiously. "Come on Frank. Five grand for risking being sent to prison for fifteen years for treason, and you're talking about probably having to feed the groups as they come through, no doubt being the paymaster when they want money for subway fares or whatever. You said five grand. I'm assuming you were talking about a regular monthly amount here as well. If so, ten grand would be more like it... I mean, let's get real here for fuck's sake!"

Frank glanced in the rear view mirror. "What d'you think Mohammed?" he asked.

He frowned. "It's a lot of money for just a promise so far. Sure he's good at unarmed combat, and this will be useful. He'll probably need a car as well to pick up our people coming in, so it could end up being a bottomless pit if we're not careful Frank. Give him some funds for the flat and to set up the bank account, and in a months' time we'll have a better idea of how valuable he can be to us, then we can hammer out a deal with him."

Danny shook his head and swung sideways, his face angry.

"Oh man, you chaps are something else! You know something? All I've got so far is two hundred quid in my hand and a gun stuck in my face. I might as well be back on the fucking street. In fact, why don't you just pull over right now and let me out. Oh by the way, I've contacted my friend in Belfast and he's currently sniffing out the possibility of getting his hands on some weapons and C4."

Frank raised one hand off the wheel. "He's got a point Mohammed. We've been somewhat rough with him. Now, Jack, when is your friend coming back to you?"

Danny was silent for a moment then answered grudgingly. "Two days he said. He's hungry, but very skittish about getting caught in a sting operation. Luckily we have some history. So..."

Frank exchanged eye contact with Mohammed momentarily in the rear view mirror, then he nodded as if coming to some decision.

"Right Jack, here's the bottom line. We'll raise that amount to seven and a half grand paid each month, to be revised at the end of the first month as long as you're on the team. That's my top offer and I'd advise you to take it."

Danny bit his tongue, staying silent again for a long moment.

Then he started nodding. "OK, you got a deal Frank."

The American grinned, took his hands off the wheel and clapped them twice.

"That's my man Jack. Now let's get started on the flat and the bank account. Zain's sister lives in a nice apartment block, where the basement flat is available right now and would be ideal. It's got a rear entrance as well which could be useful to us."

Down the street in the surveillance van, Alina started breathing again and turned to her new colleague Clive Spooner.

"Oh my God, I could see Danny as a hostage negotiator quite easily. I can't believe the risks he's willing to take."

Clive Spooner the other MI5 Agent, looked stunned. "Listening to him has given me some new ideas when I go in for my annual review next week. I'm going to increase the amount of that pay raise I was going for."

She smiled gently at him. "Sure, go for it, but remember, you're no Danny Quigley."

CHAPTER 36

The rest of the morning went by in a swirl of activities as the two Jihadists brought Danny around to the new proposed flat in the docklands area of London. This surprised him, as it was a relatively new development, but the American pointed out that a number of successful Asians had moved into some of the apartment blocks and were well accepted by existing English residents.

He met Zain's sister briefly and could see she was not particularly impressed with his association with her brother. However she brought them down to the Manager's office where he signed the contract and Frank produced the necessary cheque for down payment and rent. He promised to return in the next few days, with his banking details for the automatic rental payment arrangement to be set up.

The fact that Zain's sister was already a reliable tenant made the process smoother and the Manager waived the usual credit check. Basically, he was glad to rent the last flat available, which as a basement, had less light and was more exposed to street noise. The previous tenant had left after a short stay.

Danny received his key, and a duplicate one was held by Frank, who planned to cut some extras for new Jihadists coming in. Surprisingly the flat, which was three bedroomed, was still sparsely furnished due to the previous owner getting married and moving to a house, where his new wife had no use for his old stuff.

The Manager said he could get rid of it by calling some charity shop, but Frank said to leave it. He planned to move in some more furniture to facilitate sleeping arrangements, within the next couple of days.

Danny opened the fridge and reared back…the last tenants had left more than old furniture; there were a number of food items that had been left in the fridge, which was not hooked up to the electricity, and the contents were rotting.

Zain slammed it shut again. "Don't worry I'll have my sister chase up the Manager and have this cleaned up. No problem Jack, we'll set it up right, you wait and see. Anyway, I can tell you that our warriors coming home from Iraq and Syria will think this is the Hilton after where they've been."

Then it was on to a Lloyds Bank where the American, sitting in the car, wrote out a cheque for seven thousand five hundred pounds and handed it to Danny.

"There you go Jack, that's our part of the deal. Now let's see if you can deliver, Buddy."

Zain reached forward from the rear seat in the vehicle and grasped his shoulder strongly.

"If you don't deliver Jack, it's back on the shitty streets for you, even if you did save my bacon the other night from those punks. You hear me?"

Danny opened the door and climbed out without answering.

Then he stuck his head back in and looked back. "Yeah, I hear you," and strolled up the steps to the bank.

Zain leaned forward. "You know, there's still something about him that I don't like."

Frank laughed. "Sure, he's an Infidel, that's why. When Jack's usefulness is over, you can chop his head off as well, like the ones you did back in Iraq."

He yawned. "No skin off my ass, either way."

Inside Danny went through the process of setting up a new bank account using the false identity provided for him by Thames House. He made sure to get a photocopy of Frank's cheque. MI5 would be very interested in having a close look at that particular account.

Assuming he was now fully accepted by the Jihadists, he said goodbye to the two men and walked away, ostensibly to do some more work on the possibility of finding a weapons cache in Belfast. He explained that he preferred doing this in the back room of the Sally Ann where the phone was available for street people to keep in touch with their families who still wanted to hear from them.

After strolling round for a good fifteen minutes, and confident he was not being followed, he finally hopped into the surveillance car and was brought back to Thames House.

He needed updating on how Allison was doing, and how the Police investigation was proceeding.

Rebecca had cleared the decks and was waiting for him, along with Jerry Sackville of counter terrorism and investigations, and Phil Dawson who was responsible for placing listening devices in suspects' residences. Peter's position had not been filled, as it was not known the extent of his shoulder injuries or expected recovery time. They had, however, pulled in a temporary replacement: a retired Scotland Yard detective called Dave Jones, already a member of the surveillance section who had extensive experience in this area and weaponry. His role would be either organizing the surveillance teams, or accompanying Alina in her vehicle when he was available. Otherwise Clive Spooner would be accompanying her on surveillance duties.

The Director General, as usual, didn't waste any time.

"Right People, let's get an update for all of us. For Danny, his daughter Allison has come round after a sedative last night and a good sleep. She's a chip off the old block for sure. She demanded to know all about last evening's events in full detail. Naturally I didn't and couldn't at this stage, but suffice it to say she's pulled round amazingly fast for someone so young who just saw her mother shot dead... and let me say also" she looked directly at Danny, "she's asking to see her father right away, which is not unusual for someone who has just lost one of her parents. You got that?"

He nodded. "I hear you and that's my next port of call after I get out of here."

Rebecca pointed to Jerry. "Let's hear what's happening with the Police investigation at this early stage Jerry?"

"Well, as you can imagine, and as Dave Jones there, with his Scotland Yard experience will confirm, the Police are not a happy bunch right now. Go figure…they've got eight dead bodies, one being Danny's ex-wife, three of them MI5 Officers, the Gate Guard - an experienced ex-Military type, and three bad guys… and get this, all three of these presumably killed by Peter Sanderson who suffered only a shoulder wound after all that combat!"

Rebecca frowned. "As you can imagine the Detective in charge nearly blew a fuse when I pulled the carpet from under his feet by producing a National Security blanket on the whole situation. Go on Jerry."

"Right Ma'am, Oh I forgot one more body! The driver of the abandoned cab on the street outside the safe house was found dead, dumped in some garbage bin round the back of a restaurant, three miles away."

There were murmurs from around the table.

It was Dave Jones who cut across the sudden chatter.

"Not surprising that the Police feel you're effectively putting shackles on their investigation. As you know most of the breaks come from the initial speed of chasing up suspects before they get their stories right, or dispose of evidence."

Jerry held up his hand. "Let me finish, then we can get your views and experience on this. First, some good news. The three bad guys have already been identified as ex-Military, discharged last year, and get this, they were all ex-Military Police, whose last postings were in Afghanistan. The odds are there was a further bad guy left on the gate after they killed the Guard. Danny also saw one person take off in a vehicle, similar to our surveillance ones, and head towards the gate."

"Fast work for the investigators" Jones commented.

"That was my initial reaction," added Jerry "but apparently, these chaps had their ID's in their wallets in their back pockets!"

"Not exactly the practice of paid assassins, and certainly they never expected to end up dead" Danny pointed out.

"Oh, and one more thing that might be relevant. The man who jumped in the car and took off, stared right at me for a moment, and I would be ninety percent certain that he was an Afghan."

"Afghanistan again… it keeps popping up here doesn't it." Rebecca muttered.

Jerry looked around wearily. "Come on guys let me finish. I have some more little gems for you. I'm ahead of the Detectives on the next lot. They did provide me with the three Military names. Their names don't matter at this stage but, using some of the beautiful equipment we have downstairs, illegally I might add, I located the bank accounts of all three of them and guess what? Twenty five thousand pounds had been deposited in one account, and ten thousand pounds in each of two other accounts over the past week."

Rebecca lifted her hands. "Bottom line is, folks, this is going to blow up in our faces if we're not careful. Already leaks to the press have resulted in the big dailies and TV stations sniffing around."

"So what are you proposing Rebecca?" Danny enquired.

"To bring them into the situation as far as possible. Admit that another of our Officers was present, who is to remain unnamed, and due to the nature of his present covert operation, he can't be interviewed. He will provide a statement unsigned, and agrees to appear in court on camera when the enquiry is held, which hopefully will be delayed as long as possible."

Jones looked doubtful. "All I can say is to keep Danny as far away as possible from this whole Police investigation. You'd be surprised just where the Police and the media have their paid informers… and dare I say it, even here in Thames House. I'd suggest that he stay away from here completely in the interim."

"Point taken. Any comments so far?" Rebecca asked.

Danny nodded. "The individual who escaped from the front of the house: I'd like to look at pictures of the Afghan personnel from the Embassy here. I suspect he's the one, who organized the whole thing which, may I remind you, resulted in the deliberate execution of my ex-wife Fiona, the mother of my daughter. This chap is on my personal agenda whether he has diplomatic immunity or not" Danny pointed out with terse anger.

The DG's face looked sternly across at him.

"Danny, I have to say that I and everyone here feel absolutely terrible about what's happened. You're ex-wife and mother of your young daughter, murdered right in front of you both. That's a hard one to forget and let pass, especially for someone like you who believes in direct and deadly action. Having said that, I have to warn you that any vigilante action by yourself in this matter, resulting in death, will result in immediate dismissal from MI5 and criminal charges being laid against you. You have to let the forces of law and order take their course here. This is particularly sensitive if that Afghan you saw taking off, as you mentioned, turns out to have diplomatic immunity at their Embassy. I have to emphasize again, that we cannot be associated with any illegal action taken for personal reasons, against individuals involved in your wife's death. I hope I've made myself one hundred percent clear on this!"

There was silence in the room. People looked around uncomfortably.

Finally Danny broke the silence and nodded.

"OK, I understand your position and I appreciate that it couldn't be otherwise."

To get past the difficult position that he created for the DG who he regarded as a true friend, he decided to change the atmosphere in the room with something that had been puzzling him about the previous night's assault.

"Rebecca, ever since last night's series of events occurred, I've been trying to get my head around one thing, and it's this. As you know, the camera which I gave to you, was recovered from the scene, and I believe it was dropped by a person who blinded me with the flash inside the front door and subsequently dropped it when I lashed out with the fire iron. Why was he there with a camera instead of another weapon, which he could easily have killed me with right then?"

There was a chatter of conversation and speculation for the next ten minutes, without any particular conclusion.

Finally the ex-Scotland Yard Detective Jones coughed to get their attention.

"It reminds me of a case we had some years back where a family in Italy wanted revenge on a man here in London, who forced himself on a member of their family, a young girl who was over here to attend university. He was subsequently freed by the court when their defense lawyer produced so-called evidence that the sex was consensual, and that her mode of dress was such that she was essentially asking for it. The Italian family, who were rumored to have some mafia connections, apparently hired some contract killer to execute the man involved.

They wanted him killed in a special way, which involved mutilation of his genitals, and wanted a picture of it. Hence, the killer brought along a camera with him. He didn't however appreciate the number of CCTV cameras around London, and was caught trying to fly out of Heathrow Airport the following day. He's still in prison here in the U.K. The Italian connection denied any involvement, and escaped prosecution."

Alina looked shocked. "So you're suggesting that Danny and his family were to be executed, and whoever's organizing it, wanted it on camera?"

The DG cut in. "That's exactly what he's saying, and furthermore, it ties in with other information that's come to our knowledge recently. As a matter of interest our people downstairs have been looking at the camera, and it does have a picture of a rather startled Danny in it. They're examining it for fingerprints as we sit here."

She quickly filled all of them in on the suspicion that an air strike Danny had called in back in Afghanistan while in the SAS had killed a leading terrorist. The man's Pashtun family had a code of vengeance, and they had only recently found out through the change of Government in Kabul, who had been responsible, Danny Quigley!

There was a clamor of comments around the room and Rebecca called for a short break with some refreshments.

She walked over to Danny as he was getting up and caught his arm, a smile on her face.

"I have a surprise for you, next door."

It certainly was.

Standing there grinning was his old friend from the SAS Regiment, Sergeant Scotty McGregor.

CHAPTER 37

Danny and Scotty went back a long way.

They had spent a number of years in the U.K.'s Special Forces, the SAS, and had been involved in many dangerous and demanding operations overseas, including Iraq and Afghanistan. They had worked in numerous situations where Scotty had prided himself on 'keeping Danny's back', and to the extent that he almost appeared to read his mind and anticipate his every action. Now a Sergeant, he spent most of his time training new recruits up in the brutal Brecon Beacon mountains in Wales. Only five foot seven inches in height, he was as lean and hard as an oak tree, and an awesome warrior in battle. In street fighting, he used his bullet-like head with devastating effect to completely destroy an opponent. He was also efficient with a crossbow and throwing knives, having worked with his father in a carnival show.

While in the Regiment they had both been seconded to MI5 for some challenging missions, after completing a condensed MI5 course at their training camp.

More recently, Scotty had been in Nigeria supporting his brother a priest, whose church was under threat of attack by Boko Haram. Danny had joined him with some other ex-SAS colleagues, and subsequently took on and destroyed one of their highly trained terrorist units.

"What the hell are you doing here Scotty?" he demanded when they had stopped hugging and pounding each other's backs, and had moved over to a private corner.

"Well, I got a call from your DG that she needed me to come and save your ass again" Scotty replied, grinning.

"But you're in the Regiment for God's sake! You can't just drop everything and toddle off up here to London."

Scotty smiled innocently. "Not any more I'm not. I just took my discharge and was on my way up to Scotland for a number of weeks, including accumulated leave, which I hadn't taken. I was going to visit my brother before taking that big job in Nigeria with the oil company. You remember that? You were very much involved in setting it up for me Mate, so here I am, ready to kick ass again. Just point me in the right direction."

Danny was still in shock. "But how come you're here this morning Scotty?"

"The DG just caught me packing my gear and told me the story. You were doing some covert stuff, so there was no time to contact you. I jumped on a train from Swindon and here I am. I can give you some time and catch up with my brother again. Oh, I'm invited into the next part of the meeting, by the way."

And so he was.

It was Rebecca who briefed the group on Scotty's background in the SAS and his previous association with MI5. Danny filled the group in on some of the operations they had carried out while serving members, and after he took his discharge a few years ago. He could see a growing respect on the faces of the group and their anticipation of his potential involvement.

Rebecca stepped in again.

"OK Danny, you asked for Scotty to be involved. Now, how d'you want to position him in this evolving situation as we go forward?"

"With your approval of course Rebecca, initially I'd like Scotty to be located at the new safe house where my daughter Allison is right now. She's obviously still under threat, and he could stiffen whatever defenses you've set up. After the debacle of the safe house the other night, I'm sure you've beefed up the protective details."

"Already being done...go on" she commented.

"I'd want Scotty armed, whatever that takes, and when not at the safe house, I'd like him placed in the surveillance vehicle that'll be monitoring myself when I'm with the Jihadist group. From my recent experiences, I've had a weapon stuck in my face twice, and may just need bailing out in a hurry. This is especially important with the arrival of a new group next week, which may be even more volatile. I need to talk to Phil Dawson about getting some listening devices planted in the flat at Canary Wharf, but I'll have to suss this out when the sister of one of the group, who lives upstairs, will be out. Next, is my proposed trip to Belfast to create the impression that I can, perhaps, organize some weapons and explosives for them. I don't know if you've managed to get Scotty's Regiment Mate to play the part of a contact that may be able to produce a weapons cache, but will pretend to be suspicious of a possible sting operation. Any news on Jimmy Patton?"

Rebecca threw her hands up. "Phew Danny, you're coming at us too fast here. We're civil servants after all, bear that in mind!"

He knew she was really kidding. The group chuckled quietly.

None of them could forget losing so many Officers in the recent attack and were prepared to do what was necessary to get payback, whatever it took.

She carried on, ticking the points off on her fingers. "As for Scotty staying at the safe house, that's fine, also being close by and armed in the surveillance vehicle to support you if necessary. The Belfast trip, I've spoken to Jimmy Patton's CO and there's no problem right now in releasing him to play this role in Belfast. You have to contact him and provide a full briefing, or we can have him come up here and fly him over there. If we can record the meeting in Belfast with the Jihadists that would be useful in any future prosecution where they're seen to be trying to buy weapons. D'you know who would be going with you from the Jihadists?"

"Probably the American, Frank Skinner. Any Asian face over there right now with all the media coverage might raise questions or create problems. On the other hand he might bring one of the others with him and have him keep out of sight. As far as recording the actual meeting is concerned, my belt could be utilized, but we would still need a vehicle nearby to record the conversation. Oh, I'd figured on Scotty being a backup for me, and armed, bearing in mind that Belfast can be a rough area, not part of Jimmy Patton's role, but hanging loose around the perimeter, so to speak."

Jerry stuck his hand up. "Sorry to interrupt, but seriously, you're not planning to actually provide weapons and explosives to terrorists here are you Ma'am?"

She shook her head. "No way. We're trying to keep them busy, off on a false trail as it were, until we find out what the strategy of this new Jihadist group actually is. It's got a different feel to it, and quite frankly, we're worried. We hope Danny can get so far in that they'll bring him in deeper and confide in him. Now, to cover another point brought up by Danny, apparently another bunch of Jihadists will be coming in by Euro Tunnel next week. Jerry, have you any intelligence on this from Interpol or elsewhere?"

"None at present Ma'am. They must have some good cover on their journey overseas, perhaps genuine attendance records at some madras in Egypt or elsewhere. As I understand it, Danny hasn't been given the names as yet, but it was mentioned that he might be involved in picking them up. This would be a bonus for us if he did."

"OK then. Jerry a further question, have you looked at that bank account on the cheque that Danny deposited, yet?"

"Sorry Ma'am, just too much coming at me right now. I'll get onto it when I go back down."

Danny raised his hand. "I'm still not happy with letting these Jihadists back into the country, to radicalize and train other young Muslims. We should snatch them up when they

214

get off the train, and lock them away under the present legislation."

Rebecca sighed. "Many would agree with you Danny, but we're still a democratic society and need proof of their Jihadist activities first. Equally, I have a bad feeling about this American and his presence here in the U.K. We need to discover what their plan and strategy is, and right now Danny, you're a player in the only game in town. You have to hang in there, and with Scotty here, you'll have a solid presence covering your butt."

They spent a further half hour tying down specifics and Dave Jones organized a vehicle to take Danny and Scotty round to the safe house.

CHAPTER 38

Belfast

Danny and the American flew over two days later, arriving in the evening, and checked into the Ramada Encore Hotel in the city center on the recommendation of Jimmy Patton who would join them for a meal when they had arrived and settled in. Frank had booked two single rooms, which surprised Danny who thought that he would want to keep a closer eye on him.

He had taken the opportunity to contact Patton from Thames House, and spent thirty minutes briefing him on what he wanted from him when he met Frank Skinner. He was pretty good at playing it by ear and winging it when necessary. They had agreed that a public place would be ideal for a first meeting, and then suggest that they go to a Belfast bar with some atmosphere, as Americans seemed to love that.

Rebecca had been in touch with the MI5 office in Belfast and they had arranged for the necessary recording vehicle to be parked in an appropriate place outside. With the hotel's co-operation, the team had rigged a listening device under the table, which Jimmy had reserved for their initial meeting in the lounge. She had also arranged for the telephone in Skinner's room to be bugged, on the off chance that he might make some calls from there. One of Scotty's procurement requests was for an automatic pistol and some extra clips, and he was pleased to be presented with an Austrian Glock 17, a weapon he had a particular affinity for, and had used many times in the past in real life situations.

Jimmy Patton on the other hand, was a solid five foot eleven Irishman from Belfast. He had also worked on the same SAS team as Danny when he'd served in the Regiment. Known as a creative expert in explosives, rumor had it that he had learned his skills before joining. He was still in the Forces, and the only concern he had about this new role was his short Military haircut, which could be a dead giveaway to an ex-Marine like Frank Skinner. However the local MI5 team brought in a makeup professional that fitted him with an incredibly realistic looking scruffy wig.

Danny had been warned about this, as he might have had difficulty in keeping from bursting out laughing when he met him with the American. However his major worry was that Patton would, during the course of the evening, call him by his correct name rather than the assumed one of Jack.

They had agreed to meet downstairs at 7 pm and had stepped out of the elevator when Danny spotted Patton already there in the lounge waiting for them. He was glad he'd been prepared, because the man waiting for him looked anything like the usually impeccably turned out Jimmy Patton from the Regiment.

The hair-do was brilliant and showed signs of an effort to control it, but it still stuck out in places like a rebellious school boy, and his black shiny leather Dockers jacket had seen better days.

Danny noticed Frank's pursed lips when he introduced him.

"Frank this is Jimmy Patton that I mentioned, Jimmy, meet Frank Skinner, the American."

Both men shook hands, measuring each other, and engaged in the usual conversation of two people sounding each other out. Danny and the Irishman shook hands briefly and mumbled some appropriate remarks to each other.

He was relieved when he called him 'Jack'.

Finally Skinner looked around. "So, where are we eating then and having our chat, ah Jimmy?" he asked.

"Follow me" Patton answered and proceeded into the good-sized restaurant where a small number of tables were occupied, to a table that had a posted reserved sign on it, up near the far wall.

Frank was nodding his approval. "Nice choice Jimmy. I wondered what you were thinking about meeting in a public place and discussing the topic that I'm here about. This is ideal."

The waiter was over quite smartly with menus and took their orders for drinks. All three ordered beer, but it had been pre-arranged that Danny and Scotty's drink would be of a non alcohol-variety. MI5 had considerable influence in the city and Danny wouldn't have been surprised if the waiter himself was an Agent. Probably not, because when he returned with drinks and took their meal orders, he was either a genuine waiter or a superb actor.

Jimmy took a quick slug of the drink, looked around nervously and glanced across at the American.

"So Frank, Jack's filled me in a bit on why you're here, but can you first broad stroke me on your own background? Quite frankly, I'd like to know who I'm dealing with. I mean, we're talking here about a pretty dangerous topic. I'm a bit long in the tooth to just blabber on to a complete stranger."

Frank nodded in approval. "Point taken Jimmy, and I'd be disappointed if you were not showing signs of caution at this stage. I can't afford to get involved with anyone who might have a loose mouth either. My background is a good chunk of time spent in the Marine Corps. I did some tours in Iraq and saw the futility of our efforts when I saw my buddies blown apart and shipped back home in body bags, only to see the Iraqi army that we'd trained, run at the first sign of a fight and abandon all that weaponry and gear behind them. You could say that I've now seen the light and want to make some real money from what's happening over there right now, but tell me, what's your main concern Jimmy?"

Jimmy's face took on a frustrated expression. He took another long drink and set the glass down hard.

"My concern? Look, you're an American right? You could be fucking CIA for all I know, trying some sort of sting operation. I'm nicely set up here in the city, and I don't need this kind of trouble."

Frank laughed. "Me CIA? Come on! I gave my all for my goddam country, and when I got back home could I get a job? Could I hell - myself and a whole slew of my buddies. The bankers, the stockbrokers, and the techies in Silicon Valley were coining it, and the poor working slobs could get a job in MacDonald's for a pittance, so quit pissing about. Either you can locate some weapons and explosives for me, or I'm outta here. You got that?" he finished harshly.

Danny stepped in.

"Hey look Frank, here in Belfast they've gained considerable experience of how the Security Forces work. Look at all the court cases where informers were feeding back information on so called secret meetings, where the participants ended up in prison. Believe me, Jimmy's got a point. All I can say here to both of you is that I know Jimmy from of old, and he's the genuine article. If anyone can get what they're after, it's him. Also Jimmy, this chap Frank is a genuine entrepreneur who is out to make money, and you and I can benefit. I might add that I already have, to the tune of several thousand pounds, so let's cut to the chase and stop sparring around. I know you Jimmy, and I also know that you wouldn't be here unless you'd got some sort of lead on a possible cache of weapons, right?"

Patton looked somewhat mollified. "OK Da...Daddio, I hear you. Listening to Frank there talk about his buddies being sent back in body bags, he was either the genuine article or should be on stage making a living."

The American looked puzzled. "Glad to hear that, now what's this Daddio thing you called Jack a second ago?"

Danny slapped the table. "You son of a bitch Jimmy, I told you never to call me that again," he snapped angrily.

Turning to Frank he went on. "When I was meeting Jimmy in secret a few years back, I insisted on playing a music tape just in case there was a bug nearby, and guess what? I used to play the same song every time...Elvis's rock around the clock, so Jimmy here starts calling me Daddio when we meet, just to get my goat. I swore to kill him if he called me that again!"

Frank relaxed and grinned. "Yeah, I can see why some hard ass in the Airborne Regiment might be somewhat pissed off being called that."

Danny kicked Jimmy under the table. That was too close for comfort!

Jimmy looked up at the ceiling for a moment as if coming to some decision.

"OK, here's the situation. I'm willing to run with this and see where it takes us. I haven't spoke to Jack about it, but after we're finished the meal here, I've prepared a small presentation for you, as it were. Jack knows me as a wheeler and a dealer over the years, so I know the score when it comes to supplying a need to a customer, as it were. People like to have a look-see at the product first, if at all possible. We can do that this evening, and I think you'll like what I've set up. We'll go for a short ride, about forty minutes, where you can take a wee look at what may be coming on the market, assuming that Frank here has the wherewithal to make a purchase. How's that sound?"

CHAPTER 39

That was how the three of them were going northwest out of Belfast with Jimmy driving, and both Danny and the American in the back.

Frank was getting increasingly nervous and was shifting around. Finally he leaned close to Danny and whispered.

"Are you sure this is kosher, Jack. Why weren't we told about it earlier?"

Danny patted his arm reassuringly.

"Probably security Frank. He's probably not his own master in this whole thing."

"Are you carrying, Jack? This could be a set up!"

As if sensing the American's disquiet, Jimmy shouted back at them. "Hey, not to worry lads…we're nearly there."

Five minutes later the car crawled up a small stony track that ended in what looked like a disused quarry with a small hut standing at the entrance where they pulled in.

They jumped out of the vehicle and looked around.

At the far end, about a hundred yards away, they spotted two old cars parked up against the hillside of the quarry. On top of the old cars they could see numerous tins, bottles and empty petrol cans laid out on the roof.

Danny was starting to see where this was going.

Jimmy led them across to the hut, opened a large brass lock and went inside. He emerged a moment later dragging a collapsed table which he pointed to, and Danny started setting it up. He went back and came out, this time with two bundles under his arm wrapped in some old oily blankets. Like a stage presenter, he slowly unwrapped the first and revealed a sleek rifle, which he passed to the American.

"Shit, an AK 47, and it looks like new!" he breathed in awe.

Jimmy did the same with the second rifle, and handed it to Danny.

"Ammo clips on the table lads. The targets are on top of those cars. Have a go and don't worry about the cars. I tried to get my mother-in-law to come and sit in one to make it more interesting, but for some reason she refused" he joked.

Danny wasn't very interested in trying out the weapon, so he left it for Frank to have a go, using both weapons.

The American didn't waste any time. He grabbed the ammo clips, rammed them home and started blasting away at the targets on top of the old cars.

Danny had to admit, the man could shoot, as the bottles and cans went flying off the roofs of the old vehicles. When he had finished off half of them, he stepped back and nodded to Danny to take his turn.

"Have a go Jack."

"Hey, you're the buyer man. Here try this one as well just to make sure."

Frank shrugged. "Why not? The old AK 47 has been pretty dammed reliable over the years, even when they've been used and abused."

With that he took the second weapon, slammed a clip in and blasted downrange at the remainder of the targets, sending them flying. He finished and looked down at the weapon, nodding in satisfaction.

"Nice weapons Jimmy, I'll give you that, now what about...?"

Jimmy silenced him with a finger to his lips, picked up the two rifles and stuck them back inside the hut.

"That's only the first demo lads. Now step over to the side of the hut here and get your bodies behind it. You can peek around the side and keep your eyes on those two old wrecked cars" he instructed.

They did as he said.

Jimmy didn't bother taking cover. He took a monitor out of his jacket pocket and looked back at them. "Ready lads?" He pressed a switch.

The first car exploded with an enormous blast and shot into the air, landing twenty feet away.

He looked around at them again.

"I didn't like where I parked that one. I'll try for another spot" and he pressed the switch again. The second car flew up into the air with an even greater noise, and landed twenty yards away in the opposite direction. Parts of the vehicle with stones and dust were flying around in all directions.

Jimmy hardly seemed to notice, but he did have a bout of coughing from the dust that had been kicked up.

Danny looked sideways at Frank who was shaking his head in wonder.

"Jesus Jack, this guy's a real find. I just saw our car bombs go off outside the House of Commons. This is exactly what we need, Buddy!" he chortled.

Danny's head reeled...The House of Commons! Oh man!

A grinning Jimmy was waiting for them when they emerged from behind the hut.

"Like our little demo lads?" he enquired.

Frank nodded vigorously. "My God Jimmy, that was superb! I wish you were working for us, the way you blew those cars in two different directions. C4 was it?"

"Yep, you got it in one. Now let's wrap this up before some farmer round here gets curious and calls the Police. We can talk business on the way back. Frank, you sit in with me this time and I'll lock these weapons up again, back in the hut."

They were in the car and heading towards the city within three minutes. When they got back on a main road, Frank turned to him.

"OK Jimmy, you know darned well that I'm interested. Now talk to me, Man."

223

"I thought you'd like my little demo. OK, here's the deal. My contacts claim to have a cache of weapons across the border in a safe place. They wouldn't tell me just how big the store is, but they're apparently in good shape as you've seen from your recent use of those two rifles. If you want to take this further, they'll itemize the cache and give us the numbers available. They'll come up with a price, and you have to decide whether you want to deal or not. If you want to deal, they'll want thirty percent down, and the balance on delivery. They'll bring them back across the border, and you can collect them here in Northern Ireland. Payment is to be in Pounds Sterling 'cos they don't trust that Euro any more. How does that sound?"

"Whoa there a moment Jimmy. First, have your suppliers got any shorter weapons, MP5's or machine pistols? AK 47's aren't that easy to carry round under a jacket for example?"

"Look, bear in mind that these were whipped away across the border when the Northern Ireland Peace Agreement was going down. There were curious eyes and informers everywhere. The cache was fortunately kept inside in a dry place and serviced regularly. There were only rifles in this lot, but I understand there's some machineguns as well...perhaps half a dozen, with ammo of course. The C4, as you saw back there, is still in perfect shape. Oh, and they have some grenades as well, but these haven't been tested recently at all."

"OK, beggars can't be choosers. Now two more points. One, I'm not parting with thirty percent up front and run the risk of your people disappearing into the hills of Antrim. I can't really go to the Police and complain, can I? I'd go ten percent, seeing as how I know Jack and he knows you from some previous time you worked together. Ten percent, that's my max. Secondly, I'll need the cache delivered to the U.K. I have no way of figuring out the details of shipping stuff across to the U.K. There must be many problems involved there that your people can surely get around and sort out."

He stopped, looking across at Jimmy who was shaking his head.

"That could be a no gamer for my suppliers. They keep pretty well under the radar in all their dealings, and an export effort like this could be a flag up for the security people. I'm not sure about this one Frank."

Danny cut in. "Just a thought Frank, what about delivery south of the border in the Republic? Have you any contacts down there who could facilitate this for you?"

He shook his head. "I don't think so... hmm...wait just a moment... there is a possibility down there, now that you mention it. OK, let me check it out further and get back to you. How does that sound?"

"Sounds like a plan. I'll get back through Jack here on the amount of the upfront payment, which could still be a deal breaker."

The American looked skeptical. "Your friends have been sitting on those weapons for years, and they must know there's a sell by date on them by now. They won't have many offers like this, my friend. I think they'll go for the ten percent. Now where's that Irish bar we were going to end up at? I'm thirsty all of a sudden."

CHAPTER 40

In the MI5 vehicle a mile behind and listening to the conversation from the bugged vehicle in front, Scotty got a High 5 from the Officer monitoring the conversation.

"We can't lose on this one. We got him trying to purchase weapons and explosives in the U.K. and he even mentioned a target, the House of Commons. That's one American that's going down for sure."

Scotty would be up next when the group went to the pub.

It was in a rough protestant part of Belfast.

Skinner the American loved the rough camaraderie, the noise and the music blasting out Irish rebel songs of the protestant genre in The Fox and Hounds that Jimmy Patton brought them to.

They managed to push through to an annex, off to one side near the toilets, and grabbed one of the last small tables available. It was Patton who took their orders and disappeared back into a mass of people crowded around the bar, shouting at the sweating, busy barmen and women who were trying to keep up.

Danny made an effort to keep the conversation going, but stopped when he saw how wrapped up Skinner was in the atmosphere around them. Every bar in Ireland has it's resident drunk, gossiper or opportunist, perched at one end of the bar or the other, where he can keep an eye on people entering, who he can scrounge drinks from or run out and place a bet for them, or do some other errand. In this pub Wee Willie Rawlins, a slight wizened man of indeterminate age dressed in a scruffy raincoat, held the title. He always appeared to be half asleep, but in fact behind those half closed eyes was an alert brain at work. During 'The Troubles', he had been a double agent for the British Forces and the protestant Ulster Volunteer Force. (UVF). His real master was the UVF who were briefed by him on what the crown forces were up to. With the coming of peace, Wee Willie's regular supply of cash dried up to a small trickle. Now he was always on the lookout for any edge or opportunity that could generate some income, illicit or otherwise.

When Jimmy Patton pushed away from the bar carrying a tray full of drinks, Wee Willie got off his stool and weaved his way after him in an apparent drunken stupor, passing the table where he saw the drinks being deposited in front of two other men. He stumbled past, seemingly immersed in some conversation with himself, and totally disinterested in the people around him.

However, for an instant his eyes flicked sideways and registered something that made him catch his breath.

He went inside the toilet and waited until the two people who were there had left, then he straightened up, suddenly alert, whipped out his mobile phone and dialed a number.

It was a quick conversation.

"Yes, Yes SAS, I'm sure of it, one of them, sitting with two others. I've seen him in Castlereagh Barracks years ago when I was in a meeting with the Brits."

He listened for a moment.

"Right, right, I will Sir… count on it."

He put the cell phone back in his raincoat pocket and hurried out of the washroom.

Scotty McGregor had been riding around in the MI5 vehicle that had followed Danny, Jimmy and the American, when they came back into the city. The vehicle was now parked back up the street. Scotty had got out and positioned himself in the darkened doorway of a small shop across and at an angle from the pub. The shop was closed for the evening. Anyone chancing to spot his vague figure would see a street person with a bottle of wine in his hand.

He shook his head in disgust. 'Boresville, stuck in a windy road in Belfast when Danny was inside quaffing ales and listening to good music' he muttered.

A certain quietness had fallen on the area as the numbers inside had maxed out and taxis stopped dropping off regulars and tourists.

An hour after he had taken up his station he became aware of a small scruffy man who started coming out of the pub and looking anxiously up and down the street. Scotty wondered if he was looking for a taxi for some group inside who were on the verge of leaving. Finally a dark colored van pulled up and double-parked directly across from the pub, about twenty feet from where Scotty was posted. The small scruffy man darted across the street and spoke to someone through the van window. Then he turned and ran back into the pub. The van stayed double-parked, and the occasional car had to drive around it.

'What's going on here?' Scotty wondered and using his collar mike he sent a brief message back to the team in the car.

Another twenty minutes passed, then the pub doors shot open and the small scruffy man was there again, waving his arms at the parked van before running off up the street.

Scotty tensed, taking out his automatic and jacking a round into it.

Three men wearing balaclavas and carrying firearms, leaped out of the back of the van and lined themselves up along the far side of it, their weapons facing the pub. One of them carried a shotgun, and the others had pistols. The driver stayed in the van.

The front door of the pub opened and Danny, Frank Skinner and Jimmy started coming through onto the street.

A number of things happened at once.

The man with the shotgun tensed and leaned forward, pointing towards the pub.

228

Scotty fired at him from the side, slamming him into the gunman next to him, whose weapon went off, sending two shots high. He then caught this gunman with a shot in the hips, sending him screaming to the ground.

All three men coming out of the pub froze at the sound of the gunfire, smashing above them into some glass windows. Then as one, all battle trained, they dived to the ground as additional shots cracked out.

The third attacker turned, sensing Scotty's presence, and lifted his weapon.

Scotty didn't believe in taking chances.

A double tap to the head dropped the assailant like a bag of cement in the street.

The driver of the van put the vehicle in gear and raced away.

Scotty didn't hang about. He belted back up the street and jumped into the MI5 car.

"Let's get the hell out of here!" he gasped.

"Are the others OK?" the team leader asked.

"Yeah, no problems, unless they got hit by some flying glass." Scotty replied.

"Jesus, what the hell happened back there?"

"I haven't a clue Mate. All I know is that the lads would have been totaled if I hadn't been right there."

Back at the pub the three shaken men picked themselves up from the ground and looked around.

"What the hell's going on here?" The American demanded.

"I've no idea." Jimmy replied, "but I see three bodies lying over there and cops will be here any minute. The best plan of action for us, I can tell you right now, is to get the hell out of here. Let's get back to the car and skedaddle, lads."

That seemed good advice so they turned and ran, as the first face appeared cautiously around the pub door.

They sped off minutes later as sirens sounded in the distance.

Frank turned to Jimmy, who was driving. "What the hell did we run into back there?"

He shook his head.

"You know what? I haven't a fucking clue right now. All I know is that we nearly got our heads blown off."

Danny leaned forward from the back seat.

"Could we have been caught in the middle of some turf war? You know, three strangers come into a pub and somebody gets the wrong message and makes a phone call?"

Jimmy thought about it.

"Anything's possible in this city. Since the peace deal came in, it's been all about gangsterism, protection rackets, turf wars and settling old scores. Something may have been going down, and what happened was probably a lousy case of mistaken identity. I brought you there on the recommendation that Frank would see some crack in an Irish pub, with some good music thrown in. I guess I was wrongly advised on that score."

Frank was still looking puzzled.

"Then who was the other party across the street who obviously stopped us from being shot to pieces?"

Danny stuck his head forward again.

"If you were to buy my comment about a turf war, what if there was an attack planned for some of the players inside the pub and it leaked, resulting in that group waiting outside for it to go down. The attacker just happened to be lurking back there behind them in a shop doorway. He seized the opportunity to take down some of the opposition, who effectively appeared right in front of him."

Frank wasn't convinced. "Still doesn't make sense to me. Why shoot at us unless your mythical gunman hiding behind them started shooting, and their automatic response was to pull some triggers by accident and hit the windows above us."

Jimmy nodded. "Could be. Those shots were way too high to catch us, and we were pretty clear targets under the door lights of the pub."

The American still looked annoyed. "I don't believe this! I get out of the Marines and put all that crap behind me. Now I've got people taking pot shots at me as I come out of a fucking pub. Jack, tomorrow I want you to get me the hell out of here. You got that?"

"Yeah, sure Frank, no problem. We'll be on the first flight out."

"Hey, what about the weapons cache and our deal?" Jimmy demanded.

"I'll have to see about that. One thing's for sure, I'm not coming back to Belfast. Now get me back to the hotel. I need a strong drink of that Irish whiskey before I can get to sleep after what we've been through."

CHAPTER 41

Scotty decided to fly direct from Belfast, and visit his brother in Scotland for a couple of days. Jimmy Patton decided to take advantage of the break and visit some family while awaiting the call for him to play the role of an arms procurer, if it was still on.

Back in London, Danny's double life had finally caught up with him. His daughter Allison was still in a safe house, and from all accounts, she badly needed him right then. His ex-wife Fiona was in the morgue, and he had asked Rebecca to try to determine whether some family members would be making arrangements, or if her new boyfriend would want some involvement. He was prepared to pay for the funeral costs himself. There was the whole situation of probating her estate, which presumably would go to Allison. Someone, probably

Danny would have to be the guardian for this arrangement. Did Fiona actually draw up a new will when they were divorced some years back, he wondered?

He was supposed to take ownership of the flat being prepared for the incoming Jihadists, who he was expected to meet off the Euro Train in the coming week. There was still the outstanding ransom demand from Afghanistan where he was required to place an advertisement in The Times newspaper.

Danny also had his own personal vendetta to follow up.

He intended to find the man who had set up the assault on the safe house and was responsible for the cold deliberate murder of Fiona, his ex-wife and mother of Allison.

He couldn't get that blurred face out of his mind, staring through the car window at him as it drove away.

He hadn't had time to go back into Thames House at Jerry Sackville's urging, to examine photos they had of Afghan Embassy personnel, to see if he could get a match for this person. In the interim, he did have an idea. However he needed transport, took a chance and picked up his own vehicle from his house, hoping none of the Jihadists would spot him in the city, however he doubted it as he would be travelling in the opposite direction to their location. The American Frank Skinner, was supposed to arrange a vehicle for him that afternoon, in which he was to collect the incoming Jihadists from the Euro train in a couple of days, as yet unspecified.

Jerry had told him that the three bodies of the attackers had been released to the families, after the autopsies had been completed. They had been advised to keep a lid on the details of their deaths and publicity at this stage. This suited all the families concerned, as there was a question of their Military pensions being stopped for any involvement in criminal activities after discharge.

Jerry had kept a close eye on the whole situation and informed Danny where the funeral for one of the attackers, Al Sinclair, was being held the day after they returned from Belfast. Danny knew that, while it was supposed to be low key, the word would have got out among Sinclair's ex-Military colleagues, and they would be there for sure. He planned to be there as well, to see what information he could pick up.

He suspected that a fourth man, who was manning the compound gate on that fatal night, might be there. Wives would be there too of course, but it would not be the venue for asking questions. However he knew the pattern for the funeral of friends in the Forces: after the burial or cremation, most of the men involved converged on some pub to talk about the deceased, re-live old times, and drown their sorrows.

He had asked Jerry to do some research for him on the postings of the three dead attackers, and had concocted a story in his mind as to where he might have bumped into them during his own service.

He was dealing with the Military Police establishment, so he appreciated that their training made them pretty alert, and as investigators they would have pretty sharp bullshit detectors.

The MP's were also a tough bunch of people. They had to handle some very hard men in their day-to-day work schedule, including Special Forces, when they got out of hand, as they did occasionally.

Normally Special Forces guys kept pretty well to themselves and avoided any altercation with others, be it Military or civilian. Occasionally when too much booze was involved, or a girl friend or a wife was insulted, all rules could be broken, including some heads as well. He had witnessed some pretty tough SAS people being hauled out of pubs by equally tough Military Police, which had affected their careers in a severe way, when brought up on charge in their Units.

A highly trained SAS trooper could easily, in a flash of temper, kill or disable another individual, so any loss of control or stepping over the line, could result in serious repercussions for that soldier. Therefore it didn't happen very often.

He got to the church as the funeral directors were wheeling the coffin in and up to the front. Inside he found a small group of people, concentrated in the top left hand side. He had learned from Jerry that the deceased had been divorced in the past year, but he assumed that the woman in the front row surrounded by a number of people was Sinclair's ex-wife.

After the coffin had been settled, and while they were waiting for the Pastor to emerge, a number of people were going up and shaking hands with the family seated in the front row.

Feeling a bit of a hypocrite, (he had after all killed the deceased) Danny muttered something comforting to the family, as he went along the line. He was also conscious, coming back down the aisle, of a number of eyes appraising him, probably wondering if they could place him from some time past in their Unit.

It was a speedy service, with a very brief and sketchy homily from the Pastor.

There was a short announcement from a family member at its conclusion, to the effect that the deceased was being cremated, and referring people to a nearby hotel for a lunch afterwards. Danny chatted to someone at the back as the church was emptying, and learned that most of the people were going directly to the hotel and having a drink while waiting for the cremation to be over.

That sounded exactly like the opportunity he was looking for, and he drove over, parked, and waited until he felt most of them had gone inside. Then he slipped inside also, rehearsing his story, which he knew he would have to repeat a number of times. He had to sign in at the door. There were already over twenty men in an annex leading to a larger room, which was laid out for the meal later on.

On one of Sinclair's tours, to Afghanistan, he had been tasked with escorting British soldiers, who were in custody for certain crimes against Afghan citizens, to where their Military trial was being carried out. Jerry's research showed that the other men killed at the safe house had not been posted there at the same time. Danny recalled that the Parachute Regiment, like all Units, had to take turns providing personnel to man the Military court and take custody of the accused on delivery by the MPs. He was going to claim that he had met Al Sinclair at that time and had built up a relationship with him. Hence his attendance at the funeral under his present pseudonym of Jack Fisher whose 'legend' or background, MI5 had already set up.

There was always a chance that someone else in the group had been there, and would quickly realize that he was a plant and an imposter. In a worst-case scenario, the fourth man, from the gatehouse, could very well have been there in Afghanistan at the same time.

He always liked the company of ex-Military and was not happy being here with an ulterior motive. However, thinking about Fiona stiffened his resolve as he strolled up to the bar in the lounge and ordered a beer.

He turned back from the bar, hoping that things would be taken out of his hands. If not he was prepared to take the initiative.

He needn't have worried. A solid, balding, forty-five year old pulled away from a group, came across to him and observed him warily.

"With the party then?" he queried.

Jack knew that, probably not recognizing him, they might have thought he was crashing the free bar that was available for mourners.

Danny stuck out his hand. "Oh, Jack Fisher by the way...nooo, I served in Stan in the Para's and got to know Al when he was bringing down our lads who were in Military custody, for their trials. I got stuck there for a few months duty... shitty duty. We were there to give the Afghans democracy, and in thanks they kept reporting our chaps for so-called crimes, just to get their hands on some compo."

The man's face cleared up. "Ah, that's why you're here. Good lad yourself. I'm Jim Perkins, an ex-MP like Al was. The family needs all the support they can get, even though poor Al did get divorced by that bitch of a wife of his who stuck him for everything."

Danny made a face. "Oh, I get it... not the first of us to come back after eating sand for a few years and freezing our balls off, only to get a nasty reception when they came back.

You can add me to that number too Jim. Were you a close mate of AL's then?" he asked casually.

"Yep, on a few U.K. postings. I did Iraq and Stan at different times than Al. Sank a few ales with him here and there. He was like a number of us coming back and getting out.

Just working with these goddam civilians here is so hard to get used to. They had no fucking idea what it was like over there" he grated angrily.

"You got it in one. If I had to do it all over again.... say Jim are there any of Al's other old Mates here today? I wouldn't mind a quick chat before the meal starts which I

236

haven't time to stay for, by the way?" he remarked, looking around the room.

The man looked around, stroking his chin. "Let's see then… close Mates you say. Well as you know we in the Military keep getting moved around all over the place at a moment's notice, so you might say we deliberately avoid making close friends most of the time. You know how it is Jack. However, that small group near the back door might be the closest you'd get to that. Did some time in Stan with him I believe, and have stayed close back home here as well. Come over with me and I'll introduce you."

They skirted around the people congregated in the center of the room and approached the group by the door. As he got closer, Danny was struck by the noticeable Police presence of the four men, who almost looked like clones of each other - short hair, solid builds, alert skeptical eyes and defensive stance. They were now watching him and Jim approach.

"Lads, this is an old friend of AL's from Stan…Jack Fisher, ex- Para, who was handling the custody end of soldiers escorted across by Al for trial. He and Al bumped into each other a few times. He's just here to pay his respects, and has to leave before the grub…wanted to say hello to a few old mates of AL's, before he left."

There were handshakes all round, and two of them used the moment as an excuse to head for the bar and some more free drinks before the funeral party came back. Danny was left with two of them, as Jim headed for the bar as well.

Danny did a quick study of the two men.

While he had initially thought they looked like clones of each other, now he could see a distinct difference between them.

The first was a tall trim forty year old with shrewd watchful eyes, called Eoin Purcell who had apparently lucked into an investigator's role with the Metropolitan Police.

Danny could see him as a very able interrogator, and took an immediate liking to the man. His handshake was warm and his demeanor, while watchful, was friendly.

The second man named Malcolm Watkins was a chunky, slightly overweight man with a pair of bleak watchful eyes. Danny noticed that his handshake was brief, and his hands were sweaty. There was little warmth in him and he looked uneasy with Danny's approach.

"So tell us about knowing Al over there. What was your Regiment doing there before you got stuck in custody duties?" Eoin Purcell asked.

"Let's see. I try to forget most of it. Basically as a Regiment we were up country mostly, supporting various initiatives such as re-construction projects in some of the more friendly villages, if you can call them that. They called it winning hearts and minds. We would provide protection for the re-construction teams who worked with the elders in building community centers and schools, and sometimes drilling wells. We would have regular potshots taken at us during the time we were there from the surrounding hills. Of course, as you all well know, when we left, the Taliban came back in and blew up the community centers and schools and poisoned the wells that had been drilled for them. The custody work, while boring was a nice break for the few who were tasked with it."

"What was Al like?" Watkins asked abruptly.

"Al? Hmm, lets see…a good soldier. I'd say competent, on the ball, missing home like a lot of us, a bit worried I thought about his home situation, though he never said anything specifically about it."

"Did he like to drink?"

Danny recognized that Watkins was testing him and was obviously having some reservations about him.

He didn't have that piece of information on Al's drinking habits and realized he could bury himself on his next answer.

Despite the situation Danny chuckled. "I've no idea about Al's drinking habits. We never met off duty, more's the pity, but if he was like the rest of us, including MPs, he would kill for a cold beer after a day sweating in the temperature over there."

As Danny answered him he was looking directly into his eyes and saw them defocus slightly. He didn't know how, but he was suddenly aware of something with absolute certainty:

Watkins was the fourth man in the attack on the safe house.

Danny broke off after a few moments and proceeded outside.

"Wait up Fisher." He heard a sharp voice behind him.

He turned and saw Watkins standing six feet away from him.

His face was red and his lips tightened and Danny recognized his aggressive stance as signaling a possible attack.

"You forgot that we're Cops and always have that bullshit detector in place. You, my friend, just failed the test. What the fuck are you doing here at Al's funeral? That, to me, is disrespect big time."

Danny easily slipped into a casual defensive posture, usually undetectable by an attacker and replied.

"Why, have you something worrying you right now, where you need to have that bullshit detector in place? I thought you were just here to say good-bye to poor old Al. It's a funny thing in life isn't it, you never know when your time's up, do you?"

Watkins swung at him. A massive blow in a black and fearful rage.

He was a hard, tough ex-Military Cop, but he was in the wrong league.

Danny blocked the blow and slapped a crushing wristlock on him, bringing him to his knees. He could have carried through with a smashing knee to the face and a savage kick to the stomach, but he just held him there as Watkins struggled and tried to stop himself from screaming with the pain.

He leaned forward and whispered in the man's ear. "Keep looking behind you Watkins, 'cos one night when you do, I'll be there to bid you good night."

He put his boot to the man's shoulder and pushed him forward into the gravel, where he lay groaning.

He heard a voice from the door of the restaurant. It was Purcell. "What's up Malcolm, are you all right?"

Danny turned and left.

CHAPTER 42

"Can't you shut that bloody kid up, for God's sake?" Malcolm Watkins shouted as his two year old kept crying non-stop, in the playpen.

His wife turned, as she was placing his supper in the microwave.

"Mal, she's just a child for Pete's sake, and you know she's starting to get some new teeth."

"All she seems to do is cry when I'm around. How come Tommy didn't fucking cry like her when he was her age?"

His wife Annie shook her head wearily. "Because they're all different, that's why. You even heard your mother say that last week. Stop complaining for God's sake, she'll be over it in another six months. Anyway, I asked you not to swear in the house. It's surprising what they pick up. Before you know it Tommy will be effing and blinding around here."

"Six months!" he exclaimed. "I'll be in the nut house if she keeps that up for another six months."

She put the plate down on the counter without starting the microwave and sat down opposite him, a concerned look on her face.

"Look Mal, I know it's been a lousy day for you with Al's funeral and all and the death of your other Mates, but I have to say that you haven't been behaving normally for the past few weeks, and especially last week when you were out late and wouldn't tell me what you were doing. You're in some trouble

241

aren't you? Were you there when they were killed? Is that what this is all about Mal? If so then we're all going to suffer, and that means little Tommy as well. Please tell me I'm wrong" she pleaded, as tears started to trickle down her face.

He started to answer her, only to be interrupted by the doorbell.

He slammed the table. "Who the hell can that be at this time of night?" he growled angrily, getting up and going out into the hallway.

He could make out a muffled shape behind the glass on the door. Suddenly he thought of the man at the funeral earlier in the day and shuddered. The muffled shape on the outside doorstep didn't look big enough.

He opened the door.

Standing there with a large smile on his face was Omar Bashir.

"Ah Malcolm, good, you're home. We need to talk about the ten thousand pounds I put in your bank account. You still haven't earned it yet my friend."

"Shit, you shouldn't have come to my house for Christ's sake! What the hell were you thinking?" he whispered.

His wife's querulous voice came from the kitchen. "Who's at the door Mal?"

Mal leaned forward. "Look I'll meet you at the same place you met Al and the lads. Give me ten minutes."

He slammed the door in his face and turned, just as his wife came into view. He held his hand up.

"Look, forget the supper. I have to go out for a while. Something I forgot to do earlier at the funeral."

He reached for his jacket and keys, opened the door and was gone. His wife watched him leave, ashen faced.

"Oh no, please God no" she whispered. "It's all coming apart, just when I thought we had a chance to get over all the bad stuff that's happened to him in the Military."

She heard his car start up and take off from the driveway.

CHAPTER 43

Danny was glad he'd waited for Watkins to eventually emerge from the hotel. Others were heading off too, as the meal finished.

While waiting, Danny had taken his bag of disguise kits, slipped into a busy bar down the road and went to the washroom. There he quickly changed his appearance, to look like an older man, slipped on a hairpiece that was long and scruffy, and he made sure to alter his walk when he came back out. He topped this off with a rough, well-used jacket, a cheap pair of glasses, and an old pair of runners. Counter surveillance experts had pointed out that many people in the surveillance business didn't change their footwear, and that sometimes gave them away to a trained target.

He doubted if Watkins knew his car, which was deliberatively mundane to blend in with his previous role with MI5.

He hadn't been certain that his quarry would drive himself home, or cadge a lift, because he was drinking. From his previous experience with Police, both civilian and military, they generally felt somewhat untouchable, and were prepared to risk the chance of being stopped.

Watkins didn't appear to take any precautions to check out if he was being followed as he headed home. Danny made a note of the license plate number. The man he was following was smart enough to stick to the speed limit and avoid jumping the traffic lights. The journey took about forty minutes in a southerly direction, and the man ended up in a small tidy estate of about a hundred similar type two-story houses. That presented Danny with a problem in that there wasn't any parking place close by, or coverage to hide his car.

He was lucky to spot a 'For Sale' sign fifty yards up from Watkins's house. The place appeared to be unoccupied, and he backed in.

He took out a pair of binoculars with a built in night vision, though there was still lots of daylight left, and settled in to wait. He was glad he'd used the washroom back in the pub as he had seen many people carrying out surveillance, who had paid the price for drinking too much coffee and had to dash off and find a toilet or a friendly tree nearby, sometimes to return and discover their target had flown, or the surveillance vehicle, containing their colleagues, had gone as well. The experienced male surveillance people always had an empty milk bottle handy.

He had achieved one goal and that was to discover where the ex-MP lived, and he didn't expect much more action from him. However he had decided to give his task at least an hour, and he was glad he did. Another vehicle pulled up behind Watkins's car shortly after he'd got home, and a man got out. Closing up on him, he could only see the back of the man, who was small in stature, as he went up to the door and obviously rang the bell. Watkins was easily recognizable as he opened it, and even from where he sat, Danny could see the angered expression on his face.

Ha, not a happy bunny!

The face-to-face meeting didn't last more than a few minutes. The door appeared to be almost slammed in the face of the visitor who turned and proceeded back down the driveway.

Danny gasped in surprise.

The face he saw was the one he had briefly seen fleeing from the scene after the assault on the safe house. He did indeed look like an Afghan. Danny now had a better target to follow. His target's vehicle looked like it was fairly new and he wondered if it might be able to give him the slip on the way back, presumably into London. If the man was with Intelligence at the Afghan Embassy, he might very well be a lot more aware of being followed, and take evasive action.

As the man's vehicle moved past where he was parked, Danny crouched down out of sight. He started up his car and was about to pull out and follow him, when he spotted Watkins backing his out of the driveway and speeding up the road behind the Afghan.

Watkins was obviously following the Afghan… better still.

He pulled out, and when they got onto a major road, he placed himself a couple of cars back. After a few times at traffic lights where Watkins appeared to be in no hurry to keep up with the Afghan, he realized that the man was probably going to some meeting place, just arranged by the caller to his house.

He relaxed somewhat.

Twenty minutes later Watkins pulled into the parking lot of a major hotel chain, got out and proceeded inside.

After a few minutes Danny, having parked, headed into the building. He stopped for a moment to memorize the Afghan's number plate. No diplomatic sticker, he noted with satisfaction.

Conscious that the Afghan might be shrewd enough to be watching from inside, he wandered off to one side of the hotel, as if heading elsewhere.

He was also aware that he wasn't properly dressed to be visiting a major hotel chain, and wouldn't even get past the doorman. He managed to haul out some more appropriate clothing, changed his wig to a better one, and placed a better class of glasses on his face.

He remembered to switch his runners, and went inside.

He spotted them at the far end of the bar lounge which only had a small number of people frequenting it. The two men were huddled together and appeared to be in heated discussion. He wished he had some way to listen in, but it was not to be. He was lucky to have stumbled on Watkins and the Afghan in the first place. It looked like the meeting was underway, and they were not expecting any more people to join them, so he figured he was looking at the two remaining people who were responsible for killing his ex-wife.

He couldn't afford to hang around the hotel for long without arousing the curiosity of Security, but there was one more thing he could do.

Back outside, he retrieved two bugs and slipped them without being noticed, underneath the vehicles. If they weren't discovered by a professional sweep, he could keep a close eye on them and give the knowledge over to Jerry and his team. MI5 had lost four Agents and had a long memory. They wouldn't waste any time in following up on the information.

Danny still had his own personal agenda to take care of, where those two men were concerned. He wasn't intending to leave them to the tender mercies of the law. He had other ideas in mind.

CHAPTER 44

Omar Bashir didn't like what he saw in the man sitting across from him.

Malcolm Watkins smelled of drink and sweat, looked disheveled, and frightened. Bashir ordered two coffees, and having added four spoons of sugar, he stirred and raised the cup delicately to his lips and observed the man across from him.

Putting the cup back down, his lips tightened as he appraised Watkins.

"You look upset my friend. What have you been up to?" he asked.

"I've been at a bloody funeral today... for poor fucking Al! So much for a well-planned operation where we would get in and out. You're responsible for killing all three of them" he snarled, his face red with anger.

"Wait a minute. As I recall, you four signed off on the plan, and had your friends been half as good as they claimed, it should have been a cakewalk. Basically, you took my money and didn't deliver. I'm here to put that right."

Watkins stared at him. "Just what the hell do you mean 'put it right'?"

"Your target on that particular evening is still walking around large as life. You and your friends agreed to the contract, and as the sole survivor, I'm holding you responsible.

I want you to complete the deal you signed up for and were paid for. There's no such thing as a free meal my friend."

Watkins stared at him. "You must be fucking kidding! All my Mates are dead, thanks to you. I'm in no shape to complete any goddam contract, and I don't have any more Mates who would get involved, for starters. Look, I'm happy to give you the money back if that's the problem."

"Not an option my friend. The only way out for you is to kill this man. I'll supply the intelligence, the where and when, and you do the killing."

Watkins looked around wildly, sweat popping out on his forehead.

"Stop calling me your friend, you bastard. I'm not your friend. You're responsible for killing my Mates for Christ's sake. If I have to, I'll go to the Police and take my chances. After all I didn't kill anyone, just guarded a gate, that's all."

"As an ex-Policeman, I'm sure you understand that your involvement in a crime makes you equally guilty under the law. No, it would not go well for you my friend, or for little Tommy…"

Watkins's eyes widened. "What do you know about my family? You stay away from them you hear?" he hissed, leaning forward. Then thinking of something, a half smile came to his face.

"You couldn't touch this chap anyway, he's one scary son of a bitch, I can tell you!"

Bashir's face changed. "What are you saying? You've met this Quigley? When? Where?"

"I thought that might get to you. Yeah, Quigley… he was at the funeral today and guess what? He twigged that I was the fourth man, and even threatened to get me some night. He's one dangerous looking dude MY FRIEND."

The Afghan's cup dropped noisily to his saucer, causing people in the lounge to look over at them.

"Quigley knows about you? Did he say anything about me?" he whispered, leaning closer.

Watkins was enjoying seeing the man's fear.

"Oh, it's Watkins now is it? Where's 'my friend' gone? No, he didn't ask about you, but I wouldn't be surprised if he wasn't sniffing around your heels pretty smartish, looking for you MY FRIEND, having been responsible for killing his ex-wife, the mother of his daughter. I'll bet he'll have something real special in mind for you."

Bashir's eyes were flicking around, obviously thinking hard.

Finally he stirred. "And did you even take any precautions driving home afterwards, to make sure he didn't follow you? You were probably half drunk already, and haven't a clue have you?"

Watkins looked stunned. "Shit, I never thought…"

Bashir shook his head. "How could I have been so stupid to get involved with an incompetent bunch like you and your friends, tell me that?"

"You've killed three of my friends and ruined my life, whatever happens. I wish I'd never set eyes on you. And you know what? I wish I'd taken out a whole bunch of you fucking Afghans when I had the chance over there" he said feelingly.

Bashir was silent for a long moment, regarding him thoughtfully. Then he shrugged. "Win a few, lose a few. OK I understand. You don't want to get involved any further. You're a family man and have responsibilities and have just seen your friends killed. Tell you what; let's call it a day. You can keep the money I sent to your account, and to encourage you to keep your mouth shut and not go to the Police, I'm prepared to give you an additional bonus, which I have in my car outside. Then we'll call it quits. I'll never bother you again. How's that sound?"

Watkins face lightened.

"You mean that? It ends here? You won't come round bothering me again? That's pretty decent of you. Shit, yeah man, I'll buy into that."

Bashir smiled and leaned forward, shaking his hand.

"All's well that ends well. Isn't that what you English say? Let me get that ah, envelope from my vehicle, and I'll join you in your car in a moment."

Watkins went outside and across to his own vehicle. He was humming quietly to himself when Bashir slipped into the back seat, but he didn't hum for long when Bashir slipped a steel wire garrote over his head and jerked back viciously.

CHAPTER 45

Danny drove over to the Sally Ann and discussed some ideas with his contact Kevin, the supervisor, who understood the covert role he was playing. Then he went into the back room and called Phil Dawson, the bugging and burglaring specialist, and talked through a procedure he wanted to put in place the following morning. He also managed to get through to the counter surveillance manager and passed on the information about placing the two bugs in the vehicles shortly before. They would access the details of the owner of the second car as well, and jumped at the idea of following up immediately on the information. Apparently the teams watching the Jihadists were getting bored stiff with nothing happening.

He would have them disengage from that job and head over to where the vehicles were last seen for starters. In any event, there was no hiding place for them now, with the bugging device attached.

Danny had already briefed the DG on returning from the Belfast trip, but he called her again and filled her in on the new developments with Watkins, and his meeting with the person he had recognized from the safe-house attack.

She was pretty excited about the breakthrough, as it might be bringing them closer to have the Police make an arrest. Before he broke off, he shared his plans for the following morning that he had arranged with some of the in-house staff.

He had no sooner rung off when the phone rang.

It was from the surveillance team.

They had got to the hotel, and the car belonging to Watkins was still parked there. They watched it for a while, and sent one of the team inside to check the lounge where the two men had been meeting, according to Danny's account.

There was no sign of two people having a meeting.

Outside, one of the team casually walked up past the car, and in doing so, spotted what looked like blood splashed on the inside of the windscreen.

On checking closer, and peering inside the vehicle, they could see that the driver had obviously been killed in a violent manner. They had no option but to call the Police, who were already there, asking questions and demanding answers. After the MI5 cover up at the safe house, they wouldn't be satisfied with being blind-sided again on this new development.

Peter wanted to know what he could divulge to the Police at this stage. Could he tell them about the man who had just had a meeting with the deceased, and details of his plate number, and the bug installed on it?

Danny's mind flew in all directions at once. The investigators would very quickly find out that a Jack Fisher had turned up at the funeral and had an altercation outside the hotel with Watkins.

He would be immediately under suspicion.

If the Police pulled him in, he couldn't afford to drop out of sight, with the Jihadist operation where it was right then. He hated to do it, but suggested to feed the information to the Police about the second vehicle and its driver, in the hope that it would distract from his involvement. His plan had been to find this individual and extract the ultimate penalty himself.

It might still be possible.

Even if there was proof of the Afghans involvement in the death of Watkins, and he was arrested, he would no doubt, with a good lawyer, be out walking the streets in no time at all, awaiting trial.

That would give Danny an opportunity to settle the score.

Rebecca herself called him back some time later.

"Pretty shitty news Danny. We ran the number plate on that car and it belongs to a man called Omar Bashir, and guess what? He's with the Afghan Embassy and has full diplomatic immunity. In other words the Police can't touch him."

"Can't touch him? After being responsible for what, at least ten deaths so far including Watkins tonight? I can't believe this Rebecca! So what happens to him then?"

"Basically, if the Police believe they have evidence that can justify court proceedings against someone with diplomatic immunity, they can request a waiver in order to arrest, interview under caution, and if appropriate bring charges. This is done through the Diplomatic Protection Group via the FCO, (The Foreign and Commonwealth Office), to ask for a waiver of immunity for this individual, to the Head of Missions concerned, in this case Afghanistan. If they refuse, the FCO can ask this person and their family to leave the U.K. within 31 days I believe. At this early stage in the investigation, I've no idea if the Police will ask for a waiver."

"What about the fact that he was driving a car with no diplomatic plates on it? Could they pull him in on that basis?" he asked.

"There's nothing against any Diplomat getting a private car. A lot of them prefer it to drawing attention to themselves, for example dropping kids off at schools, shopping and so on. If this Omar Bashir was in Intelligence, he could slip around the U.K. pretty well unnoticed, which might suit him in his role."

"So he walks?" Danny whispered, "after what he's done? No way Jose, no fucking way!"

"Danny!" she said warningly "Leave this one alone. It would only get you in a real heap of trouble, and need I remind you, MI5 as well."

He wasn't listening.

He hung up.

CHAPTER 46

His daughter Allison squealed with delight when she saw him, but Danny's heart filled with remorse when he saw in her face the pain from seeing her mother shot right in front of her, and re-living the on-going trauma of her death. It came home to him forcibly that she was already showing the physical signs of growing into a lovely young woman. He wondered how he would cope with all the areas that Fiona would have handled so efficiently and with such ease. Allison had proved in the past that she was a pretty tough and resilient person, and he believed she would rally after this tragedy as well and get on with her life.

When she finally stopped clinging to him, he went and talked to the two Agents manning the safe house. They had no problems with him taking her out for a few hours to get her away from the confinement of the situation. In fact they welcomed the opportunity to do some pressing personal tasks that had been building up. He collected the re-entry details, including the alarm codes, in the event that he returned before them, and set off, trying to put all the other demanding situations in his life on the back burner for the moment.

Rebecca had advised him that she had managed to contact some relatives of Fiona, and they had suggested arranging the funeral the following week as some other members were off in Greece on a holiday. Fiona's boyfriend was very upset and was planning to move out of the house, realizing that it wouldn't be practical to stay there and take on the role of Allison's guardian. This task, he assumed, would now fall on Danny as her father. He did however, want to be informed of the funeral details when they were organized. Rebecca hadn't heard any suggestions of anyone else taking on the cost or the arrangements, and contacted a funeral director on Danny's behalf.

He took Allison for a walk in Hyde Park, where she enjoyed feeding the ducks and watching the graceful swans gliding across the waters. She had many questions too. It was then that he filled her in on the proposed arrangements for her mother's funeral and tried to address some of her anxieties and fears about the future. He still wasn't sure how this would play out, in particular, his own role in her life and how it would manifest.

He'd had his own flashbacks of his earlier life with Fiona, and while they were initially exceedingly happy together, he realized that it was his increasing Military commitments, that eventually eroded their marriage to the extent that the Military became his number one 'family'. It was thanks to Fiona's insistence that he take his discharge or else, that he had left the Service.

He was glad he did, as he'd re-discovered a beautiful young daughter who adored him and needed him as a father. Fiona, despite his discharge, still divorced him, but he never neglected his new and increasingly fulfilling relationship with Allison.

They stopped for some goodies at one of the refreshment stands and, despite everything, Danny felt part of himself relax inside. There was a limit to what he could disclose about his current operation, as that would have increased her insecurities, having just lost a mother to the people who were still at large and a danger to him.

All too soon, it was time to head back to the safe house where the two Agents had got in shortly before them.

When he hugged her goodbye, she wouldn't let him go for a long time, and eventually the female Agent gently took her arm and led her inside.

Danny didn't look back—he couldn't.

His next job was to contact the American, Frank Skinner and fill him in on a few ideas he'd had about furnishing the new flat on Canary Wharf. He told him that the Sally Ann had just received a delivery of used furniture that was apparently in excellent shape, and that they were willing to pass it on to Danny for a small contribution. He was heading down to the flat and would contact Zain's sister while he was there. Frank told him he would be coming round later in the afternoon with a used seven-seater van they would use for picking up the new expected Jihadists and transporting them around.

It was all in the timing.

He belted around to the flat and met Zain's sister on the way out to do some grocery shopping. Her black eyes still regarded him suspiciously, and she sniffed derisively when he told her of his offer of some furniture from the Sally Ann.

When she disappeared round the corner, he hauled out his mobile phone and called the team that Phil Dawson had thrown together. They already had the used furniture in the Sally Ann van, which arrived promptly, with all four Agents, wearing off-white working coveralls.

The furniture was basically dumped around the flat without any specific planning. He figured that he'd leave that to the suspicious sister to arrange.

Then they went about the real purpose of the visit, quietly and efficiently, while Danny kept an eye on the street for any unexpected visitors such as Frank turning up early, or inquisitive neighbors in the building.

He needn't have worried.

The work was completed inside twenty minutes.

Even Phil Dawson, the manager and overseer of the operation was rubbing his hands in satisfaction.

"We've got them here, covered from all directions. Even if they do a sweep it's the latest gadgets that we've picked up from the CIA via MI6, and it's undetectable. Unfortunately there's no phone installed in the flat, but not much will go on around here without us knowing. Stick a bug on that new vehicle the American friend's bringing round this afternoon, and we'll have all the bases covered, as the Americans say. Anything else Danny, or should I say 'Jack' to keep you in the proper ID?"

"I just remembered that my ex-SAS colleague in Belfast started to call me Danny and stopped just in time. I dummied up some story about how he used to call me Daddio in the past, which really pissed me off. The American swallowed it."

They both laughed and he could hear Phil sharing the story as the team headed off down the corridor. Within moments they had disappeared from the street outside. When the sister returned over an hour later she walked into the flat using her own key, looked around and sniffed again. Then she left, still saying nothing. He got the feeling that he shouldn't look forward to building a long-term relationship with her.

When Frank came round later with Zain and Mohammed in tow, he was glad that neither his MI5 colleagues or Zain's sister, had settled in the various bits and pieces of beds and cupboards. The Jihadists knew exactly what they wanted and set about arranging the stuff in various rooms.

He was surprised how good they were.

Frank laughed at his astonishment. "Zain used to be an interior decorator at one time. He has his uses. Nice job on the purchases by the way. What did they charge you?"

"Five hundred pounds including delivery with four chaps lugging the stuff in. They were in and out in twenty minutes."

"Not bad at all...Yeah, I could see they didn't have much imagination as to where they put the stuff. Probably some of your old friends from the street. They couldn't wait to get back and buy their next bottle of plonk with the money you gave them."

He was obviously pleased, looking around the lounge with some satisfaction.

"Yep, it's coming together Jack... I like that. In a couple of days I'll have the arrival details of the new people for you. Let's go outside and you can take over the new vehicle."

It was an old model, unremarkable seven passenger SUV with tinted windows.

Frank still looked proud of it. "They had to access this from somewhere in Wales, to get me one with tinted windows. Not too popular today I'm told, and probably illegal."

Frank handed him the keys and showed him where the vehicle documents were, then he turned to Danny.

"I need to check that you have a current license Jack, to validate the insurance and make sure if you're stopped, that you're legal. OK with that?"

Danny shrugged. They were still checking him out.

"Sure, no problem there Frank." He hauled out the Jack (John) Fisher driving license that MI5 had arranged as part of his legend. Frank laughed when he looked at it. "Even the Brits follow the lead of John F. Kennedy...calling yourself Jack. I don't blame you, John in my opinion, is a rather insipid name, don't you think?"

"You got it in one Frank... I learned that early on in school. Now what about our friend in Belfast, if he's not still running after being shot at the other night? Do you still have an interest in trying to chase up that cache of weapons?"

"Hmm... you know what Jack, there's something about that whole thing that doesn't smell right. I don't know what it is. I'm out of my league here. Is it the sense that there are things going on over there that I'm dubious about? Are there parties involved that are just setting us up to get their hands on our money? This sixth sense, if you like, has never let me down in the past. I'm just not comfortable about the whole thing."

"Fine by me Frank. Is the deal dead in the water, or is there some way they could satisfy you at this stage?" Danny queried, studying the man's face.

"Well, nothing is ever over my friend. I mean if they arranged a nice clean delivery here in the U.K. and we could verify what we're getting...who knows, but right now it's no longer on the cards. I do have other irons in the fire that will amaze you. More about that later."

They chatted some more, but despite Danny's casual efforts, he was unable to tease out any further details. He was particularly interested in the man's statement about 'having other irons in the fire'. MI5 would be going spare on hearing that remark.

Did the Jihadists have a delivery of weapons en route to the U.K.? With what in mind? In particular, what were they targeting?

CHAPTER 47

Alina looked delighted to see him at the front door and drew him inside, giving him a long hug. He didn't realize how hungry he was until he smelled a tempting aroma coming from the kitchen.

She raised an eyebrow.

"Want something to eat? I just did a nice mild chicken curry and some rice, and apple pie for desert."

"You betcha! I didn't realize how hungry I was until I came in here. As long as I'm not taking your meal, fantastic, bring it on" he exclaimed.

The next half hour sped by as they shared the food together and he filled her in on how things had blown up in Belfast.

She was shaking her head in disbelief.

"There's no doubt about it… trouble really does seem to follow you around. A simple sting operation turns into an attempted assassination on the three of you. Remind me, who was it made that statement?"

"My ex wife Fiona actually. You probably heard it from Rebecca."

"Ooops, sorry didn't mean to bring her name up."

"No, it's OK, I was filling Allison in on the arrangements for her funeral next week. I'm not quite sure of the actual day yet, and I'm hoping that I'm not involved then with the new bunch of Jihadists coming in any day now. At the moment I'm meeting myself coming back, as it were."

"Speaking of Jihadists, I just finished reading in the Telegraph that the number of them who travel to Syria to fight with the Islamic State of Iraq and the Levant (ISIL) has exceeded seven hundred. Further bad news is that three hundred and twenty 'dangerous' Jihadists have now returned to the U.K."

He grimaced. "There's no doubt we're heading for serious trouble here. I really worry about what's ahead for Allison and young people like her."

"How is Allison taking it Danny?" she asked, taking his hand and moving them across to the settee.

"Like a flipping trooper actually, but I suspect she's suffering in her own way. Imagine seeing your mother shot right in front of you."

She shuddered. "I'd rather not, if you don't mind. What's happening on that front? I understand this man, what's his name?"

"Omar Bashir."

"Right, Omar Bashir, from the Afghan Embassy, probably in Intelligence, can't be pulled in for questioning unless the Police ask for a waiver through the Foreign Commonwealth Office. I don't fully understand this procedure. Have you heard any more on it?"

He shrugged. "I just talked to Rebecca and she didn't actually say it, but it's probably a non-starter. Even if it was, it would take a while and give this creep time to cover his tracks and get rid of any evidence."

She smiled in sympathy. "Well, you know the odds in breaking cases, they're either cracked in the first forty eight hours or don't get solved. What happened with his vehicle you bugged?"

"The Police have confiscated that, and you can bet your boots, it'll be examined thoroughly. If this Bashir is actually in Intelligence, he probably has enough smarts to make sure he's left no evidence in the vehicle."

She nodded, looking closely at him. "So, he could get away with this? I mean, ten people that we know of, murdered, including Fiona, by this bastard! How d'you feel about that?"

"Off the record Alina, he's a dead man walking around right now. I just have to catch up with him at the right time and place."

"Whew, you don't mince your words Danny! Does Rebecca know how you feel?"

"Yes, and she told me in no uncertain words to leave it to the Police, or she would see that I was charged in the criminal court. I hung up on her in the end" he said bitterly.

"Danny, Danny, get real here. She probably knows how you're feeling right now as I do, but she couldn't say anything else. She's the head of MI5 for Pete's sake, and could never be involved in having someone killed. She's sworn to uphold the law and can never step outside of that. If she did, the word would get out sooner rather than later and her career would be finished. She'd probably end up in criminal court herself."

He nodded. "Yeah, I got a bit hot under the collar. I should have said nothing at all and taken care of this Bashir in my own way. What's your thoughts on it Alina?"

Her face tightened. "How do I feel about it? We lost four good Agents that I'd come to know quite well - men I respected and liked. All have families who miss them dearly. Personally, I couldn't turn my back and let this cold murderer leave the country. If there was any chance to even the score on this Danny, and you have some idea how to make it happen, then I want in. You got that?"

"I got it, and as a matter of fact I do have a small job for you to take on, which I was sure you'd turn me down on when I first thought of it."

"OK, tell me…"

He pulled her close and kissed her… for a long time.

"Hmm… you know what, you're something else" he whispered, and kissed her some more. "How about we leave this topic till later?"

They never left the couch.

Dessert was forgotten.

CHAPTER 48

"Where the hell have you been? I've been trying to contact you. I even tried that chap at the Sally Ann, but he hadn't a clue." The American snapped when he came into the house which he, Zain Waheed and Mohammed Shareef shared.

Danny stopped in his stride.

"I woke with a bitch of a tooth-ache this morning, and had to queue up in one of those emergency clinics for a few hours. Jeez, sorry about that Frank. What's the big rush anyway?"

"Our people are coming in this afternoon off the Euro Train at St Pancras, and you're supposed to be picking them up, that's what this is all about. I even ran over to the flat at Canary Wharf looking for you. I can't afford you disappearing like that in future Jack. I'm running a tight ship here, and I've invested quite a lot in you already, so shape up from now on. Am I loud and clear?"

Danny lifted his hands apologetically. "Hey Frank, I'm cool with that. I thought they weren't coming in for a couple of days yet or I would have stayed closer."

Frank looked only slightly mollified. "Change of plans… connections fell in place on the airlines and they're on their way. You need to be there ahead of the 3pm arrival this afternoon. Try to get a parking spot close up, which won't be easy at that location."

"Fine, I'll be there. Now, how will I recognize them or will I hold up one of those signs that people do waiting for groups coming in?" he enquired.

Frank went and picked up something that had been lying behind a door into a storage cupboard. It was a sign on a handle that read 'Horizon Tours'.

He handed it to Danny. "This should do it—they know to look for it. Now it's not a meet and greet. When you have the six people assembled, you turn and head out of the station with them in tow, and load them and their stuff into the vehicle. Then bring them to the flat at Canary Wharf. I should mention that Zain's sister has been tasked with getting a supply of food in for the group, and she'll take on the job of cooking for them."

Danny nodded. "Sounds straight forward. They wouldn't have liked what I would have bought in the supermarket anyway. Now will you be at the St. Pancras station as well?"

"I'll be there with Zain and Mohammed, but we'll be keeping well back and observing what's going on. Will there be Immigration or Police interest? Will any of them be detained or taken aside for questioning? Will you be followed when you exit the station?"

"OK, you brought up a point Frank. If any one of the group are pulled aside, and there are only four or five people waiting, do I wait around for the other to turn up?"

"We talked about that very possibility Jack. If one's missing, it would be normal to wait for ten to fifteen minutes, but anything beyond that time span could mean some problem. I don't want someone who's raised suspicion, to lead back to the group."

"Makes sense. Will the group understand that if the situation arises? You told me it's not a meet and greet situation. However, if they're missing a colleague, they may want to discuss it with me and hang on past the fifteen minutes."

"Jack, you worry too much. These guys are Military trained. They understand discipline and they've been scripted on this. After that short time span waiting, they get the hell out of there pronto. Any more queries?" he sounded weary.

He didn't.

Down the road in the surveillance vehicle, Alina picked up her phone and called Jerry Sackville, counter terrorist investigations at MI5, and filled him in on the conversation she had just heard.

He sounded surprised. "Six of them coming in this afternoon? I haven't heard a thing from Interpol, or our contacts abroad. They must have pretty good cover for their trip then. We'll have a team there of course, and record the meeting with Danny. Critical to have pictures of them. Now, d'you want us to arrange with Immigration to hold any of them or let them all through?"

"I haven't discussed this with anyone at this stage. Danny got hit with it only moments ago. I'd suggest letting them all through, but make it real as well, otherwise they might get suspicious."

"OK, I get it, but not to extend the questioning beyond the ten, fifteen minute time span. Would that be your take on it?"

"Yes, on the assumption their clearance is smooth through Immigration, but as you know anything can happen. One of the terrorists may not be too well versed in his story and let slip something that an Immigration Officer can't let pass. Danny's instructions are to bail out with the rest of the group if it appears that one of them's being detained for too long."

"OK, got it. This doesn't give me much time Alina. I have to move my ass... Bye."

CHAPTER 49

Danny lucked in when circling the streets around St. Pancras station, coming upon someone pulling out, and managed to slip into the vacant parking spot. It was situated a nice 60 yards from the station and he made sure to pay for a parking ticket that extended beyond the time period he expected to be there.

London Parking Inspectors were notorious for getting bonus travel rewards for the number of tickets they wrote, and because a number of them couldn't even speak understandable English, harassed motorists had learned the futility of even trying to communicate with them. The Inspector's favorite retort, by rote, when a car owner tried to complain was: "you go see lawyer!"

He'd heard of a painter and decorator business that spent one week in every month in traffic court. This, despite the fact that they were permitted to park and unload materials for a short time span. Unfortunately, the Inspector turned a blind eye to it and dinged them anyway.

Still with time on his hands, and being familiar with the layout of the station from previous trips, he went off and ordered a pot of coffee from one of the small restaurants inside.

He kept a sharp eye out for the American and his fellow Jihadists but never spotted any of them. With ten minutes before the arrival of the Eurostar, he made his way across to the area where people were already gathered to greet arrivals. He positioned himself up near the left front, and as people started to straggle through, he lifted the 'Horizons' sign up so that it would clearly be seen by the arrivals. He did a quick sweep around the area behind him, but still no sign of Frank or his friends.

The crowd thickened and he scanned the faces carefully, his focus primarily on Asian looking men, though it occurred to him that there could very well be white Jihadists among them as well. He hadn't clarified this point with the American, but he needn't have worried about missing them.

They saw his sign first and pointed over at him, pushing through the milling passengers, four of them with Pakistani appearance, though there was one that could have been of Somali or African descent. They crowded around him, saying nothing, and the incongruity of it struck him.

All about were the happy smiles and greetings of people being met, while beside Danny were four silent individuals with one distinct difference: the thousand yard stares of men who had just come off the battlefield.

Two missing.

He glanced backwards and caught a fleeting glimpse of Zain's face peering across from behind a pillar.

The crowd kept flowing past.

Other hotel greeters were holding up signs offering transport back into town.

The four men still stood silently, but one of them, possibly their leader, glanced at his watch, starting to look tense. Danny didn't need to, he was facing a large clock on a wall directly in front of him.

Ten minutes had passed.

In five minutes he would have to leave with the four in front of him. Then he heard the first sound from the group… a collective grunt or release of air.

The two missing men rushed up, breathing hard.

The leader leaned forward and had a brief conversation with them. Then he turned, his cold eyes fastened on Danny, and he nodded.

With that Danny turned and made his way swiftly outside, and up to the car, getting the trunk and side doors open. In minutes the men had thrown their backpacks in the trunk and climbed inside. The person he assumed as the leader sat in the front with him. He was aware of a pair of gimlet eyes focused on him.

"How far to go?" he asked.

Danny glanced across. "Oh, thirty minutes, give or take. You probably know London, it depends on traffic."

The thousand-yard stare looked right through him.

"Just drive and shut up!"

Hmm, someone else who didn't want to build a long-term relationship with him. This chap would get along really well with Zain's sister, he thought.

It was a quiet trip.

Checking in the rear view mirror, he was conscious of hard, hateful eyes looking back at him.

He stopped himself from shaking his head. Why in God's name were they allowing these radicalized and brainwashed Jihadists, whose sole aim was to destroy the whole system, back into the U.K.? These men were straight off the battlefield, and had seen and perpetrated every cruelty known to man, without any compunction whatsoever. For some reason he recalled a story on the news recently where a killer tiger in India had killed hundreds of villagers before a professional hunter was brought in and killed it. He was more than willing to take on the job.

On arrival at the flat, the group followed him inside where they were greeted by Zain's sister who spoke to them in what he assumed was the Pakistani language. The first sign of life came from them when she pointed to the set table waiting for them, and they smelled the aroma of cooking food.

The American with his two colleagues hustled in the door within minutes. Danny slapped the keys to the vehicle into his hands.

He looked startled. "Hey, what's this Jack?"

"I get enough crap in life without taking it from these guys. They could use a lesson in manners, especially their leader... I'm off."

"Hey, wait a minute Jack, look they've had a long lousy trip back here, not knowing if they would be picked up coming back in. Lots of tension. Give them a break OK?"

Danny shrugged, saying nothing, and moved towards the door.

Frank followed him.

"I was hoping we could use you tomorrow to give an unarmed combat session to Zain and Ali and the new arrivals. The leader you mentioned is apparently well qualified in this...has some sort of black belt, so it could be more interesting for you. I was thinking around noon in the same place as the last time. That sound OK with you?"

Danny glanced sideways and was immediately aware of the leader's black eyes watching him. 'Why not?' he thought 'it might be an opportunity to teach this Jihadist some manners', then he realized he had just made a fairly common mistake, under-estimating an opponent's skills.

He nodded to the American. "Yeah, sure, I'll be there" he replied somewhat grudgingly.

CHAPTER 50

Danny Quigley had amassed quite a load of useful experience over the years about various styles of martial arts. In his leave periods in the Military, prior to him getting married, he had travelled to various dojos in Japan, South Korea and Germany to perfect his skills in judo, which had been his first preference. He had also taken time out from his judo practices to take courses in some of the other aggressive martial arts systems such as karate, taekwondo, and others. He hadn't been interested in being graded in all of these particular arts, just interested in taking on board some of the moves and techniques involved, and dovetailing them with his own highly effective techniques.

He had learned basic unarmed combat skills when he joined the Parachute Regiment before qualifying for the elite Special Air Service (SAS).

The advanced Special Forces training further enhanced and honed his own martial arts skills to a whole new level. The focus then was different: disabling or killing an enemy quietly and with deadly efficiency.

One of his advantages lay in the remarkable speed of his reactions in unarmed combat. One of his SAS instructors remarked that it seemed he had some sort of in-built computer that enhanced his reaction time when fighting.

His Commanding Officer made no bones about it when commending him to a U.S. Military Police Colonel who wanted Danny's help in sorting out some troublemakers in the local pubs in the U.K. - "Quigley's a walking killing machine," he stated.

Danny had been interested in a competition he had heard about in South America between the various top-graded martial arts proponents, to see who came out on top: The judo specialists came out streaks ahead of any other fighting skill. It came down to the fact that sooner or later opponents fell into a clinch as they bumped into each other. It didn't matter what system they were following. Then the judo people used that instant to slam them on to the ground with a high hip throw... a win!

When he came into the building they had used the first time for training, he was surprised to hear the sound of activity out on the floor. The American met him, wearing a look of concern on his normally relaxed face.

"We ran into a bit of a problem last night after you left, when I mentioned the combat training you were putting on this morning."

"What sort of a problem? It's no big deal is it? Just like the last time, only a few extra bodies."

"Well, it's like this. One of these new people Syed Hussein, I believe he sat in the front with you last night, is apparently some sort of karate expert."

Danny looked puzzled. "So what, that's great, we can bring him in as well and make the work-out even more interesting. I don't see any problem?"

Frank looked embarrassed. "Hussein has apparently been training large groups of Jihadists over in Syria and Iraq and is highly looked up to. He feels that it's below them to have an infidel training his warriors with inferior teachings, when he's here to do it. He wants you to defer to his experience. He already decided to start them off this morning. In fact he's stated that he's quite willing to challenge you on the mat to prove the superiority of his teachings."

Danny looked surprised. "Hmm, unusual attitude I must say."

"Why d'you say that Jack?"

"Well most of the really top rated people rarely make a boast about how good they are. They're willing to learn from everyone, and show respect for whatever level of grading one has attained. All I can think of is that it must be a Muslim thing… correction Jihadist, because I've met a number of really competent Muslim practitioners who have no attitude problems. Anyway, let's take a look at the inside."

The five of the new arrivals plus Zain and Mohammed were out on the floor working through some routine.

He spotted Hussein right away. He was the one wearing the karate uniform with his belt grading clearly marked.

Danny knew that the grading process for karate was not unlike that in judo, where one worked through various stages, reflected by the colors of the belts earned. In karate, he was aware, one worked through ten Kyu grades, starting at ten and going down to one, which could take from four to five years.

After that it took eight to eighteen months to work up to first black belt level, known as Sho Dan. It took two years after that to get up to second grade black, known as No Dan and a further three years to third black belt level, known as San Dan…

He stopped there at this level as he spotted that Hussein wore a third Dan black belt.

"Interesting" he commented.

The American's head shot sideways. "Interesting, what do you mean?"

"Hussein's wearing a third degree black belt."

"How d'you know that, and what's interesting about it?"

"Third degree level can wear one gold stripe for each level attained, and Hussein is wearing three. What's interesting is that most black belts, out of humility, don't actually display the gold stripes, indicating their level attained. It's still quite an achievement, and you're probably talking about at least ten years of classes for Hussein to get there."

"So he's pretty darn good then?"

"Oh yeah for sure, and with his height and long legs he'll be quite an opponent to face out on the mat."

"So you defer to him then? Wise decision I'm thinking."

"Actually no, and for two reasons: one, I always like a challenge where I hope to learn something about fighting, and two because he pissed me off last night treating me like a door mat."

Frank grunted. "Better to suck it up Jack than getting your ass kicked all over the place. This guy Hussein looks pretty damned mean and you could get hurt out there. You're no good to me if you're banged up. Remember I'm still paying you. These guys will be gone up to Birmingham in a couple of days and be out of your hair."

Danny grinned. "Thanks for the advice Frank, but I'll go and change into my gear and warm up inside. I'll be out in about ten minutes. You figure out who's going to be the referee and the rules we're working with."

Danny normally used more time for warm up, especially where he faced imminent combat from an aggressive opponent as soon as he stepped on the mat. Today he speeded this up and went through a mental rehearsal as he did so. He recalled all the competitions he had been involved in and the tactics that had won the day for him. He went over the very valuable lessons he had learned in various dojos around the world. He re-visited his SAS combat training and recalled the stances he had used in blocking brutal attacks. He recalled karate competitions he had watched, and the deadly blows from hand and feet that had finished off the contests.

He saw himself as a solid rock facing his opponent… and defeating him.

He was ready.

Outside, the activity had stopped and Hussein stood erect in the middle of the mat with one of the new Jihadists, a chunky Pakistani, beside him, speaking quietly to him. This stopped when Danny strode out onto the mat and stood in front of them.

Frank hurried across and stood between them.

"Right, I'm the referee here but why we need one is beyond me. Hussein, tell Jack what rules you're working with for this match?"

The man lifted his head and looked directly into Danny's, his black eyes reflecting hatred and confidence.

"No rules... no rules for Infidels... anything goes" he snarled.

Frank glanced at Danny. "OK with this Jack?"

Danny looked back directly into the cold eyes of Hussein.

"Sure, fine with me. Only problem is that those seventy virgins might not like what I'm going to do to him by the time I'm finished."

Danny was trying to unsettle him with the taunt.

He succeeded.

Hussein started to lunge forward, but was restrained by the American and his colleague.

"Just for that, I'm going to...." he hissed.

"Yeah, yeah, sure. Why don't you stop talking and let's get to it."

Frank saw that he didn't need to say anything more and indicated to Syed's colleague to leave the mat.

He pushed both opponents back and literally scuttled off the mat to allow the battle to begin.

It had started even before he reached the edge.

If Danny hadn't been prepared, the first swinging high kick would have taken his head off. Hussein, still enraged, came at him like an express train looking for a fast kill. The kick had too much power in it to block, so he stepped back as it zipped past his face. It was followed by three kicks directed at his lower body.

Danny moved out of the way of two of them, and half blocked the third with his elbow, swiveling sideways. He was looking for an opening to try to unsettle Hussein early on, and he saw one right then.

As Hussein's half blocked kick slapped back onto the floor, Danny did his famous leg sweep, that had won him many contests, and Hussein crashed to the floor.

He was only down for an instant, fearing an attack, and leapt to his feet.

There was a murmur of surprise from the Jihadists squatting along the side.

Hussein looked furious, and hurled himself back into the fray, this time driving Danny back with a combination of punches and kicks, most of which Danny managed to evade or block. One body kick did catch him on the side of his ribs and he gasped.

'Oh man, Hussein could kick,' he thought. 'I'd better not get caught with too many of those.'

As if reading his mind and spotting a weakness, Hussein directed a number of savage kicks at his lower body, again driving Danny back as he weathered the storm. He let his attacker force him to the edge of the mat and decided to start fighting back.

As Danny blocked a right hand blow to his head, and the left fist that started to follow it, he smashed his right elbow into Hussein's face, stunning him and making him stagger back.

He followed his opponent swiftly, closed with him and attempted a hip throw, which failed.

He was caught a stunning blow to the head by a straight punch from Hussein and gritted his teeth. He deliberately clinched and held on to his attacker until he regained his balance.

He tried again for a foot sweep, which was avoided and stepped back.

Both men circled each other.

Danny didn't want the bout to settle into a bunch of flurries where each became so defensive that neither would win.

He caught the next right hand that his opponent threw and drove straight through, his head catching the man on the bridge of his nose, smashing it.

Hussein screamed in pain.

Still holding onto the arm, Danny chopped down directly onto it, just below the shoulder muscle, snapping the bone.

Hussein didn't have time to scream this time.

Danny swiveled and brought him up and over in a high hip throw, smashing him down to the floor where he lay groaning.

He stepped back from his fallen opponent.

275

"Look out Jack!" he heard a voice coming from behind him.

He only had a peripheral glimpse of a figure hurtling directly at him, and without thinking, dropped like a stone to the floor, seeing a body flash across above him and lash down at him with some sort of weapon. The attacker's feet got tangled in Danny's and he sprawled to the floor.

Both men jumped up.

Danny could now see that it was the Jihadist who had been talking to Hussein before the contest, and now he was coming at him with some sort of weapon... it was the wooden leg of one of the old chairs left behind in the vacant flat.

It was coming down in a vicious circle towards his head.

Without thinking Danny blocked it with his left forearm, and struck down with the edge of his right hand onto the man's collarbone, breaking it.

The man sunk to his knees shrieking in pain. Danny wrenched the weapon from his hand and tossed it across to the edge of the mat.

It was over, at least that part of it.

Frank was across in an instant, his face stricken.

"Shit man, I didn't mean this to happen. I'm supposed to be forming an attack squad here, and you've just taken out two of them, and one of their leading trainers at that! What the hell were you thinking? Did you have to go that far Jack?"

"What? I'm supposed to let this bastard take my head off, or let Hussein there have his jollies by beating me to a pulp? Remember, I didn't start this. I agreed to come in this morning, like the last time and give these chaps some exercise and training. Hussein decided to hijack the whole thing. I hope he learns something from this Frank. Oh, by the way, my old army training tells me that you should bundle them into the vehicle out there and get them around to the ER. I'm outa here. When things have cooled down leave a message at the Sally Ann."

He turned and left, leaving the American standing there, shaking his head dazedly.

Danny went round the corner and located his own car where he had parked it earlier.

He didn't take any particular enjoyment in hurting people.

However he felt a certain satisfaction in the outcome.

He remembered the story of the tiger in India.

He had taken two Jihadists out of the equation who wouldn't be wreaking havoc on innocent people going about their business in a mall or building, in the coming weeks. In the process though he may very well have sabotaged any future role with the terrorists.

He wondered what Rebecca would have to say about it.

CHAPTER 51

She didn't like it at all.

"Danny, Danny, you may have just sandbagged yourself in terms of being accepted inside with this Jihadist group. I can't see them wanting you back in when you've just put two of the group into ER!" Rebecca exclaimed.

She examined him closely. "You didn't have to defeat them so permanently did you? I know what you can do and I'm sure you could have beaten those two without crippling them. What's going on here?"

He ran her remark through his mind, wondering how to explain his actions.

"OK, you haven't met these people, especially this latest group. They're trained, cold-blooded killers who, I've no doubt, will shortly be making the headlines for some shocking massacre in a mall or some other vulnerable places here in the U.K. I saw an excuse to take two of them out of the equation, especially one of their top trainers in martial arts, who would have gone on to teach some dirty tricks to these new radicalized recruits. What I'm saying again is, that it's a mistake to let these animals loose here in the country. We should grab them at entry and fire them far back in some remote prison where they won't emerge until they're old men. So there."

Rebecca shook her head sadly. "I'm sorry to hear you say that Danny, because as much as I dislike having to say it, it could mean that we can't use you any further on this operation. The policy decision we made here at MI5 was to allow some of these Jihadists in, and keep them under surveillance until they led us to others who share their beliefs. Then we would arrest the lot of them, or as many as we could collar. We can't have one of our Agents making changes of policy on the hoof that contravenes the plan we'd agreed on. Can't you see that?"

"Yeah, I can see where you're coming from. However just a short hour ago, two of these Jihadists that you're talking about, were virtually trying to kill ME, one with a club in his hand. I believe I was justified in what I did in protecting myself. How much good would I be to MI5 if I'd allowed this third Dan karate expert to break a number of bones in MY body? OK, perhaps I erred somewhat in the old police rule, using as much force as is deemed necessary, or something like that. In any event, I think this American Frank, will be back for me. That's the impression I got when I left him anyway."

She was still shaking her head as she reached for a document on her desk.

"Well, let's see where this goes. Just remember there's a whole team working on it as well as you, so they won't thank you, nor will I, if it turns out that you screwed up the whole deal with your cavalier attitude out there this morning. Enough said. Now to other business: this Omar Bashir chap at the Afghan Embassy. The Police have put in for a Waiver of Persons Diplomatic Immunity for him, through the Foreign Commonwealth Office (FCO), in order to arrest and interview him under caution, and if appropriate, bring charges. However, this takes time and if the Head of Missions concerned, the Afghan Government does not agree, then we have no option but to kick him out of the country."

"Let him go scot free? So, what are the chances of this waiver coming through?"

She wrinkled her forehead. "I wouldn't hold your breath Danny. Remember this is a new, fresh Afghan Government, and the last thing they need is bad press like this, but who knows, miracles do happen."

Danny felt a turmoil of emotions flash through him, primarily the thought that his ex-wife Fiona, had been brutally murdered, in front of her young daughter Allison. At this stage, he knew better than to share his thoughts with her.

He wasn't giving Omar Bashir any waiver for his actions. He planned to extract full payment from him, even if he had to pursue him back to Afghanistan.

She took his silence as his acceptance of the status quo and carried on.

"Now, this situation with Jamilla and her kidnapper. As I recall, the ball's in your court on that one. An advertisement in the paper agreeing to meet was the next step, when you have the ransom available. I have those fake diamonds on order, just so you'll know, though you believe she's already been killed. What's your thoughts on that Danny?"

"As of this moment, let's see where I am with the Jihadist group first. I can't just disappear right now, or that would really put the abdabs on any future involvement. In a similar vein, have you managed to get those funds out of the Cayman Islands and disbursed to those people and situations that I asked you to?"

"Not quite there yet my friend. Getting the money out is no problem, just your signature that we've forwarded to the bank. The problem is getting it back in to the U.K. as legal tender, prior to disbursing it. Look at the problems David Cameron had over the Panama papers, some time back. If we try to process it through your back income you're going to be hammered. We're checking through with our tax people, but we haven't discussed anything with U.K. Revenue as yet. If those chaps get a sniff of this they'll take you to the cleaners and there won't be much left to disburse to anyone. There's a possibility that I'm discussing with one of my own personal hawk-eyed accountants, that I'm getting more information on, so leave it with me for the moment."

He sighed. "Jeez, I never knew that having money could be such a pain in the ass Rebecca. I'd really appreciate it if you could sort it out. Now about our Belfast trip. The American, Frank, is suddenly gun shy on the whole deal. He says that something smells about the whole thing. I don't think it's going to go anywhere."

She leaned forward looking concerned. "So does this mean he has reservations about you, or you leading him over there?"

"Strangely, I don't think so. Getting shot at didn't help the situation. I was on the ground as fast as him then, I can tell you. No, he just feels he's out of his depth. He was looking for a nice clean deal, and now feels there's elements involved which he has no control over."

"At least you're not coming under scrutiny for the whole screw-up. What about Jimmy Patton? Do we ask him to hang in there or send him back to the Regiment?"

"Actually, I'd like to bring Jimmy to London to join Scotty as protection in the surveillance vehicles. Our teams are very exposed with these Jihadists coming through."

"O.K., I'll inform Patton's Regiment. To get back to the American for a moment, any other news?"

"No, but he made an interesting statement that'll interest you. He said he had weapons coming in from some other source. He didn't enlarge on it, but something's in the wind for sure."

"Shoot Danny, this is bad news… a cache of weapons coming into the U.K., and battle hardened Jihadists ready and willing to put them to use! God, I hope you haven't screwed up your relationship with the American and that group. We need you in there more than ever!"

He nodded. "Let's keep our fingers crossed. Oh, the American mentioned that the present batch of arrivals will be heading up to Birmingham in a couple of days."

"Hmm, to further radicalize the people there and probably train them in creating mayhem here on the ground."

"Hey, I suggested we take them off the streets down here. Anyway what about the Police Investigators who were looking into the safe house killings, and that other bastard that was garroted?"

"I've managed to hold them off for the moment, telling them you're involved in an undercover operation and not available. Same with that ex-soldier you believe was the fourth man involved, apart from the man Bashir. Your statement will keep them at bay for the moment, but not for long. The Police well know that cold cases don't get solved. They want every morsel of information they can get right now. Don't forget, this is a massive case with all of those that were killed, including our own MI5 people as well."

Their meeting ended as her secretary came through with the arrival of the people she was expecting.

He waved as he slipped out of the room.

CHAPTER 52

Syed Hussein was sitting on the edge of the bed in the ER treatment room when his mate Abdul pushed his head through the curtains, and seeing him, walked through. Abdul himself was wearing some sort of shoulder harness to support his broken collarbone, and the morphine shot had obviously taken the pain away when they re-set his shoulder. Syed glared at Abdul.

"So what have they done to you?" he demanded.

"I just finished getting my shoulder re-set. The doctor said that broken collarbones usually heal up pretty good. No lifting or aggressive sports he told me, or it could come back on me, so I'm not going to be much help to you going forwards. What about you?"

Hussein frowned. "Had my arm ex-rayed up the hall. I'm slated for an operation in the afternoon. My nose was ex-rayed as well, but it's a different surgeon, someone from ENT who'll do the operation tomorrow morning. He has to come across from a different hospital, and he's chock a block with operations in three different hospitals, so I have to sit here in pain while he treats all these bloody migrants from all over the world. I think U.K. citizens should be put at the head of the waiting list."

Abdul leaned forward and examined him closely.

"You look bloody terrible brother, that must be very painful - your eyes have turned black and blue already. That bastard Jack really did a job on you. I hate to say it, but that's the end of your training role. Rumor had it that when the American, Skinner went back home, you would have been a shoo-in for taking over the top spot. That's probably a no go as well, with your present injuries."

Hussein's black eyes stared balefully across at him. "I have a score to settle with that infidel Jack. He broke the rules and caught me unawares, otherwise I would have put him down within the next five minutes. I had his moves all worked out and he must have realized it when he cheated and head butted me."

Abdul raised his eyebrows skeptically. "Agh…cheated did he? I thought you said you weren't going to have any rules, when we were talking before the match."

"You must be mistaken. I don't recall making that statement to you. Anyway, I need you to do something for me. First, find out where this bastard hangs out, and second, get your hands on some sort of weapon for me. I know you have contacts in one of the mosques here in London, so use some of your contacts and get back to me. You hear me Abdul?"

"I hear you, and I have to say that trying to settle a personal grudge could de-rail the timeline the American has in mind for the U.K. operation. You need to go carefully on this."

Hussein grabbed him with his good left arm. "Look, you owe me, after protecting you over there in Syria and keeping you away from those areas being bombed by the Americans, so don't give me any shit about Frank's timeline. I'm out of the battle now, but I can still get my revenge on this Jack, and for that to happen, I need your help, so come back tomorrow with some news for me. I'll hopefully have my op. over by then and be in a better mood."

"You in a better mood Brother? I've followed you through Iraq and Syria and I've never once seen you in a better mood - just pissed off at the world all the time. OK, I guess I do owe you, so I'll see what I can do. Don't forget we're all off to Birmingham shortly, and I plan to go with them. There must be something I can still do up there for Jihad."

CHAPTER 53

Danny had arranged to meet up with Alina Tariq at her apartment after she had finished her surveillance shift with Dave Jones, the retired Scotland Yard Detective.

Her place in the vehicle had been taken up by Clive Spooner and another MI5 operative who were keeping a listening brief on the Canary Wharf building. The fact that the newly acquired Jihadist vehicle had a bug placed on it, lessened the need for a fleet of vehicles keeping a tight surveillance on the group. This might change if Frank Skinner bought a second vehicle.

Alina had one piece of news that was disturbing. She had overheard a discussion in the group to the effect that on the day Danny had picked up the newest group of Jihadists, who came through on the Euro Train from Paris, a second larger group had sailed from Calais in France, to Dover. They had, according to the conversation, already travelled north to either Bradford or Birmingham.

Danny whistled. "Shoot, it sounds like Skinner doesn't trust me a hundred percent. He didn't mention a thing about this."

"Perhaps not. It could be that he's had lots of training in compartmentalizing different sections of the operation, for safety purposes. This small cell method works as you know, on a need to know basis, and is being used effectively by all the terrorists in every country they operate in."

He nodded glumly. "I don't know Alina. Skinner's pretty shrewd. He could be playing me for all I know. Rebecca could be right...I may have sabotaged myself by taking out those two Jihadists on the mat. I did go well beyond merely defending myself by putting them in hospital. A good trainer wouldn't have done that, or he'd run out of people to train pretty fast."

She placed her hand on his.

"Hey, don't be too hard on yourself. Sure they pissed you off, but don't forget, your ex-wife was shot to death in front of your daughter, not too many days ago. With this Omar Bashir, seemingly leaving the country scot free, you were probably pretty damn frustrated right then!"

He straightened up, suddenly alert. "You've been watching him on your off duty hours and I really do appreciate that. Now...."

She smiled triumphantly, reaching for a small writing pad in her purse.

"I think I've found out where he lives. He's been dropped by an chauffer-driven car at this address, three days in a row, and on two other occasions pulled out from an underground parking lot there in the vehicle where you planted the bug."

"Nice work" he exclaimed. "Did he go anywhere in particular?"

She shook her head.

"He went into a couple of sleazy pubs that I couldn't have followed him into without giving myself away. Oh, and he went back to one of them just yesterday evening. He's obviously trained in counter surveillance as he keeps changing direction, slips through lights deliberately as they change to red - the usual bag of tricks. With the bug in place of course, he hasn't a chance. He did park a few hundred yards away from the second pub he visited, and was very alert when he was on foot. I could have used the team with me or someone who fitted into the pub scene. I assumed he was heading for the same one, and hung well back. He was out again within half and hour, and I broke off at that stage. I needed a shower and some food by then as I was on the job all day on the Canary Wharf location."

"You did a super job Alina, and thanks a bunch. Now show me those pub addresses."

After looking at them, he nodded.

"I know of them, but I've never been in either. One of them rings a bell though: the Wolf Tavern. It had a reputation some years back of being a gathering place for what they used to call mercenaries, and some of the hard men from the Paras...even some ex-SAS people who'd crossed the line on some of their operations and were kicked out of the Regiment."

She made a face. "I really wouldn't have fitted into the pub then."

He grinned. "I've no idea what it's like now, but it used to be a hangout for some old slags who liked so-called dangerous men. If you'd walked in there, it would have been like the nice girl walking into a saloon in one of those Westerns."

The doorbell rang.

Being in the business she was in, she was well versed in checking out who was outside before opening the door.

Danny turned and looked at the visitor and laughed.

"Hey Alina, we were talking about finding someone scruffy. I believe we've found our candidate."

Jimmy Patton walked into the room. He had picked up the tail end of Danny's remark and took a mock swing at him.

"Who are you calling scruffy, you civvy bastard."

The next fifteen minutes were taken up with bringing Jimmy up to date on where the London operation was at this point in time.

Rebecca had now tasked him with working closely up front with the surveillance teams to avoid another abduction such as the one carried out on Danielle, and her subsequent murder.

It took a further half hour to acquaint him with the attack on the safe house and the imminent departure of Omar Bashir back to Afghanistan.

Jimmy Patton had worked with Danny on numerous operations in the SAS, and some situations that Danny had pulled him into.

Now he regarded him closely.

"I gather you don't intend to just let him walk away from this whole thing and go back to Afghanistan, without some sort of reckoning?"

"You'd better believe it Jimmy. However, I don't want to get MI5 in the frame when it happens. It'd finish Rebecca's career for starters."

Jimmy looked away thoughtfully. "Hmm... why do the words 'a tragic accident' come to mind? It's an awfully dangerous world out there today you know."

Alina looked from one to the other. "Why do I get the feeling you two are up to something?"

Danny shrugged. "We were just talking about it a few minutes ago... need to know, you said. Let's leave it at that for the moment shall we?"

Both men grinned at each other.

Alina shook her head and headed for the kitchen.

CHAPTER 54

Silence did fall inside the Wolf Tavern when Jimmy Patton eased through the front door, stopped and looked around. He had decided not to wear any disguise for the visit such as the scruffy hairpiece he had worn in Belfast. He did however look distinctly different from the inhabitants of the pub. In the main they appeared to be out of work layabouts, construction workers coming off site and having an early drink before heading home, and a motley crew of ex-Service people trying to bask in the battles of the past in the Falklands, Northern Ireland and the first Gulf War. Some tourists had drifted in and were buying the odd round for former so-called action men, where the closest they had ever came to action had been being rejected by the Recruiting Sergeant, not to forget chatting up the old female slags, who frequented the pub.

The conversation started up again as Jimmy walked over to the bar and shouted an order through the stacked group clustered there. The barman went away, came back in five minutes and slapped a pint of Bitter down.

"That'll be five pounds sixty Mate," he shouted through the packed men.

Jimmy took a tenner out of his wallet and reached through with it.

"Keep the change Mate," he shouted back, waving the barman with the usual sign to hang onto the change. One of the men standing beside him gave him a sharp glance.

"Hey, don't start tipping these bar people, the beer's expensive enough already."

Jimmy made an apologetic grimace and headed over to a table that had just become vacant in the back of the pub. He sat back taking in the atmosphere and the flow of people going back and forth. No one stopped to talk to him or asked if they could join him, however a number nodded to him in passing. He had nearly reached the bottom of his glass when three pretty young women came round with trays and paper plates, offering free food. He eagerly grabbed some and asked one of them if she could get him a fresh pint when she was through with the food round.

She smiled. "After the tip you gave to Colin, I'll be happy to do just that." He tossed another tenner on the tray, getting an even bigger smile.

Fifteen minutes later he was beginning to think it had been a mistake giving the money up front, when she hurried across to him with the pint, and again he waved off the change. Before she turned away she leaned forward and spoke quietly in his ear.

"There's a chap in the back room over there, the one with 'Private' written on it, who would like a word with you if you wouldn't mind. He's called Tommy, Tommy Jones."

He didn't rush… took his time bringing the glass down a quarter, then strolled casually through the milling crowd, to the door.

He didn't knock.

When he walked in he saw four men seated around a table playing cards. Before he could even close the door, three of them got up and brushed past him. The fourth man stayed seated. He looked in his late thirties, and sitting there, looked like someone who might have been a former athlete, now starting to pack on some weight.

He stood up and Jimmy could see that he was tall as well as bulky, with the look of someone who could handle himself.

He gave Jimmy a measured look, then extended his hand.

"Tommy Jones. My barman says you have a Belfast accent, so I thought I'd say hello to a fellow Celt."

Jimmy took his hand. "Ah yes, of course Jones... from good old Wales no doubt, though it seems the Sassenach has robbed you of your accent."

Jones laughed. "I'm back in the valleys for only a weekend and I'm told it comes back. Anyway a smart Celt knows that to do business with the British you have to blend in, hence this beautiful London accent. Now sit down and finish the rest of your pint."

Jimmy looked around. "Am I to gather that this is your establishment then?"

A flicker of a smile crossed the former Welshman's face.

"I'm awfully glad you didn't refer to it as a dive, as a lot might. You obviously know a thing or two about trade."

"Well, there's a saying back in the bogs 'where there's muck, there's money', and from what I saw back there in the bar, you're selling a hell of a lot of booze. Now that is smart trade," he replied with emphasis.

"Pretty observant for your first visit. You're either from the Inland Revenue or a Cop, working undercover."

Jimmy choked on his pint, blowing some foam out of the glass.

"Oh man, don't do that to me! No one has ever pegged me for that lofty status." He paused, finishing his swallow.

Jones continued to look at him, saying nothing, but his face held a question - an important one for him.

Jimmy sat there for a long moment nodding, and struggling with what he was going to say.

"Yeah, fair comment. I'd probably be asking the same question if it was my business. No, nothing as dramatic as a Cop or the Taxman. In fact I've just spent twelve years in the Forces, eight in the Paras and four in the Saas. They've just let me go after me giving my all, as they say for my country...Iraq, Afghanistan, Kosovo, and many other shit holes not even worth mentioning. Now the Government's cutting down at a time when the Ruskies are flying up and down the Bristol Channel, and we can't even go out and greet them."

He shook his head disgustedly.

Jones shrugged. "So why are you here in this pub of mine right now?"

Jimmy made a face, slightly embarrassed. "Well, it's like this. It wouldn't sound right coming from an ex-Saas type, if I said that I was scared. Of what you might ask? Of bloody Civvy Street, that's what. I thought, lived, tasted, and smelled Military for twelve years, and now I haven't a bloody clue how to go about getting a job. Some Mates of mine got out and went to the job center and they just laughed at them. Suggested getting a job as a Security Guard, checking trucks coming in and out of a construction site. Can you believe it? The overseas security jobs have practically vanished, with Afghanistan reducing NATO troops, and Iraq of course falling apart. The Government spent millions training myself and all these people in all sorts of valuable skills, and this is how we're treated! The uncertainty of Brexit doesn't help either. I tell you it's absolutely unbelievable!"

"Oh I can believe it all right Mate. Politicians will do whatever it takes to stay in power, and if that means slashing the deficit by giving you chaps the chop, no skin off their noses. I understand the numbers of our Military will be down to fifty thousand soon. About the size of the New York Police Department. You can go back as far as Wellington at the battle of Waterloo, to the last time we had such a small Military, but again, to get back to my question, what were you looking for here in my pub?"

Jimmy shook his head. "Yeah, stupid when you think about all that… OK, I heard some time back that some ex-Saas types congregate here over a beer, and I thought I might get steered in the right direction. Like, how did they make it, for starters?"

"Hmm…I'm sure that, in sitting out front drinking your pint you must have realized that most of the people out there were losers, not people who'd taken life by the scruff of its neck and made something of themselves. The only place they'll steer you to will be to where they go to renew their unemployment benefit when it comes up. As to THEM working, forget it."

Jimmy finished his pint and sat with his head down looking dejected.

"Well, I guess that's it then. Anyway, thanks for taking the time to straighten me out" he said, starting to get up.

"Just a thought, but don't you ex-SAS people have your own club in town? Wouldn't you be better trying there?"

Jimmy made a face. "Well, if one had just retired, or had sought a discharge for his own reasons, that route would be fine. I was kinda let go, so to speak."

"Ah, they kicked you out in other words. What for may I ask?"

Jimmy sat down again, shifting around in the seat.

Jones pushed him. "Come on Jimmy, what did they kick you out for?"

He squirmed again. "Well I had this little thing going with a middle aged waitress down in Hereford…"

"Screwing her in other words."

"Well, yes, but that wasn't the problem. You see she offered me her sixteen-year-old daughter for a hefty price, and then threatened to go to the police when I didn't cough up. I didn't have the money right then, and I thought she was bluffing anyway, but the bitch put a complaint in to the Regiment. They arranged to keep the whole thing quiet, but they kicked me out. I pushed and got an honorable discharge because I said I'd go to the press if they didn't, so you see…"

Jones sat there shaking his head. "Oh man, you are one stupid bastard! Twelve years of putting your life on the line, taking all that parade-ground bullshit, and you throw it all away for a piece of underage ass, and I'd bet my boots you weren't the first one either. They saw you coming my Celtic brother."

Jimmy stood up and turned slowly towards the door.

Jones's voice stopped him.

"On the other hand Jimmy, I might have something for you. Apart from screwing young girls, do I take it that you can still kill people?"

CHAPTER 55

Kevin was used to all sorts of people coming into the Sally Ann. It was that kind of place. You couldn't be a racist, and work with street people from various backgrounds wandering in for assistance. Some of them might be passing through on the way to somewhere else in the country, while others, might be regulars who almost regarded it as a social meeting place to get together for a quick bite of food, before hitting the street and heading for their favorite pieces of turf outside subway stations, or places where the Police wouldn't be moving them on every hour.

The two who pushed their way in that morning were different.

For starters they looked like they had just been involved in a traffic accident. One had a bandaged nose with discolored black and blue eyes and appeared to have an immobilized right arm. The other wore a sling supporting his left arm.

Kevin guessed they were of Pakistani extraction, and both looked nervous and on edge. One of them cut a large and imposing figure and looked decidedly angry. His companion was of smaller build. He wondered if they had just been released from some ER in the city after some sort of accident.

They both stepped forward past his table and quickly glanced around the room, now filled with drop-ins eating their breakfast.

The small one leaned across the reception table.

"We're looking for Jack Fisher, I believe he hangs out here?"

Kevin was immediately on the alert.

For starters Jack (Danny) always made him aware of the imminence of visitors coming in for a quick meeting, or dropping some piece of equipment, but he hadn't mentioned anything about visitors when he'd arrived earlier.

Kevin's old Cop nature suddenly came to the fore. He took a closer look at the two men standing before him.

He didn't like what he was seeing. Both men had their good arms held inside their loose flowing shirts, and something about their eyes started alarm bells ringing. These two weren't the usual types that dropped in for a handout.

Danny was back in the room that he used, but there was no alarm bell that Kevin could press to alert him. There was something wrong here – most decidedly.

His only option was to stall the two visitors in the hope that Danny might check the entrance before emerging, and spot them, or that some of the street people might mill around at the desk, as they occasionally did for a chat before they left, and he could make a quick call inside.

"Hey, look lads, I'm not sure who you're talking about here…Jack Fisher?"

Pointing back down the room.

"There's hundreds of people drift in here every day and guess what? How many of them even want to let me know their name? I can't really help you here I'm afraid."

The next moment the big man had jumped around the side of the table, and his left hand emerged with a handgun that he pressed against the side of Kevin's head.

"Be very afraid Infidel, because in one minute I'm going to blow your brains across the wall behind you, unless you get Fisher out here right now. Your choice, you English bastard" he hissed.

Kevin froze, in total shock at the unexpected turn of events.

Not so the group back down in the room, who, a moment before had been deep in conversation and finishing their breakfasts. In an instant they were on their feet, shouting, chairs and tables flying in all directions.

One of the closest shouted "what the fuck's going on there?" He hurled the chair he was holding, up the room at the two men, but he was too far away and the chair merely skidded across the floor, stopping twenty feet away from the two terrorists.

Startled, the smaller man withdrew his hand from his loose clothing.

One of the street people screamed a warning. "Shit, he's got a sawed off shotgun, and he dived for the ground as the smaller man pulled the trigger, spraying the room with lead pellets that ripped through the people standing in the front row. The bedlam increased as the wounded started screaming, and the rest of them dived for the ground and any cover that was available. Some turned to run towards the back of the room, and were caught by the next two blasts of the shotgun.

For Danny, back in the room, the first sign of trouble was the sound of the blast from the front of the Sally Ann.

He recognized the sound, - a shotgun, being used outside in the reception area.

Two quick blasts followed, but he was already moving to his locker across from him, where he had stored the weapon MI5 had arranged for him and the surveillance team escorts to carry after Danielle's murder, to provide protection. It was a Heckler & Koch 0.45 Mk 23 (SOCOM Special Forces Command Pistol) with a 12- round box magazine capacity. While it came with a sound suppressor and a laser-aiming module (MAM), he didn't have time to attach these to the weapon. Instead he started running, notching the magazine in and setting the selector switch to single shot, then clicked the safety catch off.

He could hear the bedlam from inside the breakfast room, but ignored his urge to crash straight through into the room.

The shotgun rang out again as he knelt down, carefully opened the door and peered through. As he did so some shots rang out and splinters flew from the sides of the doorway.

'Shit, there was someone with a handgun out there too. Just as well he'd knelt down to reduce himself as a target.'

He couldn't wait any longer…people were being shot in there.

He kicked the door open further and hurled a metal doorstop lying on the lino, straight at a table full of dishes, stacked against the far side of the room, hoping to distract the shooters for an instant. Then he dived straight into the room in a forward roll.

Coming up onto his knees he factored in the two gunmen's positions and weaponry.

The shotgun was swerving away from the broken dishes in his direction. This was the most dangerous weapon in terms of the potential damage it could inflict on a roomful of people.

He would have loved to deliver a double tap to the head, but couldn't risk it with the chance of a miss from that distance, so he settled for two quick single shoots delivered straight into the man's midsection. The guy crashed backwards, the weapon blasting harmlessly up into the ceiling.

He was out of it. Then two things happened.

Kevin was retired, but he had still done his time in Police uniform, and some things one never loses: trained reactions when confronted with a dangerous individual.

As the large terrorist, distracted by the noise from the broken dishes and the subsequent shooting of his colleague, turned away to take aim at Danny, Kevin kicked the back of his leg joint, making him stumble.

His pistol fired, tearing holes in the reception table.

Danny wasn't risking chest shots this time with Kevin still a potential casualty from a wounded terrorist. He put two shots into the man's head, holding the pistol with two hands to steady it.

He was already dead, as the weapon dropped from his hand and he collapsed onto the floor.

Kevin's training kicked in again. He was already on the direct dial to the Police and Ambulances.

The screaming and shouting was coming at an increased level from the dining area.

Danny grabbed Kevin's arm.

"Kevin, I can't be here when the Cops come. All you know is that some chap you never saw came in to have a shower back there, came out shooting, then left in a hurry."

"Kevin made a face. "Jesus, Danny, that won't hold them for long. The men back there screaming right now, know you, and have seen us talking for Pete's sake."

"Yeah, I know, I know Kev, but I'm hoping the old street code of playing dumb with Cops will still be in play. Look, call Rebecca at MI5 and she'll give you some cover. Stall them as long as you can. I'm off, but first I have to close my locker inside and grab whatever might give me away. Take care, and oh, well done there with that bastard. You stopped me from being shot and gave me a chance to take him out."

Sirens were coming closer as Danny slipped out of the building and dived down into the closest subway. He didn't think it was a good idea to collect his car round the corner, with the street blockages that would already be clamping down around the area.

He had, of course, recognized the two assailants. Probably pissed off and taking unilateral action against him.

He wondered how the American would react to it. At least, hopefully, he couldn't hold Danny (Jack) responsible for the debacle... or could he?

Skinner hadn't informed him about the other Jihadists coming through by ferry.

Was there some hidden agenda at play here?

He'd better put in an appearance at the flat in Canary Wharf and find out where things stood right now.

Rebecca would be spitting bullets when she found out where his actions in putting Akmal Hussein and his pal in hospital, had now led. His brief career with the Security Service might shortly be coming to an end.

He had to get rid of the pistol he was carrying as well. All he needed was an alert Transport Police person to spot the bulge under his jacket and check him.

He didn't need any more attention right then.

CHAPTER 56

Jimmy Patton wasn't kept in the dark for long.

The pub owner, Tommy Jones, asked him to wait outside in the bar area and have a drink on the house. He declined the drink, but moved back outside into the packed bar.

It was over an hour later that he spotted a man entering the pub who didn't look quite like the usual customer.

He also recognized his face from the picture that MI5 had shown him.

It was Omar Bashir.

The barman had obviously been waiting for him, and waved him straight through to the private room at the back. Jimmy kept his eyes down as he went past. Another fifteen minutes passed before the barman came over and told him to go back inside the private section.

Once through the door, he was confronted by both Jones and Bashir, the latter eyeing him speculatively.

Bashir didn't offer to shake hands.

He just stood there silently, taking the measure of Patton.

Finally he nodded and pointed to a chair.

"O.K., you certainly look the part. Tommy tells me you are ex- SAS who got into a bit of trouble and now have difficulty getting a job. He tells me he was pretty direct with you by asking you if you could still kill people. You're still here, so I gather that's a yes?"

There was a question in his voice.

Jimmy sat down, realizing he would now have to play this very carefully, but it was Jones who interrupted them.

"Just a minute Omar, you asked that we scan him first as a precaution. Hang on while I get one of the lads in who's a whiz at this and has the necessary equipment."

He picked up the phone and spoke into it briefly.

Patton and Bashir sat there without any comment, until the door opened and a squat, long-haired man came bustling in, carrying what Jimmy knew to be a regular scanning device. Knowing the routine, he stood up and lifted his arms out sideways as the man slowly moved the scanner up and down his body, and out along his arms.

Jimmy was glad there was no 'ping' sounding from the device, especially as he was wearing Danny's special belt that could transmit a message to the car outside where a team headed by Alina was listening.

Finally the man with the scanner nodded to Jones.

"He's clean boss, nothing on him."

Then he turned and left.

Jimmy turned to Bashir. "Back to your question of a moment ago. I've been killing people for the past twelve years with Her Majesty's blessing. I always thought it was a great stretch of the imagination when people left the Regiment, that one could supposedly turn a switch and stop doing what one had been conditioned to carry out without a second thought. The answer to your question is unreservedly 'yes'."

Bashir's eyes bored into his. "OK, that sounds good but I've recently come to realize that people can be in the Military and never see any real action. They might have served, but never came close to actually shooting someone, the enemy for example. Tell me some of the operations you've been on?"

Patton shuffled in his seat. "Well, you know, we've all signed the Official Secrets Act, which means we can't divulge details of operations we were involved in."

Jones cut in.

"Look Jimmy, stop messing about. Either you're the fucking goods or you're not. Give Omar some details of what you can do, or just move your ass out of here" he snapped.

Bashir nodded his head.

"Let me know what kind of operations you've been on, and how you carried them out. I'm not about to invest in you until I know you've got what it takes to carry through on my instructions to finish someone off. To kill them in other words."

Patton raised his arms as if in surrender.

"OK, I get it. I guess I'd be the same in your place. It's just that we rarely talk to people about it, even the chaps we were with in the middle of it. We just park it, 'cos it's the only way we can deal with it. We get hit with the flashbacks later, which is where all that Post Traumatic Stress shit comes from. Right, details…."

He paused for a moment as if gathering his thoughts.

"OK. Operations… in Columbia where myself and my sniper partner were staked out for seven days waiting for a drug lord to appear. We shot him and a half dozen others around him, and killed at least another dozen who chased us back through the jungle to the Exfill point."

"Exfill point?" Bashir enquired.

"A helicopter, to get us the hell out of there. To carry on…. we had several similar ops in Kosovo, where we were laying up in hides, moving frequently, and taking out Serb fighters who were murdering Muslims in droves, and assaulting their women. I probably killed at least twenty top Serb fighters and some of them we identified as wanted war criminals. We were instructed to arrest them, but everyone knew that was not expected of us in any way shape or form, so we just took them out. In Iraq we went out nightly in teams, following up information on Sunni tribes people, gathering for attacks on the Shia Militia who were on our side. Sometimes two or three raids a night. With Saas training and equipment of course, we didn't encounter much real opposition. You can imagine, an eight-man Saas team dropping down on them from the sky.

Similar stuff in Afghanistan. We often teamed up with U.S. Seals or Delta Forces to go out on nightly raids, grab Taliban or Al Qaeda leaders, and bring them back for interrogation."

301

"You fought alongside Seals and Delta teams?" Bashir asked, his eyes widening.

"Yep, we sure did, and the Rangers as well. I can tell you, the targets we were after didn't come easy. They were usually surrounded by their fanatical supporters who didn't mind dying to protect them, so we quite often fought our way in and out again, and suffered casualties on a number of occasions. We might do two or three of these nightly, so you can imagine how strung out many of us were after a 6-month posting over to that hellhole. In addition, we had several ops in to Africa to rescue people who'd been kidnapped. We had to bail out Embassies that were being evacuated in an emergency, and on occasion we were called upon to train other countries' so-called Elite Forces up to some sort of professional standard. We were always on call, even when we got back to the U.K., absolutely wrung out. A number of the chaps just got out, as either they or their wives couldn't take it any more."

He looked up at the two men who had fallen silent as he talked. "Is that enough? Is this the stuff you wanted?" Jimmy asked.

He detected what might have been a gleam of sympathy in the Welshman's eyes. The Afghan had sat forward more, as Patton had gone over his story.

He looked excited. "This is exactly what I wanted to hear. That you have the background to plan your actions and carry through with them without any holding back. I can see, watching you as you told us of your experiences, that you were a machine carrying out orders, and nothing could get in your way. Killing was second nature to you, and of no real consequence to you. That's what I'm looking for. Now to the money side and the target."

The Welshman raised his arms. "Hey, I'm outta here. You know, deniability - I don't want to hear any of what you chaps want to discuss."

He got up and left the room. Bashir pulled his chair closer.

CHAPTER 57

The first chance Danny had, he tried to call Rebecca at MI5 and failed to get through as she was in an important meeting. He asked to be put through to Jerry Sackville, the man in charge of counter terrorist investigations and research.

Luckily he was there and able to take his call.

He listened as Danny filled him in on the recent developments at the Sally Ann.

Jerry whistled. "Shit Danny you're a regular 'Stormin Norman'. Trouble really does seem to just follow you doesn't it?"

"Tell me about it" he answered wearily.

"OK, so what do you need from us right now?"

"Right, I tried to get through to Rebecca. She'll need to know what happened and give some sort of story to the Cops. Jack Fisher will be identified pretty smartish when those Sally Ann casualties start being questioned. They all know me, and saw me speaking to Kevin over there on a number of occasions. Kevin's on tenterhooks because he can't cover for me for very long without being charged himself. I have to go round to Canary Wharf and let the American Skinner know what happened. This might be the last straw for any further involvement they might want with me. In fact they may decide that I'm more of a liability at this stage."

"They might just decide to get rid of you now," Jerry said, with concern in his voice.

"Yeah, I've thought of that, but I have to find out if I'm still in the group or not. If I'm not, they couldn't let me wander off, especially if there's a Police alert to pick up a Jack Fisher. Rebecca would have to contain any linkage between Jack Fisher and Danny Quigley for starters."

Sackville sounded doubtful.

"She's pulled in a lot of favors already with the Police on your behalf. I'm not sure how much more they're willing to play 'hands off' where you're concerned, especially with all the bodies piling up. This is England after all, not bloody Chicago in the old days."

"So, what can you do Jerry."

"Right, decision time. Firstly, I'll contact Alina who is, I know out on a surveillance operation on that Bashir chap. I'll get her to nip across to Canary Wharf, if she can pull away from there, and record you meeting with the American. Unfortunately, I can't organize a SWAT team at this late stage, but you're still armed I take it?"

"Yes, I am, but I was planning to stash the pistol in a locker here in a subway station. I could keep it, as Skinner will assume I'm carrying it when I tell him I've just shot two of his men, but I still have to come up with some story as to why I had the weapon in my locker at the Sally Ann in the first place."

Jerry groaned. "Jesus Danny, you have so many holes in your story at this stage, I just can't see it holding together much longer. OK, my advice is to go in with that pistol stuck in your waistband or somewhere. It might give you an edge. Secondly, I'll barge into Rebecca's meeting, privilege of my role in MI5, and brief her on what's happening. Oh, one good piece of information, Scotty McGregor's come back and is sitting drinking tea downstairs right now. Says he tried to contact you on your mobile."

"Oh shit, I rushed out of the Sally Ann in a hurry, as you can imagine. Now listen, you've given me an idea. Have Alina pick up Scotty and take him with her to that surveillance at Canary Wharf. He's authorized to carry a weapon, so make sure he has one. I'll watch for them and won't go in until I see the van there. I know most of the number plates by now anyway."

"I hear you and that's an excellent idea. How will Scotty know that you're in trouble?"

Danny laughed. "Good point. OK, firstly, if he hears shots, tell him to hit that basement as fast and as hard as he can, and to watch out for me. Second, if I'm inside for too long as far as he's concerned, to come and knock on the basement apartment door and pretend to be looking for an apartment. It was on the market up to last week, so it might just be long enough for me to show my face, if I'm still OK. If not, Scotty knows what to do."

"Heck Danny, we normally plan for three months for something like this. You're making it up on the spot as we talk. Well, I have to go and start contacting people. All I can say is good luck Mate."

CHAPTER 58

Jimmy Patton had left, and the Welshman came back in and sat down across the desk from Bashir.

"So, he's the goods then?" Tommy Jones asked.

"I believe so. What d'you think?"

"I believe in old President Reagan's statement - 'check and verify'. While you were talking to Patton, I had someone outside who used to be Saas, call the Regiment headquarters, asking about Patton. He said he's heard that he was job-hunting without much success, and had come across something that might interest him. They just played dumb with him saying that, yes he'd left, but had no idea where he was at the present moment. They asked for my contact's name outside here, but he just hung up. So, Patton existed and was in the Saas, but they're playing coy. It sounds like our boyo is in deep shit as he claimed."

"As he laid out, I believe he's just what I'm looking for Mr. Jones."

"Hey, say no more. I really don't want to know. Now you were talking about a fee, in cash I recall, for setting this up. Can we finish this side of it then I can get us a couple of drinks in here?"

Ten minutes later they both sat back, after Jones had slipped an envelope of cash into a drawer.

It was Bashir who brought up the topic that seemed to interest him.

"You probably guessed what my profession is outside of the fact that I work at the Afghanistan Embassy for the new Government in Kabul, who are just one year in power right now. I won't elaborate on it, however part of my brief is to pick up rumors, whispers even, on what the major powers are thinking and planning for our country, and where the power shifts are occurring in the world."

Jones grinned. "You're a spook, in other words."

Bashir shrugged. "Whatever you say. However, it's common knowledge that the U.K. is cutting their Forces down to practically nothing: This could very well have certain implications for my country, especially with the upsurge in Taliban attacks. Where would the U.K. and more importantly the U.S. stand if the Taliban got tied in with ISIS and went after us, the new Afghan Government?" he queried, having a long drink with obvious appreciation.

"OK. For starters, Omar, I'm not a political animal. As long as those greedy corrupt bastards up there in the House of Commons, keep their paws off my business and me, I really don't give a shit. As to your question, let me tell you what my old Welsh Grandmother said, when I saw her last weekend. She has a reputation as a physic and a prophet if you like, and a lot of what she says actually comes true. She's held in some fear and trepidation, I can tell you. Probably the old witches had similar sway in their village way back in the last century."

"I'm not really interested in old wives tales Jones. Give me something I can put in a dispatch back to Kabul, that might be useful."

"You're not going to like this my friend."

Bashir shrugged. "OK, let's hear it."

"Right! I'm told that she can go into a trance at any time, and predict future happenings… small things usually like the sex of a new baby in the womb; who might win an election; or is someone a suitable match for a lad or lassie in the village? Sometimes she can predict a health issue, a heart attack, or occasionally even a death, not necessarily the name of the person who will die but, for example, she might say 'a young man will die this year in a car accident'. I have to say that quite often she's right on...sometimes way off as well, but anyway, that's not what you want is it?"

"As the English say 'You're buying,' so keep talking."

"Right, here's what she predicted: the Russians launched three nuclear missiles at the United States, hitting Washington, New York, and one other city that she couldn't name. A newly elected President was killed in the attack and his Vice President, who was a committed Christian, had been sworn in and had been sworn in as President. Despite the urging of the defense Generals, he refused to use the black box to retaliate in a return strike against Russia... he just couldn't push that trigger, which would have resulted in millions of people dying. The Generals were out of their minds, trying to chase up the person who should replace him because he couldn't carry out his Presidential role. The Speaker of the House who would normally have stepped in, had also been killed in the attack. They finally managed to organize the next replacement, pro tempore of the Senate. Then they found that the President had already sent a message to the Russians, asking for a cease-fire and a truce, in order to avoid the further death of millions. On hearing this, the Brexit U.K. declared it's neutrality in the developing conflict, and the European Union followed suit, followed surprisingly by NATO. Other countries with nuclear weapons such as India and Pakistan followed suit too. Strangely it was France, an EU and NATO member, who launched a nuclear weapon at Russia, but it was intercepted and the Russians then nuked Paris.

That finished the French. It was a new world order, my old Welsh Grandmother claimed, and that the world would never be the same again."

Bashir stared at him.

"This whole thing's ridiculous! This is just some old woman, playing 'spin the bottle' or something like that. Come on, you can't tell me you believe this story!"

Jones smiled. "Yeah, it's probably a load of crap, and I wouldn't really advise you to put it in the black bag going back to Kabul. They'd probably recall you immediately."

He clapped the Afghan on the shoulder and they both burst out laughing.

Bashir shook his head. "It must be the English beer. I'm crazy, sitting here listening to this total bullshit, as you English are so fond of saying… a U.S. President refusing to fight back with all those nuclear subs out there! Come on, get real. Tell me something of some use to me, instead of this garbage."

Jones smiled with him, but deep in his eyes something had stirred as he recalled the lifeless expression, distant gaze, and monotone voice of his Grandmother when she was recounting her predictions. He might just open up that old cottage down there that one of his uncles had left him. The valley might be an ideal place to be, if things got really hairy.

He shook his head. He'd have to get rid of that old Celtic monkey sitting on his shoulder, whispering tales of doom and gloom. Whatever happened in the world, people would still be drinking beer!

CHAPTER 59

The American didn't look very pleased to see him.

"Where the hell have you been Jack? I've been sitting here pulling my hair out with people coming and going, and you're supposed to be the guy running them around. Remember we're paying you big bucks to back me up here, and now Akmal and Abdul have disappeared completely off the map, after getting fixed up at the hospital."

Danny looked away avoiding his gaze and made a face.

Skinner caught the look. "What's going on Jack? Am I missing something?"

"Well yeah, you are Frank. Sorry to be the bearer of pretty shitty news."

"Oh no, not more bad news! This operation's falling apart: Ali disappears off the map grabbed by the Police; you disable two of my men, one a top martial arts trainer and a future leader when we launch our operation here in the U.K., and now you're telling me there's more shit coming down. OK let's have it" he demanded.

"You're not going to like this Frank. I was sitting in the back room of the Sally Ann clearing out my locker, when I heard a burst of weapons firing out front in the reception area. I grabbed a pistol I'd borrowed from a chap after coming back from Belfast. After we'd been shot at over there, I thought we were going back. Anyway, I rush outside, only to have two people start blasting off at me. One had a sawn off shotgun and the other a pistol of some sort. You'll never guess who these two were." He paused.

Skinner stared at him. "Tell me, for Christ sake. I'm beginning to think I really won't like this."

Danny nodded. "You won't Frank, I can tell you. The chap with the shotgun was Abdul and his Mate was…"

"Fucking Akmal" Skinner finished the sentence for him. "Oh shit, I don't believe what I'm hearing!"

"You won't like the rest of it either. They were obviously there to get revenge on me, and they'd already opened up on a bunch of poor homeless people quietly having breakfast."

The American sat there looking dazed.

Finally, he caught Danny's arm roughly, and shook him.

"Tell me the rest," he demanded hoarsely.

Danny shrugged. "As I came through the door, they started firing away at me. Pieces of the door were splintering all around. I dived into the room in a forward roll and came up shooting…"

Skinner let his arm go. "You killed them didn't you? You bastard! They only had one good arm apiece, for God's sake. You didn't have to kill them."

Danny raised his arms. "Frank, you've been in action. You know the score and you certainly know that when bullets are flying all around you, you don't sit there working out your options. Those two were firing up a storm before I even entered the room. All you need is one arm to fire a pistol, and a sawn off shotgun can be fired one-handed as well. I was dead if I hadn't taken them out. Now, here's the thing, someone here had filled them in as to my location. They knew exactly where I was."

Danny had only slipped this in to re-focus the American's mind elsewhere.

Frank's head swiveled round towards the room where the Jihadists were noisily having a meeting.

"Someone here?" he echoed.

"Exactly, and it could only be Mohammed or Zain. The new bunch didn't know my movements, and where I tend to hang out."

Skinner sat there, mulling the information around in his mind.

"Hmm, I don't like where this is going. We were supposed to slip a large group back into the U.K. and quietly prepare for the equivalent of a 9/11 here. This could blow the lid off the whole thing: returning Jihadists opening up on a group of homeless people in a place like the Sally Ann."

He gave Danny a calculating look. "So where does this leave you Jack? Those Sally Ann people know you, and the Police will be looking for you as we speak."

"I'm screwed Frank. No two ways about it. It'll be hitting the TV screens as we speak. In addition, Kevin, the chap you met at the Sally Ann, will have no option but to mention my involvement. Even though, as far as he's concerned, I saved the day in one way, killing those two who shot up the place killing and wounding a whole slew of them."

"Probably leading them right back to this address. You signed the papers upstairs for this flat, so he'll remember you as will Zain's sister, but she'll say nothing. Jack, I have to say it, you've become a fucking liability, and one more thing, the weapon you shot Akmal and Abdul with - how come you have a weapon that I know nothing about? Why wasn't I told about it? Tell me that Jack?"

"Basically Frank, there wasn't time. I put the word out for a weapon when we got back from Belfast, on the assumption that we'd be going back over there. I had no intention of being a target for those crazy Irish bastards again, and I would have gone across by ferry to avoid the stricter Airport security. This morning, believe it or not, this guy slips in to the Sally Ann and offers me the weapon, strictly on a loan basis for two weeks. Kevin came in while we were discussing it, and I shoved it in my locker, telling the chap to come back later to conclude the deal. It was for a whole bundle of money for just the temporary loan of the weapon, and I wanted to talk to you about it. Sure, you'd vetoed the return trip to Belfast by then, but I thought you might have some other need for it. Luckily, the gun was loaded, and I'm familiar with weapons as you are, so when the situation blew up outside, I'd no problem using it."

The American was stony-faced as he sat there staring across at Danny. He looked away tapping his fingers. Finally he looked back at him.

"Are you carrying right now Jack?" he asked quietly.

"Yep, when I left the Sally Ann in a hurry, I took a few seconds to run back in and grab my stuff from the locker. I couldn't leave the pistol there either so I took it with me. My intention was to stuff it in another locker in the subway coming back to Canary Wharf, but believe it or not I couldn't find an empty one in either of the two locker sections I came across. So yes, I have it tucked into my belt at the moment, but we have to agree a price with the chap who gave it to me. These guys are fringe crime people, really bad bastards, and will be after me for it."

Frank chuckled, suddenly appearing to relax.

"That's your problem as I see it, not mine. I'm not hiring any weapon that's just killed two people. Anyway, let me have a look at it. I miss the feel of a weapon since I got back from Syria."

In the surveillance van, down the road, Alina and Scotty stared across at each other.

"Shit, if he hands it across, he might be killed on the spot!" Scotty said reaching for the door.

Alina grabbed him. "No, not yet. Let it play out some more. Danny always has other tricks up his sleeve, if things really get hairy."

"Hey, this is as hairy as it gets, girl. You're placing a lot of confidence in him. He's probably waiting for my knock on the door, for God's sake!"

She put her hand to her lips. "Shhh, let's listen."

313

CHAPTER 60

Frank Skinner, the American, hefted the weapon with the ease of someone who was used to handling handguns.

"H.K. M 23 pistol, with a twelve round box magazine. In my Marine days we associated these with Special Forces' armaments. In fact they referred to them as SOCOM pistols. Jack I must admit I'm baffled as to why some street hawker of weapons here in the U.K. would offer you one which is easy to buy back home in the good old U.S.A., but here in England where all weapons have been confiscated some years back by the Government, how would they get their hands on this high-end type of gun? Can you tell me that?"

Danny shrugged, shaking his head.

"I've no idea Frank. If I was to make a guess, it could have come over to the U.K. with some of the U.S. R&R troops (rest and recuperation) coming in from Iraq or Afghanistan, or even our own Brit. lads coming home with some souvenirs and flying in our Military aircraft with little checks on them. I've personally seen many of them slipping stuff through, drugs as well of course, that were spirited away off Base as soon as the aircraft touched down. The pistol might have been sold off quietly to some gun collector, from whom it might have been stolen at some later date. We could sit here all day speculating, but I would suggest we've more important things to discuss, wouldn't you?"

Just then Zain and the tall gaunt-faced Mohammed Shareef came through from the other room. Mohammed looked at the pistol in Frank's hand.

"What's up Frank? Planning on shooting Jack here?" he asked with a grin.

The American didn't return his attempt at levity.

He gazed long and hard at Danny before leaning sideways to look at Mohammed.

"Jack just shot and killed Syed and Abdul, so killing him is an option I'm seriously looking at right now."

Mohammed gasped and leaned forward on the table, as if for support.

"But that's impossible! Why, I spoke to them earlier this morning."

Danny cut in with an attempt to take the focus off him.

"You didn't happen to tell them that I sometimes hang out in the Sally Ann did you? They came in with a sawed off shotgun and a pistol, and opened up on a roomful of people sitting there eating their breakfast. I heard the assault from the next room and came through with that pistol I was planning to rent off a chap, once I talked it over with Frank here. I came under immediate fire, and just did what any soldier does automatically when he comes under attack. You don't try to reason with someone blasting at you with a sawed off shotgun. Yeah, they both went down and I'm real sorry about that, but they seemed crazy. Was it you who pointed them in my direction Mohammed?"

The man stepped back, a worried look on his face.

"Now wait a minute Jack! I didn't set this thing up, if that's what you're thinking. Sure we were kicking things around with the group and yes, as I recall your name came up. I forget who might have mentioned the Sally Ann. It could have been Zain...I just can't recall exactly, but I do recall that it was Abdul who was driving the conversation."

Frank put the weapon down on the table and shook his head.

"The shit will hit the fan for sure just as soon as the Police question that guy who runs the Sally Ann, and some of those street people who came under attack. So Mohammed, get together the group who are left, and clean the apartment carefully for fingerprints, then pile them into Jack's vehicle with you driving, and head north to some of those safe houses we discussed until this cools off. If there isn't room in the car just squeeze them in until you reach Luton, an hours drive north of here, and have some of them take the train. I have to emphasize that Muslims opening fire indiscriminately in a charity place such as the Sally Ann, on a bunch of defenseless street people, is going to create a firestorm of Media and Police attention on us, and especially our teams trying to slip back in to the U.K. We'll have to postpone them coming in for awhile, but the targets here in the U.K. still remain the same under the time-plan we discussed overseas, and will still be vulnerable to our planned attacks."

"What about my sister upstairs? She'll be staying here and will be questioned by the Police for sure. The Superintendent upstairs will soon spot Jack's face on TV, assuming there's security systems at the Sally Ann. Will she be in some trouble?"

"Does the Super upstairs know that she and you are related?" Frank asked.

Zain thought about that for a moment.

"You know what, I don't think it was ever mentioned, so she could just say she heard at the market of some people coming back from study overseas, that needed some temporary accommodation, and put a word in for them with the Super.

She can claim she didn't know them, and has never met Jack, who signed for the apartment here, and who was running the group around London in his car. It might get her off the hook, and she doesn't have to mention that we're related."

Frank sighed. "A lot of ifs there, but we have no option at this stage, so jump to it and get moving."

He looked at Danny. "Let's have your keys for Zain" he ordered.

He handed them over without comment.

After a speculative look at Danny, Zain left the room.

Frank leaned back and took a long hard look at Danny.

Down in the vehicle, Scotty opened the car door. "This is getting hairy, I'm going to knock on the door looking for an apartment, as we discussed earlier."

Alina tensed, gripping his arm.

"Scotty please, just give this situation another minute. You might set off alarm bells if you happen to turn up right now. The American is no fool. He'll sniff that something's wrong, believe me," she pleaded.

Scotty threw off her grip. "For fucks sake we're talking about Danny's life here, while we piss around."

She continued to grasp his arm.

"Just give it another minute Scotty. This is Danny we're talking about. He always thinks things through and has a back up plan. Anyway, what would happen to Frank's group packing up and sanitizing the apartment if shots go off over there?"

"OK, I'll give it another few minutes but I have to tell you, then I'm off over there like a bolt out of hell. I've backed him too many times in the past to let him down now."

Back in the apartment Frank leaned forward, picked up the weapon and looked at Danny.

'This is it' Danny thought... 'It all depends on how good a shot he is'.

He realized that his options were limited at this stage.

'Where the hell was Scotty?'

Frank slid the pistol across the table.

"Get rid of this Jack. Give it back to that gun hawker you mentioned, then disappear for a couple of weeks somewhere. I don't really care. I have to say I'm really pissed off with you, but I've asked myself what I would have done in similar circumstances. I didn't survive Fallujah in Iraq, without being in situations where I had to make split second decisions to save my butt, or more importantly, my Buddies' Asses."

Danny's face creased with relief.

"Hey Frank, I'm really sorry about this turn of events. Remember, I came in with you to make some money, and it

317

was starting to happen for me. I wouldn't do anything to screw up a sweet arrangement like this, so what happens now? What do I do after the two weeks are up?"

Frank took out a slip of paper and wrote briefly on it, then handed it over to Danny.

"Meet me down there in two weeks time if things have calmed down somewhat. I'll call you on your cell phone to confirm it around that time. I can't say for sure. This problem you created might just be sabotaging my plans to move forward. We'll take it from there to the next stage, which is probably the most important one."

Danny looked at the note. "I know this place quite well. It's on the south west coast... a small fishing village as I recall. Tell me, what are we going to be doing there?"

Frank cracked a smile for the first time. "Those weapons I mentioned coming in...I'll say no more."

Danny whistled. "Oh man, you weren't kidding! You got a bunch of weapons coming in! So you're gearing up for the big one. I can't wait to see these fucking Brits. get it right where it hurts. Hey, I like where this is heading Frank. This is mega!"

"You better believe it my friend. This will be their 9/11 for sure. Nothing will ever be the same in the good ole British Isles after it's over."

Casually Danny asked one further question. "So what are the targets going to be then?"

Frank chuckled. "You don't really expect me to answer that do you? My philosophy is that a secret is something known to just one person, and right now, here in the U.K. at least, that person is me. You'll find out when the operation has all the stages set up and is ready to be launched. Planning is supposedly one of my skills, and that was the reason I was chosen for this operation. When I give the go ahead, you can bet the attacks will be seamless and once launched, there'll be no stopping them. Keep your nose clean for the next couple of weeks Jack, and you can be part of that and make some nice money in the final phases. Now it's time for you to get your ass out of here and get out of London as your first priority. You hear me?"

He did. He grabbed the weapon and hurriedly left the apartment.

Around the corner it was a much relieved surveillance team who dragged him into the vehicle - no one as much as Danny was. That had been far too close for comfort.

CHAPTER 61

Back In Thames House the DG, who had been receiving a direct link from the surveillance van, sat back and looked at Peter Sanderson.

"Whew, can you believe this? Danny just notched up the last of his nine lives! That was very, very close. Despite what Alina said to Scotty in the van earlier, I don't think he did have a back-up plan. Scotty was his insurance policy, and she took a real risk there, didn't she?"

"Yes, but she made the right decision, Danny's still in the group, and did you hear the American's last remark?"

"I sure did Peter... about a nine eleven here on British soil! Can you imagine how big this is? Thank God Danny's still on the inside with the group."

She paused for a moment, slapped her forehead then lifted the phone, stabbing some numbers from her diary that she had opened. She turned on the speaker.

Peter sat there watching her.

The phone seemed to ring endlessly, and Rebecca was praying that it wouldn't go to voice mail.

Finally a voice came on the line.

"The Sally Ann. Look this is a bad time, we have the Police and all sorts of people here can you...?"

She cut across him. "This is the Director General of MI5. Is Kevin there, I need to speak to him urgently?"

"Director General? Oh no he's not here, he's around at the hospital. He travelled there with some of the wounded."

"Fine, OK, what hospital is that, d'you know?" she pressed.

She listened and started writing something down, then she hung up, looked at Peter and handed him the note.

"I need you to get round to this hospital, locate Kevin and tell him to say nothing about Jack, apart from him dropping in and making a few calls from that other room and using a locker occasionally, he doesn't know any more about him, no more than he would with any of the other street people. They're a pretty closed-mouthed lot when it comes to sharing their personal backgrounds."

"But Ma'am this won't be a response that Kevin will agree to run with. Heck, he's got dead and wounded being carted out of there and being operated on right now. He's an ex-Copper and will want to co-operate with the Police on this one hundred percent... otherwise HE could be charged with obstruction, and what about the security system? Danny's picture will be right there, not just from today but his previous visits there? The street people will be telling their stories about Jack dropping in as well."

"Aha..., shows where pre-planning pays off. When we set this up with Kevin we got him to agree to shut off the security system when Danny came in, so his picture won't be on there."

Peter didn't look satisfied. "The Police wouldn't buy that. Coincidental blanks when their main suspect came in to the building? Come on!"

"We were a little cleverer than that Peter. We arranged for Kevin to periodically call up the Security people and complain that the system had some sort of glitch in it, and they came round and kept testing it. They couldn't find anything of course, but there's a record of these calls to the Security company."

Peter still looked unhappy.

"Look, if it was me in Kevin's position with his regulars killed and wounded, I'd need more than a visit from a representative of MI5 to deliberately stop co-operating with the Police. It could blow up in his face very quickly. He'll want to know there's something much more important than getting immediate justice for his people, and that will protect his ass down the line when the Cops get to the bottom of it, which they will. The Media will be delivering a firestorm of pressure on the Police to get results, and fast."

She looked at him thoughtfully.

"You got a point there Peter… an excellent one."

She jumped up and went across to one of the computers on a separate table, sat down and started typing.

Peter sat there not saying a word.

Rebecca pressed the printer button and two sheets came through immediately. She picked them up, went back to Peter and placed the two copies down in front of him.

"D'you think that would do it for Kevin?" she asked.

He looked down and saw there were four lines typed on her official MI5 letterhead, which read: 'Kevin, something has come up arising from the recent incident at the Sally Ann, which could have a major effect on the national security of the U.K. For this reason I am asking you (no, instructing you) to deny any knowledge of Jack Fisher's background at this point in time. This letter will protect you from any charges of obstruction from the Police, when we can, in time, reveal the full facts.'

Peter looked up.

"Nice one. I think this should do it Ma'am, and I see you have both our names on the bottom with myself as a witness. Yes, in Kevin's position, I could accept this. A caution though, it may not keep Kevin mute for long when he starts getting the full weight of funerals and his wounded street people. Not withstanding the ongoing Police interrogations which may bring into question Kevin's apparent memory lapses."

"Fair comment Peter. Now, we'll both sign this, and you head around to the hospital and get Kevin off on his own a.s.a.p. I'll keep a copy here as a record."

"You know, of course, that he's probably already been de-briefed to some extent, by the Police."

"I'm sure you're right Peter, but it sounds like he jumped into an ambulance with the wounded and left the scene, hopefully before the Police sat him down for some heavy duty investigations. Do your best over there anyway. Fingers crossed."

He left the room rapidly.

Rebecca picked up the phone again and spoke to Alina in the surveillance van.

"I want you to bring Danny back here immediately, and if you can disguise him in some way coming into Thames House, that would be a good precaution."

Danny was back in the DG's office within twenty minutes, accompanied by Alina and Scotty. Rebecca was finishing up a phone call and gestured for them to sit down. Her secretary came in behind them and quietly took orders for drinks.

After a short few sentences she hung up and looked at them, shaking her head.

"Listening in to Danny's meeting and Scotty's close intervention, delayed by Alina's call, I came as close as I've been to a stroke since I took office here as Director General.

In fact, I remarked to Peter who sat in with me, that Danny had just chalked up the last of his nine lives!"

They were delayed from making any response as the secretary slipped back in with a tray of coffees and tea, which they eagerly grasped. Finally they settled back in and Rebecca brought them up to date on her initiative with Kevin at the hospital. She carried on:

"So, in conclusion Danny, if Kevin plays mum for a short while, you may not be the focus of a Police manhunt with the usual pictures plastered all across the newspapers. Now, what was your reaction after the American started talking about a 9/11 being carried out on British soil? Was he for real or was it just wishful thinking on his part?"

"From my short association with Frank, I'd say it was for real Rebecca. He wouldn't mouth off on something like that. There's also the plan to collect a major arms cache down on the south coast within a couple of weeks. My reading is that this is the real Mc Coy, and we need to take it seriously."

"I'd agree with Danny on this" Alina remarked. "We're lucky he's still on the inside, and I'm absolutely amazed they didn't finish him off right there and then. I mean he was there when Ali disappeared, and now he's killed two of the others after disabling them yesterday at that gym. This has got to start alarm bells ringing in the group - just too many coincidences for their liking."

Scotty nodded. "Alina's right. There's something not quite right here and I can't figure it out. The American accepted the whole incident at the Sally Ann far too readily, for my liking."

Rebecca frowned. "Hmm, wheels within wheels you're thinking? Could be right there. How would that grab you? The American, for his own reasons, dropped the word to those two that you would be at the Sally Ann?"

There was a collective gasp from the group who sat forward, their faces reflecting astonishment.

"But why would he do that Ma'am?" Alina asked, obviously perplexed.

Rebecca smiled. "I've thrown it out there, so I want to see you people start thinking this through. Working closely with the justice system as I do, I can tell you that I've seen it all when it comes to people's motivation for taking certain paths or maintaining loyalties to people who, here–to-fore were close friends, so lets have some thoughts here, People" she prompted.

There was a long silence in the room as they looked at each other for some sort of lead into the topic.

Finally Danny nodded.

"OK, I agree, something smells about Franks reaction to the bad news I brought him. You know what? Almost like he was expecting it."

Alina leaned forward.

"He's right. I picked up on it as well. How's this? The two Jihadists that Danny crippled were a liability and of no further use, and Frank would be better off without them, so he sent them after Danny, hoping he might do the necessary."

"But Danny wasn't even armed. He could have been the one killed. How d'you figure that one out?" Scotty interrupted, obviously unhappy.

"Back to the human motivation that I mentioned" Rebecca said jumping back in. "Either Frank had sensed that Danny's story wasn't standing up - here's this poor ex-Military chap, down on his uppers and self esteem, and suddenly he's demonstrating a kick-ass nature and taking out one of their top trainers. Heck, he may even have had Danny followed by some people who are good at that stuff, and seen him meet up with some of us, or drive off in his car he'd parked around the back of the Jihadist's apartment, OR, and this I like, he might have felt that Danny was undermining his authority with the group in some way. I have to tell you, human nature continually amazes me," she concluded.

Danny sat back, shaking his head. "I'm lost at this stage. Why would Frank keep me inside then?"

Scotty shook his finger. "Think about this. Frank gave you the bait about 9/11 but wouldn't share what the targets were going to be. He wants you to stay in for some reason."

Alina agreed. "He wants to use you somehow, but he doesn't trust you."

Danny nodded. "Shit he knows I'm not kosher then. Where the hell does that leave me, going forward, meeting him down on the coast shortly?"

"It means that we have to provide you with every protection we can muster, and be ready for pretty much any eventuality. You have to turn up, otherwise we've lost contact with the group. As it is, I suspect that by this time Frank and everyone else have got out of London just as fast as they could, and we've no idea as to where they'll be staying up north."

"Probably some relatives or Jihadists who've already slipped back in" Alina commented.

Rebecca slapped the desk lightly, usually an indication that the meeting was finished. After some closing remarks the group got up to leave.

Rebecca caught Danny's arm.

"I need you to stay on for a moment. Something I want to run past you."

CHAPTER 62

She smiled for the first time since the previous meeting.

"Well Danny, I have some good news, and other news I'm not sure about, though your required disappearance for some time from that Jihadist group might play into your hands."

"I could use some good news right now Rebecca, believe me" he said feelingly.

"I do believe you, and just seeing you sitting there alive and well is good news for me. For a while back there..." she trailed off.

Danny took a drink of what was now cold coffee, but he stayed silent, waiting for her.

"Right here it is. The good news is that I've managed to access your funds from the Cayman Islands and am in the process of distributing it to the organizations that you stipulated. Am I right in that you don't want to be involved in handing it over to them?"

"Absolutely, and in any event I don't want to alert the Inland Revenue and also the people in Afghanistan who killed Jamilla. If they hear of me handing money over they would assume that I don't have their funds to give to them. Apart from that, I'm very much relieved to be shut of it, for all the trouble it's caused."

She chuckled, despite the seriousness of the topic.

"Not many people would share your views on money. You're not an entrepreneur Danny, that's for sure. Fine, I'll put the finishing touches to that in the next couple of days. Now, the second piece of news...."

She stopped speaking and reached into one of the drawers in her desk lifting out a cloth pouch, which she deposited in front of him.

"Open it." she instructed.

He hefted the pouch in his hand and carefully untied the top cord, smiling as he did so.

"I know what this is. I can hear them and feel them inside. It's the flipping diamonds isn't it?"

"Well, not quite right there. It's a bunch of flipping fake diamonds, to be more to the point."

He reached in and took out a handful of them, gasping as he did so.

"My God, they look so real! Not that I'm any expert on diamonds, but they look like the genuine article to me Rebecca and they feel like..."

"Diamonds? That's the whole idea isn't it? I must confess that I was equally impressed with their appearance. I think they'll do the job for you. That is if you still want to go through with it."

He put the diamonds down and stared intensely across at her.

"I'm surprised that you even need to ask me that" he answered in a low voice. "I could never face myself in the mirror again if I didn't revenge her death. I'm going through with this and nothing's going to stop me."

She lifted her hand in surrender.

"OK, I gather you believe she's already dead, so I wondered if you considered the risk you'll be taking to be worth it? Afghanistan isn't the place you were in as a soldier some time back. The NATO troops are reduced down to operating as trainers, and providing some back-up with air strikes. You've heard of course of the northern city of Kunduz falling to the Taliban some time back, and intelligence coming out of the country suggests that Afghanistan will go the same way as Iraq. I mean, the Taliban controls more land area there now than they did in 2001 when it actually ruled the country."

"Which means what for my trip?" he asked impatiently.

"Well, getting you in there under the guise of some sort of legitimate role for starters. We haven't aircrafts full of troops flying into Bagram Airport every day where we could slip you in. How can we get you up-country if you have to travel to that village where Jamilla was murdered?"

"Let's assume I can get back in, what about travelling as some sort of representative of an NGO (Non Government Organization), supplying school material, or whatever?"

She frowned. "Getting more chancy by the day, what with the re-emergence of the Taliban. Perhaps you should get Jamilla's murderer to come to you, now you believe she's dead. Those diamonds are what he's after."

His face reflected his doubt.

"I think the relatives of that Pashtun who hold me responsible for killing him in that air strike, may want me up-country, to get their revenge."

"All the more reason to stick to Kabul or a nearby location. I mean, why present yourself on a plate for them to take you out? Believe me, from the stories I've heard, it wouldn't be a slow death. They'd let their women loose on you with their skinning knives, but look, I'll talk to my opposite number at MI6. They still have an ongoing function over there and maybe, just maybe, they might have some insights into how we might pull it off. Now, question: do you plan to go in there alone?"

He thought about it for a moment, then glanced at her.

"I'd like to have Scotty and Jimmy Patton with me if possible Rebecca. Afghanistan's a very dangerous place as you well know, and I'd need some sort of professional backup to succeed in this."

"She rubbed her forehead. "Oh Danny, Danny, why am I even considering this. Getting the SAS OK from Hereford for Jimmy to work here in the U.K. is one thing, but to get them to go along with an operation abroad? I don't know how they'll jump. Scotty may be OK as he's leaving, or has left the Unit. Mind you, you still have to get his agreement on it."

He nodded. "Scotty will be OK I'm sure, and I'll still do the trip even if Jimmy Patton isn't given the go ahead. One more thing, I'm now going to put that advertisement in The Times and will use your phone again. In other words have your people record it and track it, if that's OK with you, for their arrangements to get their hands on the diamonds. I'm assuming that the phone number we called before will be still operating?"

"Fine. Let's try it and see shall we? Now, while you put the ad in I'll make those two calls to my opposite number at MI6 and the CO at Hereford. Lets meet up tomorrow, say in the afternoon, and I should have some information for you."

Just then Danny's cell phone vibrated. He glanced down at a text that had come through.

Jimmy Patton wanted to see him right away, and named a pub they both knew.

He was out of there in a moment, after a brief explanation. He didn't mention what he had been using Patton for in London.

She wouldn't like it.

She wouldn't want any more dead bodies piling up.

He was right on top of Jimmy before he spotted him... his eyes widened.

"Shit Danny, you look like some pansy from the pub next door" he marveled, not recognizing him with the disguise the MI5 people had slapped on him with the limited material they had in the van.

Danny grinned, relaxing for the first time that day, and slipped into a chair alongside him.

Jimmy raised his hand and a pint appeared in front of Danny like magic.

"I'd primed the barman to do his thing" he explained, "but dressed like that my boyo, he'll probably be revising his opinion of me."

They hefted the glasses at each other and had a long silent quaff.

"So what's the news Jimmy?" he queried.

"I wish I could just sit here and enjoy this pint and shoot the breeze for a couple of hours" he grumbled, putting his pint glass down and gazing longingly at it, "but here goes."

He quickly brought Danny up to date on his meeting with Omar Bashir and their discussion back in the pub.

Danny listened with growing interest.

Finally Jimmy stopped talking and had another drink.

"So the chap's bought into you hook line and sinker?" Danny asked.

"It appears so, but you never know. Without getting too tricky, I tried to see if he was following me when I made my way over here in the subway. You know, if it was too obvious that I was trying to give him the slip my cover story wouldn't ring true, but it looked to be okay. I mean he really did buy into my story: a pissed off ex-Military Squaddie, down on his luck from a stupid mistake with some under-age girl."

Danny smiled his approval. "Nice work there. I always knew you were lost to the stage my friend, and now you're proving it."

"It's not funny Danny. The chap wants your ass real bad, and he's in a hurry. I got the impression that things back in Afghanistan were hotting up, and he might have to get back there soon - something about the Taliban being a growing threat to the new President Ashraf Ghani."

"Well, that could be good. He might make some mistakes if he rushes into something. Did you squeeze some money out of him yet?"

"We're meeting tonight and he's going to bring a down payment - two thousand cash up front, and another three when we do the job."

"Oh man, I see what you mean about this not being funny. Sorry about that Jimmy. So what's his plan when you meet up?"

"He didn't exactly give me any details, but he's obviously got some source that's providing information to him. He knows, for example, that your daughter is in another safe house and that you're visiting her this evening. Whether he has the exact location or not I don't know for sure, but I'd say he's working on some definite information."

Danny shot forward in his seat. "Oh my God! I thought Allison was out of harms way! How could he get his hands on these details?"

He thought for a moment. "Oh shit no, I only mentioned casually to Alina that I planned to visit Allison this evening at the safe house where she is at present! I can't believe what I'm hearing!"

"I'm just repeating what this Bashir told me. He's bringing a weapon with a silencer, and pressed me pretty hard as to my readiness and willingness to kill someone in cold blood. You'd better be prepared for the worst Danny."

Danny was already grabbing his mobile phone and pressing some buttons. In a moment he was speaking with Rebecca.

"Look, I have some reliable information that this chap Omar Bashir has found out where Allison is staying and plans, we believe to make a move on her tonight. Can you have her moved immediately but leave the whole safe house setup as it is so we can still draw him in?"

He listened for a moment to some question from her.

"I've no idea, but obviously there's a leak at Thames House from someone in there."

He listened to her for a moment longer then hung up.

He glanced across at Jimmy.

"Rebecca's not a happy bunny at getting that sort of information, - the suggestion that there's a leak in her team somewhere. I didn't mention that I'd only told my plans for tonight to Alina."

"She's moving your daughter then?"

He nodded. "As we sit here. Now, how do we work this?"

The discussion took the best part of the next hour.

They didn't order any further pints.

CHAPTER 63

Omar Bashir was pleased to see that Jimmy Patton was standing outside the subway station as pre-arranged. As Jimmy reached for the door handle on the passenger side, Omar pushed the button on the window, and as it slid down he shouted across: "take the back seat Patton."

In a moment he jumped inside and pulled the door shut after him.

Bashir handed him a bulky package. "That's the weapon and silencer. Take a look at it once we get moving and familiarize yourself with it. I need you to be ready to go shortly, with no screw-ups at the critical time."

"Fine. Don't worry about me. I'll have a look just as soon as we get away from these people walking around. By the way, why am I in the back seat right now?"

"Two reasons really: one is that you'll be harder to spot in the back when you take out that weapon to examine it, and two that we'll be joined shortly by someone who will take the passenger seat. He'll get us through the gate at the safe house, and he'll engage the Guard when he comes out."

Jimmy looked surprised.

"Can you get access without any problem? I mean, do we have to take out the Guards. If so I need to be ready for that?"

Bashir chuckled grimly.

"We've got that covered, don't worry. Our passenger has the access password and is recognizable to most of the Security staff."

Patton shook his head in amazement.

"Shit, man, you really do have some contacts in high places to pull this off! In and out fast is my motto. Get the job done and get the hell out fast."

Bashir nodded, his face looking pleased.

"Tonight we finish this. No more messing around, and we both get paid. Does that sound good to you?"

"You got it Man. Now where's the down payment you promised?"

"In the bag with the weapon. We can pull into some well-lit supermarket if you want to count it. I've got the balance for you later when you do the job. It's up to you now Patton."

"Naw, that's okay by me. It wouldn't be wise to try to screw me on the money side at this stage. I'm sure you know that."

Omar chuckled without humor.

"Honor among thieves and all that eh?"

Patton didn't reply as the car was moving and he was checking the weapon carefully, locking in the magazine and levering the first round up the spout.

Bashir glanced in the mirror when he heard the 'snicking' sound and nodded in satisfaction.

"The silencer's already attached, as you noticed" he commented.

"Yeah, it all looks good. I've used this type of weapon many times before tonight. It has a nice feel to it. I know that anything one hits stays down, assuming you hit them in the right place. Now tell me, are you carrying as well?"

"Carrying, but not what you think. I'm carrying a camera to capture the result of the kill in full living color as it were."

Patton sat up, genuine surprise reflected on his face, from the streetlights as they flashed past.

"A camera, for Pete's sake! What on earth for?"

"The client wants evidence that the job gets done. It's personal, and he wants to see it before I get paid."

Jimmy's mind raced back to the briefing he'd had from Danny some time back. In the previous attack on an MI5 safe house, a camera had been used, and this man Bashir had been recognized as he fled in a vehicle. He might still have some qualms about him allowing Jimmy to survive and possibly be a future witness against him. He had already garroted the remaining witness to the last attempt at killing Danny.

Bashir claimed he was not carrying a weapon, but Jimmy still intended to stay alert, and in any event there could easily be one stored in the front of the car that could be a threat later… if there was a later.

He hoped Danny could get the choreography right, especially with an unknown character who would shortly be occupying the front seat. Who the hell was he and what was the level of threat from him?

Right then the car pulled into a small mall parking lot alongside a number of parked cars. The door in a mid range Peugeot opened and a man got out smartly and came across to them. Briefly, Jimmy got the impression of a slim mid-forties man who wasted no time in getting into their vehicle.

Bashir took off immediately, and as he pulled back onto the main road, he pointed backward to the rear seat.

"That's Patton back there. He's already tooled up and ready to go."

Jimmy was aware of hard eyes briefly inspecting him.

Bashir glanced back at Jimmy.

"No names needed at this stage. Let's just get it done shall we?"

The next half hour was spent in silence as they sped across London and headed south. Bashir was using a GPS and appeared at ease working his way through the city.

They all tensed as the closed and barred gate materialized in front of them. A Guard came out from the hut alongside the gates.

The man in the passenger seat pushed the button on the window, which slid down. The Guard lowered his head.

"Yes sir, can I see some ID please?"

The passenger held up a shield, which the Guard looked at.

"So, who are you calling on this evening Sir?" he asked.

"Oh, a Mister Danny Quigley. I have to brief him on an emergency that's come up at MI5. He's here isn't he?"

"Yes he is Sir, but I'd have to call and check with him first."

The man in the passenger seat leaned slightly out the window.

"Look here, this is a matter of national security, Officer, and lives could very well be lost while you stand here chatting. My ID is perfectly legitimate isn't it? Now get that gate open."

The Guard pulled back and looked uncertainly up the drive, then walked over and reached inside the hut.

The gate rolled across and Bashir sped through.

Hmm Jimmy thought, slack for an MI5 Guard, but slick acting otherwise.

He was glad it didn't come to taking out the Guard, and wondered if the passenger had been prepared to do that.

Perhaps tasked to take out Jimmy later on as well.

As they cruised up the driveway, Bashir now fully alert, barked out an instruction to Jimmy.

"There's usually at least one Security person out front. Get ready in case you have to take them down."

Jimmy already knew from Danny's briefing that there wouldn't be any, and had prompted him as to what to say if this drew comment.

When they cruised up to the building, the car came to a halt at the front steps. No one moved in the car.

Bashir looked across at the passenger.

"I thought you said there might be some Security out front"

Jimmy cut in before he replied.

"Knowing Guards as I do, they're probably having a leak or grabbing a coffee somewhere."

The passenger nodded.

"He's probably right Omar. Good news if you don't have to show your hand just yet. I'll stay in the car as agreed, and you two head in there and watch for any Security people that might be hanging around. I see the lights are all on downstairs and some flickering lights on the first floor…. perhaps a TV going."

"There might be some big game on tonight that the Security detail are keeping their eye on" Jimmy volunteered.

"You British and your fucking soccer!" Bashir sneered. "Come on Patton, let's do it. I'm feeling lucky all of a sudden."

They both jumped out and started moving cautiously up the front steps, Bashir carrying a rucksack.

Jimmy was aware that the passenger had leaned forward, and he felt those hard eyes on him again.

It was Patton's game now.

He carefully tried the front door handle and the door opened easily, then he paused and looked at Bashir who gestured urgently that he get inside. Holding the silenced weapon, he eased it open and glanced inside, keeping his body well back. Bashir started to push forward, but Jimmy held him back while he took a quick look inside.

No sign of a Security Guard.

He stepped in quickly, followed by the Afghan.

They stood there briefly looking up and down the entrance hall. Still no Security. The only sound was coming from upstairs, and it was obviously a television.

Jimmy turned to Bashir and whispered.

"They must all be upstairs watching some sports program. Let's head up there, shall we, and we can take them by total surprise?"

The Afghan nodded and pushed him towards the stairs, fumbling with the zipper on the rucksack.

Jimmy led the way, climbing slowly and carefully, the sound of the TV station getting louder.

On reaching the top, Jimmy pointed to a door where the sound was coming from, a bright light filtering through from the bottom of it. They crept up to the door and Jimmy put his ear to it, then he turned to Bashir who pointed to the door with a finger.

Jimmy got the message.

This time he didn't open the door and step back. He opened it and leapt through, followed by the Afghan.

Jimmy had the pistol extended out in front of him.

The man sitting in front of the TV jumped to his feet. He looked shocked at the intrusion.

Bashir grinned all over his face. "Danny Quigley! I finally caught up with you. Now you pay the price."

He looked around "but where are your Security?" he asked with some anxiety creeping into his voice.

Danny shrugged. "Foolishly, I gave them the night off to watch the game at home. After all I was here with my daughter. They knew I wouldn't let anything happen to her would I?"

"Foolish yes, but you mention your daughter… where is she by the way?"

"Oh, I let her go to a movie with some friends" he said rapidly, his head swiveling towards a door off to one side.

"Hey, Mate" Jimmy barked, "I bet you she's in that room he just glanced across at."

Bashir smiled. "I believe you're right there. I'll get my camera out and be ready for her when she comes out. You know the drill Patton. You kill her as I get a shot of Quigley's face as you do so, then you kill him. My clients would have it no other way."

He put his rucksack down and rapidly pulled out a camera and a small tripod that he extended and fastened the camera to the top of it. Then he backed up and shuffled the tripod around until he appeared satisfied. He nodded to Jimmy.

"As soon as she opens the door, kill her" he instructed.

Danny took a step forward and glared at the Afghan.

"I'm glad you actually put that into words Mr. Omar Bashir. I have no hesitation now in killing you."

The Afghan cast a hurried, anxious glance across at Jimmy who was still pointing the weapon at Danny.

"Nice try Quigley, but you see I hold all the cards. You've run out of options and, I might add, you've run out of life as well, as soon as your young daughter puts her head through that door."

Danny chuckled good humoredly.

"Touch of reality now for you old son" replied Danny. "Have another look at your friend Jimmy Patton, and my old Regiment Mate."

Bashir's eyes widened.

His gaze shot sideways, and what he saw brought a shudder to his hands resting on the camera.

Patton had swiveled around and was now pointing the pistol at his head, a large grin spreading across his face.

Bashir's jaw dropped in shock.

"No, it can't be. I gave you two thousand pounds…!"

Jimmy laughed. "I doubt if I would have been given the opportunity to spend any of it Bashir. You wouldn't have left any witnesses. I suspect that chap you left in the car would have seen to it."

Right then a form stepped inside the door and Jimmy felt the cold steel of an automatic pistol pressed into the back of his head.

"Did someone mention my name? Kindly put that pistol down on the floor in front of you… slowly now… I know how tricky you chaps can be."

It was Danny whose jaw dropped then.

"Trevor Hawthorn" he gasped.

Jimmy noted the shocked state of Danny.

"Who the heck is he Danny?" he demanded. "He travelled in the same car with us here. Got us inside the compound."

Hawthorn's bleak eyes fastened on Danny.

"Good question. Tell him I'm the Manager whose career you destroyed with your clever moves, you and the bitch of a Director General, who's next on my list, right after I finish you off. I know exactly where she'll be in the next little while."

"But how did you know where I'd be this evening? How could you possibly have found out?" Danny rasped.

"You weren't to know that I'd arranged to clear out my locker this afternoon at MI5, Trevor responded. Then I had a small pot of tea in the staff coffee room. No one thought anything of me being there. After all, I resigned for acceptable reasons, no suspicion attached to me. In the coffee room it's surprising the little pieces of information you pick up. I admit I slipped in a couple of innocent questions - very casually of course. I think it was your very close colleague Alina who provided the little nugget that brought me here."

Bashir looked urgently across at him.

"No more talk...he's just trying to postpone the inevitable... SHOOT HIM!"

Hawthorn raised the automatic slightly higher. Two things happened simultaneously.

Danny hadn't come quite unprepared. He had trained extensively in using a Japanese weapon called Iga Ryu Shuriken, which had been a secret weapon in Japan for hundreds of years. Secret, because there were very few trainers who taught it. The word Shuriken is a Japanese term for small pieces of metal used as throwing weapons. Researchers had suggested that defeated soldiers fleeing the battlefield had picked up broken swords, arrows and cracked pieces of armor, to defend themselves. Others believed that Samurai warriors used it as a short sword in battle. Danny had, on occasions, carried his in a small custom-made scabbard, not unlike the size of a handcuff pouch used by Policemen. He had been fortunate in finding a Master Japanese Trainer in London who had brought him up to a level of skill and competence that had even amazed the Master.

Danny was carrying his Shuriken by design this particular evening. He was alert and ready when Jimmy moved.

Jimmy swept his arm upwards, striking the gun held by Hawthorn, the bullet ploughing into the ceiling.

At that instant, Danny, extracted the Shuriken and launched it at Hawthorn. It embedded itself in his throat and he sank to his knees, blood pumping out of him.

Jimmy snatched the weapon in his collapsing hand. Out of the corner of his eye, he spotted Bashir turning towards the door.

He tossed the weapon across to Danny and drove his shoulder sideways against Bashir as he tried to dodge past, sending him crashing to the floor.

Danny walked across, adjusting the weapon in his hand, and stood in front of Bashir.

"On your feet you murderous bastard….UP, UP, UP" he roared.

The man crawled to his feet, his hands coming out in front of him pleadingly.

"Look, it's all a mistake. I wasn't going to kill anyone."

Danny's eyes were like slivers of ice.

"It was no mistake either, when you had my wife killed in front of her daughter" he grated.

"That wasn't supposed to happen…I…."

"OK one last question…. who ordered myself and my family to be killed?"

Bashir looked hopeful for a moment. "If I tell you that, will you let me go?" he begged.

"Of course."

"OK, it's the family of that top Pashtun leader you killed in an airstrike that you called in. They wanted you killed, but first wanted to see your family killed to make you suffer. It's a Pashtun tribal custom, you see."

"Oh I see all right Omar, I see, however…." he cocked the weapon loudly then nodded to Jimmy who grabbed a rug and threw it across the snout of the hidden camera he had installed earlier.

"No!" Bashir screamed, "I have diplomatic immunity. You'll never get away with it. I'll leave the country tonight…"

He could see from Danny's expression that it was too late.

"But you promised…"

"Bashir, this is for my wife Fiona. Anyway you should know by now not to trust anything said by an Infidel."

He fired two rapid shots to the head, then walking across to Hawthorn.

"Is he dead?" he asked Jimmy.

"Yes he is. That weapon cut his carotid artery and his windpipe. He's a goner for sure."

Nothing more was said.

Jimmy had been instructed what to do.

Danny retrieved the camera and helped carry the two bodies, now wrapped in body bags, down to the car outside.

He grabbed Jimmy's arm.

"Take care of that loose end we discussed and tell the Gate Guard to expect the DG to come through shortly."

When Jimmy had disappeared Danny went back into the building and called Rebecca. He knew she didn't want any more bodies. Jimmy was seeing to that.

It promised to be another long night, hopefully, if he could convince Rebecca, without any further Police involvement.

CHAPTER 64

When Rebecca arrived, Danny escorted her upstairs and sat her down opposite a small screen.

"OK, lay it out for me Danny. What's happened here?"

He didn't answer, just pointed to the screen, reached across to the projector resting on the table, and pressed the button.

She said nothing as the film ran through the episode that had transpired there a short time ago. Her main reaction was a loud gasp at the appearance of Trevor Hawthorn. Her second startled gasp was when he revealed that Alina had mentioned Danny's meeting with Allison that evening.

The film stopped. They both sat there saying nothing.

Finally she stirred.

"So he called me a bitch and was going to take care of me next, and this is the chap I worked with for a number of years without a hint of how he felt about me. So did that weapon you impaled him with kill him?"

He nodded. "Yep, he's gone Rebecca."

She looked around. "In more ways than one, by the look of things. I see some blood on the floor but I don't see any bodies. What about the other one, Bashir isn't it?"

"You don't need to know. Suffice it to say that he will never be a threat in the U.K. again."

"Why don't I need to know? I'm the Director of MI5 and this is one of my safe houses. I'm responsible for everything that goes on here, so I certainly do need to know" she demanded, her eyes flinty, "and by the way, what happened to that film? It cut off at a certain stage just at a critical time."

He raised his arms." Hey, I'm no techie as you well know. I guess the filmstrip must have run out at that point. In answer to your question, someone with diplomatic immunity disappearing, might result in questions being asked. Right now you have total deniability about the situation. Oh, and no bodies will turn up. Don't forget that Hawthorn had you in his sights after he finished Allison and myself. Remember, he referred to you as a 'bitch'."

"Very clever Danny, I must say. You set this whole thing up without even a 'by your leave'. I don't particularly like that at all."

"OK, the other option was a massive Police presence here and two more bodies to explain: one an ex-senior figure in MI5 and the other, someone from the Afghan Embassy. Which one would you have preferred?"

The frown on her face lessened. "Oh shit! ... Perhaps you made the right call. If Trevor Hawthorn doesn't turn up at the appropriate time we can declare him legally dead and pay his widow her pension. One more thing though, how d'you know they wouldn't shoot the Gate Guard? He was pretty exposed down there."

"Not really. He was fully briefed beforehand and told to not be too difficult. I did have one of your Agents crouched down beside him, ready to step in if the Guard spotted any sign of impending violence."

She sighed. "You seem to have thought of everything, however you should have told me you were using Patton as a bird-dog to take down Bashir. I don't like people using MI5 to advance their own agendas, like getting revenge for Fiona's murder. However, as long as nothing comes back to haunt us on this, I'll overlook your plotting to get rid of some scum. I suppose I originally hired you to clean up messes like this so I can't complain when you make it happen.

Now, what about Alina's involvement in this? How d'you read that - an inadvertent loose tongue, or something else?"

He looked puzzled. "You know something, I haven't a clue myself…Alina of all people shooting off her mouth! It's just not in character. That's not the careful, precise, dedicated person I've got to know. Hell, she saved my bacon a few times recently and I can't forget that. OK, here's what I suggest. I'm going to call her after this and meet up with her. I'll get to the bottom of it one way or the other, don't you worry."

She fell silent, nodding, then murmured "called me a bitch did he?"

Jimmy didn't like loitering around London with two bodies crammed into the trunk of his car, but he couldn't risk leaving with some business still needing his gentle touch.

He parked round the side of the Wolf Tavern, strolled casually inside, and came up to the barman.

"I need to see Tommy right away" he instructed.

The barman glanced at him casually. "He's busy right now and isn't seeing anyone. Come back tomorrow."

Jimmy saying nothing, turned and headed for the office door.

The barman came out from behind the bar and grabbed his arm. "Look Sunshine, I said he's not to be disturbed."

Jimmy stopped and gave him a cold hard stare.

"He'll see me all right – Sunshine. Now get your fucking hand off my arm" he snarled.

The man jumped back startled.

Jimmy strode up to the door and opened it, stepping inside swiftly.

Five men, one of them Tommy, were sitting around a card table. They stopped and stared back at the figure that had just entered the room.

"I told the barman I wasn't seeing anyone. Now fuck off out of here and don't come back" Tommy barked, waving has arm dismissively.

Jimmy said nothing but strode across purposefully. Still saying nothing, he grabbed the table and hurled it across at the

Welshman and the group beside him, then stepped back, reaching his hand meaningfully inside his coat.

"All of you out now" he shouted. "Tommy, you're staying here."

The men started clambering over their seats, one of them reaching to gather some paper money from the floor.

Jimmy kicked the bundle away. "I said OUT...NOW!" he hissed.

One of the men turned sideways as he stumbled towards the door.

"Do you want us to call the Police, Tommy?" he asked.

Tommy hauled himself out from behind the collapsed chair and waved his arms.

"NO, no Cops for Christ sake. No, all of you leave...I'll handle this."

The group hastily left the room after looking at Jimmy's grim demeanor. When they had gone Jimmy straightened the table and pointed to a chair.

Tommy sat down on it. Jimmy righted another chair and sat down opposite him

"What's all this about?" The Welshman asked.

Jimmy reached into his coat and withdrew an automatic, which he placed on the table in front of him.

The Welshman looked fearfully at it, then up at him.

"Look, tell me what this is about and we can fix it Jimmy" he stammered.

"Your friend the Afghan tried to screw me on that deal. I'm just wondering if you were in that plan with him. Perhaps get part of the money he promised me" he said menacingly.

Tommy looked around wildly. "I've no idea what you're talking about. I was just the go-between. I haven't seen him since we met the other night. Look, what happened?"

"Like I said, he had someone else in his dirty little plan who was supposed to finish me off at the right time. Unfortunately, I've been playing these games for a long while and he's not in the game any longer."

He ran his finger across his throat. The Welshman's eyes widened. "You mean..."

Jimmy smiled, but the smile didn't quite reach his eyes.

"My only purpose now is to figure out if you were in this with him, Tommy. You see if you were…." he paused meaningfully.

Tommy tried to sit up but was pushed back down in the chair. "All I know is that I set you two up. Sure I got a fee for the intro. but that was all. I never expected to see that prick again. It never went beyond that initial introduction, believe me! Hell, I'm a businessman, not hiring fucking assassins" he protested weakly.

Jimmy studied him for a long moment. Finally he nodded, as if satisfied.

"OK, somehow I believe you…but…here's the thing. In the next couple of days you're going to see Media coverage of a certain individual from the Afghan Embassy that's gone missing. Under no circumstances are you to contact the Police or mention our little deal to anyone, and I mean ANYONE. If it comes out that you were somehow involved in his disappearance, and it comes back on me, I'll make sure you go down with me. Is that perfectly clear?"

Tommy's face took on a hopeful look.

"You don't have to worry about that Jimmy. Mum's the word as far as I'm concerned. No one will hear anything from me, I can assure you."

Jimmy picked up the weapon and looked across at him.

"See that they don't. I won't give you a second warning. Make sure your barman goes blind as well, where my visit was concerned. Oh, and you can keep the fee that bastard Bashir gave you."

He stood up and looked around. "Is there a back way out of here?" he asked.

There was.

Within the hour he was on the motorway heading west.

He still had a funeral to take care of. Two of them in fact.

CHAPTER 65

Rebecca never liked going to the MI6 building of British Intelligence at Vauxhall Cross headquarters, known as the Secret Intelligence Service. It made her feel like the poor country cousin, coming with her cap in hand.

The building had opened in 1994 with the purchase originally approved by Margaret Thatcher herself. MI6 was previously based at Century House near Waterloo Station, and initially came under the War Office, but now the MOD. (Minister Of Defense). It operated under the formal direction of the Joint Intelligence Committee. Its main function was Military Intelligence, working secretly overseas, developing foreign contacts and gathering intelligence, not too dissimilar to the role of the CIA.

The building itself was custom built, whereas MI5 was an office development on the north bank of the Thames. Security being one of its main focuses, a large part of the MI6 building was underground, below street level. It even had two moats to enhance its protective perimeter. Twenty-five different types of glass were used in its structure, with the windows being triple glazed for security purposes. In the year 2000 it was attacked with a Russian built RPG, an anti tank missile, by suspected dissident Irish Republicans. It exploded against the 8th floor causing superficial damage.

Luckily, her opposite number had arranged for her to meet his secretary at the front of the building and steered her to the appropriate elevator and downstairs where she followed the woman through various corridors, finally reaching the man's office.

Nigel Thornton was a late forties, six foot two, ex-Oxford pupil, who still maintained the fitness of his rowing regimes on the Thames river. The built-in gym in the building probably helped. His fitness didn't however mask the fact that he came across as a pretty cold fish... probably went with the territory, she thought.

Their roles required them to be in fairly frequent contact, and occasionally they sat in on security briefings involving matters of State, such as the visit of foreign dignitaries, where they might have to merge some resources. This was particularly important where MI6 had picked up information overseas, or chatter, of potential threats from individuals or organizations against the U.K.

Politics were of course always involved, with MI5 being responsible to the Home Secretary and MI6 to the Foreign Secretary.

Today Rebecca was asking her opposite number for a favor, but she wasn't expecting a very positive response.

The meeting started with the usual pot of tea and a few pleasantries, usually about families. The struggle they both had, was operating under the eagle eye of a suspicious media as well as ever-changing Government Ministers who were already fighting to survive the next election by covering their backs at every turn. As ever, the Ministers didn't want to be embarrassed by the Security Services, but they still expected them to thwart the goals of an increasingly vicious enemy, whose aim was to undermine and destroy the fundamentals of democracy in the U.K.

A silence fell, and they both knew it was time to get down to business. Rebecca was never one to beat about the bush, or try to sugarcoat her topic.

She cleared her throat.

After the meeting, followed by her Security detail, she pulled up alongside Danny who, by pre-arrangement was standing outside an underground parking lot near Hyde Park. The actual place had bitter memories for him as it was there that the brother of his then girl friend Jamilla, was shot and killed.

It also killed their relationship.

He never saw her again after that terrible day.

Rebecca jumped out.

"Let's take a walk Danny. I need some exercise anyway, and it solves the problem of being overheard."

They both knew, of course, that no place was secure from the ears of technology in the present age, but common sense suggested that the impromptu meeting left little time to set up a covert operation in order to overhear their conversation.

They started walking, followed by her two bodyguards, towards the pond where the swans were quite often the attraction for tourists. They turned right before reaching it, then turned left towards an empty part of the park.

Danny looked around. "You couldn't get much safer than this Rebecca. So tell me, what's the message from the chief spook? I'm not expecting much joy to be honest."

"You got it in one there my friend. There's good and bad news in this. He'll help you get over to Afghanistan and set you up with some guides, presumably reliable, if anyone over there can be relied on for this… but…"

"There's a quid-pro-quo isn't there?" he prompted.

"Right, understand that this is a CIA initiative from the word go and I have to emphasize that this is top drawer stuff… goes way beyond top secret in that it could create a whole shit-storm of condemnation against the U.S. Government in Afghanistan, if ever it was discovered."

He stopped suddenly.

"But where do MI6 come in and why would they want me involved? I don't even have a security clearance with them."

"For starters, I suspect that the CIA want a buffer between this op and themselves, in case this go wrong… so MI6 is an ideal partner. You can bet that there'll be some nice brownie points from the Americans for Nigel Thornton when this is over. Why choose you? Apparently Thornton had heard of you back when the Vice President Joe Biden gave you a decoration, here at the American Embassy in London. These spooks don't miss much, and basically he thinks you can walk on water. In addition, the CIA station head in Kabul, Gordon Burnside, was familiar with your background as well, and he wants you in."

"In what Rebecca?"

She looked back at the two men following and lowered her voice.

"Here's the quid-pro-quo. You know the big switch over in Afghanistan with the Americans is so called integration - getting the Government not only to talk to the Taliban, but to gradually pull them into running the country with them. The CIA has told the U.S. Administration that it doesn't have a hope in hell of working, but they want to be shut of the whole damn quagmire and go home completely… pull everyone out. OK so far?" she asked, looking at him.

"Sure, but where do I come in?"

"One of the Mullahs who is a mainstay of this plan, has been discovered to be in the pay of the Taliban. With his help, and at the right time, the Taliban plan to take over the Government by killing as many of them as they can in one swoop. The Mullah has already used his influence to get a good number of his own soldiers accepted and trained by the new Afghan administration. They'll be fundamental in turning their weapons on key people in the Government at the point of taking over. So Gordon Burnside, the CIA head of station in Kabul, approached MI6 over there for a Brit. to carry out the operation."

Danny stopped in mid stride. "What sort of operation?"

"They want this Mullah taken out by a sniper, and with your sniping skills and reputation, Thornton at MI6 thinks they would jump through hoops to get you for the job."

Danny looked puzzled, "but why don't they just expose him? Show the evidence, whatever it is to the Afghan top officials and bobs your uncle, he's history."

She sighed. "Not so easy to do apparently. The evidence comes from an informer inside this Mullah's camp, who is on the CIA payroll, and he would have to come forward, and then would no longer be able to stay on and provide useful information to them." He grimaced.

"Sounds like a real can of worms that could get me in deep shit. They probably want a non-American so they can claim complete deniability if things go tits up - I mean even getting close to this chap, up there somewhere in the foothills, surrounded by hundreds of his followers. It sounds like a non-starter."

"Not so fast Danny. The target will be coming down to a big meeting in Kabul shortly and this will apparently provide you with that all important shot, and all the back-up and equipment you would need." He stopped again... thinking.

"OK, a lot to go over first, including getting the go-ahead from the CIA, but it could be possible. Now what about Jimmy and Scotty and getting over there?"

"No problem with that. They can get all three of you over on an Embassy mail flight under some guise or other - Traffic Accident Investigators, I believe he said, looking into that helicopter that came down recently. It sounded a good cover. As good as you'll get at short notice really. I've set up a meeting for tomorrow morning for all three of you to meet up in one of their safe houses here in London. By then Thornton should have the go ahead."

"Yeah, I get it Rebecca. It's down to deniability again. They don't want our faces to be seen around the MI6 HQ on those cameras, in case this whole thing goes belly up. We'll be up shit creek without a paddle then, won't we?"

She shrugged. "You can't have it both ways Danny. It's not exactly a legitimate trip any way you look at it, and I'm afraid it's the only one you'll get. I'd prefer that you didn't go at all. After all Jamilla as you say, is dead. Justice will eventually catch up with that evil bastard who tortured her to death."

"What about my private trip, probably back into those brutal Afghan mountains if I have to? What support can he provide there?

"Basically, as I said previously, you'd be better having him come to you. However, your choice. Nigel Thornton talked about using one of the NGO (Non Government Organizations), as you suggested. There is one there right now who have contracted to put fresh water wells into some of the villages. It's on the up and up, and they would have the proper paperwork to get through checkpoints. Remember this is Afghanistan, and checkpoints could turn out to be pretty nasty, depending on who's manning them. It's getting quite dicey over there right now, and there'll be no SAS troops dropping out of the sky to save your bacon if things get out of control."

"Don't I know it? No worries, we'll bring lots of U.S. dollars for those checkpoints, and if all else fails, we'll fall back on Scotty and Jimmy." He stood there thinking. Finally he nodded.

"OK, Thornton has himself a sniper. I'd better round up the lads for tomorrow. Now let me have that safe house address where you moved Allison to."

The swans swam regally around the shallow water, as they left.

A short distance away from that peaceful scene, Danny Quigley's mind flew back to the end of his last tour with the SAS, at Kandahar Airport in Afghanistan: the previous six months living on the savage edge day after day and night after night. Their guts tensing every time they came across an object on the road ahead, that could be a hidden IED which could result in some of them going back to their loved ones with their manhood shredded... all of the troop counting down the days and hours... the choppers they leaped out of with blackened faces, skinning their elbows, as they threw themselves straight down on the rocky terrain to avoid possible incoming enemy fire. The day dawned when it was finally down to the wire: their last minutes in Afghanistan, never to return - the expelled breaths of relief, as they heard the aircraft door slam shut behind them, and the relief they saw on their fellow soldiers' faces. The speed of the plane increased as it headed down the runway - could there still be an RPG coming to bear on them even at this last stage? Then lifting off... more expelled breaths of relief. Still some tension in the troop until the pilot announced that the aircraft had now cleared Afghan airspace—heading for Cyprus. Cheers resounding... bodies relaxing... packs coming off... avoiding eye contact ... tough hard men with traces of tears in their eyes.

The brutal, long, hard history of Afghanistan bore testimony to the armies that had invaded, back down through the centuries: graveyards of dead soldiers, marked and unmarked, up and down the country. Danny knew he'd stretched his luck right to the limit on his last tour in that unforgiving country. Now he was going back!

CHAPTER 66

Danny made a quick call to Alina and arranged to meet her at a small pub that laid on what he called 'good army grub', but coming from a family that cooked a lot of spicy meals, she didn't necessarily agree with him about the quality of the food.

On the way there by car he debated how he would handle the meeting. He didn't believe Alina had deliberately mentioned that he was meeting his daughter in a specific safe house that very evening, with any wrong intent. However, it was always drummed into the MI5 culture that loose lips could cause problems, particularly in an environment where they dealt in Intelligence matters on a daily basis.

He was still debating this as he lucked in with a driver who pulled out of a parking spot as he cruised slowly along, hoping for a place to pull in. It was a popular area in the evening with late working professionals.

Alina was already there, tucked up in the rear of the pub, where they had been on a couple of other occasions.

She looked pleased to see him, stood up and gave him a warm hug. She pulled back and looked at him closely.

"Hey, everything okay Danny?"

"Oh yeah sure - a tricky evening, that's all. I'll tell you about it, but let me order a beer and some grub first."

He wasn't aware that he had been overly abrupt in the hug he had given her.

The waitress had spotted him coming in and was across to them before he had even sat down. They ordered quickly and chatted briefly until his pint of lager and her diet coke materialized in front of them.

He took a long swallow and sat back with a sigh.

She took a sip.

"OK Danny, tell me how your evening with Allison went at the safe house."

'Oh shit', he thought, 'the whole evening he'd just gone through was pretty high-level stuff! Would Rebecca agree with him disclosing all the events to someone who had, inadvertently or otherwise, dropped some critical information in a public place? Even if it was Alina, a highly placed Agent in the organization?'

He didn't think so, at least until the details of her disclosure to Hawthorn were sorted out.

He tried to look innocent.

"No big deal really, except that Allison was delighted to see me and spend some quality time with me."

Her eyes narrowed slightly. "You mean that was it? Just a meeting with your daughter?"

He shook his head as if puzzled. "As I said, spending some time there. Were you expecting something else?"

She leaned back. "NO, no, it's just that after your last debacle in a safe house when Fiona was killed, I thought you might have ramped up some extra Security for the evening?"

There was a question in her voice.

At this stage his initial intention of sounding out Alina re dropping secret details about his meeting in a public place, which had been picked up by Hawthorn, didn't make sense anymore. He had literally painted himself into a corner.

He opened his mouth to say something.

A hard voice cut him off in mid-sentence.

He looked sideways and saw a tall, slim Asian man standing beside their table and glaring at Alina.

"So this is where a nice Muslim woman spends her time. In a pub swilling alcohol, and in the company of another Infidel!

Wasn't your last experience enough for you? It ended in divorce as I recall!"

Her face looked shocked. "Mohammed, what are you doing here? How did you find me? As I recall, you don't frequent pubs either, and I'm not drinking alcohol. It's a diet coke, if it's any of your business."

She glanced sideways at Danny. "My brother Mohammed believes all good little Muslim girls should be at home, wearing a burka, doing the bidding of their men folk, and having loads of children."

The man leaned forward, his voice vehement.

"I followed you here, you bitch. We knew something was up when you stopped coming home as often as you did. Now I know why."

At this stage Danny felt he should intervene.

"Look here Man. You may be her brother, but she's in my company and I don't appreciate you referring to her in such a demeaning manner. Tone your voice down and, I'd suggest that you get the hell out of here. Already, the people on those nearby tables are looking across at you."

It was as if the man didn't even hear him. His hand lashed out at Alina's face. If it had connected, it would have really hurt her.

Danny's reactions had been fine-tuned in hundreds of hours of martial arts training. Mohammed's wrist was caught in a vice-like grip that stopped the blow from landing, only inches from her face.

He slid sideways off the chair, standing, in time to stop a punch coming at him from Mohammed's other hand. Very quickly he swiveled the man around, facing away from him and, slipping him into a painful arm lock, made him cry out in pain.

Alina was on her feet, moving out to confront her brother.

The waitress had also hurried across by then, accompanied by a large burly man who was probably the barman or a bouncer.

Alina was trying to speak with her brother. He continued to spit abuse at her, and in the end she shrugged and stepped off to one side.

The barman came in close. "What's going on here Man? This is normally a quiet place and we don't want any shit like this going on. Shall I call the Police? This chap looks really pissed off."

Alina intervened. "No don't call the Police. He's my brother who doesn't like me meeting with a non-Muslim. I'm sorry for the disturbance. I'd just ask you to see him off the premises and stop him coming back in."

Danny nodded agreement and shoved Mohammed across into the barman who grasped him by both arms.

"OK, let's go Mate. Out you go, and don't come back or I'll call the Police." He started to hustle him away.

Mohammed swung his head sideways, glaring directly at Danny.

"Pretty soon we'll take over this country, and people like you who even look at a Muslim woman, will be beheaded out in the street. Be warned, your time is coming," he hissed.

That ruined the evening for them right then.

Danny slapped some money on the table ignoring the food, which another member of staff had just delivered to their table.

There wasn't much conversation between them as he walked her to her car, parked nearby. In turmoil he excused himself, explaining that he was planning to have an early night.

He wondered how the evening would have evolved if he'd had time to answer Alina's unspoken question. He'd now leave it to Rebecca to sort that one out, as she surely would the following morning.

Alina's background was more complex than he'd been aware of. He wondered if her brother's apparent radicalization had come up in her initial screening for employment at MI5.

Where would it leave their relationship now, he wondered?

CHAPTER 67

Danny was back in Thames House by pre-arrangement the following morning at 8 am. Rebecca was already waiting for him.

She pointed to some equipment stacked on a nearby table.

"I've already had Phil Dawson in to set up this equipment to record your call to Afghanistan. You know of him of course?"

"Yes, he's the chap who nips in and installs the covert listening and bugging devices. He's one clever operator from what I've heard, but before we get into it, I have to share something with you Rebecca. Reluctantly I must say, but the buck stops with you, and I need to put you fully in the picture here."

She looked askance at him. "Something's gone wrong about last night, or has something else come up?"

"I was about to brace Alina about her dropping confidential information which was picked up by Hawthorn, but I couldn't do it in the end."

"Why not?"

"Well, for one I decided not to fill her in on the details of what actually happened at the safe house, until we'd got to the bottom of it. If there was some security breech with her involved, it didn't feel right, so I didn't tell her."

"That was a good call Danny. How did she react? You must have told her something."

"Merely that I'd had a nice visit with Allison at the safe house."

"Again, my previous question: how did she react?"

He thought back to the conversation the previous evening.

"You know what... she looked puzzled as if she'd been expecting something to have happened, like she doubted my reply, or something like that."

"Oh Jesus," she whispered "not Alina for God's sake!"

They both fell silent.

Finally she stirred.

There's more isn't there? OK, let me have the rest of it."

He told her about his meeting with Alina in the pub and the interruption by her brother.

Her eyes widened. "You've got to be kidding me Danny? She has a brother who appears to be radicalized, and it didn't jump out at the people who screened her? I don't believe what I'm hearing. Alina wouldn't have risen to her present status if we'd even had a sniff of this before she was taken on."

"I was as shocked by the whole episode myself Rebecca. What did occur to me was that if she was a plant inside MI5, it's unlikely her brother would have confronted her the way he did. Surely he would have liked her cover to stay in place?"

Rebecca got up and wandered across to the window, deep in thought. Finally she turned, came back and sat down.

"I know that you two had something going there for the past while Danny. I liked Alina and she was a great and dedicated worker. However, through her own naivety or otherwise, she's broken one rule that's written in stone here at MI5."

"Loose lips" he murmured.

"Exactly, and as I mentioned, two men were killed as a result. I'm not suggesting they didn't deserve it, but this is the U.K. after all, where every person is entitled to a trial by their peers, before being sentenced. In this case sentenced to death, and if this got out it would finish both of us, and Jimmy Patton would be in the dock. Not forgetting the fact that one of the two men was here in the U.K. under diplomatic immunity. After hearing what you just shared with me, I'm doubly glad you didn't tell her the details of what happened yesterday evening. That would have really clipped our wings in dealing with her."

She sat there thinking, saying nothing for what seemed to him to be a good five minutes. Then she stood up.

"OK here's what I'm going to do. You go, and come back here in three hours. Get together with Scotty and Jimmy and keep that meeting with Nigel Thornton at the safe house as previously arranged. Nigel will want to brief you on your trip to Afghanistan and will probably require details of you three for the ID's they have to prepare: pictures they need and so forth, to process them."

She continued. "When you come back I'll fill you in on the situation with Alina at that time. I have to research her employment and screening record, and speak to the person or persons who carried it out. There's something else I want to carry out as well. Then I'll decide what to do. We can make the call to Afghanistan for you with Phil Dawson's help. You're still an important, and only link in the ongoing operation with those returned Jihadists who want you to meet up with them shortly down the coast. We need your involvement to discover what they're up to. Something pretty nasty's in the offing, I'm afraid. In the meantime I suggest you cut off further contact with Alina until we sort this situation out. That's it for now Danny, I'm sorry to say."

There was no hug this time as he left.

CHAPTER 68

Nigel Thornton of MI6 was already ensconced at the safe house when Danny, Scotty and Jimmy arrived. He was drinking tea, and some coffee and cups were already laid out. Danny shook hands with the six foot two, extremely fit looking man who Rebecca had told him was a keen rower out on the Thames.

He introduced his two colleagues, and looked around.

"Hey, you've made yourself at home I see. I was forgetting that you must sometimes share safe houses with MI5 and are probably familiar with this place" he commented.

Thornton smiled bleakly. "If these walls could only speak, you'd be surprised."

There followed some small chat as the new arrivals helped themselves to some of the tea and coffee. Thornton put his cup down and glanced thoughtfully at the three of them, his gaze stopping at Danny.

"Well, I finally get to meet the famous Danny Quigley. Of course there's no secrets for long in the Intelligence field. We've heard rumors of some of your escapades, and I'd love you to flesh them out for me sometime. The CIA in Kabul have also heard of you, over some stuff you carried out for them back in Langley."

He paused, as if expecting some response.

Danny shrugged. "No big deal... really."

Thornton chuckled. "Not quite what I heard Danny. Now the CIA has OK'd your participation in this little job we want you and your colleagues to do for us over in Stan. You're still on for it I gather?"

"The answer is yes, with a number of caveats. I've been out of the Saas for a few years, however my colleague Scotty has just got his discharge and Jimmy is still a serving member. It's been hammered into all of us over the years that 'preparation is the key'. Back in the Regiment, we would spend hours, days even, going over any operation in detail, rehearsing it time and time again, including the entry and Exfil arrangements. Then we would role play it until the whole operation was seamless, with everyone knowing their roles and reactions if and when things go wrong, as they do quite often."

Thornton nodded. "I'm in total agreement with that approach. At MI6 we don't want any cock-up either that creates a shit storm to come down on us. I'm answerable to the Foreign Secretary as you know, and he'd have my ass for breakfast if we create a mess over there."

Scotty coughed. "Sir, I've heard rumors from ex-colleagues that MI6 have co-opted ex-U.K. Special Forces over in Stan, and called them 'The Increment', to provide some muscle for any black ops you carry out. Why aren't you using them?"

The smile slipped on Thornton's face.

"Where did you hear that rumor? I'd have to deny it completely. In any event, British Forces pulled out and left Helmand Province for the last time on the 27 Oct 2014, and returned to the U.K. Sure, we have a hundred British Officers still there as trainers at the Military Academy and who will remain there until 2020."

"Whatever," Danny interrupted, "we still have to get you to fill us in on our roles once we get there, and the timings for the operation."

Thornton looked relieved.

"Right, let's get down to it. That's why we're here isn't it?"

He opened his briefcase and removed a file, which he opened up.

"I have copies of the details for your team which I'll pass over to you after the meeting today. Now as to the details, we've booked you on a commercial flight from Heathrow for the day after tomorrow, which takes your team to Istanbul, and flying Turkish Airlines from there to Kabul International Airport. Tickets are in the file with appropriate visas."

Jimmy leaned forward.

"I thought we were going out on a Military flight with the mail run. We've flown out from the RAF Base at Northolt a few times on special ops."

Northolt was on the Oxford road on the west side of London, and at one time after the 2nd World War, had been the city's civil airport, then it gradually decreased in use and was utilized by private and executive jets, but while still RAF property, was occasionally in use for special flights that didn't want to attract attention.

"Be glad you're not, Jimmy! Those Military flights are an absolute nightmare and we've more hassle getting civilians on board. Remember, you're going across as civvies, ostensibly to investigate a helicopter crash. This is strictly a cover story for the curious. You won't actually have to go near any chopper or meet any of the genuine crash investigators on site."

"Thank God for that!" Jimmy retorted. "All I know about helicopters is that I've jumped out of the bastards far too many times in my life."

"Right, so that point's covered. We'll have some genuine role ID's that will cover you just in case some busybody demands them - could be an Afghan Security Policeman, for example. My opposite MI6 number in Kabul, Jack Curtis, will meet you at the Airport along with Gordon Burnside the CIA head of station. Burnside merely wants to eyeball your team for a brief introduction in a private office at the Airport, to avoid prying eyes or cameras."

Danny smiled inwardly.

He had no illusions - Burnside was making sure there was no link between the sniper team and the CIA.

Thornton went on:

"Then Jack Curtis will bring you to a secure place in downtown Kabul and set you up there. He'll provide a further briefing when you arrive, and the weapons you've asked for."

"I know you work out of the British Embassy there," Danny said. "Is there no accommodation there for us?"

"I'm afraid not Danny. As you can imagine, this is an operation that we want to stay under wraps, and the Embassy is a very busy place every day of the week. Not a good idea at all. Now, have you any timings on your own foray up into the countryside?"

"I'm making a call to Afghanistan when I get back to Thames House and will have additional information then. I'll get on to you straight away once I know."

"Fine, I'll be waiting for that call. We've arranged for you to travel up-country with that NGO (Non Government Organization). The timings are fluid at the moment, however there's no guarantee that they'll escort you right to your destination. You don't have your expected travel details up-country, as yet, but they could get you out of the city and on the route. It could get tricky though, if the three of you were stopped at a checkpoint, or even by the Taliban who are pretty active right now. With no Afghan speaker with you it could be dicey."

"Couldn't we hire one, or indeed some of those Security people who are set up at Bagram Airport?"

Thornton grimaced.

"If you have the money, anything's possible. Bear in mind, it would look awfully bad if three Brits. were captured wearing civilian clothes and out on some mission. That's one part of your plan that both the CIA and myself at MI6 aren't very happy about. The MI5 Director General isn't too enthusiastic about it either, let me tell you."

"I can understand that Nigel. If possible I'd like to conclude my business in the Kabul area and get the hell out of there. Tell me about the sniping job…when, where, and how?" Danny enquired.

"Fine, here's the deal. Your target, the Mullah, is coming down to Kabul in three to four days time, and as a sweetener the Government in their wisdom have offered him a tour of Bagram Airport. They'll be travelling in a limo, and two jeeps for his soldiers who, as you know, are now part of the Afghan army and will be wearing army uniforms. Apparently this chap has never been inside the Base and badly wants a look around. He's heard about the shops, Burger King, the Pizza place and so on. This will be your chance to take him out."

"Wait a minute!" Scotty protested. "We shoot him from inside the Base? The Base would be sealed up right away, leaving us with no Exfill plan. It wouldn't take very long to winkle us out, especially logged in as newcomers."

Thornton beamed.

"Well spotted Scotty. We've found an old deserted building, across the road from the entrance to Bagram, which was destroyed by the Soviets when they held the Base. Some of the CIA people have checked it out and have found an ideal crawl space in among the fallen cement slabs, which provides an excellent line of fire. Even you Danny, as a sniper would approve of it. We can check out the site with you again the day before the operation, so you can familiarize yourself with it. There don't appear to be kids playing around the area, or animals grazing around it, so that's one less problem."

"And getting away after?" Jimmy pressed.

"OK, now the deserted building is approximately three hundred yards from the Base entrance - a nice distance for a sniper. Behind that building is about two hundred yards of scrubland that leads out onto a secondary road running between Bagram and Kabul. One of my men will be waiting in a van there and will whip you back to Kabul 25 miles south."

Danny made a face.

"Twenty five miles? News travels fast and we could have checkpoints thrown up, looking for anything out of the ordinary. I'm not too happy about that at all, Nigel. Have you a plan two for us? That's a busy road as I recall."

"We have. For starters our man at the Embassy over there, is an Afghan interpreter, and we've arranged for him to join up with his family in the United States in six months time, so he's the genuine article, as it were. Plan two is where we head off southeast to a small town called Chanikar in the Pawan Province about ten miles away. Why there? Because the chopper you're supposed to be investigating, crashed outside the town there. It fits in with your paper work and role if you're stopped, which is unlikely on that small road. We can have a helicopter waiting to give you a lift back to Kabul as soon as you get there."

Danny and his two companions looked at each other.

Danny nodded.

"Yeah, plan two sounds better. What about the genuine chopper crash Inspectors, who might be hanging about? They would soon suss us out as not being the real deal, wouldn't they?"

"We thought about that as well. The answer we came up with was to provide you with genuine papers showing you to be merely over there working on an inspection for the insurance providers. So in effect, you chaps wouldn't even be speaking the same language. They might avoid you, thinking that your Insurance Company might be looking for an out, to avoid paying the claim. What d'you think?"

Jimmy still didn't look happy.

"My understanding is that Military aircraft and equipment are covered by the Government who owns them, not civilian coverage as you're suggesting."

"You don't miss much do you? In this particular case the chopper was leased from a civilian company in Pakistan, who were flying in some people working for a charity here. Happy with that now?" Thornton asked, looking at each in turn.

They nodded in unison. Thornton continued. "The details…the Mullah and his men, are expected to roll up at approximately 11 am on that particular morning."

"How many men?" Scotty asked.

"Well as I just said, a limo with the Mullah, a driver and probably one soldier followed by two jeeps with the usual four men per jeep. That's about ten soldiers altogether. Originally they trained twenty five of the Mullah's men."

"All carrying weapons?" Danny enquired.

"Most certainly. You won't see any soldier not carrying weapons over there. You probably heard that in December 2015 six Americans were killed by a suicide bomber riding a motorcycle just outside the Base. Everyone's on the alert there, twenty four seven."

Danny still didn't look happy.

"You know what? There's something I don't like about this. They're going to let someone who is a known enemy into a secure area with a bunch of his armed supporters, and you've already been warned about their intentions of attacking the Government at some time in the future. Tell me I'm way off on where I'm going with this."

Thornton held up his hands as if to pacify the group. He was starting to look annoyed.

"Hey, back off chaps. Leave the politics to us. Look, our informer has told us that their plans for this attack are for later in the year, so lets stay on track here shall we?"

Scotty touched Danny's arm briefly.

"Let him finish the rest of the details and we can critique later."

CHAPTER 69

Danny had to cut his visit to Nigel Thornton short, but he left Scotty and Jimmy there to get some ID paperwork completed by MI6, and to study the proposed operation for Afghanistan in more detail.

On re-entering Thames House, he immediately sensed that he was coming back into a more intense atmosphere than the one he had left. Janice asked him to sit in the waiting room, telling him that the DG was holding a meeting in the boardroom down the hall.

After fifteen minutes, Alina came in with her supervisor Peter Sanderson, and they were escorted into the boardroom. Her eyes were flinty as she glanced at him in passing, but nothing was spoken.

A moment later Jerry Sackville came out of the boardroom with a man and a woman that looked familiar. He approached Danny and leaned forward, opening a file with a picture of an Asian man on it.

"Danny, I want you to look at this picture and tell me if this is the man you met last night in the restaurant with Alina. The person she introduced as her brother Mohammed."

He glanced at it. "No, this isn't the man I saw last night."

The other man standing beside him leaned forward.

"Take another look at it" he urged. "I want you to be absolutely certain about this."

He looked again. "No doubt in my mind at all. I've never seen this man before."

"Good, that's all I want to know. I may ask you to repeat this inside in a few moments."

Jerry escorted the couple and Danny back into the boardroom.

Once inside, he found a number of people sitting around the table. As well as Alina and Peter, Phil Dawson the bugging specialist was there, Jerry Sackville the counter terrorism and research specialist, Rebecca, and two people he'd seen outside. He vaguely recalled meeting them during his months working at the screening of new employees.

Rebecca indicated he come round and sit on her right. He was glad to be in that position, until he realized he was sitting directly across from Alina.

She deliberately avoided his gaze.

Rebecca cleared her throat.

"Thanks for coming at short notice, People. We have a lot to cover, and I'm going to proceed along the lines of initially involving Jeff Paulson and his colleague Jill Stinson who, as you know, are responsible for MI5 employee screening. Then I'll ask them to leave in order for us to look at another situation. To clarify the first part of the meeting, I'll just mention what you all know here already, probably better than most people in the organization, and that is the thoroughness of our screening process, for good reason, because we are involved in matters of national security at the highest level, which can go from simply confidential in nature, all the way to top secret and even further. Now we're looking at the screening record of Alina Tariq who you all know, has worked under Peter Sanderson for the past ten months, and who has a very high opinion of her work history since joining us. Isn't that right Peter?"

He nodded.

"Oh, absolutely Ma'am. First class all the way."

She carried on.

"Security screening doesn't stop with one's initial screening. It continues on all the time one works here in MI5, in various ways that you may be aware of, but others that you don't even suspect, so, to cut to the quick, Alina's personal family background screening was carried out by Jeff Paulson and Jill Stinson. Last evening, Danny here was meeting with Alina in a pub when they were approached by a man in a rage who tore a strip off Alina for being essentially with a white person. She immediately introduced him as Mohammed, her brother, and he immediately attempted to assault her, at which point Danny stepped in and stopped it in time. This Mohammed was then escorted off the premises, but not before threatening Danny with beheading him when the Muslims had taken over the country. Danny reported this to me this morning, as was his responsibility. At this point, I want to hand over to Jeff Paulson and Jill Stinson."

Jeff stood up.

"Right, as you know our screening process involves a complete screening of all the family, including extended family, previous neighbors and work colleagues. Essentially, there's no stone unturned, as we're looking for any hint that a person we are thinking of hiring for the service, has nothing in their background that could compromise them at any time in the future. In Alina's, case everything appeared kosher, as they say. She had parents still alive, two sisters and a brother called Ahmed. We were not given any information on anyone called Mohammed."

Alina interrupted him. "I think they made a mistake. They must have got the names mixed up somehow" she said defensively.

Rebecca glanced across at Jeff, who was still standing.

"Jeff, what d'you say to that?" she prodded.

He smiled.

"We don't make mistakes like that Ma'am. It's also why two of us always carry out an interview. Jill Stinson was there with me that evening."

He nodded to her. She didn't stand, but looked around the table at the group.

"Jeff's correct. The brother was there. He was called Ahmed, and we even took a picture of him which is in the file right here, that we completed."

Jeff stepped in again, holding up the file with a picture of an Asian man. He passed it around the room, where everyone apart from Alina glanced at it. Then he took the file back.

"Here's the thing. Danny Quigley took a long look at this picture a few moments ago in the waiting room outside, in the presence of Jerry, Jill and myself. He stated quite positively that this was not the man, this Mohammed, who Alina introduced as her brother in that pub last night….."

He trailed off as everyone turned to look at Alina.

The DG cast a hard look across at her.

"Alina, stop wriggling around. Let's have the truth please" she commanded

Alina looked down at her hands. The room fell silent. Finally she looked up.

"It wasn't meant to be like this. I badly wanted to make something of my life, to do something different in a completely new field and excel at it, to make my parents proud, and our friends and relatives as well. To be in a top position in MI5 would do all of that for me, so when the ads came out to recruit people for the service I realized I had a lot of the qualifications, language etc., for it, especially the situation in the U.K. with radicalized Muslims becoming such a focus point, so I sent in my initial application and waited…and waited it seemed for a very long time. It was probably only a couple of months, but I was watching the post every day and not looking for any other positions. Then something terrible happened. Yes, I had a brother Mohammed. He had a close friend who one day just disappeared. A month later I happened to glance at one of my brother's e-mails and spotted one from his friend. He was now in Syria, fighting with ISIS, killing people and loving it, if you can believe it! Someone who'd been in and out of our house for years, a quiet respectful young man. I was shocked, and the first chance I had away from the house, I tackled him about it. Then I was really shocked! He burst out with a tirade of hatred of all things western, that we were all on the wrong path, and that true Muslims were going to take over in the U.K. when they had established the caliphate in Syria, Iraq and other Middle East countries. I was virtually speechless, and he just stormed away in a violent rage with me. He disappeared the same day. It was a week before I could tell my parents, but in that week I was called for an interview to MI5. I knew that if I mentioned anything about my brother Mohammed and where his true loyalties lay, my interview would have been a revolving door. I would have been out on the street in five minutes flat."

"So you lied then" the DG commented, "and went on lying, so it appears."

"I just didn't want my dream to end there Ma'am. Mohammed was gone out of our lives. Who knows, he might never return, with the situation out there in Syria, so when Mr. Paulson and Miss Stinson came by appointment, I just left out any mention of him. It sounds stupid now but it just seemed to take on a life of it's own."

She was looking around almost desperately, as if looking for some understanding. There was nothing but an accusatory silence coming back at her.

Jeff wasn't finished grilling her. "So your parents, both sisters and Ahmed, went along with your story then?"

"Well yes. They could see how important it was to me. Mohammed was gone in any case. How could he have any effect on my position at MI5? I'm sorry, but I wasn't really thinking straight at the time. I can see that now."

"You knew of course, that we would follow up with some of your other relatives, and even your neighbors. How did we miss finding out about him? Did you involve them in your plan as well Alina?"

"The answer's yes. The Pakistani community can close ranks when it comes to one of their own. We passed out the word, and amazingly nothing about Mohammed came to light. If it had, we would merely have said that we left him off our family details because he no longer lived in the U.K. and we thought MI5 was only concerned with U.K. residents. In any event, I eventually passed all the other tests, the training and so on, and as you heard Peter say, I was first class in my role here."

Peter Sanderson shook his head sorrowfully.

"Oh brother, the plans of mice and men" he muttered.

By some pre-arrangement, the DG nodded to Paulson and Stinson, and they withdrew quietly from the room.

She opened another file beside her and studied it for a moment, then she looked up.

"Now we move onto our second issue which, in effect, has far more serious consequences for you Alina Tariq, sitting here." She paused and looked across at her.

"In that respect I would urge you to desist from any further lying. I would expect more from you young lady."

She nodded to Phil Dawson who didn't stand, but started speaking, referring to his file as he did so.

"I have four statements from people who were in the staff restaurant at lunch time yesterday morning. There were others there as well, but for various reasons they were not available for a statement. However they all heard Alina say that Danny would be meeting his daughter in a safe house that evening. They also stated that Trevor Hawthorn had quietly joined them and, while not joining in the conversation, was sitting there listening."

He paused, glancing at the DG, who looked across at Alina, raising her eyebrows.

"What d'you say to that Alina?" she asked.

She shrugged. "OK, I screwed up. I wasn't thinking straight at the time. Pressure of work I guess. I was just chilling out with some friends."

The DG looked across at Jerry Sackville, who had a tape recorder in front of him.

"Alina, you don't need to know the why's and wherefores of the background to this tape, but it was taken last night. I'm only going to play a couple of sentences for you."

It was a recording of the precise moment when Trevor Hawthorn, holding Danny at gunpoint the previous evening, had boasted about receiving the information from Alina at lunchtime, of Danny's meeting with his daughter at the safe house.

Alina looked shocked, and at one point like she wanted to get out of her chair.

She shrugged again.

"Look, I said I screwed up, but how could Hawthorn know which safe house Danny was having his meeting in? That didn't come from me."

Dawson had the floor again. This time there was regret in his voice.

"I'm sorry to say there's more in the statements Alina. Three of them recall you saying, at least twice, and I quote 'You had to go in five minutes,' and again 'that you had a meeting starting in five minutes'. Does that have any significance for you?"

"No, none whatsoever. I'm not sure what you're alluding to Phil" she exclaimed impatiently.

The DG intervened. "Would it help if we told you that the safe house was number five? You were feeding this deliberately to Hawthorn, telling him exactly where Danny would be meeting his daughter Allison. Now stop lying and start leveling with us Alina."

"I'm sorry, but you're making some connection I don't understand" she protested.

The DG spread her hands and sighed wearily. "OK Phil, give us the rest of it."

He looked across at Alina.

"Question for you. Did Hawthorn ever call you in the past week?"

"No, of course not!" she snapped back.

He reached into the file.

"OK, I have a report from the telephone company showing a call five days ago. Does that ring a bell?"

She shook her head. "It must be a mistake. The telephone people get things wrong all the time."

The DG shook her head.

375

"Alina, Alina, I told you to stop telling lies. You're digging yourself deeper every time you open your mouth. Phil please straighten her out on this."

"Yes Ma'am. Alina, you don't know this, nor does anyone else who has gone through a selection process and started working here, but we at MI5 have a bug on your home phone and cell phone as well, for the first eighteen months of your employment here. What d'you say to that? And I have to tell you, you haven't a leg to stand on after this."

He reached for a sheet of paper in the file. "Shall I tell them, or will you? It's time you stopped lying, young woman."

Suddenly Alina collapsed in tears, her loud voice wailing in the boardroom. It seemed to go on forever. At one point the DG walked around and placed some tissues in her hand, which she pressed into her face. Finally she stopped, her head down, then gradually lifted her face and started muttering.

The DG stopped her. "I'm sorry, but we can't hear you properly Alina."

Her voice lifted higher.

"Alright, he called me, as you know now. He had somehow found out about Mohammed and threatened to tell you unless I tracked Danny's movements on a specific evening - last night as it happens. He told me he would be in Thames House by pre-arrangement to clear out his locker, and that he would drop into the lunch room at a specific time."

The DG showed her first emotion, slapping the table and making them all jump.

"He instructed you to drop the information about Danny and how to include the safe house number, didn't he? Jesus, have you any idea what he planned to do to Danny and his daughter?"

She shook her head miserably.

"No Ma'am, I didn't think beyond keeping him from informing you about my brother. That's the truth!"

She started wailing again.

As the group began to move out, Rebecca caught Danny by the elbow.

"Come back in two hours. We have that call to complete."

She then indicated that Peter and Alina stay on. The group crept out quietly, milling in the reception for a few moments, conversing in low voices.

Danny pulled Jerry aside. "Hey, I'd no idea we would all be screened for eighteen months after joining MI5?"

He chuckled. "WE don't... I was bluffing. She bought it though."

"What's going to happen back in there Jerry?"

"Not my problem my friend, or yours for that matter. Who would want the DG's job?"

Who indeed?

He still had to wait to make the telephone call to Afghanistan and organize the trip over. He wondered about the timings.

He had to carry out an assassination for the Americans, via MI6, and still arrange a meeting with the murderer of Jamilla, and also meet the American Jihadist Frank on the south coast in two weeks time.

Even the rigors of an SAS operation had never made demands like this! He was glad Scotty and Jimmy would be on that plane with him.

Back inside the meeting room, the DG stared silently at the weeping Alina. Her face was stony.

"I have a question to ask you Alina. Last night when you asked Danny what had happened at the safe house, you were surprised at his answer. Why? Because you were expecting something to happen, weren't you? "

Alina wailed louder, saying nothing.

The DG sat there shaking her head.

"Jesus Alina, I can't believe you staked Danny and his daughter out like tethered goats! Apart from your being accepted here at MI5 as one of the family, you and Danny had a thing going, for God's sake!"

Alina finally raised her tear-streaked face.

"What did happen there?" she whispered.

The DG held her gaze for a long moment.

"You'll never know Alina. You're not one of us anymore. And that leads me to my final question, which Peter and I will have to decide. What do we do with you now?"

CHAPTER 69

Things seemed calmer when he came back in to Rebecca's office at Thames House. He found Phil Dawson, the bugging and burglaring specialist, who would no doubt be monitoring the call, and Jerry Sackville, the counter terrorist, research and investigation director.

In his brief ad. in The Times newspaper, Danny had put his satellite cell phone number and a time to call him. The tension built up in the room as Phil Dawson hooked his phone up to a recording machine.

It rang exactly on time. After three rings he answered it and recognized the voice as belonging to the same one who spoke to him previously. The Afghan's voice sounded jovial. "Ah Mr. Quigley, on time as specified…I like that."

"I want to know how Jamilla is and if you're treating her well."

He had been instructed by Phil to try to prolong the conversation as long as possible, but hearing the man's voice made him grit his teeth.

The Afghan laughed. "She's fine. I'm sure your people are trying to trace this so let's keep it short. I gather you've followed my instructions as you placed the ad. in The Times?"

" OK, just tell me about the arrangements for the swop. I'm coming over to Kabul in two days time, and I have the diamonds."

"Two days time…I like that. We can conclude this within the next couple of days then."

"We conclude nothing until I see Jamilla in person" he said abruptly. "No Jamilla, no diamonds, you got that?" he grated.

"I believe you want her back more than I want the diamonds my friend, so we hold all the cards. Well, here's the arrangement. I'm assuming that this number I'm calling is your own cell phone and has a Sat program?"

"Yes it has. Now go on."

"I will call you on this number shortly after you get to Kabul, and will give you instructions from there."

"Look here, I want more details………" He was speaking to a dead line.

They sat back looking at each other. Phil shook his head.

"Too short I'm afraid. We got zilch."

"What about that previous number Phil? In Kunduz you said. Is it still in service?" Rebecca enquired.

He shook his head again.

"Afraid not Ma'am. It went dead after Danny's last call. No surprise there really."

"So what have we got then?" Rebecca asked, looking around at them.

Jerry Sackville grimaced. "Danny's going in cold Ma'am, and with little back-up. Just imagine how much coverage we would provide here in the U.K. for a kidnap swop. This is a veritable minefield. I'd suggest strongly that Danny cancel the whole thing, especially as he suspects Jamilla's dead already."

"What's your reaction to what Jerry just said? Remember he's got more street smarts than anyone else around here?" Rebecca asked Danny.

He was silent for a moment, then looked up, his face grim.

"Logic would suggest that Jerry's absolutely right. They want me dead, and to get their hands on the diamonds as well, but it's not about logic at this point. There's more to it than that. I owe it to Jamilla to get this bastard, and despite what he's got lined up for me, I won't be killed that easily. There's a lot of dead people in the ground out there who thought they could take me down, - some pretty clever and dedicated people, so I'm going in, but thanks for your concern…all of you."

He glanced sideways at the DG.

"There's something else I need from you Rebecca. I'd like a second set of identities for myself, Jimmy and Scotty."

She stared at him.

"But MI6 are providing these for you."

"True, but I have a bad feeling about Nigel Thornton's side of the operation. I need some additional insurance."

She made a note on a pad in front of her, then looked up at him. "OK Danny, have the lads come in today and Jerry will process the paper work. We need the usual pictures and so on. I probably won't see you before you go, so I'd better hand over this valuable cargo to you."

She opened the drawer and produced a small sack, which she gave to him.

"Oh, and we've contacted the Heathrow Security to let you and your team through without any of the usual x-ray machines etc. We couldn't have some Security Guard digging out what would appear as a cache of valuable diamonds, now could we?"

The meeting dissolved without further comment.

Danny went downstairs with Jerry and called Jimmy and Scotty to head in to Thames House. He made several other calls as well, while waiting for his team. He checked with Jerry that his cell phone would still have the encryption protection when he reached Afghanistan.

The countdown had ramped up.

CHAPTER 70

It could have been worse.

As it was, it took over twenty-six hours to fly into Kabul Airport, and by that time all three were squirming with being confined to narrow airline seats, especially on the Turkish airline flight from Istanbul.

Once they entered the terminal they appreciated being pulled aside, as arranged, by a tall slim, late thirties male with a military cut to his stance.

He obviously had their pictures, and nodded to the three as they straggled into the building. He grinned at their obvious discomfiture and shook their hands in turn.

"Danny Quigley and his team, I presume from these pictures. We've never met but I've heard lots about you."

"Thanks...good things I hope...you must be Jack Curtis. Look, we just need to have a shower and crash for a few hours" Danny muttered.

"I know how you feel chaps. I've done that trip numerous times, going to my family back in the U.K."

His pale blue eyes took a measuring look at the three men.

"Should I say welcome back to Afghanistan?"

Scotty looked at him in disgust. "Please don't, our memories of this place are not of the pleasant kind, I can tell you. I never thought I'd be back here again - ever" he said with emphasis.

Curtis chuckled, "and you just took your discharge from the Regiment, Scotty. You sure are a glutton for punishment. Anyway, as arranged, Gordon Burnside the CIA station chief here wants to briefly meet with your team, then I'll slip you out of here without any Security to go through."

Burnside wasn't what Danny had expected.

The man looked more like an ex-football player, trying to fight his weight, probably over fifty, with a shrewd measuring gaze and a small black beard. Probably useful if blending in doing undercover work in a country with most men sporting beards.

He advanced and reached out his hand.

"The famous Danny Quigley... I've heard the rumors from some people who know of you. No names, no pack drills."

The handshake was firm... a touch clammy, Danny thought, but then this was Afghanistan.

He quickly introduced Scotty and Jimmy.

"I should mention that these two are still hard-ass troopers, and I wouldn't be doing this operation if they weren't with me. I'm one of those dammed civvies now after being out of the Regiment for so long."

Scotty snorted. "Danny could still eat us alive... don't listen to him."

Burnside smiled, but Danny noticed that the smile didn't reach his eyes.

"Glad to hear it... we want this to be a clean operation... no fall out, just the results you got from the briefing in London. In that context, I like what I'm seeing and hearing."

And that was it.

They hung onto Jack's coat tails as he escorted them through and out of the Airport, and into a waiting vehicle where their bags were already stacked.

"Probably remember the traffic?" Jack teased.

They did.

Kabul was the fifth fastest growing city in the world, and the streets were clogged with vehicles, all ages, makes, sizes, and driven it seemed, by madmen, one of them driving the large tinted windowed Toyota SUV, that they wearily climbed into outside the terminal.

It was the stench that hit them right away, even from inside the vehicle with the air conditioning on.

The smell of open sewers, animal and human waste, and garbage dumps, some with burning material, emitting clouds of thick smoke. Crowds milled around open meat markets containing skinned animals and chickens, with the usual decoration of flies covering them.

The traffic was bumper to bumper, with numerous vehicles all engaged in what seemed to be kamikaze tactics to get ahead: old pickups, scooters, bicycles, handcarts, taxis, donkeys and military vehicles. They had not forgotten the habit of Afghans decorating their vehicles with strobes, lights, and ornaments that sounded louder than a Mardi Gras parade in Rio.

After the droning noise of the flight, Danny and his team were now bombarded with different sounds: the constant shouts, horns, bleating animals and begging children.

Jack Curtis merely smiled and sat back, saying nothing, seemingly at home in the chaos. He was aware of the futility of attempting to carry out any sort of conversation during the ride.

It was a relief when they finally arrived at the solid two story building set back from the road, which they got to after driving through a solid metal gate, and up a short driveway.

Danny whistled his appreciation. "Looks impressive… not what I was expecting" he commented.

"Yeah, a bunch of American Contractors lived here when they were building the Bases for ISAF (International Security Assistance Forces) a few years back. We grabbed it for a song when they left, and we use it occasionally for…. well, I'm sure you have some idea…." he finished lamely.

They did… It was a quiet, off the road area, with what appeared, initially, to be a relatively secure building.

When Curtis hit a monitor in the vehicle, the garage door raised, showing spaces for four cars. Two of these spaces were already occupied. The driver edged the car in between the two vehicles and the door closed behind them.

There was a linking door through to the kitchen, which they stumbled through. An Afghan male, dressed in a grey shalwar kameez and Kaffi turban met them inside. Danny estimated his age to be around thirty and was aware of a pair of alert intelligent eyes observing him closely.

Curtis started to introduce him. "This is Rahim Reza, our interpreter…"

The man stared at him more closely. Danny's jaw dropped.

"Rahim. We know each other for God's sake!" he exclaimed.

The Afghan smiled with pleasure.

"Quigley, how could I forget? All those patrols back up into the mountains, night after night! You're back!"

Curtis looked from one to the other.

"You know each other then?"

"Know each other? Man that's an understatement! He was our interpreter when we went out in our choppers, night after night, to take out pockets of the Taliban spotted by Intelligence, or to grab prisoners. We went through some rough times up in those mountains, I can tell you!"

He glanced at Rahim. "It must have been for at least 6 months on my first tour and part of my second one."

The Afghan grabbed his hands fervently and glanced at Curtis.

"If Quigley's involved in this operation you have the best with you, and I'm more than happy to work with him."

Curtis laughed. "I don't know if you're aware Danny, that Rahim, who joined us at the Embassy when the Brits. pulled out, has been watching a lot of John Wayne movies, and likes to be called the Duke. He thinks that's what the U.S.A. is like."

Rahim smiled in embarrassment. "I know it's not. My wife has written to me and told me that things are completely different than any John Wayne movie. I still look forward though to riding on one of those western plains in Colorado or Wyoming, so Mr. Curtis can't disillusion me about that. The truth is they want me to stay on in Kabul with them for a while longer."

Curtis nodded.

"With the Military mission winding down, our focus has started to be on development here in Afghanistan via DFID, the Department For International Development. Rahim is playing a terrific role in getting the cooperation of villagers who are suspicious of any western face. With the Taliban getting more brazen every day, we have to use every card we've got. Now, you'll be glad to hear that I'm leaving him with you for the duration, and you're lucky to have him, as I suspect you already know."

With the small talk over, Curtis left to return to the Embassy.

Despite their obvious weariness the 'Duke' led them into a small room off the main living room.

It looked like it might have been used to store coats and jackets or cleaning equipment. Today it contained a large wooden crate, already with the top off and filled with a number of weapons.

Danny was impressed. He had made certain requests as to the number and type of weapons he wanted in the cache. Nigel Thornton of MI6 told him that even though the country was awash with weapons, he couldn't guarantee the exact selection would be available.

Rahim seemed familiar with the contents and started hauling them out, passing them to Danny and his two colleagues.

The first one he handed to him.

"This is probably for you my friend, from what Mr. Curtis has told me." It was a Remington model 700 Sniper rifle, with a dull Military finish. Danny handled it lovingly.

"Would you look at that!" he exclaimed. "Range 820 meters, caliber 7.62, NATO bolt action, five round detachable integral type."

Rahim carefully passed him an additional small package.

"You're going to like this too - a Star-light Scope, the Star-Tron mark 303 A."

"Wow, isn't this what that incredible U.S. sniper used in Iraq before he was shot back home by a so-called friend?" he asked.

Scotty, who was busy looking at two M16s that Rahim pulled out, glanced sideways.

"Yeah, his name was Chris Kyle. He was something else— held the record for the most confirmed kills. To go home after all he'd been through, and then get killed the way he did! How d'you figure that?"

Jimmy was examining one of the M16.

"Nice one—the later version too, the MI6 A1 with the chromium-plated chamber and barrel with optional burst control. As I recall a range of 400 meters and a box type magazine that takes twenty to thirty rounds… got a telescopic sight as well. Hey, I bags this one."

"Me too" Scotty grunted. "We could give Danny excellent back- up cover if needed."

He craned forwards "Any side arms in there Rahim? I'd feel half dressed in any action scenario without some sort of back up. I've had too many rifles misfire at the wrong moment."

Rahim extracted three pistols and laid them out on the table.

Most soldiers in action have a preference for the sidearm they carry, and which might save either their life or their fellow soldiers: weight, size, number of rounds, ease of extraction, grip, carrying comfort in running and jumping out of choppers, were just a few of them, and past experience as to its reliability.

The first pistol was a 9 mm, U.K. manufactured weapon from British Victory with a magazine capacity of 17 rounds.

The second was a Smith and Wesson model 657.41 Magnum, with a 3-inch barrel, while the third was a Beretta M51 pistol, 9 m Parabellum, which used an 8 round detachable magazine box.

Danny reached for it. "I want something small and light that won't stick in my side when I'm lying down on the sniper rifle. You chaps can fight over the other two."

Rahim caught his arm. "Hang on just a second Danny. I've something that might suit you better, especially if you might be getting a pat down from some of those people you're going to be meeting, or indeed if you need an advantage with a fast-draw reaction weapon."

He reached in, drew out a small package and handed it over. Danny's curiosity got the better of him and he tore the paper off.

"Oh man, a flipping Derringer!" he exclaimed.

"Yes, it's a 'swing up, two shot' made by Davis Industries in the U.S. This one is a .22 LR caliber, and as you can see, with a 2.4" barrel length, you don't even have to cock it like some of them… it's ready to go."

Danny made a face. "A two shot with a small caliber and a .22 at that. Not a lot of punching power there, and you'd have to go for a head shot, otherwise they could still kill you."

Scotty shook his head. "Danny, you're shit hot with a pistol. No one better than you to fire a double tap into someone's head."

Rahim butted in again. "I'm not talking about a shoot pistol here Danny. Just a quick draw emergency firearm, and we have the small holster you can attach to your arm. I've tried it out, and it's quite easy to operate… a twitch in your arm and it pops into your hand ready to go. I'll show you how it works, and if you're not comfortable with it, no problem, don't take it, OK?"

He still didn't look happy about it. "Alright, tell you what, if we've time I'll try a few dry runs with it, but I still want to take that Beretta M51 pistol as insurance."

They left it at that.

Jimmy and Scotty seemed comfortable with either weapon and quickly reached forward and selected the one nearest to them.

Danny craned his head forward.

"Anything else in there Rahim?"

"Lots of ammo as you might expect, and 3 Kevlar vests. You can each take what you need, and some nice two-way radios with ear mikes - enough for all of us. However we still have one more nice little baby in there."

When he hauled it out, all three nodded in agreement.

It was the Israeli invented Uzi—a 9mm Luger with a four and a half inch barrel and a magazine capacity for 20, 25 or 30 rounds. Danny lifted it up and handed it to the Afghan.

"As I recall, even though you were our interpreter on our night ops, you kicked ass when things got messy, as they did on occasion. You take the Uzi, Rahim. I can't think of anyone I'd sooner have covering my ass."

"But you might need it yourself" he protested. " Why not keep it with your team just in case."

"It's already decided Duke, and good hunting, as John Wayne would say."

Right then Danny's cell phone rang.

CHAPTER 71

It took him a while to struggle, extract the phone and hit the button. He recognized the voice immediately.

The voice of the man whom he knew had killed Jamilla.

"Ah Quigley, you've arrived in Kabul I see. Good timing."

"How d'you know I'm in Kabul?" Danny demanded.

The man laughed. "We have eyes everywhere. Remember that. Remember also why you're there: to rescue your dear friend Jamilla as you call her, from further punishments."

Danny struggled to keep his temper under control. He wanted to scream his hatred down the phone, but that wouldn't have achieved anything.

The man chuckled. "Good, I can sense your anger Quigley, so we can resolve this quickly and we can do the swop, then you can get her the medical attention she needs."

"Listen you…!" Danny started to shout.

Scotty caught his arm and shook his head warningly.

He took some deep breaths and felt a coldness coming over him. He already knew that Jamilla was dead, murdered by the man on the phone.

"Well let me have the name of the place you want to do the exchange and we can start to plan it. I gather it's somewhere back in those mountains, so we need some time to organize it."

"No need for any trip Quigley. I want to meet with you in one hour, here in Kabul, and we can do the exchange. The diamonds for your friend Jamilla."

"In one hour?" Danny exploded. "We only arrived an hour ago and we need a few hours sleep. There's no way we can get organized so quickly. That's ridiculous!"

The voice continued remorselessly. "I'm not interested in your sleep problems Quigley. If you want the woman, you'll keep this meeting or you'll never see her again, believe me."

Danny sat back, his mind working rapidly. "As I said, one hour is ridiculous. As a matter of interest, where were you planning to have this meeting?"

"At the Kabul Zoo. It's off Asmayi Road on the banks of the Kabul river. Any taxi driver can get you there, wherever you are in the city right now."

'Ah' Danny thought, 'so he doesn't actually know where we are at the present moment'. As the call was on speaker, the group were listening closely.

Danny gestured to Rahim and scribbled on a piece of paper, which he handed to him. On it he'd written 'the Zoo, how far?' The Afghan grabbed the pen, made a swift note, and pushed it back to him. On it he'd written '20 minutes drive'.

Danny nodded and started talking into the cell phone.

"I'm afraid you've got a real problem there. Your purpose with this meeting is to get your hands on those precious diamonds, isn't that right?"

"Correct, as you well know. I don't see any problem Quigley. What is it?"

"Well, for one thing we don't have the diamonds."

"What?" the voice screamed. "You know what's going to happen once I hang up this phone, don't you? No diamonds, no Jamilla!"

"Yes, so you made clear in your calls to London. What you're obviously not clear about is what d'you think would happen at Security on any airline when you try to walk through with a large bagful of diamonds in your luggage?"

"You're telling me you haven't brought the diamonds with you?" he shouted.

Danny's purpose was to get the man off balance and keep him there. He yawned audibly into the phone.

"I didn't say that exactly. It was arranged by my company to have them sent across in the diplomatic pouch, to the British Embassy on Fifteenth Street, the roundabout Wazir Khan. I'm sure you know where that is, and it's a ways from here."

There was a long silence on the phone and he could hear the faint exchange of voices. Finally the man came back on. He sounded more subdued

"This is not good... not good at all. We're holding a prisoner here, and that will be getting more difficult the longer you wait. When did you intend to pick up the diamonds from the Embassy?"

"Tomorrow morning, as soon as they open. That was the arrangement."

"No, we can't wait until tomorrow. Why not phone them right now and see if they can be picked up today, then phone me back? We could still do the exchange?"

There was an implied question in his voice.

Danny scribbled a note to the Afghan. "What time does the Zoo close?" '4.30' he scribbled back.

He lifted the phone up. "I can try that, but you know these Embassy people have their own speed of doing things, and they have closing hours that might make it tight. OK, give me your number and I'll get back to you...that's all I can promise."

Jimmy scribbled a note and passed it to him.

'Ask to speak to Jamilla'.

Danny nodded and started writing down a number he was getting. When he'd finished, he asked the question:

"I'd like to talk to Jamilla, to make sure she's still alive and well."

"Not possible right now. She's being held in a safe place not far from here. We can't carry her around all the time with us with possible checkpoints."

Danny grunted, making himself sound unhappy.

"I don't like the sound of this, but be sure she's there when we do the swop, otherwise no deal. I hope you understand that. No Jamilla, no diamonds. You got that?"

"Perfectly. Now you get moving on contacting the Embassy. I'm running out of patience at this point, and you know the consequences. We may decide to cut our losses and leave Kabul, and you'll never see Jamilla again. Have YOU got THAT?"

The line went dead.

Silence fell inside the room as they sat there looking at each other. Finally Danny stirred.

"That was a good prompt, asking about Jamilla. He could have got suspicious if I hadn't. Now let's look at what we've got here. Any thoughts?" he asked.

Rahim jumped in. "The phone number could be a lead if we can get Mr. Curtis at the Embassy to try to locate it, though they could only try when you make the call back to them later."

Scotty looked skeptical.

"Doesn't make sense. The Taliban and their ilk know about the vulnerability of using cell phones for any lengthy calls. They'd have a drone up their ass in no time short."

"Perhaps they're not Taliban" Jimmy said. "If we get a location it would give us an edge for sure. Hit them hard and fast. If we go to their pre-arranged meeting place, we would be at a disadvantage. It could be a set up."

"Wait a minute Danny" Scotty interjected, "I thought you said you had the diamonds with you."

"I do. I was merely playing for time. For us to rush around to that Zoo at their bidding, with little or no preparation, would have been a recipe for a botched up operation. Now we have time to set up a strategy where we're in control - to some degree at least."

Rahim nodded. "You heard voices in the background, so he's not alone. He may have a team with him, considering what's at stake here - those valuable diamonds."

Danny nodded grimly. "I very much suspect that this is not strictly about the diamonds. There are a few other people who want me dead as well."

He spelled out to him how an airstrike he'd called in when he was stranded back in the Afghanistan mountains on an SAS

393

mission, had killed a Pashtun leader called Mohammed Qureshi, and his family had vowed revenge on Danny for his role.

Rahim grimaced. "These people have long memories, and Pashtun culture and beliefs make it mandatory that they get revenge, but answer me one question Quigley: what is your goal or purpose in meeting this individual you just talked to? I mean, my understanding is that your friend Jamilla's already dead."

"I plan to kill him. He murdered Jamilla after torturing her."

Silence fell on the group. Then Danny turned to Rahim again. "Tell me about this Zoo."

"Not much to tell. It was once the pride of Kabul when it was a thriving place with loads of animals and visitors. Various Zoos around the world presented them with prize animals. Then the Mujahedeen and the Taliban came in one after the other and the Zoo went down from there. They ate many of the animals and saw nothing wrong with basically torturing the ones that were left: throwing rocks at them, or poking them with sticks, and really no concept of caring for them - even the people in charge. In 2002 a lion called Marjan killed a man who went inside his cage to prove how macho he was. A day or so later his brother came in and threw some hand grenades at the lion, not killing it, but blinding it and damaging it's face and teeth. It has since died, and a large statue of it sits outside the Zoo where visitors stand and have their pictures taken. Today, better carers, housing, and provisions, combined with hundreds of new animal species being given to it, have restored its attraction, once again bringing in loads of visitors."

"I don't see how this potted history helps us in any way" Scotty muttered.

"Well, background information's always useful" Danny said thoughtfully. "However Scotty's right, we need to get round there and do our own recce ahead of time, on the assumption that we'll be going there later on today. We can assume that Jamilla's captors will want to get set up early, once we agree to a meeting time."

He turned to Rahim. "You mentioned that the Zoo closes at 4.30. Would it be to our advantage if we met inside with this group while it's open, or outside after it closes?"

Rahim stroked his chin thoughtfully.

"Good question Danny. It's got me thinking. I believe it would be to our advantage if we met inside. You'd have more close-up cover for one thing, however having loads of people around would probably inhibit any action you might want to take."

Jimmy snapped his fingers.

"Wait a minute! You just hit a very important point there. Rahim, would it be possible for you to arrange entry to the Zoo for us after it closes? I mean what authority would you need to have the Management agree to that? Could we get some Police identities arranged with Curtis, and talk our way in on some pretense...a drug takedown? Whatever?"

Rahim looked at him.

"Not impossible in real terms. There's a dirty tricks department at the Embassy that they don't advertise of course. It would depend on Mr. Curtis. It could probably be much easier to set up just for myself, as they have all my details on record, picture etc. If I could arrange it, I'd have to go around there and collect it. I'll get onto Curtis right away."

He went into the next room to use the local phone.

Jimmy lifted his hands, his mind racing.

"Wait a minute. We're missing a very important point here. IF, and this is a very big if. If Rahim gets the ID, and if he can get the zoo people to let us in to the closed Zoo and get set up, how would Jamilla's captors know they'd be allowed in? They would surely smell that it was a set up."

Danny rubbed his forehead wearily.

"Shoot, I'm bushed right now. Stuck in that goddam plane for all that time, I'm just not thinking straight."

Jimmy picked it up again.

"Perhaps we're complicating it far too much. Fundamentally these chaps want the diamonds. You say

Jamilla is dead anyway, which strengthens your hand quite a lot. When you phone them, just say you figured the Zoo was too busy and crowded when the public were inside and you paid some people to let you in after it closes. All they have to do is turn up at the front or side doors which will be open, and you'll be waiting at the lion's den or the monkey cage...whichever Rahim suggests. What d'you think Danny?"

He shook his head.

"I think we've to get round there a.s.a.p. and be prepared to wait somewhere near by, once we case the place. We'll take all weapons and ammo with us. There are too many loose ends here. It's not the way we'd normally plan an operation. I don't want to see any of us killed like our pal Clyde Stoner in Nigeria some months back. We need to get as much edge as possible on this one. These chaps live here, and have the advantage right now."

Rahim came back inside and gave them the thumbs up.

"Mr. Curtis has come up trumps. He's setting up the ID as we speak, and guess what? He's sending it round here as soon as possible with someone who'll bring enough equipment to track the phone call when you make it later. He estimates that, with the Embassy driver's knowledge of back streets, we could have the techie here within the hour. How's that?"

"Brilliant" Scotty said, jumping up and slapping him on the arm. Danny nodded. "Well done Duke."

The Afghan grinned.

He went on. "We need to get round and have a good look at the Zoo from all angles, and see how we can set this up, so lets organize the weapons and material, get it all loaded up and be ready to go as soon as the Embassy chap gets here. We'll need two vehicles to fit us all in. OK, let's move!"

Suddenly their flight fatigue was banished and it was like old times again. The potential action had started the adrenalin pumping through their bodies.

Rahim grinned.

Quigley was back, and he knew that action usually followed.

The Duke was ready for it.

CHAPTER 72

One of the details that Rahim suggested was to dress Scotty up as an Afghan for the initial walk around, where his shorter stature made it more believable.

The house had a large wardrobe with make-up kit, and with a few dabs of brown make-up, Scotty looked the part. He would blend in as he strolled around at the zoo in the company of Rahim.

Danny and Jimmy toned down their western clothes and put on more appropriate garb worn by the many European and American people moving around Kabul working for NGO's or charities. Danny decided to slip on a wig with a pony tail and to wear a pair of plain glasses, as he assumed that the man he was meeting had quite probably got hold of a picture of him from his London contacts. The looser robes, which they chose, would help if they decided to carry the rifles. In the meantime, they all tucked away their chosen side arms with full magazines.

The last load was stowed in the vehicles when the techie from the Embassy rolled up and got out. There were quick introductions all round as they moved the tracking equipment across into one of their vehicles. The techie, Fred Billings, was a middle aged, slim, slightly balding Welshman who jumped in the back of Danny's car. The convoy took off, following Rahim who was driving the front vehicle. Danny spent the whole trip practicing using the Derringer quick draw, from the forearm holster that Rahim had attached. He wasn't totally unacquainted with the use of Derringers. As part of being in Special Forces, he was able to adjust to any weapon that was available. He found it surprisingly easy to operate, and on nearing their destination he slotted it back up his arm.

Rahim glanced across at him.

"You've got the hang of that pretty fast Quigley. You look like an expert already."

He shrugged. "Any weapon's better than none at all, but if I had my choice, it would be an MP5."

"I've seen you use that many times when we headed up into those damned hills, fighting the Taliban. Oh, just a thought... if you're coming back out into the parking lot after concluding your business with the bastard holding Jamilla, get rid of that disguise. Some of them might be waiting out there for a chap with a pony tail and glasses."

Danny looked across at him.

"Shit, I never thought of that Duke...good advice."

It took longer than the twenty minutes, but they spotted the massive statue of the dead lion Marjan sprawled outside the front of the Zoo, surrounded by visitors taking pictures. They had agreed to separate the vehicles once they arrived and slip into different slots in the parking lot, which was around the rear. They arranged to meet up in half an hour back in the parking lot.

Paying their way in, they first had to join a small line-up of people, then they started moving around the sprawling Zoo area, stopping, looking, and commenting on the various animals in the pens. Some of the animals were in enclosures where the viewers were able to see them through wire fencing. The children, despite the notices, were pushing food through the wire. The frantic leaps and screams from the monkey cage seemed to gather the most families, as did the parrots and other plumaged birds.

The lion's den was set up slightly different.

The public were standing high above their area and looking down on the animals thirty feet below, from behind a four-foot cement wall. Warning signs were displayed in different languages, telling parents to keep their children well back from the wall, as the lions were quite new and unpredictable.

Despite their mission, they still found the recce interesting, and the time went quickly.

Back outside, Danny, his two colleagues and Rahim squeezed into the larger capacity vehicle after looking around carefully. Fred stayed in the other car and started organizing his tracking gear. Danny started the ball rolling.

"So what's the scoop here? How d'you see this going down for the opposition?"

Jimmy shook his head. "I can't see it Danny. Not in a busy place like this with all those visitors around, unless they see that as an advantage somehow."

"He may have a point there" Scotty cut in. "If their objective is to get the diamonds, they could plan to grab them and scarper in the confusion. If he had some back-up with him, they could take you out with handguns and achieve their second objective... to kill you"

"But what about the swap you discussed with them, you know, letting you see Jamilla?" Rahim asked.

They all looked at Danny.

"That could be it exactly. They can't produce her, so when I ask to see her, if I have the diamonds in my possession, that's when they go for me. They know that's the weakness in the plan."

Jimmy frowned. "Another possibility is that they tell you she's in a car in the parking lot and invite you go outside. There they have more options. His friends pop out of a vehicle or vehicles and take you down. Less people around as well."

Danny knew that Scotty had a nose and an instinct for these types of situations, which had proved itself many times in the past. He looked at him now. "What's your take on this Scotty? Are we missing something here?"

"I like number two as being their plan. It's cleaner. They can't set you up for a kill with certainty in a milling crowd of visitors, who start screaming when they see guns produced. They lure you outside on the promise of seeing your friend Jamilla, but actually to give their shooters a nice target. We know she's already dead, so myself and Jimmy could be set up out there to take them out when they make their move. You would have to deal with Jamilla's murderer yourself."

Danny nodded grimly. "You can take that to the bank Scotty! He's mine!"

Rahim nodded his agreement. "I agree with Scotty. With respect, I know my fellow Afghan brothers a lot better than you probably do. I think they would run a mile rather than meet in an empty Zoo arranged by you. It would look like a set up to them. Number two would make sense, but you'd have to be on the alert in case they do have a go at you inside, probably up close and with handguns, I have an idea about that though which might appeal to you."

"OK, let's hear it" Danny instructed.

"I noticed some workers in the Zoo who, in some cases, were actually in the cages cleaning up manure, tossing in straw, filling water containers, or in some cases feeding the animals. There are two places, which I noted were close to these workers and a possible meeting place: the monkey's cage and the lions enclosure. My thought is that I use my Police credentials to replace either one of these workers, which puts me in a position to provide you with some cover if they start things inside. Oh, I won't go to the Management who might decide to check with the local Police first - I'll just give the worker some money to disappear for an hour. I think that'll work. Danny's already given me some envelopes with different amounts of cash for such an eventuality."

Jimmy leaned forward, looking excited.

"I think we're motoring here lads. Danny's got some cover inside with Rahim, and Scotty and I are set up outside with rifles if the action takes place there. I'm starting to feel better about this."

"How would you know which one they'll agree to meet you at? Scotty asked.

"No problem there" Danny responded. "When I negotiate on the phone, I can steer them towards one or other of those two places. If they box clever and call me back with an alternative meeting place, or indeed when we first come face to face, I have my two way radio set up and all of you can hear what's happening, though I'd more than likely hang tough and stick to the two areas we've chosen…the lions' enclosure or the monkeys' cage."

Jimmy looked happier.

"Speaking of your telephone call with them, what about your hope that Fred there can locate where they are? Do we drop this plan and do a SWAT approach to their location wherever it is, and try to take them down there, and avoid all this Zoo plan, which we all admit could get a bit out of our control?"

Danny clicked his fingers.

Scotty recognized it as indicating that he had made a decision.

"OK, here it is. I make the call, stay loose, and see what Fred can get for us with the tracker. The call itself may be the deciding factor as I see it. If we go for plan two, we make it for as soon as they agree to meet, while the Zoo is still open… say in an hour's time as they suggested initially. If it's a go, we'll have to move fast. They may send some scouts around here early, unless they've already done so - yesterday for example. We need to establish our firing zones out here in the parking lot out of sight, and Rahim has to do his thing inside with the workers, so let's do it!"

That was it. They jumped out and headed across to Fred's vehicle.

CHAPTER 73

The man must have been sitting there waiting for the call.

"Quigley?" the voice asked.

"That's right, I've got the diamonds with me. When d'you want to meet up?"

"As soon as possible. We're under pressure holding Jamilla and having to move her around."

"Fine with me. We asked the taxi driver who drove us back from the Embassy where we collected the diamonds, what was a good place to meet up with some family friends at the Zoo and he mentioned that either the lions enclosure or the monkey cage would be most suitable. I'd like to visit it and see for myself before setting a time."

"We're running out of time Quigley. Forget about going and checking out the place. We meet in one hour's time at the Zoo or we leave Kabul right away and take Jamilla with us. Now, your taxi driver mentioned two places to meet. You choose which one" the voice grated, "and you'd better have the diamonds with you this time—all of them" he commanded.

Danny opened his mouth to say the lions' enclosure but heard a small voice in his head saying no, choose the monkey cage.

He didn't have time to think it through and heard himself saying 'the monkey cage'.

There was silence at the other end, and he heard the mutter of voices in the background. The man came back on again:

"make it the Lions' pen Quigley. We prefer that. Now how will I know you?"

"Ah, I thought your friend Bashir in London had sent you a picture" Danny teased. "Whatever, I'll be wearing a pony tail and some plain glasses and will be waiting around the lions' enclosure. How will I know you?"

There was no reply. The man had switched off the cell phone.

Danny caught Fred by the arm.

"Any luck with the trace?"

"Not enough time I'm afraid. I suspect that your caller deliberately cut it short. They obviously know the score where tracking devices are concerned."

"Right, thanks for trying anyway Fred. Now, I want you to take this van, drive to the safe house, grab your own vehicle and head back to the Embassy. Tell Curtis I'll be in touch when we're done."

He turned to the group.

"OK, let's take our positions, and you shooters stay out of sight in the parking lot. We don't know how soon they'll get here, so we must get into position fast. First, lets test our radios one last time."

There was a flurry of activity as the team jumped into action. Fred took off in the van and Rahim went inside the Zoo to try to replace one of the workers near the lions' enclosure.

Scotty and Jimmy had chosen an old shed, for their position, which was on the other side of the fence circling the parking lot. They positioned their remaining vehicle near a second exit at the back of the Zoo parking lot and established that, as they had already paid for the vehicle coming in, there would be no delay in leaving.

They had done all they could do.

Inside ten minutes, they had moved off to take up their positions, then Danny turned and walked back inside.

CHAPTER 74

"Quigley!"

Despite being on hyper alert, he was caught unawares when he heard a voice coming from behind him. He recognized it, spun round and was confronted by a middle aged, slim, short- statured Afghan, with hard gaunt features and wearing traditional clothing, who was observing him with shrewd eyes.

From a quick scan around, he appeared to be unaccompanied, despite the milling crowds going past in both directions.

He recovered quickly, and unobtrusively moved into a more defensive posture.

"So, I see you had no problem finding me in this crowd. I'm at a slight disadvantage here, not knowing who I'm talking to."

"I think Quigley, that names are irrelevant here, don't you agree?"

"Sure, I've no problem with that. Now then, to the business at hand: you have Jamilla with you as agreed?"

The man's lips tightened.

"The Afghan way, as you may know, is to sit down and show you our hospitality with a drink of tea and some food, engage in some light conversation, then get down to business. Alas, the situation doesn't allow me this opportunity, so shall we assume we've gone through all the preliminaries and move on?"

Danny's eyes narrowed slightly.

"By all means, a torturer of women is the last person in the world that I'd want to sit down and share anything with. Let's move on as you suggested. I want to see Jamilla!" he demanded.

Danny saw the man's lips twitch again.

Good, he was getting to the bastard!'

"First things first Quigley, I want to make sure that you actually have the diamonds on you, before we produce your ex-lover. That's the starting place for me, so let's see them" he demanded loudly.

Danny looked at him closely for a moment, then reached inside his coat with his left hand and drew out the small sack of diamonds. He loosened the drawstring on the top and, holding on to it tightly with his left hand, held it out cautiously, a small distance in front of him.

The Afghan had to lean forward to glance into the sack. He started to straighten up, and Danny noticed his eyes imperceptibly flick sideways.

Instantly Danny's mind screamed 'attacker' and he was already spinning sideways, his right hand nudging the Derringer activation movement.

For a split instant, on turning, he gazed into a pair of intense black eyes filled with hatred, and saw the weapon coming up towards his chest.

Without thinking, he squeezed the two-barreled Derringer trigger twice and saw what looked like two birthmarks mushrooming within an inch of each other on the man's forehead. At the same time, the crowd started screaming and scattering, and Danny felt the diamonds being snatched from his hand. The Afghan turned and started running, dodging between the crowds, heading towards the corner of the lions' enclosure.

Danny started after him, leaping over the prostate form of his attacker.

'Where the hell was Rahim?'

The Afghan could easily make his escape in the crowd, but fate took a hand. As he came up to the corner wall of the lions' enclosure, a small boy had attempted to jump up on the wall and rest on it with his elbows. He couldn't make it, and staggered back, directly into the path of the fleeing man who collided with him. To the father standing there, it looked very much like his son had been deliberately kicked. Instinctively he shoved the man as hard as he could, back against the wall. The Afghan hit it, and the strength of the shove sent him flying over the top of it, into the lion's enclosure.

Danny jumped to the wall and looked down—thirty feet down, where the man had landed on his back on a cement ledge.

'His back looks broken' Danny thought.

The lioness sitting with her cubs, roared and, leaping up, sprang on the helpless Afghan, it's mouth fastening over the fallen man's throat. In his final seconds of life, the man's hands shook erratically, sending a shower of fake diamonds to the ground all around him, glittering in the intense sunshine like some sort of halo.

Danny shuddered. He wouldn't have wished such a fate on his worst enemy.

He felt strong hands on his shoulders.

'Shit, the Police' he thought.

It was Rahim. "Let's get to hell out of here fast Danny. We only have moments...let's move!"

Danny shook his head, tearing his gaze away from the horrific scene below, and allowed Rahim to steer him across to the side door. As they went through it he tore off the wig and glasses and was about to dump them in a nearby bin, but Rahim stopped him.

"No, not here Danny - fingerprints."

"Fingerprints?" Danny said puzzled.

"Yes, on the inside skin of the wig, and those glasses as well. This is one of the first places the investigators will look. Let's keep moving."

It was General Eisenhower who had said "plans are useless, but planning is indispensible."

He knew that few plans survived the first contact with the enemy. In this case Danny and his team were fortunate they had taken the time to brainstorm and plan.

When they emerged around the corner of the back parking lot crammed with vehicles, two men jumped out of a van parked half way up the lot, and started firing with rifles. Danny and Rahim dived behind a solid pick-up truck, which was immediately raked with gunfire, exploding the windscreen and flattening the tires.

They both tried taking out their side arms, but were kept busy trying to make themselves smaller as the bullets tore under the vehicle.

They heard a second set of weapons start firing from further back, continuing for a full minute, then silence…until they heard a voice shouting

"Danny, the shooters are down, let's get our Asses out of here!"

It was Scotty.

They jumped up and raced through the parking lot towards their car, past two still forms lying sprawled on the ground.

Scotty was waving to them, and their vehicle materialized swiftly with Jimmy behind the wheel. They piled in, and Jimmy efficiently steered the vehicle out through the unmanned rear gate.

The trip back was taken in virtual silence. They waited for the sound of sirens or for roadblocks to go up.

They were lucky.

They got back to the safe house, moved the vehicle into the garage and closed it.

Rahim took the plates off and disappeared for five minutes as he disposed of them and replaced them with another set. Then they sat there just looking at each other, with the adrenalin still pumping through their veins.

It was Scotty who finally broke the silence.

"Oh man! To have pulled that off without a scratch on either of us, and to have got completely away! No Cops or Security people pulling us over with a cache of weapons on board! We sure lucked in. Holy Shit!"

Jimmy jumped in: "And get this - Danny's taken out Jamilla's murderer and his accomplice with the Derringer, and Scotty and I probably took out those Pashtuns who were after revenge on Danny. That's probably the end of that."

Danny nodded. "Yeah, the bastard that murdered Jamilla is dead. I didn't kill him, but he couldn't have had a more appropriate end - his throat torn out by a lion, and surrounded by a circle of fake sparkling diamonds that he gave his life up for. I couldn't have planned that better in a million years. It's true what they say - what goes around, comes around."

Jimmy looked up. "Rahim, where's the beer for fuck's sake. We've got some celebrating to do."

Danny raised a warning hand.

"We still have to go out to Bagram Air Base this evening and look at that site for the sniping op. tomorrow, so we'll have a quick beer, get some sleep, have a meal, and head out later on. So far lads, this has been one shit hot day!"

CHAPTER 75

It was his cell phone that woke him.

He struggled to sit up and glanced at his watch. Two hours had passed since they had all flaked out from exhaustion of the trip and the operation at the Zoo.

It was Jack Curtis. "I see you've made the local newscast Danny."

That really woke him up fully.

Curtis laughed.

"Didn't mean to alarm you…no worries. Just the story of some shooting, and a lioness killing someone. As a matter of interest, there's more fanfare about the lion killing some man than the shootings. Even the South Africans are involved."

"The South Africans?"

"Well, they recently shipped the lion family over to Kabul, and now the local authorities are talking about killing it. All diplomatic hell is breaking loose over this Zoo situation."

Danny breathed a sigh of relief.

"Thank God for that! No sign of us being fingered at this stage then?"

"None, from the news or my brief chat with some Police contacts downtown. Nice job there. Anyone on the team hurt? I understand there was a reception committee waiting for you outside."

"Not a scratch, I'm pleased to say. We'd pretty well prepared for any possible eventuality. The lads were right on the button and those bastards, whoever they were, didn't get a chance to pin us down outside, otherwise there could have been Police on our asses real fast."

"Nice work again Danny - augers well for tomorrow. I won't discuss any more over the phone, even though mine's encrypted, and I gather yours is also is from your Thames House work. If they get their hands on your cell-phone though, with all those breakthroughs in hacking, they might glean some information."

"Message received. We're having a little trip in that direction shortly with your chap and the lads. A question regarding tomorrow: where does our target sit in the vehicle.... keep it vague."

"He likes to imitate our British Officers and sit in the back right seat" Curtis replied.

"OK, how do I get a clear shot at him then. Is the window tinted and bullet-proofed as well?"

"It's not tinted but it is bullet-proofed against standard ammo. Your A.P. (Armor Piercing) will do the job though if needed. It's normal practice now at the Base Security Gate to have all passengers alight from the vehicle so they can properly check it out. This procedure is to guard against the possibility that an ISAF Officer is in the vehicle and being held at gunpoint, so you should get a clear shot."

"Fine, any change in details, timings etc. for tomorrow?" Danny asked.

"Game's on...timings as per discussion. At this stage, after the events of today, it seems we picked the right person for the job.

Good luck." The line went dead.

He got up, headed off into the bathroom and spent 15 minutes washing off his tiredness in the shower. He grabbed some fresh clothing, wandered through into the kitchen and was surprised to find that Rahim, apart from his other skills, was an excellent cook and had a large meal ready to go.

Scotty and Jimmy staggered through, and their eyes widened when they saw the feast set out on the table.

They all dived into the meal with little small talk until the food had disappeared. Scotty sat back in obvious satisfaction. "Rahim, if you weren't going back to your family in the States, I'd take you to the U.K. with me and we'd start up a restaurant together back in Old Blighty (the UK)!" he exclaimed.

Rahim laughed.

"Before I got the interpreter's job I worked in a restaurant in Kandahar as a chef. I soon learned that I prefer this side of things much better - the action I mean. Oh, the extra money helps too."

Jimmy shook his head.

"We only came over for a six month tour at a time Mate. You had to stay on and handle this shit without a break. You must be sick of it by now and ready to get on that aircraft out of here for good?"

Danny reluctantly broke into the conversation, though he recognized it as useful in bringing them back out of the adrenalin-fused activities of the morning.

"Right lads, two things...three actually. Jack Curtis called and said we appeared to be completely clear of any traces of our operation at the Zoo. A funny side effect is that there's more concern about the lioness under threat of being shot by the Police, than the dead bodies lying around. Well, this is Afghanistan after all. What are a few more casualties with IED's and car bombs wreaking havoc every day? Good luck for us for sure. Now firstly we have to do what we always do after an op."

Scotty chuckled. "Clean our weapons, right?"

"Got it in one. Then we have to head out to Bagram and do a thorough recce of the area for tomorrow's job. We were lucky today as one of you said earlier, that we got away cleanly and without a scratch. A wounded man would have presented us with some real problems. So we have to be as thorough in planning this op. as we were with the one earlier today in so far as we can, bearing in mind that we're not in control of all the pieces on the board."

"You mean our target?" Rahim volunteered.

411

"Exactly, and by the way Rahim, I need you to come with us to help us get familiarized with the layout of the area. I have some more phone calls to make and will brief you on them as we travel out there. We'll leave the long guns here and carry side arms on the recce. We'll keep the actual planning segment and walk through until we come back this evening when we'll have better intelligence to hand. So, let's get busy... and Rahim, thanks for the meal. It was spot on and what we all needed. Oh, and can I have a quick word before you get stuck into something else - probably washing dishes for starters, since you have no weapon to clean."

They moved off into the lounge and sat on a settee over by the window overlooking a grown-over neglected garden at the rear of the building.

Danny was feeling uncomfortable with the subject he wanted to bring up, and spent a couple of minutes talking about the events of the morning. Rahim knew Danny wasn't one to spend time chatting, especially with impending action.

"Rahim, thanks again for your help in backing up our operation this morning. Thankfully you didn't have to kill anyone, but your back-up was quite important, especially dragging my butt out of there when that chap went over into the lions' den. I was frozen there for a moment... oh, and stopping me dumping my wig and glasses just outside the Zoo. It never occurred to me that a wig could hold fingerprints! As you pointed out the inside skin would pick up prints quite easily too. I admit I'm a bit out of touch on some things, so thanks again on that."

"No problem Danny. When you chaps used to go home after a six months tour and then fly back in again, we had to knock some rust off you for the first week, then you were back into you're 'kick ass' ways again, but I gather you want to speak to me about something else right now."

Danny looked out into the garden for a moment, then turned back, facing him.

"I don't want what I'm going to say to you to be taken in the wrong way Rahim. We go a long way back and have been there for each other many times. I've trusted you with my life

412

in the past, and I want to emphasize that I still do, without question. Shortly I need you to take us out to Bagram Air Base and walk us through the set-up for tomorrow. I gather Jack Curtis has already been out there with you for this?"

"Actually no Danny. It was two Americans, Wade Coyle and a second chap called Steve Hanson. They looked Military with their haircuts and bearing, and I automatically assumed CIA. They walked me through the whole operation as they envisaged it from the sniper's position, across from the front gates of Bagram Air Base, to the road where they would wait for you to carry out the Exfill."

"Over to that village where the chopper picks us up and brings us back to Kabul Airport?"

"Right, and as to timings, they emphasized that the Mullah and his group would probably be on time or even early, as these things can be, you know running into road checks and so on."

"They would have priority I assume in situations like that though, wouldn't they?"

"Yes of course, but you sometimes see a check-point set up on a narrow road to have more control, and it would have to be cleared to let their Government vehicle through."

Danny nodded thoughtfully. "Got it, so we need to be set up early then."

"I must admit the whole thing looks like a straightforward operation, comparing it to some of the shit I've seen in the past.

Was there something else you needed to talk to me about Danny? You mentioned something about me not taking it the wrong way."

"No easy way to say this Rahim, but I don't want you to come out with us tomorrow on this one. I…"

Rahim's mouth opened in surprise, even shock, and he started to say something. Danny held his hand up to stop him.

"I want you to head over to the Embassy after we leave in the morning, and hang around there for the duration. Make yourself busy and visible, however you do that. You clear on that?"

"But Danny, Mr. Curtis told me to stay with you for the few days you're here. I was supposed to run you over to that chopper when you took the Mullah out. What do I tell him?"

"Just say that I felt it would be cleaner with fewer bodies to get out of the area, and that you had done more than your bit in setting us up, not to mention the Zoo action where you played a big part in getting us familiar with the landscape."

"But Danny...." he started protesting, then stopped and looked at him for a long moment.

His face cleared of his anger and confusion.

"You don't feel good about tomorrow's operation, do you?" he whispered. "I know you Danny, there's something bothering you."

He shook his head.

"You're imagining things my friend. Look, your family is waiting for you in the States. Keep your head down for the next little while and you'll be heading back there before you know it. The last thing you want is to get your ass caught in a fire fight Rahim."

"Like tomorrow you mean? I said it looked straight forward after my walk about, but you obviously have some misgivings about the whole thing. If there's some problems out there tomorrow, I'd like to be there."

Danny looked down at his watch.

"Time to get the lads out of here. I'm sorry, but that's my final word on this topic. Sorry..."

He got up and walked back into the kitchen leaving the Afghan sitting there looking after him.

CHAPTER 76

It was a subdued Rahim who led them out to the site for the takedown the following morning. The actual area looked exactly as he had laid out in his earlier description.

The partially collapsed building where Danny would take up his firing position was ideal in terms of accommodation - it offered the elevation and a clear view of the target area.

They crawled up to the building to avoid any possibility of being spotted by the Gate Security people, who might be passing their bored duty hours by swinging their binoculars around the area.

They hadn't brought the long guns with them in case of running into a checkpoint, but they could see that the inside space offered lots of room for all three to have a clear firing area.

Test firing the Remington Sniper Rifle was not an option at this stage, but Rahim had assured Danny that the rifle had been checked out by him a few days previously and was working smoothly. Danny intended to use AP (Armor Piercing) rounds in his magazine, for the shot the following day.

They looked carefully at the area outside the collapsed building where they would make their escape. Initially they would have a flat thirty yards to cross, through long grass and chest high scrubs, to a man-sized barrier of hard clay and rocks. Then they would face a two hundred yard section of scrubland and further solid mounds of earth, interspersed with a number of large and more mature trees.

This would bring them back close to the road where the two CIA men would be in their concealed vehicle, ready to drive them to the waiting helicopter in a nearby village.

Rahim showed them the area where their vehicle would be stowed out of sight, across the other side of the road, and separate from the CIA vehicle. The road was seldom used except by the odd farmer, or their kids possibly chasing up any strayed animals grazing on the verges.

Jimmy queried - "does this mean we could run into a bunch of goats or cows? That could slow us up, and anyone herding them would have a chance to get a good look at us."

Rahim looked apologetic.

"No, not like that at all. When I did a dry run, we saw a couple of goats that must have escaped from some enclosure. Sure some kid might come looking for them at the days end, but no flocks, don't worry."

They had pulled their vehicle off the road into the concealed area the CIA would be using the following morning. Danny got some maps out, opened them up on the hood of the car, and studied the broader outline of interlinking roads.

"Hmm, looks straight forward enough."

He looked at his three colleagues.

"So what am I missing here, if anything? Remember, this whole thing has already been set up for us, not like the brainstorming and soul-searching we go through on our Regiment ops."

Jimmy pointed to the road they would be escaping on.

"We have no plan two if something goes wrong?"

"In what way." Danny asked.

"For starters, we're relying on two people we don't know. I'm sure they're totally reliable, and this whole operation has been set-up by MI6, but what if they're not here for whatever reason when we've finished haring across from the old building back there? The CIA chaps could have been delayed by a checkpoint or worse - a surprise IED placed by the

Taliban back down the road to Kabul. They've been getting pretty damn bold recently, as Rahim can confirm."

Scotty tapped Rahim's arm. "What d'you say Mate. Have we got a problem here? We'd be up shit creek if we barreled out of the scrubland and there was no Exfill vehicle waiting. We'd be sitting ducks for the first patrol coming across from the Air Base to investigate."

Rahim looked carefully across at Danny.

"I didn't intend to bring this up, but earlier Danny told me he didn't want me out here tomorrow. Something about not exposing me to a possible firefight, which could affect my plans to rejoin my family in the U.S.A. However your views Scotty are exactly along the lines of what's been going through my mind. What if something doesn't go according to plan? Sure you'll have the vehicle you came out in, to get here, but you don't know the roads around here, especially the shortcuts, if you have to make a run for it on your own."

He paused for a moment, before continuing.

"Whether you like it or not Danny, I'm going to be here tomorrow as insurance, in case things don't go according to plan, I can be your fallback option. Let me worry about getting out of Afghanistan when the time comes. Remember, as previously mentioned, I've survived six years tackling worse situations than this, and I'm still alive, so that's my plan for tomorrow, take it or leave it."

Danny knew he'd lost the argument on this one. He tapped the Afghan's arm, and held his gaze for a moment.

"Thanks Rahim. OK, I'll feel much better if you are here, and I'm sure the lads will do as well. Now lets kick this round some more so that we're all comfortable with our movements for tomorrow."

It was an hour later that they headed back to Kabul. They would do one last check on their weapons.

The die was cast.

The evening was spent with a final sorting out of weapons, ammunition and material. When it came down to the Kevlar vests Danny decided to hand over the sole ceramic plate to Scotty, and stick to a batch of paper-thin sheets of Kevlar.

"Far too bulky for me lying down in a sniper position" he explained. " Here Scotty, you have it."

"Sure about that Danny? You might need it when you head back to the Exfill point."

"You know what it's like, lying there with perhaps one very narrow chance to make a hit. Anything that interferes with one's concentration is out as far as I'm concerned."

"Fine with me. I'm your spotter for the hit, unless we go for secondary targets."

They finished and packed as they were taking their entire luggage with them after the Bagram operation. Originally, the plan was for Rahim to bring the weapons back to the house, after the operation, to return to the MI6 armory. Assuming everything went according to plan, he could still do this.

Danny picked up his phone and went into an empty bedroom down the hall.

CHAPTER 77

Prior to embarking on the MI6 arranged operation in Afghanistan, Danny had been having misgivings about the whole plan to take down the Mullah. He'd still wanted to settle the score with Jamilla's murderer, but something didn't feel right about the sniping role he had taken on. There was nothing specific about it, just a feeling in his gut that things weren't quite right about the operation. He'd had similar feelings about previous undertakings when he was in the Regiment, which had turned out badly when he ignored them.

In this situation, particularly with the responsibility of having Scotty and Jimmy involved, he decided to arrange some sort of an edge, if possible. His first efforts to locate ex-members of the SAS Regiment, who might have contracted with Security companies over in Afghanistan, came to nothing. He had hoped to hire the services of a couple of them to provide extra insurance in the event that things didn't go according to plan.

After a number of phone calls, he vented his frustration to Scotty.

To his amazement, he had the key.

"You should have come to me first Mate. After all I just left the Regiment and am up to date on the chaps who got out."

Danny looked embarrassed.

"Well, you know, I didn't want to start raising any worries in yours and Jimmy's minds. If I could have set up something,

I would have brought it into the briefing when we got down to it."

"Jesus Danny, you're like a bloody parent worrying about their kids going to summer camp. We're big boys now and by the way, our experience with the Regiment is recent. You've been out going on five years. Jimmy and I are like fucking trained Dobermans. Just point us and we take em down!"

"Yeah, OK I get it. I'm still hung up on that Nigerian thing when I lost Clyde Stoner. Anyway, tell me what you have for me Scotty."

"Well, you know our CO at Hereford, Major Wainwright was coming to a situation where, if he wanted to move up on the promotional scale, he had to move on from the Saas? Well, he was made up to a half Colonel and was given the task of taking on the role of heading up the new Military Training Academy, at Camp Qargha for Officers, just outside Kabul Airport. It used to be called Camp Phoenix when the Americans were there. The training's pretty well based on our elite Officer training at Sandurst in the U.K. and the Brits make up seventy five percent of the staff. I read that ten thousand Afghans applied for the first Officer's intake, out of which they only accepted over two hundred and seventy five or so. A hell of a challenge for the Colonel, but I'd say he'd do anything for your good self. Hell, he used to refer to you as 'a walking killing machine.'"

"Wainwrights in Kabul?" Danny marveled. "Now, that's an answer to prayer. I'll get on to him right away. I don't suppose you have any contact numbers, do you?"

Scotty shook his head.

"You're no techie for sure. Just Google Camp Qargha near Kabul in Afghanistan, and the contact number'll be right there. Look, give me a few minutes and I'll get it for you."

He was as good as his word.

"Hey, tell the Colonel I asked for him. He was one shit hot CO, I'll tell you - saved my ass a number of times when I got in trouble outside the camp!"

Danny, after waiting for 3 hours while Wainwright finished a training class, heard a chuckling voice come on the line.

"I couldn't believe it when they told me at the break that a Danny Quigley would call back later, and here you are for God's sake. I can tell you Hereford wasn't the same place after you left. Now, my mind's been spinning around all afternoon, wondering what on earth you're looking me up for after all this time."

"Well Colonel, it's like this…"

"Danny, please call me Paul. You've been one of those wimpy civvies for the past number of years."

"OK, Paul. Seems strange just the same. Oh, Scotty said to say Hi to you. He said you'd saved his ass more times than he could remember."

Wainwright laughed. "I did that all right. He sure knew how to get in deep shit off the Base, but he was one ass-kicker when I needed one. Not to mention yourself, of course. Now how can I help you? I only have thirty minutes before I go back in."

"Ooops, sorry to mess up your lunch hour then. OK, question: how secure is your line? I'm encrypted here."

There was silence on the other end.

"So, this isn't a pleasure call then Danny. Why am I not surprised? I've heard of some of the rumors about your activities since you left us. To answer your question, no it's not secure. If you gave me an hour's warning I could get the use of one that was set up in a special room by the Americans when they were here, but why not give me a broad stroke on what's going on and stay off specifics?"

"Right, here goes. You know that course I did over in the U.S.A. at one time?"

It had been the U.S. Marines Sniping Course. There was a moment of silence. "Right, I got it."

"Good. I've been offered some work in that line recently, over in Stan actually."

"Ah, by your present employers is it? Doesn't their name start with M or something…Monarch something?"

421

He's picked up on the MI5. "Well yes initially, but a relative of theirs actually."

He got that as well. The CIA were referred to as 'The Cousins' by MI5 and MI6. "OK, I got it. Where do I come in?"

"I'm a trifle worried about the roads over there, especially if we have an accident. I wouldn't have any health care coverage."

"Yes, that could be a problem" Wainwright said. "It's a dangerous place especially with the resurgence of the Taliban. People are being shot in their vehicles at un-expected road checks that the Taliban throw up. I'm not sure if I can help you there Danny. We do have a medical clinic here in Camp Qargha, but we could only help someone who was in the Military. If it needed more than a patch-up there's an ISAF compound of the Kabul Air Base a half hour from here, and with their own ISAF entrance for emergencies, but as I say, you'd have to be in the Forces."

"Understood. Where would that put Scotty? He just took his discharge, but he's still officially listed as being in for some weeks yet with his saved holiday leave."

"Sure, no problem there. Anything else on your mind Danny? I have to dash in a minute."

"One thing Paul. Remember the chap who got in trouble with Cheltenham on his computer? Have you anyone there with a similar skill?" Danny asked.

It was the GCHQ listening post that this Trooper had foolishly tried to hack.

"God, this is like twenty questions Danny. Wait a minute, I get it. I'll have to chase that one up. Wouldn't surprise me...I'm told we have some smart techies here. Look, call me when you hit the ground and we can tie something up. Bye for now."

He'd got most of what he wanted on the call: medical help for Jimmy and Scotty if they got wounded, and a possible fast way onto the Kabul Air Base. He'd learned from the travel agent that one had to turn up at the Kabul Air Terminal four hours early, and that one could be waiting an hour outside the terminal.

That could put any fast exit from Afghanistan in jeopardy when an alert went out after the assassination of the Mullah.

CHAPTER 78

Some hours later, he was waiting for a secure call with Colonel Wainwright, to discuss final details.

His phone rang. It was Wainwright.

"OK Danny, we're secure, so fill me in on what's going on. No more 20 questions please."

Danny knew he had to completely level with him as his career could be on the line if it got out that he had, in some way, provided resources or information in an assassination attempt. He went through his involvement from receiving the call from the Afghan who was holding Jamilla prisoner, his belief that she had been killed, and his desire to get revenge on her killer. How MI6 had offered him a way of doing this for a quid pro quo by killing the Mullah, who was suspected of planning an attack on the Government and it's Military. How he had already settled the score with Jamilla's murderer at the Zoo in Kabul.

Wainwright whistled.

"Jesus Danny, you really do get into these situations! I can't believe what I'm hearing, even for Danny Quigley! Question: now that you've taken out Jamilla's murderer, why do you need the CIA any more?"

"Good question Paul. Probably because Rebecca at MI5 stuck her neck out going to MI6, who in turn found the answer with the CIA. I just can't see walking away at this stage, after all MI6 got us over here initially under the guise of being investigators for that chopper crash."

"People you haven't even contacted I gather, since you got here?" Wainwright queried.

"Right. Things just took on their own momentum once Jamilla's killer contacted me on the day of arrival. Now here's my problem. I had a bad feeling all along about the CIA's method of setting this operation up. They wanted complete deniability, and loved the idea of an ex-Saas type doing the job with no connection to them. My concern is that they might want to wipe the boards completely, after I take out the Mullah."

"Sorry, how would that work? Explain your thinking here. I'm not quite with you."

"OK, perhaps I'm being paranoid, but what if there was no chopper waiting after we do the hit, and they take us out. Rahim says the two Americans were very Military types and one of the pieces of information I would value, is if you could find out whether a flight path has been requested for tomorrow to that village where the crash occurred. That would tell me something for sure. I could be totally off the mark here, but as I said, I've had a nagging feeling about this op. since I agreed to take it on."

"OK Danny. If you hang five I can check that from right here on my computer. Oh, what did you want the computer hacker for that you asked about?"

"That was for tomorrow. I wanted to know when and if a security alert went out, and if our names had been compromised in any way. We have a second set of IDs if we need them."

"We can certainly run this tomorrow. Just a quickie: did you sign in at the registration desk at Kabul Airport when you landed?"

"We went to the registration desk all right, but it wasn't manned."

Wainwright laughed. "Those bastards, they haven't a clue about Security. Now that's good news for you because tomorrow, you won't have to register out on the name you

425

came in on. In other words, you could use your new IDs. I've had another thought on you and the lads getting out. I'll check that flight plan first."

He hung up.

He was as good as his word and rang back inside five minutes.

"No flight plan request for a chopper tomorrow morning Danny."

"Shit! The CIA, as you know Paul, can be slippery. Could they in some way arrange the flight over there without a flight plan from traffic control?"

"Not in this location with all the civilian and military aircraft in the air. I have to say that the Air Traffic Control people here are shit hot, and challenge any unidentified aircraft they spot up there."

"So we seem to have a problem then."

"I would say you do Danny, for sure. My advice is to get the lads and yourself on a plane a.s.a.p. and get the hell out of here Mate."

"Hang on a minute. I now know that this Mullah, at some time in the near future, is going to attack ISAF troops and the Afghan Government, in no doubt a well planned and timed attack. I'm still a Military man at heart and I couldn't get on a plane and wash my hands of it."

"So what's your plan two, as we used to ask in our briefings back in the Regiment?"

"Between myself and the two lads, we'll have to take these two CIA people out, if they turn up and have a go at us."

"Whoa a minute Danny! I warn you, you're over the line here in terms of my helping you out. Killing Americans and especially CIA Agents is the last thing in the world you want to do. They already know who you are and will chase you to the ends of the earth until they get you. I want no part of this if that's your Exfill strategy. Jesus Danny, you're off the wall here!"

Danny shook his head, as if clearing it.

"Shit, you're right Paul. What am I thinking of - and Jimmy and Scotty would go down with me. OK, let me think about this for a moment."

He got to his feet and walked across the room, then came back and sat down.

"Right Paul, thanks for that reality check. You got it in one. I'd be walking into a wrecking ball for sure. How about this: if we encounter these people, and I suspect we will, we make every effort to take them alive and tie them up somewhere out of the way until we get out of the country. We could run their vehicle off the road into the brush somewhere on the way back towards Kabul, and leave information for you to phone in after we get out of the Afghanistan airspace. How does that sound?"

"You'd have to leave me with clear instruction as to where you'd left them. I'd hate the Taliban to come across them. That would be the same, or worse than you taking them out. You know what these Afghan women do to prisoners, especially Americans. I have to emphasize, I can't help you if it turns out that you and the lads had to terminate them. That would put me between a rock and a hard place Danny."

"OK, message received and understood Paul. Now what was that other idea you had for getting us out of the country, without getting picked up?"

"A very simple solution really. I'm responsible for arranging R&R for our British Officers back to the U.K., and I use a helicopter to fly them from Camp Qargha, over to Kandahar, which is much quieter than the Kabul Airport. Before our troops left Helmand Province completely, they used to fly out of Kandahar in our old Tri Star planes to Cyprus, then on to the U.K. The problem was that those Tri Star planes were falling apart by then, and at least thirty percent of the flights were delayed. One group of soldiers heading back on R&R was stuck at Kandahar for seven days, and others at Cyprus. In the end the troops started paying their own air fares from Cyprus back to the U.K."

"So what are you saying then?"

427

"We have a chopper going out tomorrow afternoon with a few Officers, and we could get the three of you on board over to Kandahar. You would have to arrange your own flight out of there, where I doubt there'd be any security alert."

"Hey, that sounds like a super plan Paul, but won't these Officers wonder about myself and the lads?" He chuckled. "We have all sorts of people slipping on these flights believe me. These Officers know better than to ask any questions. I'm the CO here anyway, so they wont mess with anyone I place on board."

"Sounds better and better. D'you know what airlines fly out of there by any chance, and the approximate times?"

"Well, lets see… there's Arianna Afghan Airlines that fly to Dubai International Airport. Fly Dubai, as the name suggests, goes to Dubai as well, and Kam Air also goes to Dubai, and Mashad in Iran. Some airline goes out to India I understand, but that's in the wrong direction. As I was saying, there are numerous flights going out daily, and not all full. You might consider taking different airlines, or flights if you suspect a deteriorating situation is building up here. For example, if you're tied up Americans got loose sooner than you thought and started trying to muddy up the waters…."

Wainwright stopped for a moment.

"Are we getting this wrong Danny? I mean if you take out the Mullah, that's their goal attained. If they'd planned to take you out and failed, why would they want you scooped up by the Afghan Security, where their role in the assassination might emerge? I think they might just want to see you get out of the country, and hope you keep your mouth shut."

"Or catch up with us later?" Danny suggested.

"Don't think so. Too many people involved: you, Scotty, Jimmy, MI6 in London, your friend Rahim, the local chap Curtis at the British Embassy. No, their best shot of a complete cover up if they want to play dirty pool, would be that you and your team were taken out here in Afghanistan by unknown forces. However if you and the lads slipped through the net, that would make a cover up virtually impossible."

"Hmm...I'm liking this more and more. From your experience Paul, how far could this termination policy go back? Am I to assume that MI6 here and in London are in on this?

I know for sure that Rebecca, in no way shape or form, would have agreed to the operation on that basis?"

"That's a tough one. There might have been no collusion by MI6, especially here in the local Embassy, but who knows whether the MI6 in London had any suspicion of what might happen. The Intelligence people operate on a different set of rules... layers within layers. They might just turn a blind eye to it for some future quid pro quo. It's a dirty business. I'd leave it to your friend Rebecca at MI5 to suss out. You stay clear of it my friend, it's a losing proposition. Now, the last thing, timing for tomorrow."

"Right, the op. is supposed to go down at 11am and we're assured that the Mullah's group are usually on time. We take him out, sort out the two CIA types, and follow Rahim back to your Camp Oargha. He splits and heads back to the house and claims he was there all the time and not involved, but I've no idea how long that trip would take, Paul."

"Right, I'll have the front gate alerted to your arriving some time, hopefully before noon, and they'll escort you round to my office where we'll assess the situation from there. I can delay the chopper for a short time if you run into some problem, but not for long. Oh, and the chopper should get into Kandahar which is over an hours flight, around 2.30 pm, if you want to book some more flights. Other than that, I can't do any more. Remember, don't kill the CIA people, otherwise all bets are off."

The line went dead.

Danny now had to do a full briefing with Scotty, Jimmy and Rahim.

They were in for some surprises – stunned would be a more appropriate word!

CHAPTER 79

Scotty's jaw literally dropped, while Jimmy's eyes widened, and he sat back abruptly in his chair. Rahim stood up and stared at Danny in shock. It was Scotty who broke the silence.

"Let's get the fuck out of here Mate. We didn't sign on for this! On the CIA's kill list? These people play for keeps!"

Jimmy was equally taken aback.

"You believe these bastards have set it up to take us out after the op, and you're saying we can't defend ourselves, that we have to take them alive and keep them safe? Even Wainwright should know you couldn't stop two highly trained people coming at you with assault weapons without some blood being spilled. Quite possibly ours! This is turning into a fucking suicide mission!"

Rahim merely stood there shaking his head.

Danny held his hands up and leaned forward.

"Wainwright's initial reaction was the same until I explained that this Mullah planned to make a sudden attack with his group, and the target was the Coalition Forces and the Government. They know the weaknesses of the set-up here and could do some serious damage. A great number of people would be killed - no doubt a high number of our fellow soldiers in uniform. Now we have a chance to stop this attack - to save lives. My question to you is, do we just walk away

430

from this, when we're in a position to do something about it? I'm saying yes, and I'll do it on my own if needs be."

Silence fell on the group.

Scotty started to say something but Rahim cut in.

"I have an idea Danny, that might make it more possible to take those two CIA men alive, without any of us getting shot to pieces."

"Hey, I'm all ears Rahim. Go for it." Danny looked interested.

"I have a cousin from the same village as myself originally, who works here in Kabul for a vet. They have those guns they use to tranquilize animals. I've seen them take down mad dogs and even cattle that have made a break from a slaughterhouse. Pretty powerful. I even helped him once when he asked me to work a weekend with him some time back."

Jimmy didn't look convinced.

"Just how would you see that working Rahim? I'm afraid I'd take a lot more convincing. A mad dog sure, but someone coming at me with an AK 47?"

Danny intervened. "Wait a minute here, let's give him a chance to explain. Rahim?"

"My role, as I understand it, was to get out of sight upon arrival, across the road from where the CIA men have planned to pull in their vehicle. I'll have them under observation from the moment they arrive. Danny's assuming they'll make an attempt on your lives. That could be quite true, or is there another explanation, closer to the original Exfill plan? In any event, I'll find out pretty quickly. After the shots from your sniping endeavors, successful or not, if they mean you harm they'll go forward to set themselves up as you bail out from your position at the old building. At that time I'll radio you a warning, start to stalk them carefully, and get as close as I can in the cover that's available. As we expect, they'll open fire on you as you come barreling out of there. That's when I open up with the Vet's takedown guns."

Scotty didn't look convinced. "Taking out two chaps with assault weapons, with a tranquilizer dart? Come on! If you hit one he probably doesn't go down straight away and might still get off a burst at you, or the second chap spots it and turns on you before you get off a second shot, presumably from a second weapon. I appreciate what you're volunteering to do Rahim, but I need some more convincing."

Jimmy held up his hand. "Wait a minute chaps, I think he's got something here that might work with a different twist."

"The floor's yours Jimmy," Danny encouraged.

"As it happens, I've used one of those tranquilizers on, would you believe it, a fucking elephant in Africa on an R&R once. Myself and three mates went on a cheap safari and helped the owner of an animal farm over there. Their elephant was going mad with a bloody toothache. The point I'm making is that it's the dosage you put into the dart that brings them down and real fast if you want to. Now, I'd suggest I take the second tranquilizer gun and be prepared to move up on the flank of these two. Using radio comms, we attack them at the same time. Rahim and I arrange which one to take down. What d'you think lads?"

Scotty shrugged. "You could still murder the bastards if you give them too big a dose, and then we're up the creek. Still a bit dicey Jimmy, but, lacking any other way of taking these bastards alive, let's take a look at this and see if we can fine-tune it. I'm beginning to see possibilities here."

The next half hour was taken up with further discussion followed by Rahim making a brief call to his friend at the vets. He did a thumbs-up to the group, and Danny took the moment to pull him aside and explain his side of the Exfill plan in more detail: taking both vehicles in the morning, and later hiding the immobilized CIA men in their own vehicle off the Kabul road, as well as leaving visible markings for Wainwright's information.

When the team arrived in Kabul, Rahim was to split off in his vehicle taking the weapons, go to the safe house and stay there. He was to claim that Danny had refused to take him on the operation that morning. In this way his trip back to his family in the U.S.A. would not be in jeopardy.

Danny was familiar with the route over to Camp Qargha and, hopefully, events would fall into place around Wainwright's plan. They couldn't do anymore.

Tomorrow was in the lap of the Gods.

CHAPTER 80

They were in position an hour early.

Danny had settled himself comfortably on an old sleeping bag that he'd scrounged from Rahim. He was carefully scrutinizing the main gate of the Air Base through the Remington scope, and the movements of the Security personnel. There were six armed soldiers outside, two in a small sandbagged square and the rest posted on both sides of the road. He suspected this was more than the usual complement on the front gate, with the imminent arrival of the Mullah and his group.

As planned, Rahim had pulled their vehicle well back into some thick trees across the road from where the CIA Agents would park. The other one was tucked in close to where the CIA Agents would be as Danny's group had to show evidence as to how they had arrived there earlier.

Scotty, as his spotter, was alongside him. Once he had the lay of the target area, he laid out his own weapon, an M16, and sat back on a block of concrete.

Jimmy had found his spot and played around with the scope on his target area.

All three weapons were laid out with extra ammo clips, which they hoped wouldn't be needed. The time crawled past slowly, as it does when one is waiting in a heightened alert state for action to take place.

Suddenly the lead vehicle was there, easing up, and stopping about ten feet back from the Security Detail. It was followed closely by the Mullah's vehicle.

'A bit far back' Danny thought.

No sooner had the thought occurred to him than the doors of the lead vehicle exploded open and four soldiers jumped out. They wore Afghan Military uniforms, with assault rifles pumping a fusillade of bullets into the four Security personnel by the roadside, then at the two others who were partially visible over the sandbags

The Security Detail never had a chance.

Complete surprise left them totally exposed and easy targets.

"Jesus" Scotty exploded. "What the fuck's going on?"

"This is their attack that we heard they were planning. Shit, they're going to go for the Base!"

"With four people? They haven't a chance...." Jimmy shouted. "Oh shit, look back down the line behind them!"

"No jeeps as we expected...a whole truck load of the bastards! Must be the Mullah's total team" Danny screamed, as soldiers started bailing out of the vehicle.

He clapped Scotty on the shoulder. "Let's start taking them down," he ordered.

With that Scotty dropped the spotters binos, (binoculars) grabbed his rifle, and with Jimmy, started coolly and carefully firing on the group.

Danny's thoughts momentarily, were all over the place, his focus on taking down the Mullah momentarily confused.

Clarity rushed into his mind as he realized that the Mullah's traitorous actions would finish him with the Afghan Government in any event. He wouldn't miss a chance to kill him though, if the opportunity presented itself to him.

The first task was to immobilize the truck.

His first shots took out the two sets of tyres in the lead vehicle, which faced him. His next two slammed into the engine block, causing a geyser gush out of the hood of the vehicles.

435

With the last of his five shot magazine, he took down the driver of the Mullah's vehicle who had been the first to jump out, weapon blazing.

He ejected the magazine and slammed in another. His next took out the tyres of the Mullah's vehicle.

Scotty and Jimmy, between them, had concentrated a deadly stream of lead on the remaining shooters at the front gate and the exiting truck soldiers streaming towards it.

The truck exploded in a gigantic flash of flame, soldiers burning as they threw themselves off the inferno.

Danny focused on the window of the Mullah's vehicle.

"Come on, come on, you bastard! Show your face. You're finished here anyway, but you organized this whole cold-blooded killing of colleagues in uniform. I'd love to give you your just desserts."

As if the Mullah had heard him, the back door slammed open and the man himself jumped out.

He was looking back frantically at the burning truck.

Danny didn't hesitate.

He squeezed the trigger gently and saw the Mullah's head explode.

An AP round (Armor Piercing) … no need for another shot.

Danny had a quick look at the front gate and saw Security Personnel streaming out and taking aim at the thinned down soldiers on the roadway.

Danny's head jerked back…three words popped into his mind: 'Get out now!'

He didn't question it. It wasn't that kind of voice.

He leaned back and slammed Scotty and Jimmy on their backs.

"Out now…lets go…" he screamed.

They looked up at him.

"But we've got them on the run" Scotty protested.

"NOW...OUT...MOVE!" shouted Danny.

They didn't question it, just grabbed their rifles and spare mags. then scrambled on their hands and knees out of the narrow space, dragging their rifles.

436

The two men stood up uncertainly, looking round at Danny as he crawled out and jumped to his feet. He grabbed them by the shoulder and violently pushed them away in the direction of the clay bank, thirty feet away.

"Move, for God's sake, move" he shouted, as he started racing away from the collapsed building.

They had no sooner thrown themselves against the clay bank than there was a massive explosion behind them as the building they had just crawled out of disappeared in a flash of flying rocks, showering them with debris.

They lifted their heads a moment later. Scotty's face was in shock and disbelief.

"How the hell did you know to get our asses out of there?"

Danny never had a chance to answer. His two-way radio squawked. It was Rahim's voice.

"What's happened over there Danny? What was that explosion? Are you guys OK?"

"Roger to that Rahim. They must have set charges and had a spotter somewhere up on the security perimeter of the main gate. When they saw the Mullah go down they just pulled the plug on us. There wouldn't have been very much of us left in there if you saw that blast. Now, where are the two CIA men?" he asked.

"Moving slowly towards you as we speak. Probably heading for that embankment which would give them a good overview."

"OK Rahim, stalk them carefully. Don't get spotted, whatever you do. Get ready to go into action when we do. Give me one squawk when you're in position. I'll give you two when I want you to fire. Over."

"Roger that. Out"

He turned to the two men. "Slight change of plan. Despite what we've just seen, we still can't kill them unless we have no option - Wainwright's condition on helping us get out. If we have to, we have to. They're coming towards us as we speak. If we move, we can get into position in front of the embankment they're heading for. I'm going with Jimmy and his tranquilizer gun on the right flank, and Scotty goes left. Questions?"

Scotty nodded. "What if we can't?" He meant, take them alive.

Danny looked at him. "I don't want any more of us to die here...understood? By the way, these guys should be pretty relaxed after that explosion."

They moved carefully over the brow of the embankment and headed off in different directions...Scotty like a wraith disappearing into the shrubbery.

Jimmy had slung his rifle over his shoulder and had a firm grip on his tranquilizer gun.

They approached the second embankment and Danny indicated that they take up positions on his left and right flank. They sped off. An idea had started forming as they were advancing. He decided to take up a position behind a large bolder perched on the top of the embankment.

The two CIA men were relaxed, chatting loudly as they came forward.

Danny, crouched down in the center, could hear them clearly:

"I'd have loved to have seen their faces when that building went   up.
"Won't be much of their faces left after that blast. You make a good bomb my friend... nothing left to chance."

They laughed again.

Danny had hoped he would be approximately in the path of the two CIA Agents coming forward, with Scotty and Jimmy in their positions. He inched his gaze cautiously around the side of the boulder, watching them approach, and eased back. He couldn't have chosen better. They were heading directly towards the large boulder he was now squatting behind.

He squinted around the boulder again.

They were ten feet away and would be on top of him within moments.

"Shit!" his plan was falling apart. 'Where was Rahim?'

Just then his radio squawked.

Rahim was in position.

438

He returned it with two.

Within ten seconds he heard a voice directly in front of him, roaring out in pain.

Danny stood up, in time to see one of the CIA Agents desperately reaching around his back to feel where the dart had imbedded itself in him. His partner spun round, his assault rifle coming up and, turning towards Jimmy who had risen with his weapon.

Jimmy's tranquilizer dart should have been winging towards him at the same time.

It wasn't. Something had gone wrong!

Then Scotty stood up and shouted.

The CIA Agent spun towards him, his finger tightening on the trigger.

Danny had only one chance. He still wanted to avoid killing the man. Without thinking he heaved his Remington, with the heavy wooden stock pointed like an arrow, directly at the Agent, now standing about six feet away. One could never rehearse such a move, but by good luck or chance it caught the man directly with a loud smack, and he slumped to the ground like someone poleaxed.

In a moment, three anxious figures were gathered around the fallen man.

Danny couldn't bear to touch the man he'd felled. "Scotty, please tell me he's breathing, for God's sake?"

Scotty knelt down then looked up. "Lucky again Mate." Turning to Jimmy he asked, "what the hell happened to you? If I hadn't stood up and Danny lobbed his rifle, we'd probably both have bought it."

Jimmy looked in shock. "The fucking thing didn't fire when I pressed the trigger."

Rahim leaned forward, took his dart gun and examined it.

"Would help if you'd taken the safety off" he said grinning, as the pressure of the moment started to slide off them.

Danny brought them back to focus.

"Right, plastic cuffs, duck tape their mouths, get hoods on them so they can't ID Rahim, put them into their vehicle, and we're off…all three vehicles. Let's go. The Security people at the Base will have spotted the explosion and will be heading over as soon as they clean up the Mullah's men. Let's move it."

Some miles up the road they ran the CIA Agents' vehicle back into some brush, well concealed. They made sure they were secure in the vehicle, with extra flex cuffs, and unable to make an attempt to release each other. Then they laid some unobtrusive signs out on the roadway, which could only be detected by someone who had the information.

When they reached the fork in the streets in Kabul where Rahim was supposed to split off, he signaled a stop and ran back to Danny's car. The traffic around them had become chaotic, as can happen in that city.

He leaned in the open car window. "Look, you won't make that chopper flight on your own Danny. Wainwright will have to send it off without you. There's only one chance. I know these streets like the back of my hand, especially all the small side streets, and if you allow me to show you, I think we can make it."

"OK, go for it Mate. At this rate you're our only chance. I can't even handle London traffic, which is kindergarten compared to this. Don't lose me!"

He didn't.

The tension eased when they arrived at Camp Qargha and a grinning Wainwright was waiting.

He had good news:

No security alert was out. The chopper was ready to go.

After a quick handshake all round, Rahim took off with the weapons.

Everything worked like clockwork. The one-hour trip to Kandahar went without incident.

Danny called Wainwright when they were boarding for the two-hour flight to Dubai.

When they were out of Afghan airspace, Wainwright would make an anonymous call to the American Embassy, with directions to locate the CIA Agents.

It was a long haul back to the U.K. from Dubai. No one slept a wink. The adrenalin was still pumping. At one time Scotty leaned across.

"How did you know to get our asses out of that old building?"

Danny stared at him and shook his head.

"I've no idea. I just heard a voice telling me to get out."

"What did it sound like?'

"Like a Sergeant Major reaming my ass out on the parade square. You don't question it!"

"Glad you didn't Mate," Jimmy said fervently, "or we wouldn't be heading back on this flight right now."

He turned to Scotty. "Did you hear a voice as well when you stood up and that CIA bastard turned his weapon towards you? You really saved my ass there!"

He shook his head. "If I'd heard a voice telling me to do something that stupid, I'd have told it to fuck off. I just stood up, and Danny there saved the day with his incredible javelin-like throw."

"Yeah, sure Scotty, I believe you. Thanks Mate, I owe you one."

CHAPTER 81

London

He thought it was the cell phone that woke him. When he picked it up he realized that it was the doorbell ringing.

He was still fully dressed, having come straight round to his flat with his two colleagues, where they had all crashed. As he staggered to the front door, he glanced at his watch.

He'd had four hours sleep.

There was no sound from the other room where Jimmy and Scotty were no doubt dead to the world. He didn't even peep through the eyehole. He was too tired.

It was Rebecca standing there, a look of concern on her face.

"Shoot Danny, you look awful!"

He snorted. "I feel even worse than awful Rebecca. We just got in four hours ago."

He stepped aside. "Come in won't you."

Once inside she looked around. "Where are the lads? Are you all OK?"

"They're sleeping in the other room and yes, thanks for asking, but we are all OK. What brings you here?"

"Well, we got the newscast from Afghanistan, which told us nothing. It sounded all garbled: the Mullah attacking Bagram Base; most of his men killed; some prisoners taken; vague suggestions of some intervention from an unknown force, and thankfully no mention of your involvement. I was going out of my mind, and had a watch for you coming back to the U.K using the new ID's we'd set up for you. Yes, there you were, and here you are, thank God!"

"Yes, thank God indeed!" he said fervently, "or somebody… you'll never know!"

"So what happened? How did the whole thing turn out in the end?"

He went across and turned the electric kettle on.

She sat down on a settee as he came back. Then he told her the whole story from the time he had left the U.K. right up to the time when Wainwright put them on a helicopter to Kandahar. It had taken an hour, and he had ignored the whistle of the boiling kettle, despite his pounding head and terrible thirst.

He went across and clicked the water on again, then stood and waited until it boiled. He made two coffees and brought them back to where Rebecca sat, ashen-faced and silent - but not for long.

"Thank God for old Saas Mates Danny. Wainwright saved your bacon over there! Holy mackerel!"

"You got it in one Rebecca."

She glanced over the top of the cup.

"Was MI6 involved in this? Did they know about the plan to take yourself and the lads out? I can't believe it!"

"It was a CIA plan to terminate us for sure. That explosion wouldn't have left evidence or witnesses for that matter. That was their goal- a complete wipe out and the Mullah killed.

A good result as far as they're concerned. Was MI6 involved? Wainwright had met Jack Curtis the Afghanistan MI6 chap, on the Officer's drink circuits that they have over there. He thought he was a decent type - didn't think he might have been involved."

"What about Nigel Thornton?"

"He doesn't know him and couldn't offer an opinion, though he did suggest that while they might not have had direct involvement, they might have had an understanding and been under no illusion as to the final solution. He said it could be a quid pro quo between Thornton and the CIA, but would take a lot of proving."

She got up and started moving around, obviously agitated.

"I can't believe this Danny! I was involved too in setting you and the lads up with Thornton. I have to accept some responsibility here as well. If you three had been killed, I don't know what I'd have done!"

"Well, for starters, you wouldn't have known the full score, unless Wainwright contacted you and passed on his conversations with me. Makes me wonder how far they'd go to keep the lid on this. I advised him to watch his back in the interim."

"Hmm, they'd be tangling with one capable soldier in him. He's one bad ass if they go after him."

She stopped moving around and stared at him.

"What about me Danny? Does that mean they might decide to clean house entirely? Could I be in some danger myself?"

Danny blinked.

That hadn't occurred to him.

"Jesus Rebecca, I don't know where this is going! I can't imagine the DG of MI5 would be targeted. Your connection with us was limited to merely introducing us to Thornton. They may regard that as a clean cut out...I hope. Nonetheless, get those Security types who follow you around to double up and stay on hyper alert. Don't slip off on your own for shopping trips, as I know you do occasionally. Perhaps have the surveillance team follow you for a few days to see if there's anyone watching you."

She looked anxious. "I can't believe it's come to this Danny: that a friendly Intelligence Agency, the CIA, would make a decision to have you and the lads blown up, and may now be a real threat to me. It beggars belief, I have to say!"

She thought for a moment.

"OK, OK, lets stop right there. What do I say to Thornton when he calls me, as he will for sure? How do I handle that situation?"

"Just play dumb: You haven't heard from me. The ID we went out on hasn't been used to date. All you know is what you've heard on the television. He may think we're on the run for the Pakistan border for example. As far as he probably knows, our CIA arranged Exfill plan didn't happen, leaving us with no time to improvise."

Her breathing slowed down.

"Right, that might give me some time or he may not believe me - we'll see. Now what about the Jihadist operation? As I recall, you were supposed to go down to the south coast and meet with that American and collect weapons. We have to stop that, whatever it takes: armed Jihadists here in the U.K.? That makes me shudder! When was that supposed to happen?"

He shook his head.

"My head's still spinning Rebecca. As I recall, originally, I should be down there at a specific pub or hotel in approximately two weeks, which is four days from now. He said he would contact me around that date with specific timings. I'm keeping my cell phone with me in case Frank contacts me prior to that. For now I'll stay away from Thames House in case Thornton or even the local CIA are on the lookout for me. That's all I can do for now, except to get some more sleep. How does that sound?"

She stood up and gave him a hug.

"Oh Danny, I feel so much better knowing that you're back here in the country and safe."

Right then the other bedroom door opened and the two men straggled in. "You two talking woke us up, for Pete's sake" Scotty teased "and the Director General of MI5 no less! We're honored indeed!"

Any chance of Danny getting more sleep was shattered.

Rebecca grinned and settled back in. She had them go over the whole operation again in complete detail.

Danny went off and had a shower. He would need to wake up and stay alert himself. He was out of Afghanistan but not out of trouble.

Not by a long shot.

CHAPTER 82

Nigel Thornton loved his stroll on Sunday evenings, down through the woods and along the fifty-yard stretch of his property, which ran parallel to the river Thames. The moon shone brightly, filtering through the trees around him. The sound of the swift running tidewater helped wash away any small gremlins of stress, regarding the upcoming week.

The role of being the Director of the U.K.'s Secret Intelligence Service MI6, had it's challenges, none more than right at the present moment, which was causing him some disquiet:

a bungled operation that could explode back in his face.

He'd underestimated Quigley by a long shot.

His brief conversation with Rebecca Fullerton Smythe at MI5 confirmed his suspicions that she was privy to information she was not disclosing to him. Unusual to say the least, and disturbing. Nothing he couldn't take care of though.

He suddenly stopped in his tracks as a shadowy figure stepped out from behind a large chestnut tree. As the figure took some further steps, rays from the moon caught its face.

He gasped.

"Quigley, what the hell are you doing here? This is private property and I've two Security Guards back there at the house!"

Danny stepped closer until he was about four feet away, then halted and chuckled.

446

"Knowing what you know about me Thornton, they're in no position to help you."

"I don't frighten easily Quigley. Tell me what you want and then get the hell out of here. In any event you're finished here in the U.K. Even Fullerton Smythe won't touch you with a barge pole when I'm finished with you."

Danny laughed again. "You'll have to do better than your pathetic attempt over in Afghanistan. I'll bet you're not looking too good with your CIA friend Burnside over there. The CIA don't like screwed up operations. Right now you must be looking like an amateur. You certainly read this one wrong didn't you NIGEL?"

"What the hell are you talking about Quigley?"

"If you're out here strolling along the Thames to calm your mind about things, forget it. This is far too big for you to contain. There are too many people involved here."

Thornton was about to say something but changed his mind and jumped back two paces, reaching behind him and pulling a handgun from his belt.

"Not smiling now are you Quigley? You've just presented me with one big part of the puzzle - accosting the director of MI6 in a threatening and violent manner outside his home.

No one will blame me for defending myself. With you dead, Burnside or myself will soon take care of your two SAS friends, and that useless cow Fullerton-Smythe will be the only loose end to take care of. As a matter of fact, we shadowed her when she was horse riding yesterday. Our chap could have reached over and touched the rump of her animal. He saw an ideal spot where she could have a fatal accident shortly: a place called Maggie's Curve, as I recall"

Danny's face looked relaxed.

"Oh yeah, we spotted your people following her around these last two days. Pretty sloppy if you ask me, Thornton. You can't even train your people properly in surveillance procedures."

Thornton lifted the weapon, a look of anticipation crossing his features.

"I'm going to really enjoy this one Quigley, and seeing the look on your face when I pump some bullets into you."

Danny yawned.

"Hmm, 'fraid not NIGEL, you see there's blanks in your pistol."

Thornton's eyes dropped down momentarily to glance at his gun, then took another step back.

"Oh no you don't! I know you sneaky Saas people... distract me and then disarm me. Not this time."

He held up the weapon and fired two shots. Blanks... they didn't even make a sound. He looked down in disbelief.

Danny stepped up in front of him.

"Forgot to mention it Nigel. I broke into your house last night and switched the bullets. Sorry about that, but not about this."

He spun Thornton round until he was directly behind him, locked his right forearm around his throat and his left one behind his neck in a choke hold, then dropped straight down, hearing it snap.

He moved quickly, removing the weapon from his hand and stuck it in his coverall pocket. He physically lifted the man onto his shoulders and walked the dozen paces to the edge of the swirling water of the river Thames, now in full tide.

He eased him carefully into the water and watched the body swirl away, then he pulled the weapon out and removed the rest of the blanks, replacing them with live rounds before hurling it as far out as he could into the river, hearing it splash. Unlikely it would ever be found, but if so, it might add to the puzzle of Thornton's disappearance.

Turning and searching for the two blank rounds, he managed to spot both and pocketed them. Then he carefully made his way back through the woods to the place he'd selected earlier to conceal his vehicle. Once there he took a moment to remove his gloves, coveralls, footwear, and rubber gloves, stuffing them in a brown paper bag. He removed the blank shells from the coveralls first. Underneath he was wearing a black tracksuit, and he now complimented this with a fresh pair of runners.

Then he silently left the area.

Five miles from there he stopped on the edge of a small village and dumped the brown bag in a large garbage disposal bin. Making sure there was still no one around, he switched plates on the vehicle, in case someone in that rather upmarket area had spotted him. He drove further and dropped the old plates and blank shells into another dumpster before heading home.

CHAPTER 83

Danny had planned to be up early in order to drop Jimmy off at a railway station for the trip west to his Regiment at Hereford, and Scotty at a subway connection for a journey north, back to Scotland. They understood they were his witnesses for the previous evening, in case such a situation would ever arise, but he doubted that it would.

As he was turning back into traffic after his last drop off, his phone rang. It was Rebecca. She wanted him in straight away at Thames House.

He managed to slip into the underground parking lot, having been waved through by Security.

There was no warmth in her greeting. She didn't waste time.

"I was wakened at 1 o'clock this morning, Danny, with disturbing news. Nigel Thornton has disappeared from outside his home, sometime yesterday evening. It's more than merely a missing persons situation with someone from the Secret Intelligence Service disappearing. An alert went out to myself, which is standard procedure for this type of situation. As you can imagine with the increasing level of terrorist activity, Paris Belgium and others, it could signal the start of a new campaign, striking the heads of Security and Police."

Danny tried to look shocked.

"Oh man, Thornton missing! Where did this happen? I mean, you said outside his home. Had he just come home from being out somewhere?"

"Apparently he took a stroll out into the garden or something like that. I didn't quite take it all in. As you can imagine I was woken from a deep sleep by a call from Scotland Yard. I offered to come in, but they were informing me also that they were sending a squad car around to provide additional security for my home."

"What time did he actually disappear? Who became aware of it?"

"He has two Security people at the house. They knew of his movements and were aware of his nightly stroll outside in the evenings. Whether they were more engrossed than usual in a football game or not, they apparently didn't notice that he hadn't come back in after his normal interval outside. They went looking for him. There's the Thames going past below his property as well, so they scoured along it's edge and, finding no trace, came in and woke his wife who had apparently gone to bed earlier. Thornton works late in his home office most evenings according to the Security Detail. Then they called the Police and that led to further searches and area road blocks. Learning of Thornton's stature, Scotland Yard and the Special Branch were alerted. A command post was set up at the house which is on-going as we speak."

"Hmm…Sooo… is there some reason you brought me in this morning? I can't imagine how I can help out on this one, with Scotland Yard and Special Branch involvement. Unless of course you want some additional close-up protection. I can't imagine that, with my present assignment, which is at a pivotal stage."

She stared directly at him.

"Where were you last night Danny?"

His jaw dropped. "Good grief, you got to be kidding Rebecca!"

"I asked you a question. Where were you last night, or yesterday evening to be more specific?" she repeated.

451

He shook his head. "I can't believe you're asking me that! I was at home, all evening, as a matter of fact, seeing as how you seem to think it's important."

"Do you have any witnesses that can verify that?"

"Well yes, as it happens, I do. Scotty and Jimmy were there with me all evening."

She heaved a sigh of relief. "Thank God for that! Not that I think it will come to it but, are they still at your place?"

"No, I dropped them at the subway and train station. We agreed last night that they could rejoin their lives, with the trip to Afghanistan finished. That was the reason they were here in the first place, as you can recall. They were both chomping at the bit to get going."

She pursed her lips. "Very convenient if I may say so Danny."

He spread his hands wide in frustration.

"Look, they're both easy enough to contact if you need them to verify where I was last night. Scotty's gone back to Scotland to see his family and pack up for his Security job in Nigeria. Jimmy's heading back to the Regiment on the train as we speak."

She relaxed somewhat, then called for her secretary to bring in some tea and scones.

She had him go over some of the past few days' events in Afghanistan again, and asked a number of questions.

They talked through his pre-arranged trip to the south coast to meet up with Frank the American, where they would presumably collect a cache of weapons. Danny would need a large team in position if and when this occurred.

Then he got up to leave and walked to the door.

He turned back to her. "Is that all?"

She nodded. "Yes, that's us finished."

"Good. Oh, by the way, Thornton referred to you as an old cow and a loose end that he planned to take care of. As a matter of fact he said he had a rider shadowing you on your horse on Saturday - could have reached over apparently, and touched the rump of your horse at one time. Even picked a place where he said he could make sure you could have an

452

accident - a fatal one at that - Maggie's Curve as I recall. Not a nice chap Nigel, when you think about it."

He turned and left.

She sat there in stunned disbelief, but not for long. Rebecca's mind always worked at high speed, like a steel trap.

She picked up the phone and dialed a number from memory.

A woman answered.

"That sounds like Tina, this is Rebecca Fullerton-Smythe here. I have a question for you, if you have a moment."

"Oh, good morning Rebecca. Sure, it's quiet right now, go ahead."

"After I booked in on Saturday morning, did someone else register for a ride?"

"Yes, a nice young man… might just be a regular as it happens."

"Fine, now what can you tell me about him: his approximate age, his accent, appearance and manner for example? Oh, and the name he registered with and how he paid… by cash or credit card for example?"

"Wow, you're getting me real curious now Rebecca…dare I say concerned even. Let's see, I'm checking the register as we speak. He wrote his name down as Jim Bowman, paid by cash, was approximately thirtyish, looked like one of those gym jockeys, fit I mean…."

"Wait a sec, I believe I actually saw him there. Was he the one who came in after me and was over in your small shop looking at riding gear and stuff?"

"Yes, that's the one. That's why I mentioned he might become a regular. He had to borrow riding gear from me for the ride on Saturday, but said he'd probably buy his own for the following week."

"OK, did he ask about me specifically?"

"Let me see how that went. He mentioned the lady who had booked in before him and if you rode regularly. When I said Yes, most Saturdays, he asked if you were booked in for next week and I told him that you were. He then booked in as well. Ma'am, was I wrong there?"

"No, not at all Tina. You were just doing your job. What happened then?"

"Well, he asked what ride you were going on and I said the usual one, over five miles with rough terrain and some challenging jumps."

"He then asked if it would be OK to trail along behind someone as experienced as you and get a feel for the course, or even a section of it. Apparently he's ridden before. I didn't say anything to you as you were getting your mount ready in the stable. I didn't see anything wrong or sinister about his request or manner, for that matter."

"No, I'm not suggesting anything you did was out of order Tina, just chasing up something that's come up in here. Last question: what was his accent?"

"No problem there. As the Australians would say he was 'dinky-die American'. No doubt about that."

Rebecca sat back in her seat thinking.

"Are you still there Rebecca?"

"Oh, sorry, just thinking. Tina, if I send out someone with some pictures, will you have a look at them and pick out, this Mr. Bowman if you can. It'll be sometime this morning. Will you do that for me?"

"Rebecca certainly I will, but you're getting me all worried about this now."

"Not to worry at this stage. I'm just being cautious. One thing more, don't tell anyone about our conversation, and especially if this American contacts you for any reason - to confirm the ride Saturday for example. Mum's the word, OK?"

Rebecca hung up, held on to the phone and dialed direct to Jerry Sackville, the counter terrorism, investigations and research Director, and asked him to come up.

He was through the door within five minutes and sat down, looking questioningly at her.

"Right Jerry, I'm sorry to interrupt whatever you're on right now, but I have a rather sensitive task for you. I can't tell you all about it at the moment, in fact I may never do so. However here's what I need right now."

She filled him in on the situation where someone was shadowing her, without going into the periphery details of the disappearance of the MI6 Chief. Most intelligence heads were well accustomed to 'needs to know' briefings, to protect them in potential enquiries or media leaks at a later date.

He listened intently, making notes as she spoke.

"Right Ma'am. I think I get it. My first question is, of course, should your personal Security team be informed? I gather they don't follow you to your riding trips on the weekend."

She sighed. "Shoot Jerry, if I let them invade my whole life, I'd never have a moment's peace. Think of the personnel that would be needed as well: a woman to accompany me to the washroom, and places like that. I get that during the work week. No thanks! Now here's the initial task I want you to attend to personally. It may seem trivial initially, but I want to exclude any more people at this stage. Here's the brief: I assume you have personal details of most of the CIA people posted here to the Embassy in London?"

"Standard procedure Ma'am. We do make every effort with all countries, as you know, to collect these details. Mind you, we might not know the ID of a new arrival for some time until they surface somewhere. In theory they're supposed to tell us, but with the CIA, you never know; someone might fly in for a special timed assignment that we wouldn't know about. However the information gives us a heads up, when our politicians are circulating at the rounds of Embassy parties and so on. Useful to know who one's talking to, sometimes even to plant misinformation when required."

"Exactly Jerry. I'd like you to put together a list, and especially photos of the CIA Intelligence group here in the city, and take it out to Tina at my riding club. She's expecting you, and see if you can get her to identify the person who was there last Saturday. Obviously, what I'm looking for is to find out his real name. I doubt very much that it's Bowman. Don't reveal his name to Tina, or share anything else, but I'd like you to call me from your vehicle outside with your encrypted cell phone. That's it for now Jerry, and I'll be here waiting for your call. Good luck."

He left the office with alacrity.

Jerry knew when something was on the boil.

CHAPTER 84

Rebecca had great difficulty in concentrating on anything for the next couple of hours. She knew Jerry would have to fight his way out to the riding club in the slow moving London traffic. She was on tenterhooks for the whole time but still jumped when he called back later in the morning.

He didn't waste time.

"You were right Ma'am, Bowman wasn't his name."

"So Tina recognized him straight off then?"

"Spot on, no hesitation. Oh, his name is Colt Devlin and he was, as you suspected, on the CIA list - came over ten months ago to the Embassy. We've no further information on what he does in there. By the way, Tina offered some additional information. Her brother is in the Forces, and she thought this Devlin had a similar Military cut about him... the way he moved and spoke... sort of clipped, but she was so taken with his accent, it hadn't occurred to her when you were on the phone. That's about it. Anything else on this you want me to follow up on?"

"No, not at the moment, though I may have to drag you in later, on where to go from here."

"A word of caution then. Watch your back… we could get some of our people to tighten up even further until you resolve this. We could even get some surveillance set up on this Devlin in the meantime. What d'you think Ma'am?"

"The extra cover makes sense, as I'm apparently a person of interest to the Americans at the moment. I wouldn't slap any cover on Devlin for the moment, as it might stall him if he spots it. I'd sooner get this resolved a.s.a.p. Jerry, as you can well understand."

She hung up, having thanked him for the speed of his follow up.

What to do?

Danny Quigley would no doubt have his own personal solution to the problem. She might still use his rare but deadly skills, which he had obviously used to take down Thornton.

However, Danny had gone out of his way to avoid killing Americans over in Afghanistan on the advice of his old Commanding Officer Wainwright.

Rebecca agreed with him. The Americans had long memories, a bit like the Israeli Mossad in that regard.

Killing people in the wild west of Afghanistan, as Danny had done at the Zoo, was a lot simpler than terminating someone here in the U.K. Special Branch and Scotland Yard had the sharpest investigators in the world, and had the tenacity to continue a case with even the most slender of clues. Time was of the essence: a case got cold after three days and was stored away in the cold case file. She hoped Danny had not inadvertently left any clues that might come back and bite him in the ass. For that reason, she was not sharing his information about the MI6 Director's disappearance with any other soul.

A plan was beginning to form in her mind.

It could work. She hoped it would, otherwise she might have to go on the offensive and that would mean bringing Danny Quigley back into the picture in a serious way.

She shuddered.

When Wainwright had been his Commanding Officer in the Regiment, he had referred to Danny as a walking killing machine, and since leaving he'd got even better at his craft.

She wondered if the word 'better' was the appropriate word.

The following Saturday.

It was a beautiful morning as Rebecca, arriving early, checked in with Tina who, looking a bit strained, still made no mention of the conversation they had earlier in the week.

She went out and spent the next twenty minutes getting her mount ready, and having a few words with the stable manager.

Then she saw the American, who she now knew was Colt Devlin, dressed for a ride. He walked out and proceeded to the stable where another young lad brought a horse out and slapped a saddle on it. There didn't appear to be any other riders preparing for the exercise, and Rebecca gave no indication of being interested in him. She casually walked her horse out to the front and climbed up on the mount.

She unobtrusively activated the small mike attached to her collar.

"Subject's here" she spoke quietly, leaning forward as if adjusting the reins.

A single squelch of acknowledgement came back.

The American had come out behind her, already mounted.

'Here we go' she thought.

She pulled her horse round and trotted back, stopping alongside him and smiled.

"Oh hello, I saw you here last week. Colt Devlin isn't it? Just a note of caution: watch it when you get to Maggie's Curve... a bad place for accidents."

She couldn't tell if his jaw dropped with the headgear strapped on, but she saw his shock as his whole body went rigid.

She smiled again.

"Enjoy the ride." She rode off swiftly.

He didn't follow as his horse spun round a few times, anxious to get running. Five hundred yards out she glanced back, and saw that the horse and rider were still there... this time the horse was standing still. She activated the collar mike again. "Not following me."

One squelch returned.

She looked back once more prior to entering some woods where the real trail began. Still no sign.

She wasn't out of the woods yet.

Ahead, Danny Quigley had concealed himself in a position earlier, across from Maggie's Curve. He was armed with a tranquilizer gun, which he had come to appreciate as a result of his experience with Rahim in Afghanistan.

He had planned to take down the American if he still attempted to carry out some sort of attack, even after Rebecca's attempt to sabotage him psychologically back at the stables.

They speculated as to whether Devlin would call off whatever plan he had in mind, especially once Rebecca had made him aware that his identity was discovered, and possibly his plan. Under pressure, would he still make a decision to carry on, assuming he had no other options?

They had also considered a further possibility: that the American might have organized a colleague to carry out the task, (or bring down Rebecca's mount), while he coasted along behind to clean up the site or even to finish her off.

Danny had been carefully crawling through the areas that might be used, but found nothing indicating a possible attack position.

He was satisfied there was no one there.

He gave two squelches and received two back.

In seven minutes Rebecca rode into view, riding alone.

Danny stayed alert and tensed until she pulled across into the brush where she knew he would be positioned.

She climbed down, and without thinking they embraced.

"My God Danny, I think I pulled it off" she exclaimed breathlessly.

"I believe you did Rebecca…nice job! I'd have loved to have seen his face, the bastard!"

He walked carefully back to the trail and looked both ways, listening carefully, then came back.

"Yeah, looks like it… no sign of Devlin or any other bad guys out here. How d'you read this now?"

"As we discussed when we were planning it, what would you do if you had an operation planned and suddenly realized you were rumbled, and that any number of people could be involved at that stage. Killing me then would just muddy up the situation considerably."

"I'd walk away for sure. No other option for them as I see it. On going, I wouldn't see any further attempt on your life. At this stage you couldn't be removed from the Board without all sorts of shit hitting the fan."

"Thank Goodness for that! I'm glad we avoided killing an American on English soil. There were bound to be links back to me with Tina involved. We couldn't stand that scrutiny."

"Agreed, but your mention of Maggie's Curve, would surely clue them in that you'd had some contact with Thornton and his disappearance. I'm presuming only he and Devlin were involved in this plot to 'take care of that loose end', as he referred to you."

She grimaced. "We'll have to hold our breath on this one Danny and hope they get the message. The CIA have their own black ops. when needed, but they need to learn that they shouldn't mess with us either, certainly not here in the U.K. They know that as MI5 Director General, I have a Sass Saber Team standing by 24/7, and as you well know those chaps don't take any prisoners. The CIA knows you guys from Iraq and Afghanistan, and that you can be a pretty nasty piece of work when required. In fact, I hear that at the end of the original U.K. mission in Stan, NATO Officers were calling specifically for the Saas to carry out missions."

Danny shrugged. "We were run ragged in the end: out night after night in those choppers, contact with the Taliban on every mission - our asses were dragging. The best thing they did was to bail all of us out of Helmand Province and bring us home."

"Speaking of being run ragged Danny, weren't you supposed to head for the south coast to meet up with that other American Jihadist, Frank?"

"That was the plan, and we need to organize some resources for down there to interdict the weapons and ammo that Frank hinted were coming there. As you know, he's supposed to call me first, before I head out "

"Right… so lets go back to Thames House and get that set up, then you can head off. See you there."

She climbed back on her mount and trotted off.

Danny cut back four hundred yards where he had run a vehicle in earlier. Then he headed back into central London.

CHAPTER 85

When he got back to his apartment he found the answering machine blinking. There were two messages. The first one was a surprise: a three-word message from Naomi Richards, in California "I'm missing you."

He wondered about the new reality in her life, with her kidnapped husband rescued, and how the knowledge of his 'coming out', was affecting her. He knew that she was a tough-minded, ex-Military Policewoman, and was convinced that she would successfully go forward with some new career move - perhaps back into Police work in some capacity. Her contacts with Mike Collins and Cole Ranger at the Police Department might open some doors for her.

It was too late to call her, so he made a mental note to do it the following morning. He had also made a mental note to spend some quality time with his daughter Allison before getting involved with the MI5 operation.

It wasn't to be.

The second call was from the American Frank Skinner, who was in charge of the newly arrived Jihadists coming back into the U.K.

The message was short: "call me" and gave a number.

Somehow, despite the knowledge that he should expect the call, he felt surprised. So much had passed since Frank and his crew pulled out of London in a panic: his trip to California and

Afghanistan; his settling the score with Thornton, that he had shoved the Jihadist problem to the back of his mind.

Now everything rushed into his head.

The American was planning a 9/11 disaster for Britain, and Danny was the only one who had a link inside the group.

Reluctantly, he picked up the phone and dialed. At the same time he made an effort to lift his energy and interest level.

"Frank, Jack here… got your message…what's up?"

The American's voice sounded tense.

"Right Jack, things are moving here. We're heading south shortly and I recalled that we'd taken the vehicle you were given when we loaded up and left the city, so we want to meet you at the subway station just a hundred yards or so from that Sally Ann you love to hang out in."

"Sure, I can manage that no problem. What's the plan then?"

"Simple Jack. We take you down with us to the south coast and that solves the problem of your lack of a vehicle. On the way we can discuss our next operation with you that I referred to briefly - the 9/11 op. which is coming together nicely. You're going to love it AND some more funds coming your way as well, which I know is your big motivation."

"Well, I like the sound of that for sure. I'll grab some gear and get over there. What time will I meet you Frank?"

"Immediately if not sooner Jack. Myself, Zain and Mohammed are around the corner from the subway, eating some take-out, but hanging round here for very long isn't a good idea with the state of alert in the city after that Sally Ann shooting."

"Oh man that's fast, I had a few things planned for this evening Frank."

"Un-plan them and get your ass around here. What plans can a recent street person have that are so important? It's not as if you have a large group of people looking for your company?

Remember we gave you a large chunk of money and you haven't exactly earned it during the past number of days."

464

Danny thought quickly.

Frank was right and, being the only insider in the Jihadist group, Rebecca was relying on him to find out what they were planning.

"Yeah, I get it…OK, I'll fire some stuff in a kit bag and head out. You're probably talking about thirty minutes for me to get there. See you then."

The American said nothing more. The phone went dead.

Danny leapt into action.

His first and only call was to Rebecca, and he was lucky to get her at home. He explained the present situation to her.

"Fine, you have to run with it. I doubt we can get a team together and over to that location in time to catch your meeting with them. We don't even know if it's the same car they're driving, which we previously bugged. You still have that belt we used to monitor you before it all came apart, so hopefully we can get something set up from that. Otherwise we watch for you down at that pub where we've already prepared some resources to stop them getting weapons. Anything else Danny?"

"Yes, please give Allison a call and explain that I'm still on the job and can't get to see her."

"Will do Danny and good luck."

He hung up and dashed around the apartment shoving some gear in a bag that would suffice for what he expected to be no more than two to three days. Then he dashed down the stairs and out the front door.

It was dark and he couldn't see any people around as he headed out the gate, planning to turn right on the street.

As he turned he saw a van parked out in front.

The passenger door opened.

"Hey Jack, we thought we'd pick you up…save you time."

It was the American.

Danny shook his head, suddenly confused, and drifted a few steps towards the vehicle.

Things were shooting through his head; 'How did they know where he lived? They believed him to be a homeless person. What was going on?'

465

Frank was grinning at him.

Something was wrong, terribly wrong!

He started to turn away and got hit with a massive Taser burst from Zain, who had slipped up behind him.

He didn't know what happened after that.

CHAPTER 86

Danny felt he was in a confused dream with fleeting pictures bombarding his senses: awareness of being on the floor of a van which was moving at a high speed; the vehicle stopping and his clothes roughly torn off his body; a knife being used to cut through his trouser legs and shoe laces; the back door opening once and a hand reaching in for his shoes and clothing.

Leaving him lying there in his underwear, plastic cuffs holding his wrists behind him.

Someone punched him a number of times… more than one person…the sounds of cursing.

He blacked out again.

Gradually he started to come round and felt the movement of the vehicle beneath him. He held himself still and gradually opened his eyes in a narrow slit.

There was only one person in the back with him: Zain Waheed, the slim, teacher-like Jihadist.

He appeared to be dozing with his head back against the metal side of the van. He could hear voices from the front of the vehicle, Frank and Mohammed?

He wasn't certain, but he was sure about one thing: he hadn't a hope in hell of attempting an escape with his hands cuffed behind, and he realized that his legs were also tied with some restraining item. If his hands had been cuffed in front he might have tried attacking Zain and hurling himself against and out through the back door of the van.

They weren't taking any chances.

Despite his cramped position, he steeled himself to stay still.

Gradually he became aware of having sustained blows to his face and probably kicks to his rib cage.

He hoped no ribs were cracked, but he doubted it, as the pain wasn't sharp enough... probably not enough room to do a proper job on him in the back of the van.

He felt sure they would get around to that when they arrived at their destination.

His mind started working. Where had he slipped up? How long had they known? Why hadn't they taken him out sooner?

Where were they actually headed now?

He doubted it was to the south coast.

If they had known who he worked for, had Frank used him to send MI5 on a wild goose chase, while they collected assault weapons from somewhere else?

His clothes and shoes had been handed out the back door of the van and probably discarded. Had they suspected there might have been tracking equipment hidden somewhere and got rid of them?

Certainly his bugged belt could no longer be relied on.

What options did Rebecca and the team have now?

Would she presume that the pick-up had gone ahead and hoped that Danny could re-establish contact somehow?

Frank had been clever in planting the seed again about the proposed meeting place on the south coast.

He must have known that the information would be passed on.

He'd certainly underestimated the American. All the time Danny thought that he was leading Frank by the nose.

Just how clever was he?

Was he actually capable of wreaking the havoc of 9/11 equivalent on U.K. soil?

He wondered why Frank had taken him alive, now that he had served his purpose of misleading the Security Forces.

He'd find out soon enough.

Rebecca had gone back into Thames House later in the evening to meet up with the surveillance team, Dave Jones the retired Scotland Detective and Clive Spooner.

There was little joy there.

The team felt they had made it to the meeting point in time to observe the proposed pick up.

It never happened.

They waited half an hour and contacted Rebecca.

She urged them to get around to Danny's apartment and try to find out if he was still there… perhaps even in the company of the American.

They never made it inside.

Coming up to the gate they came across a man looking puzzled and holding a kit in his hands.

He looked up at them. "Did you come back for this? I just discovered it lying here on the sidewalk a moment ago when I came out"

The surveillance team looked at each other, alarm crossing their faces.

Jones reached in and took out his Security identity card.

The man glanced at it.

"Oh, I guess I better give this to you then" as he passed the kit back over to him.

Now at Thames House, Jones unpacked it on the table.

Rebecca slumped down on to her chair.

"Oh shoot, that's Danny's gear, I recognize some of those shirts. This means he's in serious trouble. We wondered whether the American and his group were on to him. Probably fed him information on the south coast meeting place again to have us focusing our resources there, but where does this leave us, and more to the point, Danny? He's in deep trouble, isn't he?"

Clive Spooner nodded.

"We left him out there too long, even though we started wondering about the Jihadists. He's taken out three of them already and they must have started looking more closely at him."

"But what option are we left with now?" she asked.

Jones frowned and shook his head.

"Ma'am we don't have any, I'm sorry to say. Danny's been lifted, and God knows where they've taken him. Certainly, I wouldn't send resources to the south coast. We don't even know what vehicle they're in. Are they still in the city or have they gone to some other location to take delivery of the weapons? All you can hope for is that Danny somehow manages to contact us."

Clive Spooner was fiddling aimlessly with the kit bag items.

Rebecca looked off into the distance, shaking her head.

"He kept pushing the envelope out and seemed to come out smelling of roses. His luck just finally ran out. He went over to Afghanistan and pulled off the impossible. I can't tell you about it but you would need to be super human to survive what he and his two Mates, Scotty and Jimmy pulled off. I've had a bad feeling since he came back. He's been living on the edge far too long."

She paused, taking some deep breaths.

"But you know what? You can never write off Danny Quigley. It's not over until it's over. Now let's see what we can start putting in place and be ready if he does contact us."

They both looked at her.

There was little hope on her face.

CHAPTER 87

He made a rough guess and reckoned they had been on the road for three hours or more.

Zain had been fully awake for most of that, and gave him a few rather un-enthusiastic kicks, more to remind him that he was a prisoner and there was worse to come.

The van finally slowed down and drove on to what were obviously rougher roads with more bends. Finally it slowed way down to a crawl and stopped. He heard shouts from the front and the sound of a barrier or gate being dragged to one side. The van moved off again and stopped. The back door was pulled open. He was unceremoniously shoved and pulled from the back of the van and hustled in through a doorway. In that brief moment, as his gaze flicked sideways, he could see that the house stood on it's own, out in the countryside.

He filed it away.

Inside he was thrust into a kitchen chair.

Mohammed looked in some cupboards and came back with some thick twine and started to tie his hands.

Danny looked up into his face. "Hey, what about a chance to use the washroom?" he asked.

Zain's reaction was to backhand him viciously across his face.

"What chance did you give to Syed and Abdul when you gunned them down, and probably Ali as well for all we know?"

Skinner came into view then.

"Whoa there a moment guys. I'm with you on this one hundred percent. He's gonna get his later for sure when our other friend gets here. In Iraq we used to tie those bastards up and let them crap in their pants, to soften them up for interrogation. Now, if some of you are going to be staying here for a couple of days, leaving him to do his thing, I can tell you that the smell in here will be like a blocked up sewer."

Mohammed looked up.

"So what are you suggesting Frank? He's far too dangerous to let loose."

The American chuckled.

"He won't be with a shotgun duck- taped to his skull around the edge of the toilet door. One false move and you have my permission to pull the trigger. Oh, and when you come back, do the cuffs on the front, so we don't have to release them from his back each time, and he can have a leak on his own."

Mohammed scowled but went ahead and followed the instructions. For Danny, it was relief to get to a toilet after lying in the back of the van. A quick check inside showed a small glazed window, where various coats of paint had sealed it permanently closed.

Zain kept nudging the barrels of the shotgun against his forehead, determined to keep the pressure on and muttering abuses as he did so.

Back inside again he was tied to the chair and this time, his hands were cuffed in front.

Frank had unloaded some sacks from the car and proceeded to pull the contents out: food, drink and a number of other items.

Danny couldn't make out if there were any weapons there as well.

The other two Jihadists came across and opened some of the water bottles. The three sat down and started drinking and eating some sandwiches.

Frank looked across at him.

"We're not wasting any of this stuff on you... you won't need it where you're going."

The two Jihadists chuckled, as if privy to some unspoken joke.

Danny licked his lips. Right then he would have loved a long drink of fresh water, but he realized he had worse problems to deal with. He wasn't meant to come out of this alive. It didn't sound like an interrogation was on the cards either... they already knew all they needed to from Danielle's kidnapping and murder.

He needed to get the American talking... even goading him to get him to reveal some details of how they had got onto him and their plans to inflict some sort of assault in the U.K. shortly.

Goading Frank though might result in a further beating from the group. They obviously wanted to keep him alive sooo...

The American must have had his own agenda as he strolled across to where he was trussed up.

"I can see you have lots of questions Jack, or is it Danny? I would too in your position. I don't mind bringing you into the picture, cause you won't get an opportunity to run your mouth off to anyone, after your friend gets here."

A snigger from the two over at the kitchen table.

Danny made a futile effort to shrug, but settled for raising his eyebrows.

"What is that old saying in those movies 'You got me', and so yes, I'm dying to know how you rumbled me."

"Wrong choice of words my friend, however I believe we can take care of that small detail. Rumbled you say? Oh, yes we rumbled you all right. Let me share some of the details with you."

He grabbed a chair and pulled it across directly in front of Danny, straddling the seat and leaning forward on the back of it.

"For starters, we'd gathered quite a lot of information from that sweet little lady, what was her name? Oh yes, Danielle. Sweet is right, we all enjoyed her Danny boy. Surprised you didn't get into her pants on that trip across to Amsterdam."

473

"So you had her too?" Danny hissed, forgetting for the moment that he was trying to get under the American's skin.

Frank shrugged. "Hey, what the hell! The boys had warmed her up for me... she was loving it."

Danny strived to tear his hands loose, leaning forward.

"Yeah, sure... knowing she was about to be killed and enjoying your filthy hands. You bastard, if it's the last thing I ever do, I'm going to take you down."

"Hmmm... I doubt it somehow. Now dear sweet Danielle told us about a Danny Quigley on her team. She had a very high opinion of you for some reason. I can't imagine why, 'cos here you are trussed up like a chicken, waiting for it's head to be chopped off."

There was a burst of laughter from the two sitting at the table.

Frank grinned, glancing across at them.

"Sounds like they know something Danny boy. I wonder what it can be?"

Danny had worked to bring himself back into control. His plan, if one could call it that, wasn't achieving anything. He tried again.

"OK, so under torture, she revealed some information, even about my involvement. Why did you bring me inside the group then?"

Frank scowled. "OK we screwed up. You'd rescued Zain from those skinheads and we even checked with the ER unit they ended up in. You did hurt them real bad, breaking bones and stuff. That couldn't be an MI5 set up. Then you were disguised as a scruffy street person, and we bought it. Hats off to you for that."

"So when did you start to take a harder look at me?" Danny asked, genuinely interested, despite his situation.

"When Ali disappeared some flags went up, but the press coverage confused us: he was running back to Syria? We kinda half bought it."

"I still don't get it. You let me run loose for quite a while... meeting more of your Jihadists coming in at the Euro

Tunnel, involving me with renting that apartment, so when did the penny drop?"

"Good question. We let you run because you hinted you might have a contact for weapons, and I had no option but to chase it up. Belfast is where you dropped yourself in it... or rather your Mate, as you call him."

"Jimmy? But he... how?...." Danny started.

Frank smiled smugly. "Daddio....remember?... he called you Daddio...I caught it right away, especially after sweet Danielle mentioned a Danny Quigley."

"Shit...I thought we'd recovered the ball on that, but why did you wait so long after that to take me down."

The American wagged his finger. "Aha... I'll cover that, but first what was all the shooting about in Belfast outside the bar? I couldn't see any purpose in that. Afterwards, I realized I wasn't in any danger that evening, but it's baffled me ever since."

Danny shook his head.

"To this day, I've no idea. That's Belfast for you... turf wars or someone recognizing Jimmy or myself from our days there with the Brit. Forces."

"Somehow I believe you. I enjoyed the bar scene though. What we Americans look for... how d'you say it, the didilei music? Now to your question: why didn't we finish you after that? We tried to... I set it up that Syed would kill you on the mat that day in the gym. Instead you finished him off.

Then I arranged for him and Abdul to take you out at the Salvation Army hostel, only they screwed up. We had to flee the city expecting the Police to be banging on our doors, but even then I could have shot you, when you brought me the news. I nearly did but I worried about the sound of shots attracting attention in the building."

"But you let me completely off the hook?"

"Not quite. I used you to create a possible arms delivery scenario down on the south coast that I knew MI5 couldn't resist, and gave the impression you were still on the inside with us. D'you know what we were actually doing in the past couple of weeks, knowing that MI5 were waiting for the big arms pick up and their Agent was still being accepted as Kosher?"

Danny shook his head, fascinated by what he was hearing, but staying silent.

Frank carried on. "I was assembling the manpower and working on the plans for delivering that 9/11 blow that will bring the U.K. to it's knees, shattering it's illusion of being safe in these British Isles. We're set for three days time, and all we need is one last piece of the puzzle. Can you guess what it is?"

"It's got to be the weapons. You don't have them as yet. That's why we're out here in the countryside, waiting for delivery, isn't it?"

"Clever boy Danny, but not clever enough. You're the one tied up right now... how about that?"

"So what's the big plan then Frank? Set a bomb off in Burger King or in some bus full of kids?"

The American put his finger across his lips.

"Mum's the word on that one. You'll find out soon enough... hmm, or will you? No I don't believe you'll be still around...pity, it's an amazing plan."

Danny decided he would attempt to break through that superior attitude and see if he could get under his skin.

He shook his head.

"You know something Frankie boy. You're talking about being the leader of some amazing massive blow to the U.K. Come on, call yourself a leader? You let me inside your little group after just two days here in the U.K. and take out three of your men! Oh, and did you know that we identified you the day after you got off the plane from a drone shot in Iraq? MI5 have had you on a short lease ever since then so, you'll never leave this country. You'll end your days in some bleak prison out on Dartmoor and never spend a cent of all that money you've stolen from those Iraqi villagers you butchered."

Frank thrust his body forward, his weight almost breaking the chair back. "They have no proof whatsoever, you prick... none!" he shouted.

The two men across at the table stopped talking.

476

Danny smiled. "Proof? Oh, I know they do MY FRIEND. A certain statement you came out with when you were over in Belfast - something about blowing up the U.K. The Prosecutor's given an opinion that that would be sufficient to put you away for a long time Frankie!"

Skinner lunged forward and lashed Danny across his face, sending the chair crashing on the ground.

Zain and Mohammed rushed forward and hauled the chair back up onto its legs.

The American was storming around the room and swept a lamp and a vase off a dresser, onto the ground.

"I don't fu.....ing believe it!" he raved. "Not after all I've come through to set myself up for life! The crap I've taken and the shit I've listened to from these so-called Muslim Jihadists! All they really want is an upgrade on their video games and a license to really murder people and screw anything in skirts anytime they want... some revolution."

The two Jihadists backed away, uncertain how to take the outburst. Danny wasn't about to give up.

"You know what Frank, you're talking about your big plan to bring the U.K. to it's knees, but from where I'm sitting, after your screw ups since you got here, you couldn't organize a piss-up in a brewery. What's this great plan you're spouting off about? If it's so shit hot why won't you share it with me? I'm as good as dead now anyway...right?"

Frank strode across to him looking like he was going to smash Danny into the ground, but he stopped at the last minute then took some deep breaths.

He started nodding.

"OK, you want to know you bastard? I'll tell you and then tell me how stupid I am... and your assumption is right... you're a dead man as of this moment and your executioner is on the way here as we speak. Now let me lay it out for you. I actually believe you will be impressed. Oh, and you Brits won't arrest me in the U.K. I have ways of getting out of this lousy small island. I will yet enjoy the smell of tropical trees, the sun, the sand and sweet smelling senoritas."

He sat down again. "Right, here's the beginning of the end of the U.K."

CHAPTER 88

The plan he outlined was devastating.

Danny was shocked to the core, but he tried not to show it.

Skinner started by asking him a question.

"So, tell me, what's the two pillars here in the U.K. that people look up to, that project the identity of the country?"

"I've no idea, I'm afraid... never thought about it... wait a moment, beer and soccer?"

Skinner started to look really angry, but made an effort to gain his self-control.

"Want to play word games Danny? OK, let me lay it out for you:

The House of Commons for one and the Royal family for the other. That's what the people of Britain look to for the meaning of being British. I mean to destroy both of them."

Danny felt his blood go cold.

This couldn't be happening! Was Skinner so honed in Military tactics that he had come up with the plan on his own and had the skills and organizational ability to carry it out?

He doubted that the man had birthed the idea. He had probably been introduced to the plan by top-level ISIS leaders in Iraq and Syria. They then left the ground assault and organization of people and equipment to the American. A noteworthy achievement in itself.

He immediately raised his opinion of the man.

As if sensing certain acquiescence, Skinner then went on to lay out the full scope of the plan, not inviting any interruptions or questions from him:

He covered the attack on the House of Commons first.

City Cruises ran Thames Tours from 5 piers... Westminster, London Eye, Tower of London, and Greenwich, with circular tours from Bankside. Some of the craft could take up to two hundred and fifty people on board.

Far too unwieldy and crowded for the plan.

On further research, they discovered that a small craft could be rented out for special events: corporate meetings or staff parties and other events for about a thousand pounds sterling. The Jihadists liked that the crafts were also available for weddings. One had to apply for a license with the PLA (Port Of London Authority), which could be booked and cleared on line. Skinner's team had arranged for a Jihadist couple to plan their marriage ceremony on board and had obtained the proper licenses. They even arranged a Jihadist, disguised as an Imam, to conduct the mock ceremony.

At boarding time twelve Jihadists would board with boxes of 'food and beverages' for the celebration. In actual fact they were primed RPG rocket launchers.

It was a simple plan... most successful plans were.

Sailing slowly past the House of Commons the Jihadists were going to open up on the building, hopefully blowing it to bits, and with a sitting House, a whole bundle of Members of Parliament as well.

Skinner paused and grinned when he detected Danny's dismayed reactions. He couldn't help it.

The plan was superb and could work with devastating effect.

One flag suddenly went up in his mind but he knew not to mention it.

"What do you think Danny? Like it?" he asked, not really expecting a reply.

He carried on. "We have some escape routes set up to get us to safe houses but they're not important. If they achieve their operation successfully, they're not worried about dying as they fight their way across London. They could still wreak havoc on a big chunk of the city, probably already reeling from our other attack. As you can imagine, I have my own escape planned." Danny was silent, still in complete shock at the audacity of the plan. Even working for MI5, he had no idea of what type of Security was in place to cover the Thames and the House of Commons. Even so, a small-authorized wedding party might not raise any alert. The attack could be carried out without any questions being raised by the Security people.

He looked up into Skinner's gloating face.

"What did you say about my leadership and planning skills? Why d'you think they sent me over here Danny? Eh?"

Again, he had no reply.

Skinner carried on "Now to the Royal Family."

He recounted how the assault would proceed.

Her Majesty has three garden parties in Buckingham Palace in the summertime, normally in July. There's also one in Scotland. Over eight thousand invitations go out from The Royal Chamberlain's Office, to various people as a way of rewarding public service. Various groups and corporations are allocated a specific amount of invitations they can offer to people in their organizations, and who they consider deserving of one. Everyone turns up of course.

Who would turn down an invitation from the Queen?

It ran from 4 to 6pm and the doors open at three pm: twenty seven thousand cups of tea are served, twenty thousand sandwiches, and twenty thousand slices of cake. A huge benefit of course is strolling round the extensive gardens until the Queen and her party turns up at 4 pm to the National Anthem being played, - then a chance for the people to meet the Queen, and her party. Security is apparently provided by 'Yeoman of the Guard' who people referred to as 'Gentlemen at Arms', and who work as ushers. Frank didn't know a lot about additional Security, but felt that it was there but unobtrusive.

It didn't appear to overly concern him.

Food and beverages were provided by the same private companies every year. The setting up of the garden party was a massive amount of work, and they have to get started the previous day.

Frank had arranged for one of his members to work at the food suppliers for the past year, studying the service they provided to Buckingham Palace. He had seen one big weakness in the set-up, that they intended to take advantage of: the food providers have to arrange Security clearances for all their all their staff who will be working at the Palace.

He glanced at Danny. "Think about this, their vans are coming and going into the Palace all morning, and you know what happens don't you?" This was a direct question to Danny.

"Sure they get too relaxed...lax even. They've been doing it for years without any incident whatsoever."

"Right, so after a few legitimate runs, a team of ours takes over the food processing area back in the city."

"I suppose you kill all the waiters on site then?" Danny queried.

"Not at all. That would be bad for public relations. There's a large freezer handy and we shove them in there."

"Since when did you murderers of women and children worry about PR?" Danny sneered.

 Skinner ignored the jibe and carried on.

"We substitute two teams into two vans and off they go. Of course they carry the ID cards of the detained food waiters and so on. They may inspect them or just wave them on. If a problem develops at that stage we don't care. The food hampers are full of weapons: long rifles, handguns and RPGs with grenades. We simply blast our way in."

"No explosive vests or suicide bombers?"

"Unfortunately not. We couldn't get a supply of them, but you can imagine the effect on eight thousand people crammed into one big target area?"

He could and he shuddered. The casualties would be massive.

He didn't know how, but he couldn't let this happen.

It would indeed crush the normally indomitable British spirit.

Frank clapped him on the shoulder then went across and chatted with his two colleagues.

Danny would have done anything for a cup of coffee right then.

CHAPTER 89

Holyhead docks in Wales

Colm Loftus didn't know it was his last day on earth when he carefully maneuvered his truck through the busy wharf thoroughfare and out onto the main road. He wasn't concerned about the container on the back of the truck. It had come through Customs without any problems as the company made regular shipments, and their brand name was well known. The Canine Unit was not on duty with their sniffer dogs, which was unusual, however the dock workers made short work of the transfer which was now well strapped down on the back of the rig. His only concern was the slight change in the delivery details. He had been instructed to pull over to MacDonald's, a mile down the road and take on a passenger who would accompany him on the trip. The drop-off was apparently off the beaten track, an hour's drive out of Holyhead on the road east.

In a way he had no problem with that. Being originally from Swindon in Wiltshire, he was glad he wouldn't be wandering around in the dark, in an unknown area of Wales, trying to locate some address out in the country.

He had been promised a bonus for the late evening drop-off. Normally he would have loaded up and proceeded two miles down the road to a second-hand hotel, where he would stop for the night. Still, he felt certain disquiet about the arrangements. He preferred driving on his own for starters, and the job had come directly to his home phone rather than from his boss, who owned the truck. His boss didn't permit under the table use of his rig and Colm hoped he wouldn't notice the extra mileage on the clock in the morning. Outside the dock gates Skinner and his companion Zain, watched the truck move past.

"Nice one, smooth as silk Frank."

"That advice I had about sickening all the sniffer dogs with that meat, worked a dream. That was a good investment. It probably couldn't be used again, if they suspect something amiss."

"We wont need it again Frank," Zain chuckled.

"OK, lets get moving. I want to be right behind that driver when he pulls in. You know what you have to do then?"

"Sure, when we get there we pull the truck into the big barn where you'll be waiting with the doors open. Then I top him."

Danny heard them come back.

The sound of the van and a heavier vehicle... a truck perhaps.

The van switched off. Then what sounded like heavy doors scraping back on hard ground and the truck motor running for a brief moment, then it too switched off.

The doors scraped again.

Even tied up, he jerked when he heard the shots... a weapon fired twice.

He didn't need to guess... he would be next.

They came in laughing and joking.

"Did you hear him beg just before I did him in?" Zain chortled.

"Yeah, you sure got a taste for that over there in Iraq - they trained you well." Frank retorted.

Mohammed went over to them.

"Everything go as planned?" he asked.

"Like a dream." Zain said, slapping him on the shoulder, "and I just sent one more Infidel straight to hell!"

"The driver?"

It was Frank who answered. "You got it in one. We still have to check out the truck load, but it came through without any problem."

Zain was still up.

"Those stupid Brits… letting deadly shit like that through, that's going to bring them to their knees. I can't wait to get to the next part."

Mohammed pounded him back.

"Yeah, blowing them apart with those RPG's! They won't know what's hitting them!"

Frank turned to Mohammed.

"How's our prisoner been behaving?"

"I slapped him around some just to keep him awake. He was asking for a leak but you told me not to do it on my own."

"He would have made a break for it for sure. He knows that he's run out of options at this stage. Speaking of which, any sign of our visitor, he should have been here by now?"

"Not a peep, but it's not an easy place to find, even with directions."

Frank threw off the jacket he'd been wearing.

"Let's have some breakfast."

"Yeah" Zain chortled again "Killing people gives me an appetite"

Frank grabbed his arm.

"Shoo…" he whispered, "that's a car pulling up. Hope we weren't followed here from those docks."

They scattered across to the two sets of windows and looked out. Frank carefully opened the front door a crack and peered through.

He could see a figure approaching. As it came closer he could make out a set of features and breathed a sigh of relief.

"Hey, it's OK guys, it's Mohammed… the one our guest over there has been waiting for."

Zain came across and pulled the door open fully.

"Of course, Alina's brother, coming down specially to do the execution. He's really pissed off at Quigley over there. Seems he's been screwing his sister back in London. Didn't sit well with him."

Frank shook his head in annoyance.

"Two Mohammed's here now! Can't you Muslims come up with some variety in your first names! I can't wait to get the hell out of here."

The newcomer pushed past both of them and strode across to the figure tied to the chair.

"This is all I could think of on the way down here Quigley - having you all to myself. Have I got plans for you!"

He launched into a savage assault with his fists, until the American pulled him back.

"Hey, we want that bitch at MI5 to recognize him when we mail his head to her. The video will set the scene - the first beheading in the U.K. to start the beginning of the end of this country."

He shoved him away from Danny.

"Get your camera gear set up. We have to eat, check out the load, and switch it to that big van we stowed in the barn a week ago. I want to be out of here in less than two hours."

He waved to the other men.

"We'll leave the film director to set up the scene. What he lacks in skill I'm sure he'll make up in his enthusiasm."

The group roared with appreciation.

Half unconscious, Danny could only watch as Mohammed opened a large suitcase and took out a camera and tripod ten feet in front of him.

It was when he produced the last item that Danny felt the first coil of fear and desperation in his gut. It was a large skinning knife.

CHAPTER 90

It was quiet when the terrorists finally left, somewhat later than expected, as a result of opening up the container and the slow unpacking of weapons hidden well in a load of disassembled treadmills and sports equipment.

Danny had finally come to accept that his luck had run out, but to end it like this?

As an ex-soldier, particularly in his early years, he had fantasized about dying in a hail of gunfire, protecting his fellow troopers. Later he had mellowed this down to perhaps ending some action with a light wound that wouldn't affect his enjoyment in life after his discharge.

However after he'd shipped some of his more unlucky Mates, who'd lost legs, stomachs, and genitals, onto emergency choppers and aircraft with little hope of survival, he realized that when your time was up, that was it.

His time had come.

He had regrets... his now deceased ex-wife Fiona... he knew he'd shortchanged her in the marriage. His true family was his Regiment brothers. Even when he was home on leave, his thoughts were fixed on getting back to the Unit.

His daughter Allison... one favor he would always thank Fiona for was forcing him out of the Military, at which time he discovered what a beautiful daughter he had, and that she idolized him, despite his neglect over the years.

He hadn't exactly been the ideal father since he became a civilian either. He made a half effort at a wry grin, but his face hurt too much.

Sure, if he got out of here and….

Mohammed came across with a grin of anticipation on his face.

"You're going to be famous Quigley… your beheading will be splashed all across the world by tomorrow evening. That's what all you Infidels want isn't it? Fame… to be famous. That's some survey I read …typical of you Infidels… no spiritual depth. Now try to smile, I'm going to run a couple of shots for viewers to appreciate the whole of you, so to speak. Then I'll get down to the business at hand. I mustn't forget my mask, after all I don't want to distract from the main event."

The next ten minutes were taken up with re-positioning the camera by moving the tripod and taking some video shots. He finally looked satisfied, left the camera running and focused on Danny. He pulled the mask over his head, picked up the large skinning knife and moved towards him.

"I don't think so Mohammed." The voice cut like a knife into the room. Mohammed froze in midstride and swung around.

He gasped. "Alina, what are you doing here?"

"I heard you on the phone when I visited our mother yesterday. One name I picked up caught my interest… Danny Quigley, so I stuck a bug in your car and followed you down. Good job I did, just in time to stop my brother becoming a murderer it seems."

"Not in time enough" he spat, lunging at Danny's form with the knife.

Alina never hesitated. She fired instinctively.

The bullet caught him in the forearm holding the knife, which flew off to the side of the room. Mohammed collapsed to the floor clutching his arm and screaming.

The next few moments were taken up with Alina grabbing the knife and cutting Danny loose. She also had keys for the handcuffs, which she unlocked, then slipped them onto her brother's hands.

"Hey, I'm bleeding" he whimpered.

"Well, bleed some more you moron. What do you think you were about to do to Danny here? You make me sick!" she spat.

It was Danny who collapsed on the floor this time.

She knelt down beside him.

"Danny, Danny, I couldn't come in any sooner, until the other group left…shit, you're a real mess. What can I get you?"

He struggled sideways and croaked something in her ear.

"What?" she asked.

"I need the toilet in a hurry or I'm going to really embarrass myself right here in front of you… then a telephone, in that order."

When he staggered out a few minutes later, she already had Rebecca on the line.

He spent the next fifteen minutes filling her in on the Jihadists' plan for the assaults in London. Alina sat there with her jaw agape. He finished by informing Rebecca about how Alina had rescued him in the nick of time.

Then she was all business.

As they were in Wales, Rebecca would arrange for a chopper from the SAS Regiment in Hereford (also in Wales), and transport him and Alina back up to London. As the building they were in, and the barn, were now crime scenes, she would contact the nearest Police Force to move in and take over.

They were to leave Mohammed trussed up like a chicken, and slap something on his arm to stop his bleeding. This item didn't seem that important to her.

Because of Danny's weakened condition, Rebecca informed him, he wouldn't be well enough to get involved in the containment operation against the Jihadists.

She was now activating an SAS Saber team at Hereford to head for London.

490

His fuller knowledge of the Jihadists plans would be invaluable for planning the operation.

She didn't know the real Danny Quigley.

He had some scores to settle himself.

CHAPTER 91

It was a balmy, sunny afternoon on the banks of the river Thames. Crafts moved serenely past on the fast moving water.

People were out for walks with their dogs. Joggers plodded past in one's and twos. Families were sharing picnics on the wooden benches along the banks.

A normal day on the river as the boat pulled in to the side and one man jumped out, tied it up, and waved to the other man higher up in the engine room.

The man, stocky and wearing coveralls, looked around and grinned as he saw the group waiting.

"You're the wedding party I can see, and I must say the bride looks beautiful. Haven't we got a lovely day for it?"

One of the group came across. "Hey man, you're spot on time…super" he exclaimed.

The boatman looked at him. "Oh, you're American… good, I can expect a big tip then." he said jokingly.

"Well, I mean" he said, lowering his voice "the Pakis aren't too good at tipping."

He nodded back at the group.

The American chuckled. "Oh, I can assure you that you'll be well taken care of."

The boatman blinked. "Good to hear it. Now, getting your stuff on board…quite a bit there for a short trip like this?"

"Hey, it is a wedding after all, give them some slack. Our guys will carry it on board my man, don't worry."

"Getting better and better... fine by me," he said turning and catching the ramp being lifted across from the boat.

"How many to go on board then?"

Before he could answer, one of the group shouted over. "Hey Frank, can we haul this stuff on board and get the people on there a.s.a.p.?"

He didn't reply, just waved an acknowledgement and pointed to the ramp.

"He's in a hurry isn't he? Not the groom by any chance?" the boatman asked.

Frank shook his head. "No, he's back there somewhere. Now is the crew merely two of you?"

"Yes, normal manning on a craft this size on the Thames."

"Look, some of our people have knowledge of boats and water safety rules etc. What would I need to give you to allow us to take the boat out ourselves? I assure you you'd be bored stiff with one of their weddings - their music and very un-English customs. We'd pay you well."

The boatman scowled. "You must be kidding Mate? Hand the boat over just like that? Be worth more than my job's worth, I can tell you." He glanced back at the load of boxes and hampers.

"You lot can get that stuff on board. I'm not paid to hump your baggage on, and you can stuff your tip as far as I'm concerned."

He strode up the short gangplank muttering to himself.

Frank gestured again and there was a flurry of organized activity as the gear was hustled on board.

The boatman came back down, untied the craft and nipped smartly up the gangplank pulling it up with a thick rope that was attached. The craft moved gently away from the anchorage, out into the river.

Frank immediately climbed up a set of steps and went into the engine room. The boatman was there with another man, a lean, whipcord looking individual, who was on the tiller, moving it slowly and carefully out into deeper water.

Frank coughed. "I believe we left instructions to take us on the first leg, down past the Houses of Parliament, and get in

493

close for some good pictures - great background shots for the newly weds... a once in a lifetime experience, right lads?"

Neither man looked impressed.

The tiller man grunted and stared straight ahead.

Seeing they weren't apparently interested in building a life long relationship with him, Frank leaned forward abruptly.

"Look, we paid your company well for this fu...ing excuse for a boat. Now how long until we get to that area? We need to get our camera and gear set up."

The boatman looked taken aback. "No need to get nasty about it Mate. We should be there in about 20 minutes, OK?"

Frank said nothing and giving the two men a rather disgusted look he stormed out and went back down the stairs.

The lean man reached into a drawer, took out a small radio and spoke briefly into it.

"Ten men on board, and that includes Frank that you briefed us on. There's one female, a fairly tough looking cookie despite the wedding dress. I'd watch her closely as well as the other. You've got the video scan from here from us and the other one facing the lower deck. Don't know if any will get on the roof above us but will advise. In any event watch when you come out that there are none of them above and in back of you. I gave them a timing of 20 minutes as you heard. We wait on your move, or our move in case we go to plan two."

"Roger that" the voice came back.

Down below in a hastily 'cobbled together' room that had been the bar up to the previous day, Danny Quigley whispered the information to the six troopers packed tightly inside.

The hope had been that a Muslim group wouldn't complain about a missing bar, and in fact the Cruise company could claim they were being sensitive to their culture of non-drinking.

Danny felt rough and he looked it, but he didn't accept being left out of it. In twenty minutes or less, it was pay back time.

He couldn't mentally be more ready, and he'd learned that this was half the battle. For the first time in nearly five years, he was going into action with a serving bunch of kick-ass troopers.

He liked the idea.

The twenty-minute deadline was nearly there. Up above, the tiller saw the Houses of Parliament coming into view. At the same time, he spotted some of the group coming up the ladder and proceeding to the top of the cabin roof. They were carrying long objects wrapped in blankets.

The American was on the deck below.

He spotted one of them coming towards the door and quickly whipped up the radio.

"On the roof! Out" It squelched back once before he stuck it back in the drawer, leaving it open.

The door opened and the man came in. They didn't know he was called Zain, but his penetrating gaze said it all.

He was full of hatred.

The sawed-off shotgun that he slipped out from behind some material said it all.

Surprise is everything.

Both men were seasoned members of the Regiment and had seen too many friends die because of hesitation. It wasn't the radio that came up from the drawer but an automatic, with a bullet up the barrel and the safety off.

He'd practiced it hundreds of times, and he rarely missed his target. He didn't this time either.

Zain never had a chance to bring up his weapon as two bullets drilled his head. The boatman even had time to catch the shotgun as it fell from Zain's grasp, not to stop the noise because the automatic wasn't silenced, but to get that particular weapon in his hands.

Everyone down on the deck froze for a brief second, then RPG's and weapons started to emerge from boxes and bundles.

Down below, Danny who was watching the video feeds from both areas, kicked down the flimsy partition and led the group over to the door and out onto the deck.

This was no operation where cards pointing out the rights of an armed or suspected assailant or suicide bomber were being carried.

This was their business…killing people, quickly and efficiently.

Some of the Jihadists were still holding their RPG's while others had dropped them and picked up some shorter weapons.

On the edge of the deck, four of the SAS saber team and Danny, confronted the terrorists who had been readying themselves to fire at the House of Commons. The other two SAS troopers faced back, looking upwards at the men on the roof. Inside, the boatman and his tiller man, started blasting up through the plastic sections of the roof as they spotted movement. The troopers outside and facing upwards, opened up on the Jihadists off the top of the boat, sending them flying over the edge of the craft into the river. Below, the synchronized firing power of Danny and the SAS troopers cut a swathe through the Jihadists, toppling them to the ground.

Danny spotted Mohammed Youssef turn and face him, shock anger and hatred written all over his features.

He stitched him up the middle and watched him hurled backwards with the force of the bullets.

He swung his weapon again, this time hovering the barrel over a familiar face… Frank the American.

Danny waved the weapons of his team aside as they started to swing towards Skinner.

"He's mine," he shouted as the opposition suddenly collapsed on the craft, apart from the bride who was screaming at the top of her voice, her white dress splashed with crimson.

No threat there.

He walked carefully forward, watching Frank like a hawk. He'd kill him in a few seconds but….

The American backed up against the boat's edge.

The carnage that had just materialized around him didn't seem to faze him. He leaned forward and spoke six words that chilled Danny to the core:

"Burnside warned me about you" he shouted.

"What...what did you just say?" he shot the words back without any thought.

"Your friend Gordon Burnside, from the CIA in Kabul warned me way back, about you. He'd picked up some information about you from Langley that he wasn't supposed to have access to. He said you were a dangerous bastard Danny... to watch out for you. I didn't twig you until Belfast, when your friend Jimmy started to call you Danny and you tried that Daddio crap on me."

Danny reared back, shocked. "This can't be true. Who the hell did you pick this up from? I don't believe a thing you say. I have friends in the CIA and I can't see them involved in killing Brits on the streets of London, and did he tell you, you could rape a young married woman like Danielle, with two children, while these animals looked on?" he said with disgust.

Angry and frustrated now the American finally raged back at him.

"Collateral damage Danny, collateral damage. Have you any idea of how goddam difficult it is, no impossible, to get a white man inside Isis? Well we did it... I did it... and the price is irrelevant. You want to know the purpose of all this Danny? A covert black ops. group operating out of the DIA, The Defense Intelligence Agency, was pissed off at the British Parliament's luke-warm attitude to fighting ISIS and terrorism world wide: Members of Parliament voting against fighting this scourge; your army with numbers lower now than they had at the battle of Waterloo; Russian bombers flying up the English channel, and the great RAF didn't have the resources to go out and confront them. Oh, yes, that mighty British lion slumped without any teeth or any desire to confront evil anymore. Where had that Churchillian bulldog gone to? You saw what 9/11 did to the U.S.... the patriot act... millions reinvested in Military hardware and high tech weapons. The DIA saw a way of waking up your country and your politicians, and co-opted Burnside across secretly from the CIA, to drive the project forward, and you know what, we nearly succeeded."

"Success Frank? You the big leader and planner! You didn't know that the Houses of Parliament aren't open in July. All the members are away on holidays. Your people will be shooting at empty buildings. Right now you're a dead man walking. Your friend Gordon Burnside will take care of that,"

"Welcome to the club Danny. Now that I've told you, you've got a target on your back as well. Anyway, I already told you I had my way out of here, didn't I?""

Danny started to lift his weapon.

The American's hand shot to his mouth. Something flashed momentarily and he leaped over the side of the boat into the fast moving tide.

In frustration Danny fired some shots from his MP5 into the water. Not a sign of anyone in the water. Then…. a figure loomed up at his side… a Sergeant in the troop that he'd known before. "Sorry, he was gone in a second. I couldn't get a shot in."

Danny shook his head.

"I thought he was going to shoot himself at first then…. did you see that thing in his hand? Like something flashed for a second."

"Actually I did, and I think I know what it was."

"What the hell was it? I haven't a clue?"

"I only know because I recently finished a course with the Special Boat Squadron in Poole down in Dorset. It was a small device that allows one to swim underwater for short distances without breathing."

Danny stood there shaking his head.

"Son of a bitch! He said he had his escape planned to get out of England. He was already getting ready to jump just as soon as his men here had blasted the House of Commons. He had his getaway planned from somewhere right along this stretch of water. Shit!"

"He's long gone now Danny. What did he tell you anyway? You two seemed to have quite a chat."

"He talked straight bullshit! I should have shot him on the spot."

The woman was still screaming as a horde of water-borne Police converged on them. His eyes drifted towards her as she suddenly stopped, reached under her wedding dress and produced a small Uzi machine pistol She swung it round to the troopers leaning over the side of the craft.

Danny fired without thinking, sending her crashing back and down onto the remnants of the boxes and packages on the deck.

The troopers swung round, shock and surprise on their faces.

The Sergeant shouted to them.

"She was about to blast you lax bastards and Danny got her in time - some bride!"

He then turned to Danny, chuckling.

"There's goes that great reputation of yours Mate. Now you'll be known as the chap who shot a woman at her own wedding, wearing a wedding dress. Oh, well, you've got witnesses, but I suspect someone somewhere, will find that you tramped all over her human rights Danny"

Still grinning he strolled across and fumbled around in the trailing wedding gown then turned and shouted: "Your reputation is okay Mate, the she was a man!"

CHAPTER 92

The Buckingham Palace operation, planned by MI5, Scotland Yard and the Metropolitan Police, didn't involve Danny. However his inside information on the Jihadists' takeover of the food processors was seen as critical.

Rebecca and the operational team wanted to avoid the killing of civilians at all costs. His information on their intention of merely placing the staff in one of the large freezers left them free to plan the takedown elsewhere. They had also established the identity of the contact that the attackers had placed inside the food company a year previously and had nabbed him at his home. He was now singing his head off and had been induced to phone in sick for the day. He had also presented a nugget of information, in that the attackers would retain the two original drivers of the food vans, and use their knowledge of retracing the route back to the Palace. The Security team promptly had them replaced by two undercover Officers from the Met.

The team liked the idea of having one less Jihadist to worry about and perhaps create some confusion in the group.

The second takedown possibility was to block the route they would take to get to the Palace, with maximum force, but public safety was paramount here again.

For the Police to block normal traffic along a certain route would quite probably raise the suspicions of the ISIS group.

It finally came down to stopping them at the side entrance to the Palace on the left hand side of Buckingham Palace Road. This had, however, advantages and disadvantages.

For starters, it was the entrance that the food waiters had previously used and wouldn't arouse any confusion with them.

Fundamentally and most importantly, the Jihadists must not be allowed to gain any access whatsoever to the Palace.

The country would never accept that an armed group had exposed the Queen and her family to possible assault.

That must not be allowed to happen.

Again on the plus side, was the existence of two large tents at the entrance, where an armed reception could be set up out of sight. The SAS Saber team and the Swat teams had some ideas on how they would go about this.

The down side was that this was the visitors center, where people came, queued up, and went forward through Security with their belongings.

They solved it by a simple plan to change the flow of the public to another entrance, as soon as the Security people learned that the Jihadists were on their way. By that time, the majority of garden party visitors would have already passed through, but would the attackers take note of the scarcity of visitors when they entered Buckingham Palace Road?

The feeling was that they wouldn't, not having done the route before, and their inside contact now out of the picture.

In the end they settled for a simple plan, with various scenarios looked at in case things got nasty or out of hand.

In the end the plan worked extremely.

Preparation was the key.

In a way, it was an anti climax, after all the planning, discussions and Security personnel involved.

The two vans full of armed Jihadists rolled up to the visitor's entrance and were stopped by Security Guards. The two undercover Police drivers promptly leapt out of their vehicles.

Almost immediately four massive trucks, two from each side with metal battering rams, tore through the flimsy sidewall of the tent and drove straight into the sides of the

501

Jihadists' vehicles. Simultaneously flash bangs and tear gas grenades were tossed in the front open windows by the Security Guards.. - actually saber team troopers.

The vehicles exploded instantly blowing out the windows, and black smoke billowed out and upwards.

There were howls and screams from inside.

The four trucks backed up as one, then the Swat teams descended on the doors, ripping those open that weren't jammed, and hauling out screaming Jihadists who were holding their ears and eyes.

Within minutes, they were spread-eagled on the roadway and cuffed.

By some peculiar timing, the Queen and her party had just arrived out in front of her guests, to the loud playing of God Save the Queen. Apart from some puzzled looks further back at an unusual series of sounds, no one noticed anything out of the ordinary. Firecrackers, they reasoned. It was the Queen's garden party after all.

Back in Thames House, the various Security organizers sat back and gave a loud cheer. A relieved cheer… no civilian or Security personnel killed or injured… no widows or widowers to notify with bad news.

Danny struggled to his feet, still aching all over but much relieved at the successful outcome.

Rebecca looked across at him as he headed for the door.

"Not waiting for the celebration drinks Danny? You had one hell of a lot to do with this. I'd hate to be in London today, if you hadn't telephoned me the other night."

He went back over to her and leaned forward.

"I have something to do… I'll call you…and one question, what about Alina?" he asked.

She pursed her lips.

"I've thought about that, talked to some people and we agreed that we couldn't bring her back inside MI5 under the circumstances, but what we will do is give her a reference if she wants to move on into some other line of work.

Her record will be wiped clean here at Thames House. Happy with that?"

He smiled, squeezing her shoulder and quietly slipped out of the room.

He had something to do about that target now on his back.

CHAPTER 93

He wasn't expecting an easy reception.

The Israeli Embassy didn't have a reputation of having open arms for visitors. This was speedily confirmed.

He was put through a security check and an airport style scanner before going forward to the reception desk, which fronted a large comfortable lounge. There were about two dozen people sitting there and he assumed they were waiting for visas to visit the Holy Land.

He went up to an attractive black haired woman sitting behind her computer and handed her his MI5 card, which she looked at.

"I'm Danny Quigley and I work over at Thames House. I'd like to speak to one of your Intelligence people here."

"What about?" she asked.

"Not something I can discuss out here for starters." He gestured backwards to the people behind him.

She didn't look impressed. "I can't get some member of staff out here on the request of someone who claims he's from MI5. What's wrong with the normal channels: a letter, email, fax or even a phone call? People in here are all busy doing something."

"I'm not claiming to be from MI5. You have my ID there which you are quite at liberty to check out if you want. I need someone out here who can get me in a secure room where I can talk to the boss of Mossad in Tel Aviv."

There was now an insistent edge to his voice.

She leaned forward as if to say something and he held up his hand.

"Miss, I've talked to him before, in his office over there in Israel."

She stared at him for a moment, then pressed a button in front of her.

He wasn't able to make out her side of the conversation.

She looked up at him and nodded to the waiting group.

"Sit over there. Someone will be out to see you shortly."

He wasn't kept waiting long. In less than five minutes a squat, middle-aged man with a great head of greying hair came through a door and gestured to him.

He went over, following him down a long corridor.

The man turned into a small office and indicated a comfortable chair.

"Now tell me why you want to speak to my boss in Tel Aviv, Mr. Quigley. I did make a brief phone call to Thames House and it was confirmed that you work there, but I wasn't told what your role actually is."

"You wouldn't expect them to would you? Look I've information that could be vital to the Security of Israel and I want to speak directly and privately to Kemuel, your boss over there, in a secure room. No recording of my conversation. "

"Mr. Quigley, you told the receptionist that you spoke with my boss before when you were in Israel. How did that come about?"

Danny shook his head.

"You don't expect me to disclose a private conversation I had some years ago with the head of Mossad... again vital to the security of your country as this information is. Another name I can give you is Caleb Kishcon who interviewed me before setting up a meeting with your boss. I could of course just go out and use a public telephone and try to get through, but it could blow the secrecy of this situation wide apart."

Danny had noticed the change in the man's expression when he'd mentioned Caleb Kishcon's name.

505

Without a word he left the office and he was left sitting there for half an hour. Then he came back in and gestured that Danny should follow him.

This time they took a lift down two flights of stairs to a small room with a boardroom style table and some comfortable lounge chairs. It had the usual padding that a secure room would display, and a telephone.

"Sorry to keep you waiting Mr. Quigley. As you can imagine, he isn't exactly sitting around hoping someone from the old days might call him."

There was however, a timbre of respect and even humor in his voice.

He left the room. Danny sat down and picked up the phone.

He recognized the voice... Caleb.

"As dramatic as ever Danny. I remember the first time you came in here and I wanted to show you the road. I'm glad we didn't on that occasion."

Despite the situation, he felt himself smiling.

"I remember it well actually. You chaps impress the hell out of me I have to say. Now, do I get to talk to Kemuel?"

"Unless you have powers you didn't display when I last talked to you, the answer's no. Unfortunately he died eighteen months ago of a heart attack."

"Oh shoot, I'm terribly sorry to hear that Caleb! He was some mensch! Did it happen quickly? Was he in much pain."

"Gone in an instant, sitting at his desk, the way he always wanted to. We still miss him. Now I'm his successor, so it's myself you have to talk to."

"Hah! I know why your local Agent's eyes flickered when I mentioned your name."

"I'll have to talk to him. I thought we'd broken him of giving away any information via body language. Now, talk to me. They pulled me out of an important meeting five minutes ago to speak to you."

"Right, two things, one, is this a private conversation? And two, I want it recorded at your end. I don't believe you'd like the locals here to listen in."

"You got it on both points it is private and I am recording it, so go ahead."

"Fine, to mark your cards, no doubt you're hearing the news already of the Jihadists' attempted assault here today?"

"That's what our meeting was about. Could they hit us with a whammy like that? What's your interest Danny?"

"I was right in the middle of it - got the information on the Jihadists' operation in time to stop it - led the team that took out the group on the Thames this morning - was involved in the planning that stopped the attempted invasion of the Queen's garden party."

"Oh man, now you are setting me back on my seat here. I take my hat off to you my friend. We still use your Afghanistan escape from the Taliban some years back as training for the Special Forces. You obviously haven't lost it, but where does this vital information come in that you hinted at?"

"The operation was organized by an American Frank Skinner, an ex-Marine who fought in Iraq and was now training the Jihadists in Iraq. He was tasked with assembling a team over here to wreak a 9/11 style attack on some vital targets. I managed to infiltrate his group initially, and picked up a fair bit of information on how he was going to go about it. I slipped up however, and ended up his prisoner, tied in a country house with no obvious chance of escape. I was going to be the first beheading in Britain, to run concurrently with the attacks. It was then that he felt safe in revealing the targets they were going to hit. I managed to escape and alerted MI5 in time, and today tells the story."

"And this story while good, tell me, where does it lead?" the Israeli queried.

"To do an aside first Caleb, my reading of the U.S./Israeli guarantee of backing, is in complete disarray right now. You chaps don't know where you stand with the President or current administration. Are they still in your corner, prepared to back you at any cost? Syria demands the Golan Heights back. Russia has moved a considerable amount of high tech anti- aircraft weaponry into Syria, which could really cramp that Air Force of yours. You need an edge my friend."

"And you can give us this edge Danny?"

"Right, listen up. I had the American Frank Skinner backed up against the deck of the craft after taking out his whole group. We got into a brief exchange after which I intended to top him. I taunted him about not being such a great planner after all: the House of Commons was empty, for example. Then he told me a story. He mentioned that a chap called Gordon Burnside, who is the CIA station chief in Kabul, had been co-opted by a black ops group in the Defense Intelligence Agency, to organize a 9/11 style strike on the U.K."

"But this is monstrous!" Caleb gasped "Why, why to one of their major allies as well?"

"Skinner told me that the Americans were sick of the Brits. leaving all the heavy lifting to them. The MPs in the Commons were voting against all meaningful strikes against ISIS, in any focused way - their army reduced, he said, to numbers that were at the battle of Waterloo. The Russians were flying up the English Channel and the Brits couldn't launch enough aircraft to challenge them. Oh, his big kicker was what happened to the American Forces after 9/11: the patriot act, lots of investment in high tech Military hardware. That was the reason they arranged this lovely little plan. They thought the Government over here would jump on the bandwagon."

There was a lengthy silence at the other end. Finally: "That's a game changer for sure. Real dynamite in the wrong hands. So, who knows about this and what do you want from us?"

"Just you, I, Burnside of the CIA, some unknown people back in the DIA, and the American Frank Skinner. Oh, he jumped overboard and escaped, but before he did, he said we both now had a target on our backs."

"Hmm, I see what you mean. Burnside and his team will certainly stop at nothing to shut Skinner down and he alluded that they would be made aware of you knowing as well. Does your MI5 boss Rebecca know of the real source of this Jihadist operation?"

"No, I couldn't expose her to this information. It could get her killed."

"And again, what do you want from us."

"First off I want you to phone Burnside in Kabul and tell him about our little chat. It's tremendous leverage that your country could now have, if there's any flip flop on their guarantee of security, you can threaten to drop this bomb on them. Equally, if I'm killed, I want you to pull the plug on them as well. I want Burnside to then phone me direct here after you talk to him."

"Man, you really know how to play hardball! So they have to take that target off your back and hope you don't die in any way shape of form in the next few years. What else? There has to be something else."

"Yes, I want the American Skinner. There's no better organization than Mossad to track him down, and I want the resources to back me doing it. He told me when I was his prisoner that he had an escape plan and he looked forward to sea, sand and beautiful senoritas. That may help."

"I like it Danny. It could just work for both of us. Magnificent leverage for Israel as you point out...just wait until our Prime Minister makes his next trip to Washington! Some heads in the DIA will fall for sure. I'd love to be a fly on the wall. As to your other requests...yes, we'll pull the plug if the CIA assassinate you, no matter how clever they might be in doing so, and I'll give one of my top Agents your contact details. You two can work it out from there."

The phone call ended.

Danny waited an hour, before the phone rang again.

The voice was a whisper.

"You bastard Quigley! I should have had you finished off long before now. I warned Skinner to watch out for you. You've tied my hands right now but sooner or later, I'll take care of you, believe me."

Danny snorted.

"You overstepped the line when you allowed those animals to rape a friend of mine - a lovely young married lady with two beautiful kids. I hold you personally responsible for that

Burnside, and you can't hide behind black covert op. teams or anything else… watch your back. One night you'll look round and I'll be there. I'll be your worst nightmare for the rest of your days…which may not be very long."

He hung up and sat there.

He'd bought some time, but not forever.

Then the Agent came in and escorted him out of the building.

Suddenly he wanted to be with his daughter Allison.

CHAPTER 94

Four Months later

The rubber dingy slipped through the dark moonlit-flecked sea coming into the small island. The figures of the three men, with blackened faces and apparel, were indistinguishable.

Nothing was spoken as the craft crunched up on the sand and the men jumped out. The recce the night before had taken most of the guesswork out of the mission. They pulled the dingy well up, out of any threat from the medium-sized waves.

One man led them off the beach into the jungle where he moved forward slowly but with confidence. A half mile later the leader paused and gestured back. He had stopped at an eight foot, thick wire fence.

Still no words.

The second man took his pack off removed a lumpy package and opened it. The third man took something from his pocket and put it up to his lips. It was a silent dog whistle.

All three put on night vision goggles.

The lumpy package containing meat was unwrapped and the contents thrown over the fence.

It didn't take long. There was a swirl of movement on the other side and the sound of animals feeding ravenously.

It should have been silent towards the end but one of the animals gave a couple of keening yelps.

Not good... they tensed.

No sign of an alarm or additional Security measures kicking in.

Total silence on the other side.

The first man took out a pair of sizable wire cutters and snipped a man-sized hole in the fence.

All three checked their ear buds, then slipped through the hole and disappeared in different directions.

The first man moved silently forward in the direction of where he knew the house to be.

Ten minutes later he stood on the edge of the trees and examined it. A solid, sprawling well built residence with a number of small surrounding outbuildings. No lights on, as was expected at 4am. He moved forward cautiously into the cleared space - always dangerous when presenting a clear target to someone inside with NVQ equipment.

He moved swiftly around the house checking for any possible doors that might be open and found none. He wasn't expecting any. The rear entrance beside the pool was the easiest for him to unlock with the small lock-pick unit that he had brought with him. He took his automatic out and opened the door, ready for the alarm to go off and the rush upstairs to catch a surprised man getting out of bed.

No alarm.

He stepped swiftly in and to one side then waited.

No sound... no remaining 'house pet' either, launching itself at him. A quick scout around the lower floor showed no sleeping Security Guards or occupants, as expected.

On high alert, and even more cautiously now, he moved up the stairs, his weapon at the ready.

He reached the landing and stopped.

No sound. No light coming on.

But which room?

Opening doors and checking rooms might create even small amounts of noise and wake someone up.

He followed his instinct on this and his recollection of the layout of the first floor plans his companions had obtained for him.

He opened the door of the drawing room and slipped through, easing off to one side then froze. Something wasn't right.

Through his night vision he saw the head of a figure, sitting on one of the lounge chairs.

Cigarette smoke was drifting up above him.

A voice cut through the silence.

"Might as well put the light on Danny. I've been expecting you."

He recognized the voice… Frank Skinner!

He glanced sideways, spotting the light switch and squatted down to reduce himself as a target.

Pulling the night vision goggles off and hitting the switch, aware of the momentary adjustment in sight that followed.

There was no sound of gunfire or sudden attack.

The American stood up in full view, apparently seeing something humorous in the situation.

"Ever the cautious Danny Quigley. How could I have missed it for so long, even after your friend Burnside filled me in on you, and the possibility that I might encounter you on my trip to your shores. Of course, when we planned this you weren't doing anything really important in MI5 that might bring us together: screening new employees or something like that."

Danny stood up carefully, taking in the details of the room and in particular the man himself.

Was there a weapon stuck on the seat of that chair or in the pocket of the dressing gown; a bodyguard lurking in the washroom across the floor?

"Relax Danny, it's just you and me here."

"Where are the senoritas you were supposed to be cavorting with Skinner? How about the sun and the sand? Life been a bundle of roses since you scarpered into the Thames and left your sorry little Jihadists dead around you?"

There was silence. "What, cat got your tongue Frank?"

The man sighed. "The first month was fine. I had all of that and it was great. However I'd spread out a lot of money in a net that would send me a signal if people were chasing me. I knew you'd have me on your radar Danny, but alone I also knew you didn't have the resources to locate me. Still the signals kept coming. Some big outfit with plenty of high tech material had me in their sights, but who, the CIA, MI6, one of the numerous U.S. Defense Intelligence units? I couldn't find out, yet somehow through it all, my instincts told me that you were involved, and were coming for me, so I just waited, and here you are."

"Yeah, here I am Frank. You were good though, I'll give you that... a little off on the planning, House of Commons and such."

"I heard the dog yelping out there earlier. I was sorry they had to go. I'd grown to rather like them. In a way, they were all I had in the end."

"Yeah, I feel so sorry for you Frank - all alone! Well Danielle's husband and two children are lonely as well, and will be for a long time."

He started to lift the pistol but Frank snatched up a small automatic that must have been strategically placed on the edge of the seat. They stood there, weapons aimed at each other.

"I didn't intend going alone Danny. I was going to take with me the man who screwed up the plan that would have delivered all the dreams I ever wished. Goodbye."

"I don't think so Frank." He touched his left ear and the American's head exploded. The snipers had been well placed.

The Exfill went smoothly - the Mossad never left anything to chance.

CHAPTER 95

By the time Danny boarded a commercial flight bound for Heathrow, his high adrenalin levels had evaporated and a sense of anticlimax was setting in, as well as a feeling of complete exhaustion. As he looked at the other passengers organizing themselves for the long journey ahead, he couldn't help but smile as he thought of the difference between this flight and his past Military flights into and out of many of the world's troubles spots. He could almost smell the fear and sweat again of his fellow soldiers as they boarded the flight from the danger zone, tending to their wounded as best as they could, while knowing in their hearts that it was already too late for some of them.

What would these passengers think if they were aware of the exploits of Danny and his Regiment friends? Would they approve or were they so immersed in the everyday banalities of their lives that they wouldn't even care? Danny wondered, but he himself was convinced that he and his friends did make a difference for the better. He knew that there were a lot of evil bastards out there whose only aim in life was to destroy what mankind, in it's wisdom, had created over the past 2000 years, and someone had to stop them.

The real world was becoming more and more like the virtual reality world of the computer gamers who reveled in non-stop violence, where the bodies they skewered jumped up again, took on a new identity and leaped back into the fray to resume the never-ending savagery.

Danny began to think of himself, how he had changed and what he had become. This gave him a sense of unease. Would he ever be able to live a normal life again? It was a real worry.

Suddenly he thought of his daughter Allison and began to feel guilty. She had just recently witnessed her mother murdered and yet he had gone off and left her in the care of strangers. They had not even grieved properly together.

This realization was painful and at that moment all he wanted to do was to hug and go on hugging her and promise her that things would be different in the future.

The future!

He was suddenly aware of the implication and what it would mean for both of them. At that moment it dawned on him that this was a major turning point in his life.

He started getting a sinking feeling in his stomach.

What did he know about raising a young girl...almost a young lady now? Then like a hammer blow he realized that he could no longer sign up for the type of missions he was used to. If he was killed, then Allison would be on her own without any family nearby, and he knew with absolute certainty that there was no way he could accept that possibility.

He would have to have a serious talk with Rebecca about his future.

For some reason his thoughts turned to Naomi in California and he wished she was there to turn to for help and advice. Thinking of her gave him a warm glow and he knew that by hook or by crook, he was going to see her again.

Just then the vibration of his I-Pad brought him back to the present. When he glanced at the screen he couldn't believe what he was seeing - it was a message from Naomi:

'Hey there. I'm still missing you! Proposition - I never managed to get to Cornwall when I was posted to U.K., but heard that it's beautiful. How about I come over for Christmas, which is almost upon us, and you, myself, and Allison can spend the holiday down there? Say yes!!! Love Naomi'.

He typed in 'OMG, you must be a mind reader. I was just thinking about you! Yes, Oh yes please, but get on the first available flight. I need you ASAP! Danny'.

THE END

ACKNOWLEDGEMENTS

I have to acknowledge additional help and guidance from the following people:

Ultan O' Reilly, in Ireland;
Bob Beach In Randolph, New York State;
Jon Carey in Buffalo, N.Y. State;
all for editing assistance.
Tom Rickert for his graphic design work;
Author Melissa Bowersock for her valuable assistance in formatting the material;
Morgan Coates for on-going computer and promotional help.

OTHER BOOKS

BY

RUSS McDEVITT

Available through russmcdevitt.com, CreateSpace.com, and other leading booksellers.

Also available on:
amazon kindle